PRAISE FOR JOHNNY ONCE

"With the nervous system of the upper Westside social activist and the heart of a Bensonhurst homeboy, Johnny Rosario is a New Yorker you have to love. **Johnny Once** is brisk, sexy, and as authentic as a plate of home cooked manicotti. Call it 'Realfellas.'"

—Greg Donaldson, author of **The Ville**

"In writing this gritty crime drama, Gangi has created an intriguing story with characters that we care about in an urban milieu that crackles with energy. The suspense carries you along until the final pages. Gangi's knowledge of New York's criminal justice system serves him well when it comes to depicting crime, criminals and everyday heroes."

—Michael Jacobson, Professor of Criminal Justice at John Jay College and former Commissioner of New York City's Department of Probation and Department of Correction

"In his superb first novel, Robert Gangi pulls off one of the more difficult tricks in fiction, breathing life into a place and a time, into people in their daily lives and rhythms, in this case, the Bensonhurst section of Brooklyn. In Gangi's hands, Bensonhurst becomes almost magical, and its joys and sorrows become indisputably real, as his hero Johnny Rosario grapples with the difficulties of leaving—and going—home. In the bargain, Gangi manages to sidestep the usual clichés about Italian-American life and about its relations to the mob, and create something new and heartfelt, the kind of work that can only come from lived experience."

—John Marks, author of **The Wall** and **War Torn**

JOHNNY ONCE

JOHNNY ONCE

Robert Gangi

iUniverse, Inc.
New York Lincoln Shanghai

JOHNNY ONCE

Copyright © 2005 by Robert Gangi

iUniverse books may be ordered through booksellers or by contacting:

iUniverse
2021 Pine Lake Road, Suite 100
Lincoln, NE 68512
www.iuniverse.com
1-800-Authors (1-800-288-4677)

ISBN: 0-595-33305-2 (pbk)
ISBN: 0-595-66831-3 (cloth)

Printed in the United States of America

To my family: My wife Barbara Kuerer Gangi, a Jewish doctor from the Bronx who was my first love and will be my last; our son Jess, who's an artist from Manhattan; and our son Theo, who's a novelist from Manhattan. You enrich my life in countless ways.

To my family of origin: My father Alfredo, my mother Rose, and my brother Alfred. As Chris and Jul said, we love you and miss you.

She knows how to load it.
She knows how to fire away.
She knows when not to aim to please
Or shoot to kill.
She's a full-blooded Sicilian.
"(She's a) Full-blooded Sicilian"—Zumpano

It's just a turn from now
Back down to the road
That we used to walk when
We were friends.
"When We Were Friends"—Beaver Nelson

ACKNOWLEDGEMENTS

Many people—family members, friends, and professionals—helped and encouraged me in writing *Johnny Once*. Friends Ed Peterson and Larry Stallman, my cousin Donna Davis, and my wife Dr. Barbara Kuerer Gangi read the first draft and provided highly useful and heartfelt feedback. Jane Lazare-White liked very much an early draft and was the first published author to tell me that my book, too, was publishable. Deborah Jo Immergut was kind enough to read two early drafts and her suggested edits provided invaluable writing lessons. Kathy McCormick read it too and provided smart and constructive comments. Barbara read a later draft and her inputs then and from before were the suggested changes that guided me most.

Minna Samuels helped in editing an early version. Richard Marek became involved at a critical time in the process and convinced me again that the book was worthy. His edits were enormously helpful and then he followed through on his promise to find me an agent. Joyce Engelson was also a terrific editor and her counsel led me to make the last and only significant change I made to the plot. Michael Denneny weighed in at the end with helpful guidance about the novel's structure. Richard, Joyce, and Michael have generously remained involved with this project, and have been always willing to listen to my updates and to offer advice about next steps.

My son Theo Gangi was the book's final editor and did an excellent job in proposing scene rewrites and structural adjustments. My son Jess Gangi is responsible for the book's effective and affecting jacket design.

I am grateful to Greg Donaldson for reading two versions of the book and being always willing to offer his wisdom re writing and the publishing world. Greg provided a positive blurb for the book, as did, in a thoughtful and kind manner, John Marks and Michael Jacobson.

Laura Parker Davidson has merited my great appreciation over the years for her expert typing and formatting of the manuscript. All of which she did on her own time. My thanks, too, go to Emily Heckman whose knowledgeable direction during the self-publishing process was very helpful and on point.

My agent, Judith Ehrlich, more than once pressed me to re-write, and add to and subtract from, the manuscript in ways that always led to a better book. Along with her able associate Meredith Phelan, she made an honorable and thorough effort to market *Johnny Once*. I greatly appreciate their unfailing loyalty to the book and, it must be said, Meredith's ever-ready good cheer.

PROLOGUE

1964

Frank Rosario poked his head into the kitchen. "Get your jacket, Johnny. Time for you and me to go for a ride." The boy finished the eggplant sandwich his mother made from last night's leftovers and put his lunch dishes in the sink.

"Frankie boy coming with us?" John wondered.

"Not this time."

They stood in the hallway waiting for the elevator. A beam of bleak light came through the sullied glass behind them, casting brown shadows across the elevator door.

"Your brother's getting ready to watch the Yankee game," Frank said. "See if the Mick can hit another one outta the park."

* * *

It was late spring, a dry, warm Saturday; John wished he could be outside playing ball. The white Lincoln Continental was his father's one showboat possession, though, and the boy loved it, its large sleek body, the cushy seats, the smooth, comfortable ride. "Like you're on a cloud," he'd tell his friends. He imagined angels driving the recently deceased and deserving to heaven in a celestial vehicle very much like his family's car. Still, he thought, there was bound to be a game, stickball, maybe some hoops, at the Bay Parkway playground.

His father looked solemn. Had he done something wrong? "What's up, Pop?" he asked, his fingers strumming on the car's armrest. "You going to tell me about life? We covered the birds and bees stuff two years ago."

"Do yourself a favor, don't be such a wise guy. Today we're gonna cover new ground, something more important than sex."

"Now you got me interested," John said, attempting a jaunty tone.

Frank drove to Flatbush, steering the car up Ocean Parkway, a wide boulevard with long sidewalks for strolling pedestrians and a horseback riding path. "Look at all the trees." He waved his hand at the foliage whizzing past. "Lotsa, lotsa trees, a lot more than we have in Bensonhurst."

"Sure, Dad, it's real nice here." Was his father starting the serious part of their talk?

"Lotsa Jewish families live here," Frank continued. "Lotsa houses, lotta money, lawns like manicures. It's almost the suburbs. You know, there's a bigger world out there than Bensonhurst.... or Bay Ridge even."

"Dad, if you're trying to say there's more to life than Bensonhurst," John joked, "at least bring me to Manhattan, Park Avenue, some place like that."

Frank tightened his jaw and stared at the broad street in front of him: the prosperous middle-class homes, the well-appointed little yards. It was not Bensonhurst, but it was still Brooklyn and, though he was nearly 50 years old, it was all that his imagination about the future could hold. Maybe his son was right—taking the boy here was a lame effort.

John sensed his father was strained, uncomfortable. Usually the old man chatted amiably from behind the wheel, resting one arm on the window, sometimes pointing to an interesting street scene, a lord looking over his land.

Frank shook his head. Maybe by rattling his brain he could come up with the right words to convey notions he had never expressed, words he practically choked on, that John might be too young to grasp, yet were too late now for Frankie boy, his beloved first-born.

They were coming up on Coney Island, not Frank's intended destination, but where Ocean Parkway ended. "I'm gonna open my window—you do the same," he told John. The pungent ocean aroma filled the car. Father and son grinned as the salty air teased their nostrils.

"Don't you love it?" Frank said, breathing in. "Of course, in Coney Island the hot dog smell's mixed in."

"Why don't we stop at Nathan's," the boy said, "and get a frank or two."

"Good idea," Frank replied. "But I didn't take you out here for a guided tour, so I'm gonna stop tiptoeing around."

The image of his old man tiptoeing around anything amused John. It conjured up the cartoon coyote tiptoeing gingerly from behind tree to behind tree, planning his next futile pounce on the roadrunner. "Wish you would, Pop. The suspense is killing me."

The father turned his head and glared at his son. "Enough jokes, okay." He pulled the car onto one of the tree-lined side streets that ran along the boulevard and double-parked. He paused, intimidated by the task ahead. "Johnny, what I want to say here is that you should be like me but not like me."

Father and son sat in mirror image, backs against the car doors, facing one another. They each had a leg up on the front seat, an arm resting on the seat's top. Occasionally they could hear car sounds, brakes groaning at a stoplight, horns honking at people crossing the street too slowly.

John raised the hand resting on the seat. "Help me out, Pop. What are you telling me?"

Frank took a deep breath. "I do more than run the restaurant. I actually operate what our government says is wrong…illegal. Men work for me, guys like Eddie the Head, Angie's father, Husky, and Hoot Gibson, you know, whose old man used to own a stable."

John felt dizzy. His father had applied a sudden wrench to his world, tilting it sideways. "What kind of activities?" he asked cautiously. He had overheard stories about his father in the playground and at school—but nobody ever talked about such things at home and he never bothered to pursue the truth. He was 15 now and the old man obviously decided it was time for him to know.

Frank saw dismay on John's face and hesitated. "Look, we lend money to people who can't borrow from banks. That's sometimes called loan-sharking, a nasty term if you ask me. We operate gambling joints where people play cards, the roulette wheel. We run book on the races, ballgames, stuff like that, and we control the local numbers game. You gettin' all this?"

John nodded.

"Any questions?" Frank asked.

"D'ya do prostitution too?" John's tone was soft, accusing. It was the most sordid sin that occurred to his Catholic boy's mind.

A feeling of panic hit Frank like a lightning crack. He knew the conversation would be tough, but hadn't realized how much it could hurt John. I'm breaking the seal now for his own good, he reasoned. "Yeah, we run cathouses too. No girls in the street though, a strictly clean operation. No funny stuff allowed."

"Do you hurt people, or d'you have people, you know, beat up or killed?"

"Sometimes we rough people up," Frank replied, "to protect ourselves, our interests. In this business, you do unto others before they do it to you."

His father's words jolted the boy. He was drifting, drifting. He struggled to reverse, to grab hold of something. "Why do you do these things? Why are you telling me?"

Good questions, Frank thought. Two damn good questions. A temporary melancholy slipped over him like a damp, heavy coat.

A woman pushed a baby carriage in front of the car, gently rocking it, calming her crying child. Frank remembered teaching Johnny to ride a bike. They were on the sidewalk in front of their apartment and he held the seat to steady the six year-old boy who eventually achieved balance and pedaled solo down the block. He thought as his son grew smaller in the distance that sometimes what you teach them helps them leave you.

"It was different for us, Sicilian boys coming up in Little Italy, Cherry Street, Mulberry Street. Not like it is for you now, Johnny. You're a good student, a terrific ballplayer. You have opportunities. We didn't. School was a joke, the teachers ignored or chased us. The cops hated all the little wop kids. The gang was the way for us. We could stand tall, be the cocks in the yard. Not only for the rough boys, the smart ones wanted in too."

A strong wind blew in from the ocean just a few blocks away, rustling the leaves in nearby trees. The two Rosarios sat in silence for a moment, hoping, maybe, the worst was over.

"Another thing I gotta tell you," Frank said. "I stood by my word and my handshakes, protected my friends and family. When people needed a favor, I was the soft touch on the block. You wanna get your daughter into Catholic school, I'll take care of it. Your son's in trouble with the cops or some other boys, just let me know and I'll smooth things. You need some quick cash and you're a friend or a friend of a friend, I'll see to it you get it and your fingers don't get busted if you're late paying up."

The boy looked sad. "A regular Robin Hood, eh, Pop?"

Frank shook his head. "All I know is I do my share of good deeds. Always been a stand-up guy. That's why I said, 'Be like me.'"

"You also said, 'Don't be like me.'"

"Because I don't want you involved. You don't need it. Once in, it's not so easy to walk away."

The boy felt sick with confusion, nausea coming on. My father loves me, yet rejects me. He rejects me because he loves me. John had one question left. "What about Frankie?"

Frank pursed his lips, nodded. "Never speak about this with your brother. He'll probably follow me, take over the family business. Now he's just hanging out at the restaurant, doing some errands for me. Strictly legit."

The boy gave his father a puzzled look.

"Ah, shit," the father said under his breath. "Frankie just made it through New Utrecht, doesn't have as much going for him in the brains department. He's a good boy, though, smart in his own way. I think he'll be alright with me guiding him. Remember, mum's the word."

John faced the windshield, arms across his chest, hugging himself. He turned to look at two young boys dashing by on scooters on the sidewalk. Legs churning, they laughed and shouted as they raced each other across the street.

The father asked, "You okay?"

"Not really, but don't worry. I'm not gonna run away from home or anything." But home will never be the same, John thought.

Frank turned the key in the ignition and raced the car's engine. "Considering everything, guess Nathan's is out."

"Maybe some other time," the boy said.

CHAPTER 1

1993

John Rosario woke from dreams of Brooklyn. Deep, noisy dreams of Benson-hurst Brooklyn, that gaudy Italian place, dreams that always came the nights before he visited home. He sat up on the side of the bed, feet like dead weights on the floor. He held his hands in front of his face, stared at them, and shrugged—gestures of bemusement.

Why do I still think of Brooklyn as my home? A familiar question, like an old friend he tried to outgrow but couldn't. Although it was early Saturday morning, the street below his Manhattan apartment was already bustling with sounds.

He missed his children, his pain-in-the-ass boisterous boys, how their video-game playing and goofing-around sounds and even their sleeping presence filled the apartment. Suzanne took them on the weekends he drove into Brooklyn.

John consoled himself with the thought that his sons would love the food he retrieved from the outland. They always treated his mother's cooking with special regard, sometimes slapping fives before sinking forks into the pasta filled with soft ricotta cheese or sweet meatballs and sausages covered with her generous sauce, the "gravy" of his earlier days. His boys had grown up on Manhattan's west side and socialized with Jewish people, a sprinkling of WASPS and African Americans—they rarely visited the other boroughs. They had little contact with Italians and their home-cooked dishes, except for these treasured "care packages" from Brooklyn.

His brother, whom he'd see on Sunday—he loved Frank deeply, but from a distance—teased him about his infrequent Bensonhurst appearances. "Hey, Johnny, the border guards at the Battery Tunnel stamp your passport?"

Before going into the bathroom, John put on an album, Dion, a paisan rock & roller. Food and music, he thought, ties that bind. It was contemporary Dion, "King of the New York Streets". Oh yeah, the city's gritty spirit lives. He smiled as he dressed for the day.

❧   ❧   ❧

He was driving to pick up his mother, a friend of hers, maybe a relative or two, and take them to the quiet, pastoral cemetery where his father was buried. The traffic was light, and from the Belt Parkway he could enjoy the serene vistas of the Narrows separating Brooklyn from the near suburbia of Staten Island. The ballfields on the other side of the parkway recalled his youth. His father and sometimes his brother took him there to have a catch, toss a football around or shoot hoops. He winced at the memory of his father's disappointment when the old man realized his athletic son preferred this new game basketball to the old standby baseball.

He drove past Xaverian, his alma mater, where his intellectual awakening began, where he made second team all city among catholic high school players, where valued friendships flowered—although Charles was the only one he still saw. But there were too many jerks. Tensions ran high between the Irish and Italian boys—tame stuff, he realized, compared to the black and white antagonisms of today. And, of course, no girls. *That* was a drag. Females were strange creatures to him for too long.

His car's tape deck played a wistful soundtrack. Frank Sinatra, the family cultural icon, Dion, and, of course, the Steely Dan number, "Brooklyn", that fellow Brooklyn boy Harry Glassman turned him onto years ago. *Brooklyn owes the charmer under me* goes the chorus. Indeed.

He swung his car onto the service road, slowed down to look at the old amusement park with the rickety ferris wheel and the relatively new Toys-R-Us. Then onto Bay Parkway alongside the playground where the handball courts stood empty early Saturday morning.

Up 86th Street, past the clothing stores where his mom used to buy him pants and shoes, the pizza places and candy stores with signs in red, white, green, and sometimes blue, hawking sicilian slices and egg creams. He sometimes hung out at these places as a teenager—not that much because he never felt comfortable with the local boys. Besides, he had his studies and basketball practices and games.

Brooklyn was an outdoors place, especially on a warm June day like this. The girls with their showy hairdos, tight pants and heels; the boys with their shirt sleeves rolled up, long hair and loud voices, already congregating in small groups on barely sunlit corners.

He reached his mother's apartment, out where 86th Street, liberated from the shadows of the outdoor subway tracks traveling noisily above it, became a by-way of open spaces. Italian Bensonhurst, a town of big skies and low buildings.

In a refreshing change from his Manhattan life, he quickly found a parking space across the street from his old building. Grabbing exercise whenever he could, he passed on the elevator and walked up to the 5th floor apartment. He remembered racing his friends, and sometimes his brother, up the same dark stairwells.

It was a spacious apartment, though modest by the standards set by the homes of men in Frank Rosario's line of work. John let himself in, paused to breathe in the familiar aromas wafting out of the kitchen.

"Johnny, that you?" his mother called out.

He walked to the back of the apartment, past the living room with the television console and big couch and two easy chairs covered in shiny plastic. Where does mom sit when she watches T.V.? he wondered.

He spoke to the woman behind the closed bedroom door. "It's me, not a daytime burglar." And then, child-like, "I'm here!"

"I'm getting ready," she said from inside the room. "Angie's coming with us." Angie was the daughter of his mother's best friend, Louise, whose husband had been his father's best friend. The two men worked closely together and died within a year of each other, from natural causes, and were buried in the same cemetery.

"Angie," he murmured. Then louder, "That's a pleasant surprise."

"Isn't it?" his mom said. "You heard she separated from that cabbage head Dominic?" His mother years ago adopted his father's practice of disparaging people by calling them some kind of food. Pineapple, sausage, frankfurter were among his old man's favorites.

"Mom, how would I hear?" he asked, still standing in the hallway outside her room. "I'm not exactly connected to the old crowd from the neighborhood." Angie apart from Dominic. He smiled, despite himself. He looked at pictures on the wall, mainly of his father, brother, and him at ceremonial occasions: first communions, weddings, wakes.

"She and her boy are living with Louise," his mother went on, "and she wanted to take the ride with us today. Okay?"

"No problem," he said. "I'll wait for you in the kitchen. Going to catch the meatballs in a dish as they fly out of the pot. You know, right before they hit the floor."

"Yeah," she said. "It's a rough job, but somebody's got to do it."

    ❦   ❦   ❦

He sat in the kitchen at the old table, covered by the sticky white oilcloth, salt, pepper, and olive oil in easy reach. Won't eat much of this, he thought, looking at the plate he prepared. Save the rest for the care package, good for at least two hardy meals for me and the boys. He nibbled at one large meatball, licking off the sauce, savoring the tiny bites, prolonging the pleasure.

Angelina Capobella. They grew up together, almost like brother and sister when they were kids, moved apart as they got older. She had a wonderful energy and was bolder than he. By high school, he knew she shouldn't be stuck in Bensonhurst, but didn't know how to help her get out, or even how to tell her she should get out. They had become too different.

I eat appetizer twice/Just because she is so nice/Angelina, waitress at the pizzeria. He recalled Angie's smile, how her face softened when her father mimicked Louis Prima singing those lines.

When they were teens, her assured sexuality confused him. He dreamed of having her. But it would have been like incest. Incest, mincest, he thought, annoyed with himself even now. I was just too afraid.

There was the time Angie's parents, Eddie and Louise, worried about how she was doing in school, had her do homework with John, the studious one. They were in the 8th grade at Our Lady of Perpetual Help. She was already becoming one of the wild, neighborhood girls—snapping her gum, sneaking smokes, wearing pedal pushers too tight—though she never did her hair up in those garish bouffants.

They were at his apartment, their books sprawled across the big dining room table. It was Sunday night and they were supposed to complete their weekend assignments. At Angie's insistence, they put the radio on a rock & roll station. Songs came on that they loved—"Come Go With Me" by the Del

Vikings, "Gee" by the Crows, or, best of all, a Dion track, "Ruby Baby." John knew that without the music, homework was hardly bearable to Angie.

"How could "Ruby Baby" not make it to number one?" she yelped, only half-kidding. "Or "Donna the Prima Donna", a great song if there ever was one. I wanna dance just thinkin' about it."

"You know," he told her, "they say Dion wrote "Donna the Prima Donna" for his sister."

"Yeah?" She saw a story coming. She put her elbow on the table, rested her head in her palm, gazed at him.

"His sister's name was Donna," he said, "and she was feeling low down about some old boyfriend or something, and he wrote this song to cheer her up."

"You see, he's really a nice guy and they should make his song number one, right?"

"Definitely," he said. A favorite word of the men who sometimes hung around with his father.

She fingered the schoolbooks they were studying about the differences between Greek and Roman civilizations. "I hate this stuff, Johnny. Can't do it, don't really want to. I know you do and that's okay, that's great but...."

"It's like it's not for you."

Her eyes showed confusion, but she nodded.

"I don't care what they say about his sister and all," he said. "I bet Dion wrote "Donna the Prima Donna" about you. When I hear it, I think of you, can see you move."

She nudged his shoulder and smiled. "You say the sweetest things, Johnny Rosario."

After the failed study sessions, he went on to straight A's, and she to barely getting by. He made it into Xaverian High School and its honors course, in Bay Ridge. She attended the local public high school, New Utrecht, with the black kids and the rest of the Italian punks and gumbahs. He was rarely seen around the neighborhood. She became a regular at two or three of its popular haunts.

His mother appeared at the kitchen doorway, dressed in light gray for her trip to her husband's grave. She was a small, dignified woman, her round pretty face showing the first traces of wrinkles around the eyes, her body grown somewhat stout. Her gray hair was cut in a shorter style than usual. She seemed subdued, without her usual determined energy.

"You okay, Mom?"

"Yes," she said. She glanced at his plate—he hadn't eaten enough of her food. "Are *you* okay?"

"Well, I had a rough week and was just sitting here trying to figure things out." He sat back in his chair, fork still in hand. "It's hard trying to change the world." It was the kind of flip remark he used about his work with family members who generally didn't understand what he did and why. He ran the non-profit Urban Justice Institute which, among other things, advocated greater public funding for social services. He'd gone to an Ivy League college—the first Rosario to go to any college at all—and then came back to New York to do some type of "social work." Trying to get the government to help the poor. Low wages, lots of grief.

"Why is it you who has to change the world?" she asked.

"You know pop taught us to stick up for the little guy."

"Those people are lucky to have you." She patted his head.

He got up and hugged her. "Marie Rosario, my biggest fan."

Outside, Marie struggled to get into the front passenger seat of her son's mini-van—a high step for her short legs. She had learned by now to wear a pants outfit. With his help, she lifted herself up and settled into place.

As usual, she commented on what a wonderful, spacious car he now owned—he had "now" owned it for 3½ years. Suzanne and he bought it as a last ditch investment in their family and their life together. They needed something to take themselves, the boys, and their friends on those weekend excursions they used to love—trips that regularly turned into squabblefests by the end.

It didn't help save his marriage, but John adored his van, the way it elevated him in the driver's seat, the smooth ride, the reclining seats with arm rests no less, the power windows handy at toll booths, the stereo tape deck that filled the car with his favorite music. It was the first time he had loved a mainstream, American consumer object. He would have felt almost yuppified if there weren't so much of his life that didn't fit the stereotype. Then again, if he were more of a yuppie, maybe Suzanne and he would still share a life.

They drove up Cropsey Ave—the sky grew wider, brighter as they approached the Atlantic Ocean—toward the house of John's Uncle Whiney. Marie brought John up to date on her life: the women she met selling housewares at Macy's where she still worked three days a week, her sister Dora's latest troubles with her daughter who was battling a drug habit, the old Fred Astaire/ Ginger Rogers movie she had just seen on cable—"Oh, how they danced, Johnny; I could watch their pictures every night"—and the new menu at Rosario's, which he would visit tomorrow. John was barely interested.

"What's the story with Angie?"

Marie gave John a blank look.

"What finally pushed her to leave the cabbagehead?"

"You know," she said slyly, "your father and I hoped for a long time Angie and you would…. When you were kids, you were such good friends. It was the talk of the family how much time you two, a boy and girl, spent together."

"When we were kids, that's true," he said, "but things changed. I got interested in the outside world. She stayed a Brooklyn girl, hung out with kids like Dominic."

Marie frowned. "Always thought you let her slip away."

"C'mon, Mom, it never would've worked," he snapped, not the usual way he talked to his mother. He knew she had touched a deep sore.

❁   ❁   ❁

Whiney's real name was Ernest. His mother called him Ernesto. His wife called him Ernie. Everyone else called him Whiney. John once asked his father how his uncle got the nickname. When he was about 9 years old, Frank Rosario had a friend named Whiney who moved off the block. He missed this kid so much he started calling his seven year old brother Whiney. "Helluva way for a guy to get a nickname that lasts a lifetime," Frank admitted. He had no idea why the friend who left was called Whiney.

Whiney was everybody's favorite relative, and Christmas Eve his big night. He gave out the presents stacked under Grandma Rosario's tall, bushy tree. John sat on the staircase with his brother, his cousins and friends like Angie, whose family frequently joined these gatherings, and nearly burst with anticipation. Whiney often left John's gifts till the end. He spread his palms outward to his small audience, slapped his forehead with his hand, and pretended, Oh my gosh, nothing's left. This was John's cue to jump up and point frantically to the pile of presents hidden behind the tree, while Whiney grinned, apologizing elaborately. He had no children of his own.

Whiney lived off Cropsey Avenue, not far from Coney Island, in a red brick house with a narrow porch and small front yard. He shared his home with his second wife, a Jewish woman named Shirley. He was so beloved, and had such a rough time with his first marriage, that the Rosario clan hardly objected to his non-Italian second bride. Now after so many years, she was fully accepted. Shirley was a frail woman, though, and couldn't make the cemetery trip.

Whiney's house was a welcoming place—the fragrant sea breeze blowing in from the nearby beaches; the warm, sunlight-filled living room where Marie and John sat. Shirley remained upstairs in her bedroom, out of sight.

Whiney sat in his easy chair. He was a large man for a Sicilian, with bright white wavy hair, and a leathery dark face. He seemed sad—he'd seemed sad a lot lately—the usual sparkle in his eyes not gone, never gone, but subdued.

"Let's go," he said, rising from his chair. "The beloved deceased await our arrival. We should not delay." He winked at John.

"We hafta pick up Louise and Angie first," Marie said.

"Angie," Whiney said, taking in the news. "A sight for sore eyes."

❧   ❧   ❧

The Capobella house was one of the neighborhood's biggest. It had three levels of rooms and windows and a broad shingled front, with a wood fence along the sidewalk, medium-sized yards in front and back that Angie's mother Louise decorated with patches of flowers, and a spacious porch that wrapped around the front. When they were kids, John told Angie he thought of the house as a piece of Kansas somehow blown to Brooklyn by Dorothy and Toto's twister of a tornado. She called him a "regular poet" and went into the front yard to look at her house as if for the first time. Hands on hips, she laughed. "Ya know, you're right!" She ran to the back yard to search under one of her mother's flower beds for Dorothy's magic shoes.

John entered the old house with sharpened anticipation—he felt that Marie, Whiney, and he were moving in slow motion, as in a suppressed dream suddenly remembered. They stood in the front living room with Louise, the big picture window looking onto the bushes in the yard. He recalled a brightly decorated Christmas tree in a corner by the piano filling the room with its piney aroma. As they exchanged hugs and hellos with Louise, he wondered nervously, where's Angie?

The last time he saw her four or five years ago, at his father's wake—or was it her father's funeral?—she looked dispirited, her color gone. She was dressed in black, of course, but more primly than even the occasion called for. Her hair, long and seductively unkempt in her youth, was trimmed and streaked here and there with gray. She was very sad, not only about her or his father's death, but about her life. "Time takes its toll, doesn't it, Johnny," she said and he agreed. He promised himself to call her and see her for lunch, but never did.

He hoped she was in better shape now, that the change in her life signaled a renewal. His heart pounded in expectation, like he was a boy again, before a special date or big game.

"Why don't you go see Angie?" Louise said. "She's out back, tending the flowers."

"Don't keep her all to yourself, Johnny," Whiney called after him. "Bring her in here after you get the garden tour."

Angie was bending down, digging a hand shovel into the ground. She wore an old pair of dungarees—he noted the snug fit—and a man's short-sleeved shirt, perhaps a "hand me up" from her son Donnie. She didn't know John was there and like a smoker inhaling, he took in the full view of her. Hmm, she looks good from here.

She glanced up, grinned, then stood up. She brushed her hair off her face—the streaks of gray were gone. Her movements were light, easy. "Johnny the Rose Rosario." She wagged a finger at him. "I remember you."

He gently pushed her finger away, took her hand and kissed her on the cheek. He stepped back to look at her. "And I you."

She guided him around the yard, showing him the tomatoes, cucumbers and basil. "There's the proof," he said, shaking his head. "These things *do* grow in the ground. Thought some factory made them and trucked them to the stores."

"Very cute," Angie responded. "You always were a city boy."

They stood over the flowers, which bobbed prettily in the slight wind that made its way to the back yard. Purple pansies, white powder puffs, yellow tulips, red roses. "My additions," she said, "like a rainbow, but 'stead of in the sky, they're on the ground, at our feet. Like a sign of hope." She seemed a bit embarrassed.

"Flowers, metaphors. I'm impressed." He could have teased her but decided to be kind. It was his truer feeling.

"I just thought it was time to tend my own garden…. or at least my mother's garden," she said with a laugh.

"Like Voltaire said."

"Who? Oh yeah, the French guy."

John lowered his head, stepped aside with a modest flourish, and she led the way into the house.

❦   ❦   ❦

On the drive to the cemetery, Marie sat next to John, Angie behind him. He was giddy with the emotions Angie roused in him, a rush he hadn't felt since before his break-up with Suzanne a year ago. He wanted to show off, crack wise and witty, take a turn on two wheels.

In the heat's haze, Brooklyn scenes floated past like in a film. Small delivery trucks parked in front of restaurants and food markets; stout, middle-aged women carrying shopping bags, stalking yet more shops; expressionless old men sitting on porches listening to the radio: was the Yankee game on yet?

Angie's life was the main topic of conversation—she spoke freely in response to Marie's questions. She had separated from Dominic about three months ago and got a job in the city as office manager for the Organization of Neighborhood Services, a federation of the city's settlement houses that John occasionally worked with over the years. "Next time I'm there," he said, "I'll come see you." "And you'd be welcome," she came back, "if I'm not too busy." He made an unhappy face and she grinned.

Angie worried about her son Donnie, who was generally sullen and uncom-municative and spent too much time in the street. He was barely hanging on at school—Xaverian, where, she pointed out, he played basketball like some other young man she had known—and defied many of her attempts to manage him. His father alternated between furious rages at the boy and an almost proud shrug of the shoulders, boys-will-be-boys attitude. "I don't want him to become just another Bensonhurst hoodlum," Angie said and John wondered whether she meant that literally. The mob, he figured, still recruited in Benson-hurst. Maybe he should talk to his brother about setting the boy straight, at least on that score.

From the back of the van, Whiney spoke. "Hope your boy knows that there ain't no more "Godfather" out here. Those days are over. It's all "Goodfellas" now." His voice was unusually bitter.

"I'm afraid he wouldn't know the difference," Angie said.

John thought about Angie's marriage: How could she stay with Dominic so long? A long dormant jealousy smouldered. He remembered when they were in their early teens watching Dominic beat up a tall, blond, skinny kid in the playground. Dominic and Larry Forno were in a stand-off, Larry turned around when one of Dominic's cronies called his name, Dominic tripped him, pushed him to the concrete, and kicked him in the gut and head until other boys intervened.

John thought of Dominic as a punk, loud and brutish, surrounding himself with friends he could easily boss. He was often pissy with John whom he saw as a snob, stuck up, "too good for the rest of us guinies."

What did she see in him? When they were 13 or 14, Angie said to John, "Johnny Rosario and Dominic Roselli, one the good rose, the other my bad rose." Has she left him for good?

❦ ❦ ❦

Louise fussed about her husband's small, marble gravestone, placing green and red artificial flowers, roses and geraniums, in front of it, clearing away the dirt, tidying up the shrine. Angie laid a comforting hand on her mother's kneeling figure and lowered her head. Marie joined the women at the gravestone and murmured a prayer, while the men hung back, looking solemn. When the plastic flowers appeared, Whiney whispered to his nephew, "Given Eddie's extreme condition, I personally think he deserves the real thing."

As they walked up a hilly path to his brother's grave, Whiney sighed, shook his head. "This shouldn't be, this shouldn't be."

They stood at a curve in the road that wound its way through the cemetery's tree-filled acres. A long line of black limos lumbered past. A mob funeral? John wondered. Couldn't be—Whiney would've said something.

He saw that his mother had finally arranged for an inscription on the gravestone and that a middle initial was added: Frank P. Rosario. "I didn't know dad had a middle name. What's the P stand for?" His tone said: there are some things I should know by now.

"Nothing," she replied. "They asked me for a middle initial and that's what came to me."

A 'why not' smile creased John's lips. Marie knelt at the stone, crossed herself and prayed softly. Whiney came up behind her, next to John, and said, "Let's make it stand for Placido, because Frank, my dear brother, was truly a peaceful man." John nodded his approval.

"What am I doing alive," Whiney said, giving way to his sorrow, "while he's dead? Damn it, I miss him." The old man fought back a sob. John touched his uncle's arm and a sudden melancholy came over him. He felt physically weak. Now not so much to console Whiney, but to steady himself, he gripped his uncle's arm. He pictured his father sitting in the big chair in the old apartment, reading the paper, sipping a cup of expresso. He recalled the drive to Coney Island when he was a boy, his old man's emotional appeal. He bit his lip and looked up to the sky.

On the way back to the van, Angie put her hand on John's shoulder. "How ya doin', big fella?"

"Watching Whiney brought me down. I wish, you know, my father was still around." They passed other small groups of people walking to and from burial sites, Brooklynites going through their paces in a blessed place. "Thanks for asking," he said.

She smiled. "What are friends for?"

He moved more slowly. "Where we having dinner tonight, your mom's or mine?"

"Mine, I think."

He paused, seemed distracted. She stopped too and they stood together. "Want to go out afterwards?" he asked. "For a walk and ice cream or something?"

"Sounds sweet," she said, surprised, smiling again.

❦   ❦   ❦

John and Angie were too full for dessert. Dinner had been a championship match—rounds and rounds of food: eggplant, pasta, chicken, potatoes, sausages, meatballs, and on and on. They headed for the park, for a stroll along the shore, and passed without talking small brick homes that lined the darkening Brooklyn streets. When they came close enough to the water to smell the sea, John said, "Catch a whiff. It always took me away from Brooklyn."

They followed the sidewalk at the park's boundary till they reached the concrete path that ran along the Narrows, the stretch of water separating Brooklyn from Staten Island and the rest of the world. The lights of the Verrazano Bridge gleamed in the distance. They saw lovers holding hands, walking slowly and kids, too, tired stragglers with their balls, gloves and bats going home for a late dinner.

They sat on a bench and looked out onto the water.

"Interesting where you bring me," Angie said. "I come here every so often, think about things…. my life, Donnie, my marriage. It was on this very spot"—she smiled—"that I decided to separate from Dominic."

"Should put a plaque on the bench," he said, "commemorating the moment." He was hardly joking, he realized.

"That's a thought," she said.

"Why do you call him 'Donnie' anyway?" A question he meant to ask for years.

"One of his young cousins couldn't pronounce Dominic and called him that when he was a baby. I latched onto it. Didn't want him known as Dominic Jr. But enough about me. What about your life? When did you decide to break up *your* marriage? You know, to that Protestant girl you hooked up with."

"Starting with easy questions, huh?"

"Met her in college?" Angie persisted.

"Yes, right." He told her it was like an exotic attraction, birds of different feathers coming together. "Suzanne and I were trying to break free of our families, and kind of used each other to declare ourselves, our separate identities." He paused. "Am I making sense?"

"Yeah, I think," she said. "My relationship with Dominic was different. I went with him, let's face it, mainly because he was familiar, like the corner grocery or something." Angie sat back on the bench. "So Suzanne and you used each other? You weren't really in love?" She squinted her face, as if trying to peer inside him and find the truth of things.

"No, we were. At least we thought we were." He brushed her nose with his finger, pushing her back gently. "Suzanne and I had lots of things going for us."

"Like what?" Angie moved toward him.

"Hey," he said, "you're crowding me!" He was relaxing, though, surrendering. To the warm evening air, to Angie's talk and presence. "Same politics, progressive," he continued, winking at her. "Liked to go to movies and read books together…. also had terrific sexual experiences." He stretched out the syllables of the last two words.

"I bet," she said, "that's all you were really interested in."

They gazed at each other, grinning, the heat stirring between them. They embraced, the upper halves of their bodies pressing together, and kissed at first gently, then more firmly. "That was great," he gasped.

"And long overdue," she said. "And enough for tonight." She stood up, wobbled a bit, then gained her balance. "Let's go home."

"What?" He leaned back on the bench. "Just when the fun begins." She gave him a look. "Okay, okay," he said, holding up his hands.

"Mustn't worry our moms by staying out too late, you know." She took his arm, swung him around and headed up the path to the exit. They dropped their hands to their sides when they reached the streets. Someone they knew might see them.

❦   ❦   ❦

John didn't expect the warm rush of the kiss in the park. Angie's sexuality, the re-connect to Brooklyn—they drew him in and drove him off. His psyche was relieved, but his body disappointed. His groin was sore, his arms tingled, his chest still felt the press of her breasts. He thought of the dumb old joke: The guy says to the girl: "If I tell you have a beautiful body, will you hold it against me?" He looked forward to a shower. And to his next date with Angie. He wondered what she was thinking.

"So, why'd you and Suzanne split?" Angie asked.

"Not going to let me off the hook, are you?"

She stopped on the sidewalk and poked him in the chest. "Don't think you can shake me off with a sexy kiss." She paused, appearing to savor the memory of it. "I knew you once, but who are you now, Johnny Rosario?"

Clouds began to assemble over the Narrows, slowly creeping forward like thieves to steal away whatever light the stars and moon bestowed on Bensonhurst. Suzanne and he had begun to fight more after their second boy, Teddy, was born. Except for politics, and, maybe, movies, they felt differently about most things: music, food, friends, vacations. Even her looks started to bother him: although a beauty, or nearly one, she was too tall, angular and blond.

She grew annoyed with his behavior in company, particularly among her professional colleagues; after a night out she would knock him for his loudness, his penchant for wisecracking. A successful attorney in a corporate firm, she began working late nights, and he felt neglected and thought the kids did too—though he enjoyed the time alone at home with the boys.

Finally, while he flirted off and on with a prisoners' rights lawyer, he discovered Suzanne was having an affair with someone at her firm. After a couple of nights or so of crazy pain and jealousy, he realized their marriage was over. Ultimately, he had to admit, he felt relief, as Suzanne did. They worked together on an amicable separation and divorce. Why wreck everything: the memories, especially of good times with the boys, the possibility of friendship and of parenting together. It would've been madness to toss all that away.

The strolling couple reached Angie's front gate, the night's quiet broken by music blaring from a passing car. John turned toward the noise, then looked expectantly at Angie. He was surprised at how frank he'd been—and worried about her response.

"How'd the kids handle it?" she asked.

It had been difficult, especially for the older boy, Jake, an intense child, who needed both parents, an intact family. He had a tough year at school where his mood swings annoyed teachers and kids alike. What with therapy, though, and Suzanne and him getting along, the boy seemed more settled now.

"That's good," Angie murmured. "Wish Dominic and I could do it that way, you know, reach a kind of understanding. But," she sighed, "he's such a fucking asshole."

"Sorry, Angie," John said. "But I was lucky, married New England, high-brow and sensible. You got stuck with Brooklyn, a primitive form of it."

"Yeah, that's the difference between you and me." She spoke without ire.

"Maybe we're not so different anymore."

She seemed to take comfort in his words. "We should go in now." She started up the steps. "You'll call me this time and soon?" Her tone was a mix of request and command.

He stayed back for a moment and could barely see her in the porch light. "Very soon, I promise."

❦   ❦   ❦

John dreamt that night he was a boy again, at church on Sunday morning with his Catholic school class. He felt isolated and anxious because none of his friends would talk to him, in fact were mocking him about some incident he didn't understand. Seeking refuge, he approached a statue of the Virgin Mary which suddenly turned into a swaying figure, sullen and seductive like Ellen Barkin in "Sea of Love," her hands beckoning him toward her. Drawn into her spell, he reached out to touch and feel her moving body. She knocked his hand away and scolded him for his dirty thoughts and actions. "Now you'll really have to go to confession." He woke up with the sound of those words echoing in his head. He got out of bed with an abrupt motion, let his arms hang loose and did a kind of St. Vitus dance, trying to break free of the nocturnal images.

He stopped and rubbed his head, grinning about his subconscious that turned the Blessed Virgin into a taunting vamp. He felt a quick thud of terror like a hot, sharp rock in his gut and had to go to the bathroom. He sat on the toilet. Like so many others, he thought, I desperately want something that scares the shit out of me.

CHAPTER 2

On Sunday afternoon John drove to Rosario's. Gray clouds covered the sky and cast a long shadow over the streets. The weather matched the pall-like feeling in the neighborhood: the Sunday quiet, the absence of humans and honking cars. The aroma of pasta sauces coming out of kitchen windows was the only sign of life.

John thought about his brother: Frankie, with the sad eyes. It was family lore that Frank resembled his Uncle Whiney. Dark complexion, elaborate hand gestures, bushy eyebrows, long, full nose. But the eyes were different—Whiney's sparkled and Frank's drooped.

Frank Rosario Jr. ran the family restaurant, a one-story, red brick building, old-fashioned in its menu and modest in its decor, its main door opening onto the corner of a popular by-way deep in the heart of Bensonhurst. Its one garish ornament, a flashing neon "Rosario's" sign splashed across the top of its front window, worked only intermittently and no one seemed to mind. Supervised with autocratic authority by Frank's wife Theresa, who was spelled at times by the family matriarch Marie, the kitchen yielded tasty and robust Italian meals favored by the 40 something and older folks who were the restaurant's steady customers. Things change, sure, but in Bensonhurst, some things really didn't and one of them was Rosario's.

John escaped Bensonhurst. He'd been the fortunate son, in high school and beyond. After their drive to Brooklyn's netherworld, his father never mentioned the mob to him again. The old man pointed the way and John walked through the opened door. *He never had to feel guilty about the sins of his father. That was by his old man's design. He just felt guilty about his brother.*

Frank stayed back, squeaked through high school, hung out first with the neighborhood boys, then with the old man and his gang, and inherited the family business in all its forms. Based mainly on the conversation with his father, John could only imagine the specifics of this arrangement—bookmaking, loansharking, the occasional strong-arm, prostitution carefully appointed. He did know that Frank had not challenged his life's pattern, and now when he walked, shoulders slightly slumped, the burden seemed visible, touchable.

John kept trying to talk Frank into leaving the mob. "Make the break, live off the restaurant, move to another state, that's what Dad really wanted. Whiney will cover for you with the capos uptown. It's a fucking sewer now, with low-life punks like Gotti taking over." Frank would sit there, at the table by the kitchen doors, the ballgame on in the background, and shake his head. "Can't do it, Johnny." He would raise his hand and wave toward the room, the walls, tables and chairs. "This is what I know."

Frank was like the family dog: kind, decent, lovable, and very loyal. Protective and watchful, he'd never hurt his own people, only the enemies of his family or business, often one and the same. Most of the time he hung around the house, head resting on his paws, looking up at the world and the people around him with sad eyes.

Their father was a different breed, the top dog. He was tall and slender like John, but dark-skinned like Whiney and Frank. Marie still spoke breathlessly about his looks—she could not believe she had captured the neighborhood's most handsome man. Bright, black hair, deep brown complexion, easy, almost luminous smile and prominent dimpled chin—a swarthy Cary Grant.

The old man once told a family gathering about an impressed woman who swore he was one of the best-looking men in the world along with Grant and Tyrone Power. He had laughed. "I just got one question, how does Tyrone Power make the top three?"

❦ ❦ ❦

As he did often on his Bensonhurst visits, especially on the drive to the restaurant, John recalled the last time Frank and he were together with their father. Six or so years ago the brothers went to see the old man at the hospital. What was at first a tame skin cancer, a tiny tumor on Frank Rosario's long, beautiful nose, had invaded his body and spread like a hungry fire on a dry prairie. Although the brothers visited their father often, they were shocked each time—the man, whose able-bodied presence once filled a room, diminished and shrunken by his approaching death, confined entirely by the cold, white walls of his nondescript hospital chamber.

Their father motioned with his head. "Come here," he croaked, "got something I want the two of you to hear, but especially you, Frankie. Something we've only danced around before." The old man paused, for dramatic effect, John thought. "Get out of the family business, leave the gang. It stinks to hell."

The older son glanced at his brother, then his father. His eyes betrayed his distress. "Whadyamean, Pop, get out of the business? What is this, some kind of death bed delirium?"

"It's different than when I started," Frank Rosario said. "Shit, it's different than 15-20 years ago. Too many frankfurters joining up and nobody's telling 'em to say it walking. You know what I'm fucking saying here, Frankie."

A nurse peered in, saw the three men huddled together, and swished away. John wished she had come in, tended to one of their father's physical needs.

"I know, Pop," Frank said, "I'm not blind, but...." He sought the right words to reassure his father. "I can handle it, I know my boys, keep things local. Act polite to the fucking jerks who come around, but don't get involved. It's cool, Dad, it's cool."

"It's not 'cool', not anymore," the old man said. "You can't control it, nobody can. There's too much double crossing, too much drugs, too many guys with no class."

No class guy, the opposite of stand-up guy, and, the two brothers knew, the worst thing their father could call a man.

The father's gaze shifted from his sons, seemed to light on the medical gadgets hanging over his head. "Don't you think I know what's going on? Drugs, they're pushing that fucking crap on you, want it on the streets.... girls too." The old man breathed heavily, waiting for his strength to return. The gadgets overhead burbled sounds, flashed lights. "I hurt people, drew the curtain on some of them, but that was war where all's fair, right.... heh, heh," he snickered lowly.

Maybe Frankie's right, John thought. He is in a delirious state.

"But I drew lines, kept the innocent out of harm's way, stopped that damn poison from coming into our backyard. Not when Frank Rosario was running things."

John noted the sharp intensity in his father's eyes. The old man's not talking to us, he thought, but to his gods, whoever, wherever they may be.

"Look, Frankie, I got you into this, now I want you to get out. I know it can be done because I've talked to people. My brother Whiney can help with this. Think about it for me. Before I die, tell me you'll think about it."

His sons did not remember Frank Rosario begging them for anything. His plea had a special power.

Frank reached through the plastic tubes surrounding the bed and clasped the old man's hand. "I will think about it, Pop," he said. "Gonna see what I can do."

The old man stared at Frank. "Think about it, not from the feet, but from the head, right?"

Frank grinned. "Don't worry, Pop, from the head."

"Good," the father said. He patted his son's hands and closed his eyes in a quickly achieved deep sleep.

Frank's hands shook as he put on his hat. He stood with his brother in the hallway outside their father's room. "How about the old man?" he said. "Love him like my kids, but isn't it a little late for this?"

"Don't know, Frankie. Maybe it's a better-late-than-never thing." John's guilt was palpable, like a pressure in his chest.

"Sorry, Johnny, that's not how these eyes see it." Frank pointed two fingers at his own eyes.

Three young doctors breezed by, white coats flapping, laughing about a golf game, someone's missed putt.

"It came straight from the old man's heart," John persisted. "You should think about it."

As the two brothers headed for the elevator, Frank said, "Easier said than done, Johnny Boy, much easier said than done."

On the ride down John said, "Drew the curtain on some people?"

"The hard truth, Johnny. Hope it didn't pop your virgin ears."

"Don't worry about me, big brother." Though it pained him, their father's revelation was not that surprising to John, and he resented Frank's condescension.

An orderly clad in green got on, wheeling an empty gurney. Frank and John did not mind—neither could think of anything else to say.

❀   ❀   ❀

John parked the van across the street from the restaurant, in front of a funeral parlor with the flashy sign, *Daniel George's*. Going back to Frank Rosario Sr.'s time, Danny George never seemed to age. The Dick Clark of undertakers, he was the doleful friend of every family in the neighborhood.

Since their father's death-bed plea, Frank had not referred to the family's Mafia connection and John never asked. But he noticed changes. Frank put more money into the restaurant, the legitimate front—an expanded menu with child-sized portions, a wall knocked down to make space for more tables, flyers stuck under windshield wipers. Fewer of Frank's guys hung out at the restaurant, and John didn't miss them. They were friendly but dull men who could talk only about women, sports, and, curiously, food, but who knew and cared little about the outside world. The only regulars now were Dominic Roselli, Angie's ex-husband and still Frank's right-hand man, and Fat Tony Trapani, their loyal compadre whose roly-poly girth and ready good cheer marked him as one of Bensonhurst's favorite characters.

Frank sat at his usual table in a small alcove to the right of the swinging doors leading in and out of the kitchen. A medium-sized, faux mahogany television set flickered from a small platform extending from the wall above the table. Frank occasionally glanced up at it from his paper work—the Yankee game, naturally.

Frank rose slowly from his chair when John came in, his slouch more pronounced—whatever load he carried had gotten heavier. The two brothers shook hands, hugged quickly, and sat down.

"Good to see you," Frank said. "How long has it been? Two, three months? Forget Johnny the Rose. You're Johnny Once."

John groaned, but understood the reference. Johnny Once, not the man's real name, was an old friend of his father. When John was a boy, he asked his old man about the origins of the nickname. On a detour from a rare family errand together, they were eating Italian ices at a local pizzeria. Because he came around only once in a while, his father explained.

"Be with you in a minute," Frank said.

John waved his hand. "Take your time." Frank stuck his tongue out as he crouched over his accounting sheets. My brother, master bookkeeper, John thought smiling.

In the middle of Sunday afternoon, customers were few and the usual buzz at a low level. The T.V. blared over the sounds of dishes clattering and people chatting. John watched the ballgame.

Frank lifted his head and started humming an old tune—"Nice Work If You Can Get It," John thought it was. Rosario's must be doing a good business.

"So, word is you got together with Angie yesterday," Frank said.

"Hmmm, a news leak," John said. "Who's your source?" He smiled, recognizing his own ambivalence. He didn't know whether he was pleased or dismayed.

"Take a wild guess." Frank leaned forward, slapped his brother lightly on the cheek.

John hit himself on the head. "Mom. Shoulda known, shoulda known."

"She's real happy too, hoping you returned to your senses and to your roots, she says."

"Mom's reaching," John said. "My home's in Manhattan across the water, nine thousand miles away from here."

"I suppose," Frank said in a philosophic tone. "But I'm thinking you can take the boy outta Bensonhurst, but you can't take Bensonhurst outta the boy."

Dominic approached the table with Fat Tony in tow, and Frank greeted them with energetic handshakes and pats on the back. The four men talked and laughed about baseball and the hard time Frank and John had growing up Yankee fans in Brooklyn, when most of their schoolmates favored the Dodgers. But their old man was a Yankee fan, so they never questioned the allegiance.

Dominic looked at John. "You root for the Yanks? Didn't think we had even that much in common."

An overture, maybe with an edge? John was wary, given their history and his renewed contact with Angie. He forced a laugh. "Runs in the family. Don't give me too much credit."

John rarely encountered Dominic, even during his occasional visits to the restaurant. He wanted a sense of the man. Dominic was handsome—his features had a chiseled Roman statue look. The bright black wavy hair, along with his dark complexion, set off his smile to good effect, giving it a kind of sheen. A flashy dresser, but not crude, he wore a classic Sicilian outfit: white slacks and a tight-fitting short-sleeved black shirt that showed off his muscular body.

A part of Dominic was always moving. When he sat, his fingers strummed on the table top or his knees bumped its bottom. Sometimes his eyes twitched, reminding John of high-strung Hollywood bad guys, Peter Lorre types.

But Dominic was friendly enough, even charming, and the jealous part of John was miffed. He preferred that Angie's ex-husband were an ignorant boor, an oafish Italian caricature. He felt a momentary stomach cramp at the thought of the two of them in bed, having sex. With effort, he chased it from his mind.

Dominic's son Donnie came in and walked past the four men, on his way into the kitchen where he worked. The boy said a fast hello without a special greeting for his father whose smiling face quickly contorted into a flushed, just-slapped expression. Dominic brushed past Frank's upheld hands and rushed into the kitchen after his boy. John looked at his brother who shrugged and made a calming motion with his hand.

Dominic soon pushed through the kitchen doors and sat again at the table. "Don't know what the fuck to do with that kid," he moaned. "Ignores me alla time now, treats me like a piece of shit."

John and Fat Tony gave Dominic sympathetic looks. Frank was soothing. "Like I told you, kids always go through this when their parents divorce…. he's got to take it out on someone and you're an easier target than his mother."

"You sure she ain't filling his head with garbage about me?" Dominic asked.

"Angie's a pistol," Frank replied, "no need to tell you, but she knows that'd hurt the boy more than you."

"Alright, Frank," Dominic stammered, "it's just I wish…." He sat crumpled in his chair, a Raggedy Andy doll.

Frank placed a hand on his friend's arm. "He's a good boy. He'll come 'round."

Frank's gesture and words were like a tonic. Dominic straightened up in his chair, his highly charged self again. "Know what Donnie's doin' now? He's given up hangin' out with the local boys. Now he's mainly with black kids. Why? Because, he tells me, they're the best basketball players in the city and besides he likes them and their music too, that rap shit. My Donnie. Who woulda fucking thought?"

Frank said, "The boy's right, ain't he? These black kids leap and shoot and handle the ball like they were born with it. Donnie's probably improvin' his damn game." Frank looked to Fat Tony and John for support. "Johnny, you're the basketball maestro here, talk to Dominic, tell him not to get so worked up. He should be grateful his boy's not taking drugs or drinkin' like these neighborhood cheeseheads he likes so much."

John held up his hands. "Hey Frank, this is between Dominic and his boy." His brother's pressure irritated him.

Frank glared at John and slapped the table. "If Dominic manages to cool his heels, the boy will return to the fold. Believe me."

Dominic spoke meekly. "You're probably right, Frank, but I feel like he's slippin through my fingers now." He held up his hand, fingers spread. "I'm not prejudiced, don't call blacks jigaboos like our friend Tony here." Fat Tony's big round face turned pink. Probably the first time he's blushed in his life, John thought. "I still think Donnie's askin' for trouble," Dominic went on. "He's even bringin' these kids down to the Bay Parkway playground. Some of the local gonzos don't like that so fucking much, so last time I go down there myself to watch and make sure nobody starts actin' stupid. That's the last straw for my boy. Won't fucking talk to me now, thinks I'm buttin' my nose…."

Frank sat upright in his chair. "Okay, Dominic, I get it. I'll talk to the boy and tell him to be more careful, and you, Dominic, you be patient now. I'm getting impatient with having to tell you to be patient."

❧   ❧   ❧

John was leaving, and the men stood to shake hands. Frank's wife Theresa, who worked the nighttime kitchen shift, came bustling in. Frank sat down in his seat as if pushed by an unseen hand. The uncertain look on his face passed quickly and he got up, took his wife's hand and kissed her on the cheek.

Theresa was a tall woman, slim and attractive in her youth, but grown heavy over the years. Her only vanity was her dark brown hair, which she kept in a stylish short cut. Although fleshy, her face was still pretty, especially when she smiled, which she did rarely these days.

She had a chilling effect on the men. They knew she scorned them and, without understanding their crimes, felt guilty. She said with a cluck in her voice, "Hello boys, what've you been doin', discussing America's foreign policy or who you got in tomorrow's daily double?"

John was the least vulnerable to her barbs. "Actually, Theresa," he said, "we debated serious issues today and, you'll be happy to know, dealt a blow to racial strife in Bensonhurst." Theresa gave him a quick, quizzical look. John responded with a wave. "How are your lovely daughters, what are they doing for the summer?"

Though suspicious of John's diversion, she was happy to talk about her three girls. One was an emergency room nurse at a local hospital, another a secretary for a neighborhood construction company and the third was in college and wanted to be a dancer. John reported on his boys who were about to leave home for sleepaway camp in New Hampshire. He'd enjoy the freedom, but miss how their comings and goings filled his life.

Frank joined his brother in the walk through the restaurant and out to the van parked in front of Daniel George's. They leaned against the vehicle facing each other, neither eager to speak. Frank grew melancholy, the sad old hound of his nature emerging, John thought. He wants to bring up something, but isn't sure how.

Frank blew his breath into the air. "Whiney was with you yesterday.... did he talk to you about my leaving, you know, getting out of the business?"

"Whiney said nothing to me about that, never has."

"He's been saying plenty to me." Frank shook his head. "Calls me at my house, drops by the restaurant. Pop must have talked to him about it too. Now Whiney's carrying the old man's water."

"Pop died years ago. Why'd Whiney start in on you now?"

"Don't know. Maybe he had a vision, but he's on a mission." Two grey-haired old men walked by, wearing caps and jackets despite the day's heat, local dignitaries from another age. Frank nodded, saying, "Hey Al, hey Benny." "Qui si dice, Frankie," one of them returned, hand raised in a creaky wave.

"Trying to convert the sinner, Whiney is," John said.

"Don't know what to do," Frank said. "Dominic and Fat Tony, mainly Dominic, want me to move the other way, to expand. Expand or fold up, they say."

John said nothing. He guessed his brother had more worries to reveal.

"Then there's this Tommy Arlotta business," Frank said. "Skinny kid, use to suck up to Dominic alla time. Remember him?"

"Yeah, vaguely."

"Years ago he moved up to Boston. Got on a bus and went on his way. Once in a while, though, he comes back."

"And...."

"Lately I see him hanging out with Dominic and he'll still do anything Dominic says and I hear they're getting into some stupid shit."

"Like what? What do they do?" John was really curious.

"Like you don't wanna know...."

"No, I do want to know. You don't want to tell me."

Frank eyed John, then the sky, then his restaurant across the way. "Okay, okay.... you are my brother." For the second time that afternoon, he tapped John lightly on the cheek. "This goes no further, right?"

"Whiney?" The sun was going down, but its rays creased the clouds and John had to shield his eyes from the glare.

"Not even Whiney…. It was a little extortion racket, Dominic and Tommy threatened store owners, roughed some of them up even. Like I said, stupid shit. On the other side of Fort Hamilton Parkway, not even our territory."

"Flirting with disaster, sounds like." John spoke in an even tone, not revealing his excitement at Frank opening a crack on his world.

"Anyway, Dominic's my guy, so I gotta answer for him. Sally Broadway and the other Brooklyn major domos made that clear."

John nodded.

"So I bawl Dominic out and chase Tommy back up the New England Throughway."

"Case closed, right?"

"For now." The brothers turned to look at a family coming out of Rosario's. A little boy and girl skipped ahead of their mother and father down the street. "The pain of this for me," Frank went on, "is that I know about these two, their little thirst for violence, for the dark side of shit. And I used it once, helped create them maybe."

"When?" John was uncertain. *Maybe this is more than I want to know?*

"When I stepped in for Dad, and DiMasi, you know who runs Bay Ridge, sent over a coupla goons to negotiate some things. It was a test. They wanted me to consider…."

"Narcotics and prostitution."

"Designate certain areas, at night, playgrounds, service roads off the Belt Parkway, like a fucking meat market under the cover of dark."

"Pop's little rant in the hospital."

"Yeah, the old man saw it coming." Dominic and Fat Tony walked out of the restaurant. Dominic raised a thumb and pointed a finger at Frank, making like a gun, and lifted the finger up in a good-bye gesture. "So I used that one and his buddy Tommy," Frank continued, "to send a message of my own. You know, the best defense sometimes is an offense."

"DiMasi backed off?"

"And everybody else. And Batman and Robin got a taste of violence's rewards, and just came back for another sip from the cup." Frank seemed deflated, though not defeated, and John understood more why his brother's shoulders sagged.

"It's more agita than you need, Frank. How about walking away?" John was hopeful. *Why else would his brother take him into his confidence?*

Frank grinned nervously. "I'm thinking about it."

"Thinking about it? Why not fucking cut bait?"

"Just so you know, my reasons for standing pat have nothing to do with business." Frank spoke in a low voice, staccato-like, punctuating each word. "They're personal."

John went to speak, but Frank held up his hands. "Basta," he said sharply. "They're personal."

❦   ❦   ❦

John leaned his head against the van. Why the frigging mystery? He slapped the side of the van once with the palm of his hand. He left the conversation with Frank for a moment, dipping into his imagination, struggling to come up with what his brother's personal reasons might be. A blank page. Shit. He wished they were closer. Maybe then he could know, could understand….

"Anything I can do?" John swallowed his frustration. Above all, he wanted to be available.

Frank didn't answer right away, and the two men stood quietly for several minutes in the darkening street. A long delivery truck stopped for a light across from them. Strange sight for a Sunday, John thought. He looked the other way, spotted a young black man standing on the block's far corner. Then, not standing, jogging in place. Another strange sight.

"Listen, just listen," Frank said. "I might need somebody I trust to talk to."

Frank was sharing his burden slightly, finally, and John felt some relief at that. The brothers hugged with feeling and said good-bye.

Over Frank's shoulder, John saw the black man running down the street toward Rosario's. Waving something metal in his hand, a gun? John pushed off Frank and pointed at Dominic and Tony sitting in a car in front of the restaurant—Dominic was about to pull away from the curb. "Look out!" John thought and screamed.

Another car with two black men in the front seats moved slowly down the street. Frank turned to where his brother pointed, said, "Oh, shit."

The gunshots exploded, the loudest live sound John had ever heard. Like speakers turned on high blast. The man on the sidewalk stopped, swiveled, then fired up close at Dominic's car, as did a gun barrel protruding from the window of the slowly moving auto that paused on the other side. The crossfire of bullets hit, ripped, the back doors, tires, gas tank of Dominic's car.

John's body trembled from the sudden violent disturbance. He placed his hands across his torso, gripped each upper arm, calmed himself that way.

Dominic banged out of his car as the sidewalk shooter scrambled into the back seat of his companions' auto that had kept moving and now, horn blaring, passed Rosario's and turned quickly up the corner. Dominic had a pistol—grabbed from his glove compartment, John figured—and was raising his arm. But Frank stood in front of him—the two men were body to body. John had not seen such agility on Frank's part since his brother's shortstop turns as a teenager on the softball diamond.

"No, no, no, you fucking dummy," Frank shouted, practically spitting in Dominic's face.

Dominic stepped back, strangely subdued, John thought, considering the circumstances. "Can't let them…."

"It was just a warning." Frank continued to yell. "Didn't shoot at you. Just your fucking precious car."

"But those fuckers…." Dominic muttered. He dropped his gun hand to his side. He stared up the street where the black men's car had disappeared.

"If you shoot, if you chase 'em," Frank said, still speaking loudly, "it'll be harder to blow off the cops."

"Blow off the cops?" John stood near the two men, saw Dominic's confused expression.

"Yeah, no police reports, nobody official fucking snooping around. You know, make like this didn't happen. Get me?" Frank tapped Dominic's head several times. "This did not happen."

"I do, Frankie," Dominic said, his breathing heavy. "I do get it." Dominic grinned broadly like a proud pupil who's mastered a difficult lesson. "They wanted me to shit in my pants, but here I am laughing." Small victory, John thought. Suddenly, his reflexes and emotions triggered by a delayed timer, Dominic jumped up and down like a manic pogo stick.

The lack of fuss struck John. A few people emerged from Rosario's including Theresa who threw Frank an angry, dismayed look. But after a return nod from her husband, she helped shoo the customers back inside. Some kids gathered hesitantly. Frank said nobody got hurt and you should go home before somebody does.

Bensonhurst justice, John surmised. The mob imposes, the mob disposes. Everyone else looks the other way.

"You oughta go," Frank advised his brother.

"I'll hang around, make sure…." John viewed the scene, Dominic, Tony dazed, the torn-up car. He wasn't sure what he'd make sure.

"No need. It's over for now."

"The cops?"

"They won't want to bother." Frank shrugged, like he's embarrassed by his power, John guessed.

"Somebody making a statement?" John asked. He and his brother were standing by his van.

"But who? What for? Thought I cleaned things up with the main guys." Frank pulled on an ear lobe, narrowed his eyes. "You know, anyone big-time who had a beef with Dominic."

"Blacks? That a clue?"

"Nah. Anyone wants a job done, they're often the soldiers of choice."

The quiet had fully returned. No more echoes of noise in my ears, John realized.

"Equal opportunity, hah, Frankie? Well, this is America." Both men grunted.

Reluctantly, John stepped into the van, but before he could shut the door, Frank grabbed the handle. "Something I gotta tell you about Angie."

"Yeah?" John welcomed the switch to a lighter subject. Evidence the world goes on.

"She still likes you. When we're together, she looks for ways to bring your name up."

"Thanks Frankie…. you spend much time with her?"

"Hey, you know Bensonhurst," Frank said. "Except when you come around, not that many people here you can have an intelligent conversation with."

"Now something I got to ask you," John said. "Any problems with Dominic if Angie and I hook up?" A jealous guy, he presumed the other guy'd have similar emotions.

Frank answered quickly. "Doubt it. All the agita she gave him, he'll probably be grateful…. funny boy, my Dominic."

He sounds affectionate, John thought, puzzled. The two brothers turned to watch Dominic who was poking his fingers into the bullet holes in his car, removing them, shaking his hand in the air.

❧   ❧   ❧

Surprised at his steady hands on the wheel, John drove his van out of the Battery Tunnel connecting Brooklyn and Manhattan. On the West Side Drive, he passed the new developments popping up along the dirty old Hudson River, the restaurant with a jungle motif and bungee jump, the beginnings of a children's playground with a jumbled tower of tires for safe climbing, the handsome high school building for the town's gifted students. He admired the twilight's purple haze giving color to the river's horizon, as it slowly faded into the deep, dark blue that was the true night of the city.

When he arrived at his apartment, there was a message from Frank on his answering machine. As John listened, he thought: Frankie reborn, full of news and chatter.

The cops had come and gone. He, John, was not to tell Angie or their mother or anyone about the shooting. They'll find out sooner or later, for better or worse, from local blabbermouths. Tomorrow first thing he, Frankie, would start making calls and would let him know when he learned something, what he learned. Dominic swore on the headstones of family members loved and hated that he had no idea about the why of it and would make his own phone calls. This worried Frank, but for now he'd let Dominic make inquiries. And, oh yeah, Frank concluded, how are you? Forgot to ask, he said.

All right, John thought. All right, if a bit shaken. He sat on his bed, by the phone machine on his night table. Not used to this crazy shit. Glad again that Pop saw to my getting out. What about Frankie, though? How'd he react to the crazy shit? More persuaded to depart, or more pressed to stay? Wish I fucking knew the answer.

He lay down on his back, neck propped on a pillow. And who dispatched the wild cowboys of color to shoot up the streets of Bensonhurst? And for what purpose? He rubbed his temples, fingers going in a circular motion, attempting to soothe his head where the gunshots' noise again reverberated.

CHAPTER 3

John usually had a hard time breaking away from work for his Monday night basketball game. He'd be writing a foundation proposal for Urban Justice Institute's budget analysis work, or a board memo about fundraising when it was time to go. Like a mosquito's buzz, thoughts about his next point would nag him on the subway ride to the gym—not receding until he met his old high school friend Charles in the locker room or stepped onto the court.

This Monday night, John easily cut the knots binding him to his desk. He was eager to meet Charles and talk about his Brooklyn weekend, at least the Angie aspects.

He couldn't share the other drama, the conversation with Frank, the strange, sudden gunplay. He'd conspire with his brother and other Benson-hurst denizens to pretend nothing happened. He saw and heard the gunfire, but it now felt unreal. Not even a fucking police report. That irritated him most. If men shoot pistols in the street and no police report records it, he wondered as he descended his workplace's front steps, did the incident really take place?

Hurrying, he took a chance and hailed a cab, regretting the gamble once they encountered heavy midtown traffic. Resigned to the delay, he gazed out the car's side window, the shapes of people, buildings, other cars, blurring. He reminisced about the perilous occasion in 1966 when he introduced Charles, a black boy, to Bensonhurst.

It was Friday night after basketball practice. Charles was sleeping over, but didn't want to stay inside all night. He wanted to get some sense of this strange Italian-American country before going to bed. So they went to Tom and Vinny's, known to its patrons as T&V's, Bensonhurst's busiest pizza place. John figured the number of people there might minimize the risk. Besides, he was Frank Rosario's son, sure-fire protection in almost any situation.

Yet he was tense when they entered the pizza parlor. The kids at the tables up front grew silent when Charles and he sat at the counter. Angie was sitting in a booth in the back with her pals. She said something quickly to Dominic Roselli who sat across from her. Dominic called out, "Hey, John, welcome back to Bensonhurst."

"Always good to see you, Dominic," he called back, trying to match the other boy's tone of not so friendly sarcasm. He could hardly tolerate Dominic, despite tales from Angie, seeking to elicit his compassion, about how Dominic's good-for-nothing father showed up from time to time at the apartment and smacked the boy around.

John and Charles ordered a couple of slices—Charles giving John a "you are slightly weird" look when he asked for eggplant topping. Good friends, with a genuine simpatico—"both on and off the court," their coach often bragged—they recognized each other's growing tension and tried light banter to relieve it. *I'm glad we don't play New Utrecht, we'd have to bring special fortifications. Can you wear helmets and shoulder pads in a basketball game?* Why was it taking so damn long to get served anyway?

A tightening rippled through John's back. Shit, this is a real drag, he thought. Bad enough Charles and his neighborhood don't mix, but in the silence and stares surrounding them, he felt danger brewing. His brain was racing: These are good-hearted people, you know there's a lot of truth in the positive Italian stereotype, but it includes a propensity to turn violent when upset. "Propensity", a college board word. Slow down, he thought, be cool, eat fast and get the hell out of here.

The worst part, he brooded, is how to persuade Charles about the warmth and generosity of his people. What a fucking joke. He swiveled in his seat to look around him—*What gives?* he wanted to ask people and to tell them, complain to them, *Don't make this problem for me.*

Tommy Arlotta sat next to Dominic—Tommy, a nervous kid, decent, a follower though, who hero-worshiped bad boy Dominic. Tommy fidgeted more than usual, another sign of trouble.

Angie got up from her seat—the only real movement in the place—and headed for the jukebox. She threw John a look on the way. Did she wink at him? She walked towards them slowly, smiling, swaying slightly. She looked great, from the neck both ways, as his old man used to say. The low-heeled boots, the just above the knees straight skirt, the blouse closely fitting, the jet-black hair framing her pretty face. A young girl with a woman's full body. Sexy Angie, his oldest friend, now a virtual stranger. He loved her.

He relaxed. People got back to chewing and talking a little too loudly—a friendly buzz returned. He heard Charles behind him breathe a sigh of relief.

"Donna, the Prima Donna" came on the juke box. *We're apart.... she broke my heart*, Dion sang.

Angie stood in front of John and they smiled at each other. They were buddies again. She had seen to it, he realized.

"You played our favorite song," he said.

"Thought you'd get a kick out of it," she said. She rested her hand on his arm and swung her leg. "But it was just one of our favorite songs, I hope you remember." She was flirting with him and he did not mind.

"Oh yes," he said, putting his hand over his heart, "all those great tunes. I haven't forgotten."

She wants to be Zsa Zsa Gabor/Even though she's just the girl next door, Dion's voice rose above the din. "Who's your friend, Johnny?" Angie said. "Don't keep him all to yourself."

"Charles Walter Buford, mi amigo." John slipped into a mock formality. "Meet Angie, a childhood companion of mine. Full name: Angelina Barbara Capobella. As simple as ABC," he paused, "or as complicated."

Angie nodded, smiled. Charles and she shook hands.

"Pleased to meet you," Charles said sincerely. John could see that his friend was still shaken by Bensonhurst's cold reception.

"Likewise," Angie replied, then hesitated. "Any friend of Johnny's is a friend of mine." She had been struggling to come up with the right welcome. That'll pass, John thought.

Angie led the two boys with their slices and sodas to a booth in the back. Except for baleful looks from Dominic and one or two of his buddies, nobody bothered them. They chatted about basketball—about which Angie knew a thing or two—argued the relative merits of pizza parlors where they had eaten in different parts of Brooklyn and shared their excitement about the new music of the day. Angie loved the Beatles—the music and the films—and Motown, especially The Four Tops. They played favorite records in the jukebox. *Sugar pie, honey bunch*, sang the Tops, a happy phrase John still associated with Angie.

"C'mon, Angie, we'll walk you home," John said at the end of the evening. She yawned, stretching her arms, her breasts pushing against her blouse. She caught his eye and winked. He fought back a blush. "Sure I'm safe with you guys?" she asked. "Maybe I should take you home?"

"Very funny," he said, "but I can't allow the switch." He shrugged, palms upward.

The three teenagers stood on the sidewalk in front of Angie's house. She jabbed John in the chest with her finger. "You know I'd like to see more of you. Why don't you call me sometime?"

"Missed you too, Angie," he said truthfully. But he lied when he said he'd call.

As they walked through the dark, quiet streets to John's apartment—at that time of night, Bensonhurst seemed like a completely contained village—Charles declared, "She is very nice, John."

"I know."

"I mean both physically and personality-wise," Charles added.

"Shit, I said I know."

"How come you never told me about her?"

"It's like she's part of my past." John's words sounded silly, even to him.

"Shit," Charles insisted, "she's part of your present now, man. I was watching her. I think she wants you."

"I probably won't do anything with her."

"Why fucking not? Don't you like her?" He raised his voice, puncturing the night's quiet with his questions.

"Don't ever tell anyone I said this, "John said. "But she frightens me."

Charles said nothing for awhile. John knew his friend didn't understand. *I take on the big boys on the basketball court. How could I be afraid of a friendly, sexy girl?*

"I'm sorry, man," Charles said. He passed up teasing John for his social cowardice.

The rest of the way to John's house they walked in silence. As they rode up the elevator, Charles said, "Saved our asses back there, didn't she?"

"Definitely," John said, smiling sheepishly.

❧   ❧   ❧

John and Charles had a regular routine. Every second and fourth Monday, they joined other fathers and their boys at the Ethical Cultural School's dilapidated gym on West 63rd Street for father and sons basketball games. On alternate Mondays they met at the Society for the Advancement of Judaism's more spacious gym for games with other men only.

Since it was the fourth Monday in June, John had to pick up Jake and Teddy on the way to the game. Impatient, he hovered over his boys as they gathered up their sneakers and shorts and hurried them into the taxi he had asked to wait downstairs.

John and Charles sat off by themselves in their basketball shorts and shirts, on a bench that passed for a spectator section in the tiny gym. Their sons—Charles' Khari and Malik, 15 and 12 years old, and John's Jake and Teddy, 14 and 11—played with other boys in a fast and loose full-court game.

"Hard for me to admit anything good can come out of Bensonhurst," Charles said after John finished telling him about Angie. "But looks like you found it, my man."

"Black folks," John said. "Time to forgive a community's decades of racist conduct. Besides, what about me?" He knew he was trying levity on a serious subject.

"Forgot about you. Wonder why?"

"Well?"

"Because you knew enough to get out years ago and hardly ever go back." Charles chuckled, but his tone was unusually sharp.

"Oh, that." John looked away, leaned back against the wall behind the bench. Didn't mean to tick him off.

Charles changed tack. "I remember Angie, though. Had personality and sex appeal, something my teenage hormones could not ignore."

"Telling me," John said, bumping against his friend's shoulder.

Charles gave John a light punch on the chin. "Johnny the Rose Rosario."

The two men gave their sons occasional tips on basketball's fine points: dribbling, posting up, boxing out. But mainly they watched, sizing up the boys' growing talent as well as their errant plays. John noted that Jake sulked only once, after someone slapped the ball away as he drove wildly to the basket. Maybe the ill-effects of the divorce were fading.

"Enough of this spectator bullshit," Charles finally said. "Let's give the old men a turn," John followed-up.

The boys were panting heavily, like young pups after a long run outdoors. The fathers trotted onto the court and shot a fast round of warm-ups before starting their game. Their children lingered, sprawled and prowled along the sidelines.

Charles and John were on the same side. On the first possession, eye contact and a nod from John told Charles that his old teammate wanted to do a pick and roll. Charles set a screen to free John up for a jump shot from around the foul line. He was deadly from that spot. Or Charles rolled toward the basket for a lead pass from his friend and an open lay-up. They worked those moves all game.

Then fathers and sons joined in a rag-tag contest that ended with Khari lofting a pass toward the backboard that Charles grabbed and slam dunked into the basket. The other men and boys stood in awed silence. "Unfair," someone cried, "you've been practicing."

In the locker room, relaxed from the game and hot showers, Charles and John talked about work. As assistant director of the city's Human Rights Commission, Charles mediated disputes among neighborhood groups, including conflicts in Brooklyn's Crown Heights between blacks and Jews. He was in regular contact with City Hall and the Reverend Bill Simon, an outspoken black activist. At a moment's notice, on the occasion of a racial incident, Simon would lead a march, hold a press conference, make a provocative speech. Rev. Bill, as the press dubbed him, sported a large Afro on top of his tall, bony frame and, whenever he appeared in public, had a gleaming peace medallion draped around his long neck.

Charles told John that behind the scenes Bill Simon was a reasonable man. Sure, he wanted the spotlight, to trumpet that without justice there can be no peace, but he also backed projects to bring the two communities together. Like turning a vacant lot into a neighborhood playground that everyone could use.

John tucked his shirt into his pants. "I'm not totally surprised. He was on T.V. after they convicted Danny Parma, that pathetic Bensonhurst punk, of being the shooter in the Connie Washington killing. Simon didn't gloat. Said something like, 'While we can never be happy when a young man is sent to prison for 25 years, we feel in this case that justice was done.'"

"Yeah, remember that," Charles said, squeezing his sneakers into his sports bag. "For now, I'm impressed. Rev. Bill's being real helpful in Crown Heights." He fit a wide-brimmed brown fedora on his head. He'd been wearing hats since his college days, when he started listening to jazz and admired the musicians' playing and their style.

Charles' hat reminded John of Donnie. Maybe some Monday night I could bring the kid to the gym, he thought. If he's as talented as Angie says, he should be able to keep up. Getting a little ahead of yourself though....

They rounded up their sons and walked out into the warm June night. On the street, Charles pulled John aside. "I have a good feeling about Angie. After those anemic Ivy League females, it's about fucking time you took up with a woman with warm blood flowing through her veins."

"All good things have their season," John said.

❧   ❧   ❧

Family togetherness, Rosario style, John thought. He sat with his boys at his kitchen's formica counter eating his mother's manicotti. Faces still flushed from the games, the boys plunged into the food. "Eat slowly, like it's a delicacy," John advised. Jake and Teddy didn't need much convincing—even two days old and reheated, the soft ricotta cheese, the light, creamy tomato sauce were sweet pleasure. "Manna from grandma, nothing better, eh, boys?" John said.

In the living room after dinner, John suggested they talk a bit. After all, this was their last night together before sleep away camp.

"Sure, Dad," Jake said, "but don't get serious on us, telling us about sex, getting along with others, sportsmanship." Like a gangly Pinocchio, he sprawled his body across his chair, his knees draped over one of the chair's arms, his back against the other.

John smiled. "Already covered those things with you guys, except maybe some sex stuff with Teddy." He winked at his 11 year-old who shifted the conversation. "I love manicotti more than Garfield."

Jake frowned. "Doofus, Garfield eats lasagna, not manicotti. Another thing, it's mon-a-goth. Right, Dad?"

The boys relived the game highlights. Teddy complained about a shot that swirled in and out of the hoop. "I was robbed."

"The athlete's lament," John soothed.

Jake lept in the air, acting out a jump shot he hit, "from three-point land." His eyes widened as they had during the game.

Jake sat next to his father on the big, plushy couch and Teddy sat on John's lap. It was tight, but cozy and, given the boys' advancing ages, a rare thing. "You boys looking forward to camp?" John asked.

"You bet," they said in unison.

"Gonna watch out for each other?" he teased.

"What kind of question is that?" was Teddy's response.

"Swear I'll never leave Teddy's side," Jake said.

Teddy hugged his father. "So you're gonna miss us, Dad?"

"Sure," John said, hugging him back.

"We're worried about you, Dad," Jake said. "How you gonna get along without us around?"

John thought of Angie, a pleasing vision. "No need to worry, boys," he said. "I have a few things in mind."

❦   ❦   ❦

In a light blue summer skirt and blouse, appearing simultaneously bold and uncertain, Angie stood in John's office doorway, tapping her left foot. Startled yet pleased, John smiled, motioned her to come in. She sat in a chair on the other side of his desk. He hurried to finish his phone conversation with the chair of his board about an op ed he had submitted to *The Times* on the Dinkins Administration's jail expansion policies. "One thing's certain," he chuckled, "if they print this piece, forget about city funding."

John's intercom buzzed. "Some woman just rushed past me," Jeannette, his office manager, blurted. "Said she's an old friend."

"Thanks for the warning," John said, smiling at his intruder.

"Nice office," Angie said. "A brownstone, two floors.... classy arrangement."

"Yeah, it's comfortable here, homey." He tapped a pencil on his desk, the eraser end. "An old building, built in the 1870's. Been converted into a space for non-profits. New York Lawyers for the Public Interest have the two floors above us and the Prisoners' Rights Project is on the ground floor."

"Smart for do-gooders to stick together, huh?" she said.

John shrugged. "In unity there's strength, or something like that."

"There for the shooting," she stated with a knowing look. "Should be more careful who you hang out with." She shook her head, wagged a finger.

"Heard already?" He was only a little surprised. It was less than two days ago.

Her expression said be serious. "Any word from Frank?"

"Not yet," he replied, worried that she was worried. Did news of the violence unsettle her? Did she still care for Dominic?

Angie pointed to the walls covered with photographs of John's sons. "Nice pictures. Whatdya have, eight children?"

"No," he smiled, relieved. Maybe only people outside Bensonhurst fret about such matters. "I just like to have all ages represented." After a pause, "You don't seem too upset about the gunplay."

She rolled her eyes to startling effect. Don't often see that trick, he thought. "You did that very well, the eye thing."

She batted her lashes in acknowledgment. "I don't think anything to do with Dominic can upset me anymore."

"Those who play with fire get burned?"

She nodded. "It's Frankie I'm concerned about sometimes. Dominic and him together is good for Dominic. Not sure it's good for your brother."

"I'm working on creating some distance between them." He could tell her that much.

"Good luck, for real."

He stood up. "So, to what do I owe the pleasure?" He sat in the chair next to her and kissed her on the cheek. "Just wanted to catch up on the latest Benson-hurst doings?"

"No, I was in the neighborhood, thought I'd drop in and see what you were up to."

"Sure," he said, "I believe that." He took pleasure in her showing up, in her interest in him. Frank was right about that. He took pleasure, too, in teasing her.

"Truthfully, I was a little anxious. You said you'd call, but you've said *that* before."

"Angie, I was planning to call. Tonight, in fact. Last night was basketball night with my kids."

"I know, I know." She put her hand on his arm. "I wanted to see what'd happen if I just popped in on you. Like my father said, 'If you don't swing, you don't hit anything.'"

He laughed. "My old man used to say that too." He felt close to her, and it was happening quickly, despite the time apart. They fell silent for several moments, looking away from each other. John rose from his chair. "I am delighted you came by today, Angie, and request your company at lunch."

"Thought you'd never ask."

"First," he said, finger in the air, "I have to make a phone call." He sat in his desk chair and dialed. Phone to his ear, he asked, "Still using Dominic's name?"

She made a face. "Yeah."

He spoke into the phone. "Is Angelina Roselli there…. Well, then, would you take a message? Please say John Rosario called, and that he hopes she'll join him for a night on the town this coming Saturday."

❦   ❦   ❦

"Let me look at what you wrote for the papers," Angie said as they settled into their seats at one of John's favorite local restaurants, a modest pasta place that never had more than five of its twenty tables filled at lunch time. "I wanna check out what wild ideas you cook up in that cute little office of yours."

John handed her the op-ed—Jeanette had made a copy before they left the office—and asked her not to judge it harshly. "It's tough being a lone voice in the desert."

He picked out a spicy eggplant and pasta dish for both of them.

"Johnny 'pulls no punches' Rosario." She puffed her cheeks and let out a low whooshing sound. "Guess you're not angling for a job in Dinkins' campaign." It was an election year in New York City and the Democratic mayor, David Dinkins, faced a serious challenge from the likely Republican candidate, Rudolph Giuliani.

"I like things about the mayor, but not what he's done with the jails." John was explaining, defending his position.

Angie wasn't paying attention. She re-read the op-ed's last paragraph.

Mainly for short-sighted political reasons, the mayor has made a devastating and unnecessary mistake: to spend billions on more jails that will confine primarily poor people of color in deplorable conditions while reducing services to the inner city areas where most prisoners come from. What a sad outcome for a public official whose rise to prominence was based largely on the hopes and aspirations of those very communities.

"So this is what you do at Urban Justice Institute. Raise issues like this?" Angie held up the op-ed. "Get publicity about it. Join with other groups to pressure Dinkins to turn things around."

"You got the basics." He was impressed. "And sometimes it even succeeds."

"A man who loves his job," she laughed.

"After all, how many people get paid for speaking truth to power."

"You're unusual." She leaned forward, chin resting on her hand, elbow stretched across the table. Her posture was familiar to him. He saw the young girl in her.

"Our mothers wouldn't approve," he pointed out.

"Oh, pooh." She lifted her head to wave her hand. "Don't change the subject. You're just embarrassed 'cause we're talking about you."

"No, I'm not," he lied and knew it.

"Yes, you are." She smiled up at him, her expression curious, affectionate. He was uneasy but enjoying her attention, thinking her face was pretty enough and near enough to kiss. She made a pointing finger and touched him gently on the nose. She giggled like the playground tease she once was and he blushed like the altar boy he used to be.

The waitress carried all the food on one tray. She almost spilled Angie's eggplant dish in her lap. She spilled some sauce on the table, apologized, and, in cleaning it up, knocked over the salt shaker, and wobbled the glasses of water. Angie covered her mouth, suppressing laughter. John took on the job of soothing the waitress. "Whew, the storm has passed," he said when she left. "Guess we're lucky nobody got hurt," Angie said.

She picked up a large pepper shaker, leaned across the food, held it under his chin, and, in a fast-talking Walter Winchell type voice, said: "So, tell us now, Johnny—you don't mind if I call you Johnny, do ya—why do you do this work, why do you want to do good alla time? C'mon Johnny, your fans want to know."

He paused, worried about exposing his soul to a woman he was beginning to care for, anxious his flat, dull words would diminish the romance she attributed to his work.

"Don't be shy, kiddo," she said. "You're among friends here." She looked down and seemed surprised to see a still simmering plate.

He talked about the sense of honor passed on by his father, doing right by the people around you, especially when they needed protection.

"Frank Rosario, the man, remember him well," she said, gulping down her food. Suddenly Sinatra could be heard. The kitchen door swung open and "I've Got You Under My Skin" boomed through. The cook's CD player, John thought. *Don't you know, little fool, you never can win….* Sinatra sang in gleeful surrender.

John talked about the Church, how he took its teachings more seriously than most kids at Our Lady of Perpetual Help, especially Christ's heroics and the poetry of his moralisms. 'What does it profit a man if he gains a fortune but loses his soul' and the like. Religion's eloquent precepts buoyed him, helped connect him to a larger life vision.

"My big mistake," Angie said. "Should've spent more time at mass."

He spoke of the sixties. He wasn't an SDS'er, but went on marches and read and observed and took it all in. The war, fucked-up and hopeless, how we treated the blacks and the poor and betrayed our best ideals. After college, when the war and marching ended and the dust of the time settled, he held onto those ideals. "They became part of me, my professional passion," he said. "Couldn't shake 'em if I wanted to."

"While others became lawyers, bankers, or carpenters," she said, twirling her finger in the air, "you chose to keep the faith, to remain…. political." She whooped out the last word like a contestant on *Name That Tune* guessing the song just before the buzzer.

"Lotsa other people did the same thing, Angie. I wasn't the only one."

Holding hands, an old man and woman entered the restaurant. They each wore granny glasses, the kind favored by John Lennon, and held umbrellas in their free hands, even though there was no sign of rain. Maybe that's why it's not raining, John thought.

"You were the only one I knew," Angie said. She looked down at her now empty plate as if it were her turn to be embarrassed.

John left a big tip, a custom passed on by his father and other male elders. Outside, the light of the sun fell from the clear June sky, and they shaded their eyes from the streaming brightness. The day's warmth felt like a blessing on their new intimacy. Angie took John's arm and they walked slowly back to her office.

"Interesting," she said, "religion and the sixties. They didn't mean that much to me. I was there, got some things from them." She made grabbing gestures as if she could snatch her sixties and her religious influences like flies from the air. "But mainly I was stuck in Bensonhurst, without thinking I was stuck. The family, the way of talking, thinking, dressing, the blocks, the neighborhood, the people, you know, the paisanos."

He saw her as swimming in deep waters in a sea he knew well. She was floundering a bit—he'd sail over and throw her a rope.

He tapped her on the arm and she turned to face him. He looked into her eyes and suddenly saw her differently. A phrase came to him: she's becoming un-stuck. "Lots of people get stuck here," he said, "back in Brooklyn. Those Italian things are so powerful, they enrich our lives, but close us in too." He made his arms into a circle, fingertips touching behind her back. "Crossing the bridge to Manhattan is like a going through cold, high mountains without winter clothes, so people don't make the trip."

They stopped in front of the building where Angie worked—big, white, rectangular, housing several prominent social service groups. It was a political statement in concrete, representing the best and worst of New York's oldest non-profits: large, solid, reassuring, with no striking architectural features. It served a useful purpose, but charted no new courses.

"People back home become angry, bitter," Angie said. "They turn sour, like milk left overnight on the front stoop." He nodded and she went on. "Don't want that to happen to me. I wanna stretch out now." She took his hand, squeezed it. "That's where you come in 'cause you've been there, know what it's like. But you've also been to other places."

She giggled and covered her mouth with her hand, hiding her pleasure at her frankness. "So," he said, "it's not my looks or brains you want me for." He made an unbelieving expression. "I'm your very own personal guide to a bigger world."

"That's right," she said softly. She stood on her toes and gave him a quick kiss on the lower part of his cheek, next to his lips, what his mother would have called a little peck.

❦   ❦   ❦

On the way back to his office, John stopped abruptly and hit his forehead with the palm of his hand. People passing by shot him quick, curious glances. He forgot to tell Angie about the main reason he left Brooklyn: the car ride into the recesses of Flatbush with his father. Why didn't he tell her? What was the old mob saying about trade secrets? The best word is the one not spoken. Maybe that Sicilian male bullshit molded him more than he let on.

He sat at his desk and swirled around in his chair, a comforting habit. He began to rally: He'd tell her if the friendship maintained. It'd be a relief, like going to St. Finbar's in the old days—on Saturday afternoon, after playing ball in the park with his pals, before mass and communion on Sunday—to make his confession and secure, at least temporarily, forgiveness for his sins.

CHAPTER 4

The door offered no resistance. John stepped back as it slowly creaked open, looked up again at the nearby street signs, Prince and Mulberry. He stood on the outer boundary of Little Italy in lower Manhattan. He peered inside, his eyes taking their time to adjust to the grey interior light. Two men in bulky sports jackets sat at a small table to the right next to an old dusty bar. They were mumbling and playing cards.

The bar had nothing on it but a shiny cappuccino maker on the other end. It looked like a lit ship out on a dark night. John looked at the two men. "Whiney and Sally?" One sipped black liquid from a small cup. He nodded toward the back.

John walked through the mostly empty place, passing large framed posters of musical comedies from other ages, reassuring signs that he had entered the social club belonging to Sally Broadway, born Salvatore Benedetto, old-time Brooklyn capo, ardent fan of the stage. "Charlie's Aunt," "South Pacific", "Funny Girl," and "Guys and Dolls" with a narrow white homemade sash across it proclaiming "The One and Only." Can't argue with the man's taste, John thought.

The back room was also dreary, its raised windows letting in little light. Whiney sat alone at a large table idly shuffling a deck of cards. John settled in next to his uncle. "So, old man, where's our host? You said Sally wanted to see me."

The toilet flushed and Sally emerged from a tiny bathroom, stooping to come through the doorway. He looked much thinner, greyer than John remembered. Shit, he thought, last saw him when? Couldn't have been more than five years ago. Pop's wake?

Sally saw John's expression. "Don't make like I'm the fucking walking dead. Just a bathroom I walked out of, not a damn tomb."

"Sally's been sick," Whiney said. "Real sick," Sally put in. "But he's on the mend," Whiney said.

"Sorry, Sal," John said sincerely. "Didn't know." Then, attempting a smile, "Least you're coming back."

"Yeah," the old gangster said, slowly lowering his large frame into a chair. "Soon I'll feel like a million bucks."

Don't take any bets, John thought.

"Stand up," Sally said to John. "Meet an old friend."

John rose, turned, saw Minx the Enforcer approaching. He knew the man's legend well, from his father's and Whiney's stories. They always called him Minx the Enforcer, no shortened version, like the three words were his given name. Once the man had squeezed some joker's head so tightly, it permanently changed shape. From then on the poor guy was known as "cu-cuzz," Sicilian slang for squash. A big fucking bruiser, John could hear his father say. Must be Sally's bodyguard, a job no doubt fitting his talents.

John held out his hand which Minx the Enforcer ignored. He started to pat John down, rough hands on John's chest. John quickly raised his arms, knocking the bodyguard's hands away; then he shoved the larger man, saying, "Hey, what's up? I'm a guest here." Minx the Enforcer stumbled back, seemed unsteady. Lost something with age, John thought.

The sudden hostilities startled Sally and Whiney. The latter rose quickly, stood between the antagonists, held up two hands at Minx the Enforcer.

The old capo shouted at his soldier. "Back off, you dumb fuck. This is Johnny Rosario." He paused so the information could sink in. "He's practically one of us. No need to frisk this man." Like a child scolded Minx the Enforcer retreated to a corner by the bathroom.

"Just doing his gig," Sally muttered. "We don't carry pieces in here, so he's gotta make sure nobody else does. Pistols, wires, bombs, never know what someone may have on 'em."

John sat down, shaking on the inside, cool, he hoped, on the outside. Why the no guns in the back room policy? Probably leftover from the cosa nostra code. He was grateful the stand-off ended so fast, pleased the two old men intervened. "Yeah," he said, "can't be too careful nowadays."

"Tough guy," Sally said. "Maybe you do have some Frank Rosario in you." Why the bitter tone, John wondered.

Whiney scowled at Minx the Enforcer, turned back, and placed his hand on his nephew's arm. "John was just holding his ground," he said to Sally.

Calm restored, Sally Broadway and Whiney began playing cards with John watching. It was brisk, short for briscola, a neighborhood favorite John barely remembered. Trump cards reigned, three's beat everything but aces.... there were other odd rules.

Sally lifted cigars out of a little wooden box on the table, put one in his mouth, and offered others to Whiney and John. John declined, but his uncle eagerly accepted. The old men patiently lit the stoogies, puffed smoke between satisfied sighs and resumed the game.

John had never seen Whiney with a cigar. When in Rome, he guessed.

Sally and Whiney chatted about old friends, some names John recalled. Sally claimed the cigars were vintage, straight from Havana, Cuba to Prince Street, Little Italy. "Give those Commie bastards credit for something," he said to a low guffaw from Whiney. Sally grunted, slapped a jack of spades on Whiney's queen of the same suit, and swept the cards into his pile. "One thing I like about this game. The boys top the girls." He winked at John.

"Got a favor to ask," Sally said to John. The old godfather sat up, breathed deeply, stared straight ahead, preparing to deliver a spiel, John thought. "My niece, sweet girl, Anne Marie Salerno, my baby sister's kid, took a while to find herself...., in her late 20's now, just finished college ain't that something, needs a job, and says she wants to make the world a better place." Sally licked the tip of his cigar, inhaled and blew out a stream of smoke. He shifted his gaze to John. "Naturally, I thought of you." John noted a mean little snicker.

Whiney and John left the social club together, Whiney on the way to his car, John to the nearby court district for a meeting with legal aid officials who wanted his help in fashioning a new contract with City Hall. The public defenders knew that if Rudy Giuliani won the coming election, the former federal prosecutor would not favor a generous arrangement.

"Moody guy," John said about Sally Broadway. "Mix of shark and teddy bear." They stood together on a corner, waiting for a light. Whiney seemed thoughtful, but said nothing. "So tell me a story, dear uncle," John pressed.

"He was taking your measure, looks like," Whiney said. "Might've even sicked the goon on you."

"Pass the test?"

"That one, yeah."

They reached Whiney's car, a well-preserved Continental, the family wheels, John thought. Parking spaces are at a premium around here, he realized. Heavy traffic, narrow streets. Did Whiney get lucky or does he have connections? Of course he has connections, especially around here. John practically laughed aloud, amused at his own innocence.

"Get in," Whiney said. "I'll finish my story." Whiney explained that maybe it was sour old age with Sally—he knew something about that form of self-pity himself—that Sally's love for the Rosarios was real and deep but maybe tinged with envy about how Frank Senior carried himself, how he was in a dirty business, what business in this world wasn't, but that there were some lines of his own drawing that he would not cross. About how Frank had two sons and Sally was childless. Sally was close to a nephew who for better or worse followed his footsteps. The kid, Billy Salerno, he was a kid then, got busted in a poorly thought out drug transaction upstate for some damn reason Whiney didn't remember and Sally had no juice there. The kid got a lot of time.

Two teenaged boys, flavored ices in hand, leaned on the car's front fender. Whiney tapped sharply on the windshield, startling them. John guessed they thought twice about giving ugly looks to two men sitting in a long black Lincoln before hunching their shoulders and slumping off.

"So Billy spends Christmas in Dannemora?" John said.

"And maybe Sally grows a little more bitter about life," Whiney said with a shrug. "Anyway, if you help the niece, Billy's little sister, Sally'll feel he owes you."

"Money in the bank to draw on," John said, though he couldn't think of a time or reason he'd want to.

Uncle and nephew fell silent. John ruminated. Angie again. Frank suddenly open to me and headed maybe to a different place. Now Sally, another blast from my Brooklyn past, beckoning to me. A trend here?

"You could have worse friends than Sally Broadway," Whiney finally offered.

Maybe so, maybe no, John thought. "I'll make some calls," he said.

CHAPTER 5

John dressed with care for his date with Angie. He splashed on Old Spice, an aroma she'd love—maybe she'd fake a romantic swoon at her first sniff—and put on dark clothes that he thought made him look good: black slacks, a trim, grey turtleneck, and a light black tweed sports jacket. He applied mousse that his son Jake left in the medicine chest to give his black hair a brighter sheen. He looked in the mirror, feigned a tipping of the hat salute.

He picked out a Dion album to play in the van. *Stop on the red, pick up on the green/I'm gonna be the something you ain't never seen, babe.* Good company for his drive into the heart of Saturday night.

Gesturing excitedly, Louise Capobella motioned John inside the house. He sat down in the living room and placed a bunch of red roses on a dark brown coffee table. Their wine-colored petals shone like soft, pretty felt—the Korean florist had called them beautiful, beautiful. He shook off Louise's offers of food until she came to caponata, a sweet and sour eggplant appetizer; this he could not refuse.

On the bookshelves to his right was a hardcover set of John Updike's Rabbit books—read by Angie? Coming from the house's upper region was the muffled blare of an angry rap song—Donnie's listening pleasure he guessed. The rappers abruptly switched to a lilting reggae tune: *Everything is gonna be alright,* they crooned.

When Angie came down the stairs, he was standing, thumbing through a several months old edition of *Town and Country*—he found it next to the

Updike collection. "The Forgotten Ancient Ruins of Sicily" was one of the articles. He looked up, gave Angie a quick, friendly "Hi", and went back to the magazine. Unoffended, she stood peering over his shoulder.

He felt a subdued, carnal tension, like a loosely tied, trembling wire, between them. John held up the magazine. "This is great stuff, the historical artifacts of Sicily." She nodded and he continued. "Our homeland was conquered by many different nations…. the Greeks, the Arabs, Spain, France, and, finally, Italy. Explains why buildings in Sicily have many different looks. Mideastern, Spanish, Greek you name it."

Angie kept her eyes on him as they sat down next to each other on the white upholstered couch. She clasped her hands. "Johnny Rosario, you are something else. Would've expected a hello hug and kiss and a geez, Angie you look great. Instead I get a bit of history on the old country."

Face turning pink, he reached for the gleaming roses. She took the flowers with an "Ahhh" sigh and placed her hand on his thigh. "But don't be sorry. I am interested in the topic and, I think, so's the rest of your audience." She pointed to her mother and son who had entered the room.

Louise placed the caponata on the coffee table and stepped backwards, speechless at the sight of John and Angie together chatting, till she came to a big easy chair in a corner at the opposite side of the room and plopped down in it.

Donnie also sat on the other side of the room. He was dressed in black, befitting an Italian homeboy, a White Sox baseball cap tilted backwards on his head, a dipping wave of hair covering most of his forehead. Slouched in the big chair, framed by its large back sides, the boy was virtually motionless.

John respected Donnie's reserve, nodded and made no effort to shake his hand. At a nudge from Angie, he went on. "Sicilians resisted these foreign invaders only once. A French lieutenant insulted a young Sicilian woman on the way to her wedding and the people rose up to drive the French from the island. Legend has it that's when the Mafia first organized—it actually stands for Murder All the Frenchmen in Italy."

Mother and daughter chuckled, and even the boy's expression lightened. "You mean, it doesn't stand for Mothers and Fathers Italian Association," he cracked.

❦   ❦   ❦

Before going out—they had picked a small Italian restaurant on Carmine Street in lower Manhattan—John and Angie sat together on the front porch, on the wooden glider they played on when they were kids. They giggled as they squeezed into it, the rusty thing creaking with their weight. "So," John asked, "who's reading Updike in your house?"

"Now, Johnny, who d'ya think?" Angie tossed the question back like a dare. When he just blinked, she taunted, "A smart college boy like you should be able to figure this one out. Could it be my mother whose reading habits run to *People Magazine* and maybe an occasional Agatha Christie?" John smiled and held up his hands, but Angie continued her onslaught. With her feet she stopped the slight swaying of the swing and ticked off on her fingers the other possible Updike enthusiasts. "Or could it be my son Donnie who, if we're lucky, may finish a Calvin and Hobbes compilation this summer? Or could it be my former husband Dominic who maybe wanted to leave behind a collection by his favorite author so he could have some excuse to visit us?"

John quickly threw his arms over his head when Angie stopped to take a breath. "Have mercy, doll. I'm just a little surprised by your interest."

"And I'm a little insulted." She pretended to pout. "You didn't know I took literature courses at night at Brooklyn College?"

"Sorry," he said. "I didn't."

"I'm developing into an intellectual goil."

"In addition to your many other talents, I suppose." He made a light comment, but was pleased. Maybe they'd have more in common than he expected.

"That's right," she said. Two teenage girls walked by on the sidewalk in front of the house, licking ice cream cones, laughing and talking loudly about a boy named Richie.

"I'll never make the mistake again." John meant it.

They went back inside and Angie took care of the flowers. He watched her prune and fit them into the thin, tall vase on the living room's mantlepiece. She *did* look great. Short red boots with tiny heels, tight jeans, a light, silky blouse, and shiny black hair, stylishly unkempt. He welcomed the sensual heat rising inside him.

Sure they were out of the sight of Louise who had waved to them from the front porch, John stopped the van at the first red light and shifted into park. "You look smashing," he said to Angie.

"You look pretty good yourself," she replied. They embraced and kissed, relishing the press of their lips and bodies against each other.

❦   ❦   ❦

Several weeks passed before she unveiled "Angie the Librarian," on a Saturday night at his place. They had been dating steadily, were together most nights, missing each other when apart, talking on the phone then, their passion, sexual and otherwise, intensifying. Groundwork laid, she felt it was time they tried "something new." Besides he "deserved a reward"—*The Times* agreeing to publish his op ed was just the occasion. When he looked at her nervously, she wrinkled her nose. "Not to worry, Johnny, you will dig this sport."

There were rules to the game—the first, and only one of real importance: she gave orders and he followed them. He was a big dopey dog waiting to be fed and she the mistress in charge. He a student, reluctant at first, though obedient, and she the demanding tutor.

He had to take off his clothes and lie on his back on the bed; he could not move without permission. Her costume consisted of g-string panties with V-shaped splashes of black lace; a small, matching halter top that just barely contained her ample bosom; serviceable but sexy high heels; and a pair of glasses poised on the tip of her nose.

Book in hand, like a prowling cat, she crawled forward above him. She paused there, her body dangling near his tongue and touch. Per her instructions, his head and hands remained on the bed. She slowly settled her backside on his chest, her thighs grasping his upper torso. He felt pleasure and pain—pain at the weight of her and pleasure at the sight and feel of her. Pleasure and pain, pleasure and pain together, he was wondering, the essence of great sex?

Outstretched hand on his head, she inched forward, placing her knees over his arms, pinning him to the mattress. "Who's the stronger sex, Johnny?" She raised her arms, wrestlerette in victory.

He wriggled a bit, then became still. He said nothing, refusing to give in for the moment. Deliciously supine, he floated in and out of erotic reverie.

"I'm gonna read from *Rabbit at Rest*," she said. "Rabbit's returned from Florida and is driving around Brewer, you know, the town he grew up in, taking in the sights."

He tried to pay attention. She took a deep breath that made her chest rise a little higher. Looking down through the glasses, she read in a formal voice: *He likes cruising these streets. In April at least they brim with innocent energy. Four leggy blacks cluster about a bicycle....* The words blurred. In a groggy, sensual state, he could just pick up on images, boys flirting with a pretty girl, people sitting outside on little porches.

She closed the book, took off her glasses, and dropped them onto the floor. "Sounds like Bensonhurst, doesn't it? That's one of the reasons I like these books."

"Know what you mean," he uttered manfully.

"Guess I showed you I know a thing or two about Updike, you doubting Johnny." She pressed her behind down harder and her breasts jiggled slightly.

"You did, you did," he panted, conscious of sounding just a little pathetic.

She pulled a condom from inside her bra, turned around on his chest, and sat facing his penis. She smiled at its bolt upright position, commenting proudly on getting a rise out of him.

"Corny joke," he groaned.

"Criticize me, eh?" She bounced up and down twice. He grunted in dismay.

"Okay, okay," he blurted, "I surrender, I surrender. You're so fucking gorgeous. I want you so bad." He felt silly, desperate, and very excited. Sex with Suzanne had not been like this. He had enjoyed their lovemaking, sometimes intensely. But sex with his wife had never brought *him* to surrender.

Angie looked over her shoulder at him, tweaking his nose between two of her fingers. "Just what I want to hear." She leaned forward to put on the condom, the pink flesh of her buttocks rising tantalizingly above his face.

He was relieved she could roll the rubber over and down his member without making him come. She has the knack, he thought.

She rolled off and lay next to him. "It's your turn to do me."

Braced on the palms of his hands, he guided the tip of his penis onto the cusp of her vagina and rotated his hips in a short, circular motion. Her body was aroused, responsive; she moaned. He slipped into her—the warm, wet feel was a renewed thrill. She was ready too.

They slept late the next morning and prepared to go out for lunch and a lazy walk afterwards. It was damp and chilly for a summer's day and Angie put on a light, loose-fitting sweatshirt of John's—"I Love New York" it read across the front. "In June and every other month," she said, primping in the mirror. He looked at her in the sweatshirt and a baggy pair of her own "knockaround"

pants. She's concealed her sexual being, he thought, not minding that the world would be none the wiser.

While they ate at a small Middle Eastern restaurant on Broadway, he asked how she knew he'd go for such sexual shenanigans, humiliating aspects and all. She answered that all good Catholic boys, when it comes right down to it, love being subdued by a strong woman.

He leaned back in his chair and laughed, guffawed really. "Babes, you are full of surprises," he said too loudly. Startled, she motioned at him to hush.

"I gotta say," he continued with a smirk, "giving in to a gorgeous, scantily clad female probably appeals to lots of guys, regardless of religious background." He relished using 'scantily clad' in a sentence.

Angie shrugged—she would not be drawn into a debate.

"And how," he asked, "did you become such an expert on Catholic boys' sexual habits?"

"You don't wanna know," she assured him.

He grinned, but felt his belly tremble. Little jiggling movements, the sudden banging of worry beads in his intestines. How much sexual activity had there been? Could he handle it when, like a sucker punch sneak-smacking him in the head, her past affairs suddenly became known?

❦   ❦   ❦

Charles called John at his office the day after the op ed was printed. "You smoked the mayor pretty good," he said.

"You offended?"

"Not really. Working for the man doesn't blind me to his, er, deficits."

John was relieved, but didn't say anything.

"But I didn't call to praise Caesar," Charles continued, "only to seek his cooperation." He hesitated before explaining. At the behest of City Hall, unbeknownst to most of the world, he was working with Bill Simon to close the ethnic divide in Bensonhurst. And the good reverend wanted to enlist John in the effort.

Race and Bensonhurst—touchy subjects. John was wary of circumstances that could endanger his friendship with Charles. He rolled his chair away from his desk and back toward it, the clickety-clack sound of the wheels helping him think. Why was Simon, a noted firebrand, playing conciliator in any situation, much less in a parochial Italian enclave like Bensonhurst? He decided not to challenge his friend directly. "How does Simon come 'round to me?"

Charles chuckled. "Simon and I are sitting at a table waiting for a meeting to begin. This was yesterday. He's reading the paper, comes across your op ed blasting Dinkins, and he takes an interest...."

"Obviously has an eye for talent," John said.

"Simon shoves the paper in my direction, says something about how he's surprised *The Times*'d run such a hard-hitting piece, and asks me if I know this Rosario fellow. I allow as I do, quite well actually, and he asks, assumes really, a new outspoken Latino on the scene, eh? And I say no, Rosario's Italian and because I can't resist the temptation to shock the guy—he's always such a cool dude, you know—I tell him you were born and bred in that backwater, Bensonhurst." Charles paused for breath and effect.

"So?" John said. His intercom buzzed, Jeanette announcing his three o'clock appointment, a law student seeking an internship in the fall. "I'll be down in a few minutes," he told her.

"So," Charles said, "the reverend wants to meet you. To let you in on his plans to turn Bensonhurst into a harmonious community where African-Americans can walk, work, play, and even live side by side, in peace, with Italians and other white folks." He punctuated all this with a loud "hah."

"Dream on, boys, dream on," John muttered.

Charles retreated. "Maybe I overstated it a bit. Simon's not a fool or even, come to think of it, an integrationist. But he does want to reduce racial hostility in the city and sees Bensonhurst as a symbol of that. A do it there and we can do it anywhere kind of thing."

When John told Angie that night that he had agreed to meet with Bill Simon, she uttered a sound of disgust and said, "Oh, please." Like most whites in the city, she saw Simon as a self-promotor, a grass-roots demagogue. She granted him little or no credibility, and thought it preposterous—both John and she grinned when she used the word—that he'd set foot in her neighborhood, to promote harmony among the races of all things.

They sat on Angie's front porch. A bird landed on the railing and chirped a summer song to them or its mate, they didn't know which. John told her his reasons. Despite his doubts about Simon's agenda and any role he himself could play, what did he have to lose? There'd be no obligations upfront, and it'd be interesting to meet and appraise the guy. Who knows, maybe some good could come out of it. Stranger things have happened, right?

She teased him for using a bunch of clichés to justify his actions. "There's one more," he said. "If you don't swing, you don't hit anything."

❦   ❦   ❦

John thought of it, Angie signed off on it, and Donnie agreed to it. A Monday night in July, the boy came into the gym, wearing a walkman, head bobbing to private rhythms. He paused to look around. Where do the players undress? John's waves hello caught the boy's eye and he strolled to the seats along the side of the court, a narrow, cramped area where John and Charles were chatting and changing their clothes. The boy's taut, six foot plus frame reminded John of his own build; he guessed Donnie's short hair, the style of many white youths, must have baffled Dominic whose nervous habits included patting into place his black, wavy coiffure.

Donnie shook John and Charles' hands without smiling and, turning to watch the other men shooting warm-up baskets, stripped to his shorts. Still facing the court, Donnie said in a flat tone: "My mom says you guys used to be all-stars. Tonight I'm gonna show a coupla living Xaverian legends how to play today's game."

John groaned in surprise and Charles laughed and said, "Talking teenage trash. You're gonna regret that, boy." The boy turned and grinned at them and John thought maybe getting to know Angie's son wouldn't be such a chore.

Donnie did not smile much more the rest of the night, not because he did not play well, John guessed, but because a blank exterior was the everyday armor he wore when facing the adult world. Growing up in the embattled household that was the marriage between Angie and Dominic left its scars. Being cool was Donnie's way of covering the wounds.

It was a three-on-three, half-court game with John and Donnie on the same side with John's friend Harry Glassman, the director of the New York Civil Liberties Union. Harry was strong and lanky, a rebounder with sharp elbows and a talent for outlet passes.

Despite Charles' superior athleticism, John and Donnie's team won the night's three 21 point games. Donnie knew to get down court when Harry grabbed a rebound and looked for the fast break. John's best moment came when he stuffed a shot by one of Charles' teammates, got to the ball just before it went out of bounds, and while in the air, tossed it, like a desperate quarterback, on a line to Donnie. The boy gave John a fast thumbs up.

As the men dressed, Charles told John that he had put the call into Bill Simon, that he'd have the meeting arranged soon. "Can hardly wait," John said.

Charles told Donnie he was pleased his alma mater was still producing fine young talent. "If you can handle it, why don't you come back, to run with us again, man."

"I might," Donnie said. "Just to see if you had any other tricks to show." Charles smiled at the boy. When Donnie turned away, he exchanged shrugs with John.

In a phone call the next day, Angie told John that her son felt the best thing about John was his friendship with Charles. Deflated, he claimed successful male bonding had been built on less.

CHAPTER 6

❁

Jeanette handed John a small batch of phone messages. "One of them's from your brother," she noted. "Funny, he's never called here before—always figured he didn't want the dirt from his Mafia business to rub off on you."

Jeanette years ago read Frank's name on a list of alleged Brooklyn mobsters in the *Daily News*. From then on she assumed John dedicated himself to social service and change to make amends for his family's sins. She despised all gangsters, blaming them for the drug trade among the young people in her beloved East Harlem.

John looked down at Jeanette. She's like a lovely bulldog, he thought. Frank would probably like her. "My brother's a terrific guy," he told her. "Maybe someday you'll get to meet him."

"I can only wish," she said.

John phoned Frank and learned that he wanted to have lunch in the city and soon, the next day in fact.

"Have to re-arrange another meeting," John said, "but sure."

"I feel blessed," Frank said.

My brother, the funny man, John thought. "Just don't say I never did anything for you." They hung up.

John turned in his chair and gazed at the one picture of his brother on his office shelf, Frank with Theresa and the girls at an outdoor family gathering. Bet he's got information on the surprise assault in front of Rosario's. Maybe he'll talk about leaving Brooklyn. *Now that would be something.*

"Luciano," Frank said when John introduced him to Jeanette. "Knew some guys with that name."

"Did you," she commented.

"Doubt you're related to those fellahs," he said with a casual wave of his hand. John saw Frank was putting on a little performance—he knew he had to work to win Jeanette over.

"I wouldn't think so," she said.

"You're Puerto Rican, aren't you?" he asked. Jeanette's body stiffened. "Figured that," Frank continued. "Your people and mine often have the same last names. People sometimes think I'm Hispanic. Suppose that happens to Johnny a lot too, though I never talked to him about it." He grinned sheepishly at his brother.

Jeanette's look softened. "You boys should consider yourselves lucky to be taken for Latinos."

John introduced Frank to Leslie Kaplan, calling her Urban Justice Institute's expert policy analyst. She was a small, thin, high-strung woman, so full of her job that she ignored Frank and rapidly reported to John the latest news about child care budget cuts. Startled by her energy, Frank stepped back and cleared his throat. She turned toward him, said, "Oh my god," and apologized in a fast jumble of words. Frank said no offense was taken—at least he learned a bit about John's work.

On the way out, Frank tapped on Jeanette's desk. "Please keep an eye on my brother," he asked. "I'm not around enough to make sure he stays outta trouble." She promised him, and John said he was pleased they had bonded so quickly around a common purpose.

Outside, Frank commented: "Look at us, coming down the street, who'd think we're brothers? Me stocky, medium build and you, wiry, tall."

"You know what they say," John responded. "I got Dad's physique and you followed after the men on mom's side."

"Yeah, my great fortune," Frank said. "Heard about your run-in with Minx the Enforcer."

"Whiney reporting from the front," John said. "So what's your read on Sally Broadway?"

"A good man, peculiar methods sometimes." The brothers switched to single file to let two young women pass. Long hair, tight jeans, laughing conversation. The men's heads nodded, swiveled slightly. "Well-respected all around," Frank continued about Sally. "Always backs up us Rosarios. Best thing about him, he prizes loyalty."

John registered his family's party line on Sally: We're business allies and share basic values. "I'll be sure to keep on his friendly side," he said, meaning he'd deliver on his promise to help the niece.

"Good idea," Frank said. "Good for you, good for me."

❦   ❦   ❦

They went to the restaurant John brought Angie to several weeks before and encountered the eager, bumbling waitress. Her friendly fussing amused them, roused their godfatherly feelings. They were not even annoyed when she knocked over a glass of water, causing them to jump out of their chairs. "No use crying over spilt water," Frank consoled her. She sniffed a bit but withheld real tears, refilled the glass, and left to order their lunch.

The brothers talked about family, sons and daughters, their mother, Angie. "She came in the other night," Frank reported. "Seems very happy, says even Donnie may learn to like you."

"Charles's apparently what I got going for me," John said dryly. Then thinking he'd cut to the chase: "So, Frankie, what's up?"

Frank sipped his water, swallowed slowly. "I'm considering some changes in the business."

John knew showing his excitement would make Frank uncomfortable, even cut short his revelations. He flashed on how their father would use a calm demeanor to cover inner agita. He'd lean forward, make no other movements, and speak with a friendly inflection. "No kidding," John said. "Tell me more after you pass the parmesan over here." The waitress had managed to put their lunch on the table without mishap.

Frank had ordered one of the specialties of the house: a small pizza topped with sun dried tomatoes, black olives, and anchovies—spices he had loved forever, at some risk to his dignity. "Anchovies on pizza," John said. "*That* makes me doubt we're related."

Frank explained the pressure on him. "Theresa'd like to move out, get away from all the 'creeps', she calls them. You've been pissing in my ear for years about this, Dad on his fucking deathbed…. Whiney also, who'll help smooth the way and thinks it's all do-able."

"What's new now, Frankie? All that's been true for years." For the moment, John was more curious than encouraging. Frank's shift have any connection to the shooting?

"Strange thing happened the other day," Frank said. "Robeson Turner paid a little visit to Rosario's." He seemed to be changing subjects, but John knew better. "Know the man?" Frank asked.

John said he did, a bit. Met him in community meetings two or three times. An old school black militant, self-appointed knight for his people, wrote a column for the African-American paper the *City Sun*, had an occasional by-line in the *Village Voice*. John found him silly and intimidating. "What's he want with you?" he asked.

"Came in by himself. A man of his complexion, as cool as he was, that's unusual, very unusual." Frank seemed impressed. "Big guy, shaved head."

"Yeah…."

"He's from Brownsville, East New York, the housing projects for the poor they got there. You probably know that." Frank shook his head in apparent disbelief. "Tells me the kids he works with are getting fucked up on drugs sold by a local dealer, that he's traced this guy, Brown Sugar's his name. Turns out his supplier is none other than my boy Dominic."

The bulletin flashed in John's head, though it ended in a question mark: Robeson Turner, Bensonhurst Invader? Looks like one mystery solved, he thought. "Wandering far from home again," he said about Dominic. "More trouble for you, hah, Frankie?" Dominic's brains, John reflected. Do they take a temporary or permanent vacation?

"Smart guy, this Robeson Turner. Knows to come to me. Says put a rope around Dominic and reign him in or else it's gunfight at the OK Corral."

"Think he was behind the other day, the warning shots for Dominic, at him, whatever?" John tried recalling whether a man in the getaway car was bald, couldn't conjure up the memory clearly.

"Denies it."

"Believe him?"

"Don't know." Frank puffed his cheeks, blew out. "But he did seem disappointed when I promised to put an end to Dominic's latest escapade."

"Might've preferred a do-it-yourself approach?"

Frank grunted an assent. Whew, John thought. Dominic's ambitions, so unexpected, reckless. If Frank does depart, who'll control the fucking guy?

"Anyway," Frank said, "enough is enough. I'm handing in my walking papers."

John didn't go for it, not entirely. Dealing with his gang's bad boy was a hazard of Frank's trade, true. More aggravating than most maybe, but not enough to explain the reversal. If the shooting itself didn't induce this decision, why opt to leave once a probable explanation surfaces and he, Frankie, can take steps to prevent an encore? Nah, he's not making this move only because of Dominic.

"What about your personal reason for standing pat?" John asked. "You going to clear up that mystery?"

"My Robeson Turner story not enough for you? The gunplay and all that?" Frank's smile was chilly. "All I can say for now, is that things change."

Unsatisfied, John tried glaring at his brother. He then looked down at his food, jabbed it hard with his fork, and said, "Shit."

Frank held up his hand, a slow down signal. "Here's the thing, what I'd like you to understand," he said. John noted his brother's more accommodating tone. "I'm getting older," Frank went on, "Theresa and our girls too. Dominic's more than ready to take over certain aspects of my affairs.... and now that you're spending more time in Brooklyn."

"What's it got to do with me?"

"Someone's got to tend to Rosario's," Frank said carefully.

John's sons, his job, his life were in Manhattan. He had no inclination to alter that. What with Frank's burden and his free pass over the years, though, how could he deny his brother now? "Whoa, Frankie, whoa," he said. He threw up his hands, pushed his chair back, making a loud scraping noise.

Frank smiled. "What did that old priest from St. Finbar's used to say? Father Signorelli, wasn't it? Beware what you ask for. The devil may give it to you, then you'll be sorry."

John pulled his chair back to the table. "Look what you've done, Frankie. Got me so upset, can't even enjoy my food." He hated the whining tone in his voice. The old man wouldn't approve.

"Keep it up, Johnny. Haven't seen you throw a tantrum in years." Frank waited, chewing his small pizza.

Whatever happens with Angie, John said, he had no intention of returning to Brooklyn. Whatever happens, Frank pointed out, "you'll probably be around more." Why can't Dominic do it? John asked, annoyed immediately with his own dumb proposal. His brother made an are-you-kidding face. "Dominic's last name's not Rosario. Whiney and Mom are too old. So, Johnny boy," Frank wound up, "that leaves you."

The brothers didn't even think about selling the restaurant. It would be a betrayal, a sacrilege, relegating a piece of their father, a holy thing, to the slagheap.

At the end of the lunch, John said, "While I'm not promising anything, Frankie, I will think about it."

"That's all I can ask," Frank replied with an old world shrug—shoulders raised half a minute, eyes practically shut, hands cupped facing each other. Your avuncular ways, John thought, charming as ever.

Though he didn't let on to Frank, the Robeson Turner story spooked John. He walked into his office worried about things.

Jeanette called out to him. "C'mere, wanna tell you something." He stood on the other side of her desk. "I wish to apologize for all the shit I've given you about your brother."

❦   ❦   ❦

"Pensiera," Angie said to John as they drove to his apartment where they'd planned an evening of listening to music.

"What's that?" he asked.

"What kind of Italian are you? Don't even know what pensiera means."

"Come on. Sounds familiar, I can hear my folks saying it." It was a sore point that he knew so little Italian.

She took mercy on him. "Pensiera means headaches, stuff on your mind. Looks like you got a bad case."

"Yeah, a major affliction. Frank unloaded a bombshell over lunch. Asked for a favor, a large favor."

She edged closer to him, expecting to hear more, he knew. He was about to break the Sicilian male code of omerta, silence before all women and outsiders about the mob, but didn't really care. He broke family traditions before. And talking to Angie seemed so…. right. He wanted her to understand not just his present dilemma but the trail of circumstances leading up to it, starting with that major life event, his introduction, courtesy of his father, to the mafia and manhood.

They stopped at a red light on 10th Avenue, the quickest route to the upper Westside. He gave her a probing look, intense, but inclusive. Yet he could tell she felt uncomfortable, more like a target than a companion. She leaned back against the passenger door, as if bracing herself for other glares he'd fire her way.

He sighed heavily and she giggled, embarrassed at seeing his distress. The light turned green, he pressed his foot on the pedal, and spoke, feeling a whoosh of relief.

He described how in a parked car on the borderline between Flatbush and Coney Island, his father told him not to follow his footsteps. He recounted his old man, on his deathbed, begging Frank to walk away from the gangster world that had turned into a cesspool.

He pulled the van into an underground parking garage on West 110th Street and backed into his designated space. As always, especially after night-fall, it was dark, damp, and spooky.

"You were there," Angie asked, "with Frankie and your father?"

"Yes, in the hospital. One of the old man's last days."

"That's heavy," she said, holding out her arm. "C'mere, Johnny." He toppled over into her lap and she cradled him against her body. "So," she continued, "you always felt guilty and Frankie, I guess, felt, what's the right word, con-flicted." John nodded in her arms.

"Poor Frankie and Johnny," she whispered. "I never knew."

The evening's cool lowered like a soft curtain on the day—making for a soothing summer's night in the city. John and Angie slowly walked the 25 blocks to his apartment. He usually enjoyed the sights, sounds, and smells of upper Broadway, the mix of Latin New Yorkers young and old, with the seedy homeless and young whites, male and female, going in and out of stores, sit-ting at sidewalk cafes, palavering with street merchants in at least 2 or 3 foreign languages. Tonight the hubbub was just background music.

John explained his brother's request, "Frank's fantasy" he called it, that he return to Bensonhurst, take over Rosario's so that he, Frank, could make the big step.

"He wants you to leave UJI?" She thinks that's a lot to expect, he noted. "Such a change in your life," she said. "And the worry too."

"A huge change, Angie. Push me back where I don't want to go." He felt pain, a tearing inside, like when Frank first broached the subject.

A scruffier than usual doorman greeted John and Angie with nervous eager-ness when they entered his building's lobby. He was new to the job, which saw a lot of turnover—probably from Romania, John guessed, the super's native country. The lobby was poorly lit, its beaten up black leather furniture, the doorman's unshaven face parts of the gloomy decor.

In the elevator, she nestled under his arm and patted his chest with her free hand. "Maybe we could do some, what d'you call it, problem-solving, about your situation with Frank."

"But not tonight."

"Why, what d'you have in mind?"

"Listening to music, like we said. I wanna play a coupla songs with your name in them. But not "Angelina-Zooma Zooma"—so don't be disappointed."

"Too low-class?"

"Nah." He was surprised at her thinking. "No Louis Prima in my record collection."

"And I'd love to play the only song with your name that matters."

"What's that?"

"Johnny B. Good"

"Of course."

❧   ❧   ❧

John put on a Mott the Hoople album. Angie and he sat on his old brown couch, feet up on a wood bench, within arm's reach of the disc/record/tape machine.

He said Mott was well-known in its heyday, guitar-based rock and roll grunge its signature, long before the new Seattle groups adopted the sound. She figured he knew about the day's Seattle bands because his sons listened to their music, as most white boys did. Her son, of course, brought only rap records into the house.

John dropped the needle on "Sweet Angeline," an unruly rave-up, guitars like fire engine sirens, a heady, crashing din of sound. Mostly buried in the mix, the lyrics paid homage to sexy, sweet Angeline, queen of the New York night-time scene. He got up and danced in goofy fashion, arms spread out, spinning in a circle around the room. Angie stayed put despite his hands motioning her to join him. "This is your show, kiddo."

John played another Mott track, a cover of a Dion song about a man who beat his drug habit by getting in touch with the people and things he valued most, that he found "back in his own backyard." When the record finished, John's mood turned somber. "Why so blue?" Angie asked.

"Heard that cut on the radio, maybe 15 years ago, and knew it was a Dion song. Went out and bought the album." John spoke softly, like a man revealing a sad secret. "It got me into Mott the Hoople. "Your Own Back Yard," a corny image, but it's always kinda haunted me. Since leaving Brooklyn, I'm not sure where my back yard is."

He rubbed his eyes hard, leaned back on the couch, and chuckled. "Here I am at a loss to explain my feelings of loss." He looked at Angie. "Sorry to ruin the moment, babes."

"Don't worry about it." She flicked her hand.

The phone rang. "Don't," John said before Angie could even rise from the couch. Leslie Salzman's voice on the answering machine reminded John of a breakfast meeting with homeless advocates to plot strategies for promoting improved services and safety in the city's shelters.

"Now those folks have real problems," John said with a sad grin. "Still, this backyard thing fucks with my head. Frankie's touched this soreness. Wants me to go home to my original backyard, but I don't feel home there anymore. My life's here now."

"So what's the problem?"

"Because this really isn't my place either," he said. "All my friends are Jewish or black. Except for you, there're no Italians in my world. I've traveled so far from home, not distance wise, but the intangibles, you know, that sometimes I feel disconnected, with no solid footing anywhere."

Angie stroked his hair, spoke in a flat, gentle tone. "It's funny, because I've always thought of you as lucky, blessed even. Because you escaped so early. Now I see deeper, your father pushing you away, for your own good, maybe, but still pushing you out. Now Frankie pulling you back."

She paused, saw he was listening. "I still think you're lucky. Look, Johnny, you've made a good life, doing good, trying to make things better, with people who love you in two places." She paused again. He crooked his head, encouraging her to continue. "Maybe you feel agita, 'cause you've lost your bearings, but maybe, too, it's not that you have no back yard, but that you have two."

The bubble of agonizing that filled his gut gave way. He felt the ugly gas leave his body, saw it dissolve in the air. It was gone for now. "So," he said, "I'm rich, not poor?"

"Why not?" she said, palms held upward.

"Thanks, I think. I mean I'll think about it." He was like a vagabond who came into some money and didn't feel comfortable yet in the new home he bought. Maybe he had been on the road too long. "It'll still be difficult, won't it, bridging the gap?"

"That's where I come in," she said.

CHAPTER 7

❁

John pushed on the familiar revolving doors of Harry's Coffee Shop, a main city schmooze center. Across from City Hall park, on the corner of Chambers and Broadway, where politicos and government officials gathered along with lobbyists and service providers who tried to influence them. He was surprised Bill Simon agreed to have breakfast there: Why compromise his reputation by being seen with the mainstream likes of Charles and him?

Arriving first, John wended his way to the back of the elongated L-shaped restaurant and sat in one of the spacious booths. He liked Harry's—its dark brown wood tables, chairs and countertops and no-nonsense waiters and waitresses made for a relaxed atmosphere.

Charles and Rev. Simon arrived shortly after one another. Simon's long, narrow face wore a full beard. He maneuvered his tall, slender body lightly through and past the booths and tables, with more physical grace than he showed on television. He smiled hello to at least eight groups of people. John had greeted two. He pondered fame's blessings and realized why Simon chose Harry's for the meeting.

The Rev. Simon flashed a big, toothy grin and shook John's hand with a vigorous pump. He complained good-humoredly that most of the folks who just greeted him, once he didn't get his face on t.v. for 6 months, would take great pleasure in snubbing him in public and refusing his phone calls. John lowered his guard slightly.

Charles and John ordered light: a muffin, juice and coffee. Simon had eggs, bacon, toast, and home fries. John wished he could indulge in such a greasy meal without feeling soporific effects later in the day. At least I can wallow in the aromas, he thought.

"All us preachers are missionaries promoting a message of salvation," Bill Simon said, beginning the business part of the meeting. "Mine's just a little different than most, because it challenges the status quo and because I deliver it not only to my own congregation, but to unfriendly audiences also, some stone hostile in fact." The Reverend grinned, shifting his gaze from John to Charles.

"To what ends," John asked after a pause, "do you expose your missionary zeal to unreceptive ears?" He momentarily adopted Simon's formal speaking style.

"My purpose, John, is to commit the offense I'm often charged with. To shake things up in the hopes that when the bricks and dust settle back into place, the new configuration helps my people." Simon jabbed the table top with his index finger. "But my other objective is just as important: saving not only my flock, but all people in this city we call New York, including your brothers and sisters, Mr. Rosario."

"That's why you've gone into Bensonhurst?" John asked.

The Reverend lowered his voice. "As we used to say in a very different time, right on, my friend."

"And so," John said, "you determined I could be a helpful disciple in your grand scheme."

"Haven't determined anything," the Reverend replied. "I'm not the arrogant know-it-all I'm made out to be. After reading your op ed, after checking out your meritorious efforts with the Urban Justice Institute…. thought you might be interested in a different kind of good works, that re-connected you with your own community." The Reverend gave his companions a sly look. "Just a thought, John."

"We all know," Charles said, "that Bensonhurst could benefit from more enlightened influences, John. Your kind of social values don't get a lot of play there."

John was dismayed, bemused: Angie, Frankie, and now Charles and this new stranger in his life, all, in one way or another, wanted him to go home again.

The food was served by two men—one young, one old, both unshaven—with a we-could-care-less-about-you-and-yours attitude. John welcomed the distraction of the clatter of dishes and glasses. Saved by the bacon.

He learned Bill Simon was serious about his work in Bensonhurst. He had quietly established a base with several church and civic groups including the local merchants association headed by Nick Caesar, a restauranteur and Rosario's principal competitor. Future plans: a basketball league to bring together black and white players; an Increase the Peace/Extend a Hand Sunday with clerics preaching harmony between the races on the same Sabbath; and an all-day community forum, co-sponsored by diverse local leaders, with panels and workshops on issues, from competition for scarce jobs to musical tastes, that keep people apart.

"Helluva blueprint," John said. He slouched back in his seat. "Hardly needs me."

"You're right," Simon replied. "We don't *need* you. But there's one other constituency in Bensonhurst we have not been able to reach, the mob."

Pretty ironic, John thought. Simon sees political positives in my Mafia ties, something to exploit. I'm drawn to this, yet uncertain. My past as flame; me as moth?

"For better or worse—it's the same in some black parts of town," the Reverend continued. "A very important group in your old community, John, are the gangsters. We'd like them to give a nod to our efforts."

"What makes you think I can help with the gangsters, as you call them?" John felt a rising annoyance, yet feigned innocence, as his father often did when the subject of the Mafia arose. "What does that stand for?" the old man would say. "Don't know nothing about that organization, if it even exists. Run a restaurant, that's what I do, the best in Bensonhurst."

Charles slapped the table and turned toward Bill Simon. The Reverend spoke with an edge. "Stop blowing smoke in our faces, John. We've done some checking, a fair amount actually. We know who you are and who your people are."

"Mr. Simon, you do *not* know who I am." He's one pushy bastard, John thought.

The Reverend sat upright, wagged a finger at John. "You're a slippery dude, aren't you? What is it, afraid of associating with me? Unwilling to go home again and confront your past shit?"

"Ouch," John said. "Taking the gloves off, eh, Reverend?"

"Yes, I am. The question is, are my punches landing on your chin?"

John held up his hands. "You've gotten through, Reverend, but let's call the match a draw for now. My answer is not no and not yes. It's I'll think about it." He'd been telling a lot of people that lately.

The whiff of the Reverend's greasy breakfast hung over the table like a pleasant echo. Charles extended his hand. John grasped it. "I knew you couldn't walk away," Charles said.

"Here's one from left field," John said. "Any chance Robeson Turner's involved with the project?"

"Ah, Robeson Turner," the Reverend replied, "who vies with me for the role of the city's last remaining white man's nightmare." The waiter handed the check to the cleric who slid the paper to Charles' side of the table.

Simon was emphatic. "A cocked gun to his head could not persuade brother Turner to join us in Bensonhurst. He has no truck with conciliatory endeavors." The Reverend was also curious. "Why do you ask?"

"He's been sighted in those parts." John eyed his companions coolly. Simon groaned, Charles frowned.

Outside the restaurant, the Reverend turned a serious gaze toward John. "All my contacts had only good things to say about the men in your family. They stand by their word, never welsh on a deal, never threaten violence needlessly. And all my sources were people of the dark hue." He pointed to the skin of one of his bare arms.

"Honor among thieves surprise you, Mr. Simon?" John asked.

The Reverend grinned. "Among white folks it does."

❦   ❦   ❦

Charles walked John toward the subway. "The Robeson Turner query. Where'd that come from?" he asked.

"Like I said, from left field."

"Come the fuck on," Charles said brusquely. "'He's been sighted.' Don't be cute. You're not usually so cute."

"Can't say any more. Probably already said too much."

They stood at the top of the stairwell leading to the subway. Charles was turning away when John stopped him. "What can you tell me about Turner?"

Charles' gaze went slowly from his friend's belt to his eyes. He's thinking whether he should tell me anything, John realized.

"Powerful figure." Charles spoke in a fast clip. "Scary, but no real reason to be scared of him, if you know what I mean." John was not sure that he did. "Unpredictable," Charles concluded.

"But not so unpredictable. You know he'd reject Simon's Bensonhurst project."

"Guess that's right."

"Any more on him?" John pursued.

"Can't say. Maybe already said too much." Charles grinned.

Alone, John heard the rumble and roar of the subway. His next decision was easy: whether to rush down the steps or to take his time and wait on the platform for the next train.

CHAPTER 8

John came home late. He had worked past 9 o'clock, putting the final touches on a grant proposal for a study of the mentally ill in the City's jails—they received none of the needed services and returned to the streets in even worse shape. He turned the bedroom air conditioner on high, stripped to what his boys called his scivies, and lay down on his bed. He didn't put on music or his television and could barely hear the street traffic sounds over the air conditioner's rumble. After his long day, that's what he craved: no extraneous noises, just the purring quiet of his cooling machine.

After 20 minutes, he went into the kitchen, where he poured and drank slowly two glasses of orange juice and seltzer. Refreshed, he was ready to be a responsible human again.

Three phone messages: one from Angie asking if he missed her—this was the first night in weeks they weren't together—and two from people in his Manhattan family: Suzanne and Teddy who called from camp, unusual considering the rules prohibiting phone calls. Knowing Suzanne had just visited the boys' camp, John got nervous. What bad news was about to crash land on his happy summer interlude?

"What?….you did what?" John squawked into the phone. Suzanne had just confessed to the sin of telling their boys about his relationship with Angie. "Why did you fucking do that?"

John guessed the ill effects on his sons, who still fervently hoped their parents would reunite. He paced the floor, feeling a sudden rush of fear and seeing a wreck on the road ahead. Through his interior racket, he barely heard Suzanne's attempts to soothe him, her voice muffled, a distant sound.

He sat in the reclining chair in his bedroom, and kept the phone to his ear. The muted sounds on the other end grew slowly more distinct. The catch in Suzanne's voice, the struggle to find words to reach him were reminiscent of her behavior during their old fights. Tenderness for her crept through, dissolving his righteous ire. Maybe I'm overreacting. Maybe I should listen.

Suzanne agreed she'd been stupid, hurtful to all of them, especially the boys. She wracked her brain for a plan to make things right or at least better. She decided first to tell John the full story—she seemed disappointed at not getting credit for that but hurried on. I have a remedy to propose, she said brightly. "Your turn to visit the camp next weekend, right? Why not take Angie to meet the boys. They'll see she's not a monster or a shrew, and maybe that'll repair the damage."

He was quiet, mulling it over. She spoke again. "That is, of course, if she isn't a monster or a shrew."

He ignored her gibe. "Got a message from Teddy tonight on my machine. I suppose it's about this." He turned to look at the answering machine on his bureau. He used to keep pictures of Suzanne there—they were gone now, packed up in some closet.

"He called me, too," she replied. "All upset about Jake who's been edgy with everybody, according to Teddy. Apparently left a basketball game because the other boys weren't passing him the ball."

"Just walked off the court?" John felt a familiar internal conflict. Moved by his son's distress, pissed at his conduct. "Good work, Suzanne." He renewed his nasty tone. He wanted Miss Ice Queen to squirm more on her petard. "What possessed you to do such an unthinking thing?"

He could hear her take two deep breaths. It was tough for her to admit her own untidy emotions—she hadn't the benefit of going to confession for years. He guessed it was a combination of envy and revenge that prompted her bad behavior and wondered whether she could own up to it.

"Alright, this is no excuse," she said, "but I think it was a mix of jealousy and revenge that just got to me. I crossed a line. I'm sorry."

Put you in your place, didn't she, Johnny boy, he thought, and in no time flat. Maybe Suzanne's growing, or maybe I missed something the first time around. Maybe, too, the Ice Queen tag's unfair.

Suzanne shifted to a childlike tone, to charm a favorable response from him. Her tactic was working, along with the cooling hum of the air-conditioner, the soft cushions of his chair, and his developing judgment that things were perhaps not all that dire. He even considered telling her about Frank and Bill Simon and the pulls back to Bensonhurst. But he thought: No, better not. It's late. We're tired. She'll react coldly to any suggestions I might return to Brooklyn. Besides, she's not really my soul mate anymore.

John slipped into bed. Thoughts of Kenneth, the current man in Suzanne's life, disrupted his drift into sleep. Was he with her on the trip to the camp? Despite his best efforts, John disliked him intensely, his name (the man told people he preferred not to be called Ken or Kenny), his status as a successful partner in Suzanne's law firm, his Park Avenue WASP background.

John thought of Suzanne and their first summer together. Her white dress, as light as air to his touch, during their week on Cape Cod, Leonard Cohen singing in a low, morose voice: *Suzanne takes you down to her place by the river….* Mysterious and romantic she was in the chilly evenings by the water. He began to forgive her, her breaking up the marriage, her recent vindictive outburst with the boys, even her affair with Kenneth. After all, one thing we share: in choosing new lovers, both of us returned to our roots.

❀   ❀   ❀

John and Angie did decide to make the trip together—he'd visit the camp alone on the first day to test the emotional waters, and she'd 'go gallivanting' through the wholesale shops lining the nearby town's main street. Suzanne looked forward to these trips for the same reason. The two women in his life, different in so many ways, had that much in common.

"Your boys Knick fans?" Angie asked John toward the end of their long drive.

"Big-time. Why?" John responded.

"No reason….. So, made any progress with your struggles?"

"Pretty Miss Curiosity, all of a sudden. You mean the back to Bensonhurst question?"

"Uh-huh. What else?"

"In fact, I have."

They had left Interstate 93 and were now on the back roads of New Hampshire, heading toward the camp, passing quiet lakes surrounded by swatches of forest and ringed by vacation homes. Rolling and green farmland marked the landscape bound by the White Mountains, somber and massive, in the distance. White clouds, pure as powder, floated tranquilly across the bright, blue sky. Twilight, and the colors of all these scenes began shifting to darker shades.

John spoke easily. His right elbow rested on the arm of his seat, his left hand guided the wheel. He wouldn't take full or major responsibility for Rosario's—that meant giving up too much of his chosen life. He'd help Frank hire an experienced manager to run the place and maybe Whiney or Dominic could help him, John, supervise that person. At Dominic's name, Angie scowled, but said nothing.

He'd give Bill Simon's project a try, go to a meeting or two in Bensonhurst. Charles would be there and he was eager to work with his old friend; there'd been tension between them lately. He also wanted Angie involved—he'd depend on her critical eye. He'd even, as Simon suggested, chat with Frank about putting in a good word with the local goombahs. Who knows, as he ponders a big life change, maybe Frank would consider it. Angie had her doubts.

On the whole, though, she approved. The plan was sensible, yet venturesome. She could not, had no inclination to knock it.

"Your wisdom was my guide, babes," he said.

"How d'ya figure?"

"This way, I keep my two backyards."

One unknown still vexed him. The personal reason Frank had for remaining in Brooklyn that, apparently, no longer applied.

The young woman at the camp office had a British accent, a short-cropped, punk hair-cut, a tattoo on her shoulder advocating peace and love, and a friendly smile. She cheerily informed John that Teddy was at basketball and that Jake was sailing, though, given his attitude toward all water sports, he was likely taking a break. "You might find him in his bunk," she said in a proper English meter reflecting Camp Robin Hood's cosmopolitan ambience. With a nod from the boy's basketball instructor, John snatched Teddy from the middle of a ball-handling drill and together they headed off to find Jake.

Music blaring from some boy's speaker greeted John and Teddy when they entered Jake's bunk-house. A grunge stylist wailing, *I'm going hungry*, stretching out *hu-u-u-ungry-y-y-y* to emphasize his urgent sense of need. For what, John thought. Love? Food?

"That's Temple of the Dog, Dad," Teddy said. "White boy's noise."

Jake was not the only one who avoided water sports. Three boys at one end of the bunk played cards on a makeshift table of two plastic crates turned on their ends. The boys lifted their heads from the game and one of them said, "Jake's in his bed, I think."

John felt a twinge of pain in his chest: Why can't my boy at least play with these kids?

Jake was asleep, a thread-bare blanket covering the lower half of his body. A stuffed bull, a gift from the boy's mother, lay next to his head on the pillow. Suzanne searched for weeks for a store with a furry animal that would commemorate Jake's astrological sign as a Taurus born in May. She wanted him to be strong, like a bull, during difficult times like his parents' divorce.

Teddy bumped his brother's mattress with his leg—Jake stirred, opened his eyes. He saw his father and brother, made an unhappy face, and rolled his head back into the pillow.

"Curb your enthusiasm, Jake," John said. "Jump up too quickly to hug me and you might knock me down."

"Good to see you, Dad," Jake said through a yawn.

"What am I, dog doo-doo?" Teddy cut in.

"You, I see all the time." Jake stood, gave his father a fast embrace, sat back down on the bed, and rubbed his eyes. With John and Teddy sitting on each side of him, they talked about the camp: the basketball coaches, the meals, the outcome of sporting events. But Jake's half-hearted responses made conversation difficult. "Let's take a walk," John said.

Outside, they passed other visiting parents with their children. In one group, a boy of about nine carried a little machine that twirled a lollipop while he held out his tongue licking it. "Ever see one of them before?" John talked in a low voice. The boys shook their heads. "So, what's the story behind it?" he asked.

"There are a lot of spoiled rich kids at the camp," Teddy offered, whispering like his father. "Maybe that's what their parents buy them now."

John shook his head. "Of course," he grinned, "an automatic lollipop licker. What other gift is there for the child who has everything."

It was the first chance they'd had that day to smile together.

They took a path through a wooded area toward a seldom used part of the lake bordering on the camp. Walking quickly ahead, Teddy grabbed twig branches, pulled them forward and let them flip back into his father and brother. "Watch out back there for the attack of the killer trees," he shouted.

"Cut it out" Jake growled, "or you'll hafta watch out for the attack of the killer brother."

Teddy swung a final branch at Jake and ran. Jake charged ahead, and when John came to the sliver of lakefront beach at the path's end, he found the boys roughhousing like frisky puppies. Teddy was on the receiving end of a noogie, a headlock and knuckle rub that did not appear, at least this time, to hurt too much.

John leaned against a large craggy rock about 10 feet from the water's edge. Only the occasional boat whizzing past marred the lake's peaceful expanse. His sons crashed down next to John, panting and sweating slightly, assuming as they nestled in, the same posture: back against the rock, butt in the sand, knees up, and hands clasped around their legs. Their physical likeness was apparent: the shape of their heads, the curve of their backs, the cut of their leg muscles, their tanned, even complexions. John relaxed for a moment. Jake's kibitzing with his brother gave him hope—maybe his boy wasn't so deep into a funk.

But the strain returned—even a discussion of movies and music fizzled. Teddy announced it was volley ball hour for his group and he loved it too much to miss. He brushed the sand off his legs and clothes, said, "See you guys later, at lunch," and trotted off into the woods.

"Well, Jake, now we can talk," John began.

"Do we have to?" Jake picked up a stone and, from his sitting position, threw it into the lake. They watched the ripples from the splash idle slowly toward the shore at their feet. "You're not going to yap at me for screwing up at camp, are you?"

John shook his head. "I wanna talk about what's bothering you, what's going on in my personal life, how it affects you and Teddy…."

"Okay, shoot." Jake stood, picked up more stones, and tossed them in the lake—sometimes trying to skip them across the surface. John stood too. While he spoke, he twice interrupted Jake's rock throwing to make eye contact. Suzanne and he, despite their affection for one another, would never 're-couple'; Angie was the new love in his life, a woman the boys would like once they knew her; he'd make sure his new relationship strengthened, rather than damaged their family. He paused, worried his remarks were too formal, like a press statement.

Jake sat down again, this time on the beach's big rock. A part of his hair fell over his forehead. He folded his arms and looked blankly toward the lake. Although they were only inches apart, John felt a great distance separating them.

Jake looked at his father—too coolly John thought—and asked: "Where is she? Thought we were going to see her today."

"She stayed back in town while I got the lay of the land," John replied. "Is having a field day shopping, I'm sure."

"Like Mom, huh?"

"They do have some things in common, I'm finding," John said.

Jake snickered. "I just don't like it, Dad. Just don't want it."

Exasperated, John said, "Why, Jake? You accepted your Mom with Kenneth." He raised his voice, but not so it became a whine. How, he wanted to ask, did Suzanne and that arrogant prig get off so fucking easy?

There was a splash, and the two Rosarios turned toward the water. What was it? Someone nearby throwing a rock? A flying fish? "Maybe we should've brought our poles, caught our supper," John said.

"Dad, don't you see," Jake said. "This is more final, now that the two of you have boyfriends, girlfriends, whatever…." The boy was sputtering. "Besides I never took Kenneth that seriously. He was so different from you that I thought it was just a joke, just Mom trying to hurt you, that it wouldn't last."

"Jake," John said softly, "the truth is your mother prefers to be with that kind of man."

"And you prefer to be with your new girlfriend?"

"Yeah, I do."

Jake lowered his head then looked at John. "It's not fucking fair," he said accusingly. He turned away and walked toward the path leading back to the camp. "Fuck it," he said, then louder, "Fuck all of it."

John stood still, his feet stuck in the sand. A sadness, heavy like the sea, washed over him. What can I do to reach my boy? he wondered. Head down, muttering, "Shit, shit, shit", he paced in slow irregular patterns the small space of sand. He picked up a stone and tried to skim it across the lake.

The softball game was John's favorite activity at the camp because parents joined in and he could flex his old skills. Several times over the years, he slugged one of the slow lobs that passed for pitches into the woods in distant left field. Today, though, in his first at bat, he hit a slow grounder to third base which he barely beat out when the infielder bobbled the ball.

Teddy and he sat on the wobbly sidelines bench watching the game when the boy pointed at two figures walking across the adjacent empty field. "It's Jake, Dad. He's coming this way, I think."

John stood up to get a better look. "Who's he with?"

"Must be Emily."

"Emily? Who's that?"

"She's Jake's girlfriend. She's very nice, one of the prettiest girls at camp, the best-looking, I think."

"Girlfriend! I didn't know Jake had a girlfriend." John processed this as good news and grew suddenly hopeful again.

"Jake said he'd kill me if I told you or Mom about Emily," Teddy said. "Now he's bringing her to you."

"Seems so," John said calmly. Wouldn't do to show his excitement.

"She's French, Dad. Her name's Emily Grandperet. We call her Emily Grandpriz. You know, like she's a great prize."

John and Teddy met their new companions about 50 feet behind the backstop. Jake and the girl quickly said 'Hi' to Teddy and then Jake, waving his hands between them, introduced his father to his girlfriend. John held out his hand which the girl shook firmly. "Pleased to meet you, Mr. Rosario. Jake has told me much about you." She spoke English a bit formally, with a trace of a French accent.

"Pleased to meet you also, Emily," he replied. "Just what has my son said?" He could not keep the hint of suspicion out of his voice.

"He says you're a wonderful basketball player, Mr. Rosario. And a nice man…. in that order, I think." John grinned. Emily was tall, slender, nearly Jake's gangly height, with straight black hair, part of which fell over the front of her shoulders. She looked at Jake who chuckled and shifted his weight from one foot to another like an awkward colt. John was pleasantly amazed: his son transformed from a brooding, sullen teenager to a goofy boy.

At a nod from Emily, Jake spoke. "Dad, can I see you for a minute alone?" John said "Sure," and walked with his son away from the continuing commotion of the ballgame and the company of Emily and Teddy. Teddy and the girl strolled together in the opposite direction and the boy shouted to his father and brother: "Emily and I are going to my bunk. Come by after you're done. Got something to show you."

John and Jake settled into two green wooden chairs next to an unused horseshoe pit. Earlier in the day, parents had sat in them and cheered their children's attempts to ring the spike. "Nice girl," John said.

Jake said, "Every kid in camp was chasing her and she picked me. Guess I'm lucky she likes the quiet tormented types."

John flinched at the reference, but did not challenge it. He'd follow his son's lead in the conversation.

Jake hunched over in his chair, elbows bent on the top of his knees, chin resting on his closed fists. He gazed across the camp's grounds at the tennis courts, noisy with the hollers of players and the thump of balls against rackets. Sad and tense, he spoke without looking at his father. "Hope you bring your friend tomorrow. Guess I'd like to meet her."

"I'm pleased. She'll be too. Her name's Angie, by the way."

"Her real name Angela?" Jake leaned back and looked at his father.

"No, actually it's the longer version, Angelina. When we were kids, I'd sometimes call her by her full name, Angelina Barbara Capobella."

"Angelina Barbara Capobella," Jake repeated. "Quite a mouthful, Dad."

"Yeah, it is."

Jake leaned forward again and stared at the ground. "Emily's parents were divorced when she was about eight. It hurt her a lot, and she especially resented it when her father got a girlfriend. She refused to see him, wouldn't even speak to him on the phone for about a year, until she realized he loved her and she was just missing out by keeping him out."

Hard times can make you wise, John thought. "Kind of Emily to give you the benefit of her experience," he said. Two boys walked past, loudly gabbing, each trying to top the other with boasts about their prowess at ping-pong.

"Kind? No way, Dad," Jake said. "Emily was harsh as hell. When I told her I was too hurt and angry to see Angie, she slipped into that snobby French accent she uses when she gets worked up about something." Jake sat in a rigid, upright position, pointed his finger in the air, and mimicked Emily's stern foreign tones. "Oh no. That is not true. You do not want to see your father's girlfriend because you are scared, stupeed, stubborn, and lazee, and you know that you just cannot handle it."

"Lazy?"

"She always calls me lazy when she's annoyed with me, whether it fits or not. She likes the sound of it or something."

❧   ❧   ❧

Father and son were walking back to Teddy's bunk when a deep voice vaguely familiar to John called out, "Yo, Rosario."

John left Jake on the path and headed toward Robeson Turner who was coming his way from the tennis courts. Fuck all, John thought, the Bensonhurst Invader himself. What did Simon call him? The white man's worst nightmare? But he doesn't haunt my dreams, just my waking hours. What's that make him, my daymare?

The two men met on the grass, stood talking under a leafy green and brown tree, about 100 feet from Jake. "What…." John started, not happy about having to look up at the bigger man.

"The fuck am I doing here?" Turner smiled pleasantly. Like John was an old friend and their meeting in a sleepaway camp in northern New Hampshire was in the unquestioned scheme of things. Like dark following the sunset. "That your boy?" he asked.

John nodded.

"Nice build. Much of an athlete?"

"Holds his own. What the fuck are you doing here?"

Turner chuckled. John saw the man did not mind the edge in his voice. It helped him relax too. Turner flicked a thumb point behind his back and John saw three black boys leaning against the inside of the fence around the tennis courts. Their dark skins gleamed against their white shirts and shorts. One of them, the tallest, flipped his racket from hand to hand, eagerly waiting his turn.

"Seeing how my Brownsville boys are making out up here. Got them a scholarship for the summer. You know, man, maybe a bourgeois sports camp can do good by them."

"Dad," Jake called out, hands cupped around his mouth. "Should I stay or go?"

"Just a minute," John responded. He turned toward Turner. "So?" He was interested in Turner's appraisal.

Turner's expression became somber. "We got something to talk about," he said. "Nothing to do with this silly camp, but with Brooklyn, things back home."

"Okay," John shrugged, his ease too studied he knew. He was prepared to wave off Jake.

Turner's face contorted, baring his teeth. He spat, the phlegm hitting the earth with a violent splash not far from John's feet. John danced back, avoiding the spray.

"Lotsa years, I've been fed fucking up with white folks. Using us, abusing us. Even when helping, using us." Turner spoke fiercely, fist pumping. "Always excepted the Italians. Fucking admired 'em even. A tough, honest people. Lately, though, I'm thinking maybe you're the worst of the lot."

Turner's shift in mood and manner unnerved John. He felt movement in his stomach and tightened his asshole. He was determined not to show fear, but knew he'd make use of the first available toilet.

"Okay," he repeated. "Let's do it." He meant talk about it, whatever it was that triggered the other man's vehemence.

But Turner shook his head. "What are you? A Nike commercial?" More composed, he pointed over John's shoulder toward the impatient boy. "Tend to your son. He's fretting like a puppy." John objected to the condescending tone, but not the content. Given the day's emotional tension, he thought, I'd just as soon postpone a confrontation with this pissed-off son-of-a-bitch. He didn't turn around when he was walking with Jake, as Turner shouted his parting words. "Call you first thing next week, Rosario."

"What the fuck was that about, Dad?" Jake asked.

He too young to talk that way to his father? John thought.

"That looked like real shit happening," Jake went on.

John snorted. How to reassure my boy while keeping it vague? "Mr. Robeson Turner back there, a New York City acquaintance of mine, gets worked up about stuff. A little turf war among non-profits, this time. Got to help settle it when I get back." He eyed his boy who seemed satisfied. Mind's probably back on Emily. John patted him on the shoulder. "Looked worse than it was."

"Wonder what Teddy wants to show us," Jake said as they entered his brother's bunk. Emily was still there—Jake sat next to her on Teddy's bed and took her hand. Teddy reached behind the music box on his cubby and extracted a lollipop. He unwrapped it and licked it, his tongue making loud, slurping sounds. "Just wanted to show you guys that some Robin Hood campers like lollipops the old-fashioned way."

John smiled then asked, "So, where's the john?"

❦   ❦   ❦

The next day, polite, uncertain exchanges marked Angie and the boys' first two hours together. They were like cautious boxers circling each other in the early rounds, barely touching each other's gloves, waiting for the other fighter's first move.

Before a casual father/son basketball game, Angie surprised them with tee-shirts pulled out of her bag, bought on the previous day's shopping spree. Two with the names and numbers of popular New York Knicks' players: Patrick Ewing #33 for Jake and John Starks #3 for Teddy. "Coach Dad," said John's shirt. Each Rosario was pleased, if embarrassed, by his gift, and very willing to wear it during the game. John put on his shirt and watched his boys giggling at how theirs fit and looked. He realized how artful Angie's gesture was. After the game the boys talked warmly with Angie about the Knicks—she followed their fortunes a bit. It helped, too, that she could name several rap groups that Donnie played for her that Jake and Teddy also favored, including the Goats from Phillie, with at least one Italian-American member.

Angie and Emily took pictures and laughed together often, especially at what the boys said to entice smiles from each other for the cameras: "Just think of Dad in his underpants."

John felt blessed by the females, proud of his sons. The best family day in years, he decided.

*   *   *

The last night in New Hampshire, Angie proposed some theater, the second coming of Angie the Librarian. To celebrate the auspicious beginning with his sons.

He was interested, but had to make a point. "It was a good start, babes, but there's still a long way to go." He saw awkward moments ahead between Angie and his boys, perhaps worse.

"Angie the Librarian doesn't like it when you rain on her parade." Her voice was a menacing purr. "She wishes to reward her favorite pupil with another reading session. What else you got to do? Worry yourself sleepless about Robeson Turner?"

He sat on the bed, and she stood next to him, running her finger down his cheek. He was weakening, only one scruple left. "I don't deserve any reward." He shrugged, palms turned upward. "Credit should go to Emily and you."

"Can't very well sit on Emily's chest and…."

His raised hand stopped her. Angie and Emily, an exciting image, shameful too, and he shook his head to get rid of it. "You win," he said.

She told him to strip to his underpants and to lie on the bed. She wore the same outfit as last time: pointy high heels, g-string, halter bra and eyeglasses on the tip of her nose. He felt a twinge of disappointment—no variation in the costume. His discontent faded at the sight of her coming toward him, flesh on display and parade.

Standing at the foot of the bed, she fished bobby pins somewhere out of her skimpy apparel and put her hair up. This is the proper look for respectable librarians, she explained. Watching the smooth surface of her belly stretch as she raised her arms and the tiny lift of her breasts, he sighed. Nervous shivers rolled like a wave over his body.

She folded her arms and chuckled. "Look at you stretched out like a hunk of steak on a plate."

"Glad I rate," he said.

She mounted him in languid fashion, resting her buttocks on his ribcage, shimmying into a comfortable position. She squeezed his sides tightly with her thighs, a 'thigh vise' she called it. But she left his arms alone, no wrestlerette's pin this time.

She did not read from, but told the story of Roddy Doyle's *Paddy Clark, Ha,Ha,Ha,* a Booker Prize winner she informed him and relevant to his life. After all, it was about two boys whose family was going through a painful divorce.

Quickly bored with her tales of the youths' shenanigans, he grunted once and squirmed beneath her. Though the movement gave her a pleasing sensation, she was not happy with him. He then stretched his arms across the bed, crucifixion style. "That proves my point," she said with nasty glee. "This is a Catholic thing for you."

"What? What's a Catholic thing?"

"That you get off on being dominated, even humiliated. Whatever did those nuns do to you boys at Our Lady of Perpetual Help?" She giggled, hands on her hips, looking down at him.

"Keep teasing me and I'll lose my hard-on." He tried for a spiteful tone.

"No," she said, "I don't think so." She took the pins out of her hair, letting it splash down around her neck and shoulders. She then loosened her halter bra and shook her breasts free. He was ready to surrender.

She leaned forward and placed the palms of her hands on either side of his head—her upper body suspended above his face. He felt surrounded by her voluptuous flesh. She scolded: "Johnny, you lost interest before I could finish my story, but you won't lose interest before I finish sex." She lowered her breasts onto his face, smothering his head that wriggled under her weight. "Stay still," she hissed and he did so.

"Now you do love it, Johnny, don't you?" she said. "Why don't you just admit it?" Her bosom stifled his reply. While she couldn't make out his words, his breath, the movement of his lips tickled her flesh. Angie raised her breasts, and he gasped for air. Laughing softly, she guided her nipples in a grazing motion along the features of his face. "Now, what did you want to say?" she murmured.

"I do love it, I do, I do," he blurted without pride. Wet with sweat, he was practically delirious, at the sexual breaking point.

"Are you prepared to satisfy me?"

"Oh, yes, please, what…."

She plopped her nipple into his mouth and smiled at the look in his eyes. She pressed down, letting him feel and taste the flesh of her breast. "You may now touch me," she instructed, "with your lips and tongue, caress my beautiful tits. You do find them beautiful, don't you?"

His mouth full, he nodded.

CHAPTER 9

Robeson Turner did not exactly keep his promise. John was back in the City for a week when the black man called, on Friday, shortly after 6:00 PM. John was organizing the paper piles on his desk, preparing for his departure. Unpredictable, Charles said, and so he is, John thought.

The conversation roused John's worst fears. He would now have to meet with Dominic, and over fucking this, he brooded. After I've succeeded so long in keeping my nose, hands, and every other body part clean. He would now have to confront Dominic, another unpredictable man in his life he would like to avoid, but couldn't.

They had an early dinner on a week-day night at Lombardi's, Manhattan's best pizza place according to Zagat's, a Little Italy hold-over, around for nearly 100 years, that now found itself bound by Soho's art galleries and clothes shops. John was impressed with Dominic's choice.

Fat Tony joined them. John guessed that if Dominic knew why he asked to eat and meet, Angie's ex-husband would have kept it a twosome. They sat upstairs, apart from the crowd.

They placed their orders, two big pies with sundry toppings, coca-cola drinks all around. Made small talk, Little Italy's dwindling boundaries, the new stores do add color, will it ever happen to Bensonhurst? Probably not.

Nervous with his own assignment, John was content to let the conversation flow this way. Not so Dominic. "What's on your mind, brainy boy?" he asked. He backhanded Fat Tony's shoulder, pointed at John. "That's what we usta call him back when." John took no offense. Dominic's tone was friendly, almost apologetic.

Though he saw beasts prowling the den, John jumped in. Robeson Turner, a guy he's worked with off and on, he explained, tells him Dominic's dealing powder in his, Turner's, community. Set up a stash apartment in the projects and uses some local low-life as his street level distributor. Turner warns it must be stopped or else.

John gripped the table, partly because of the moment's tension, partly to prevent Dominic from hitting him with it. Dominic stayed seated though, muttered lowly, "Fucking so and so, fucking so and so," cast an anxious glance at Tony. Lucky the fat man's here, John reflected.

I'm coming to you, John went on, because Turner says, he believes Frank already talked to you and that unless you back off and out soon, he's left with two highly disagreeable options. To let Sally Broadway, or whatever downtown capo Frank's accountable to, in on things or to kill you himself. Unspoken, because it had to be, especially in Fat Tony's presence, was that Turner's warning shots gambit had also failed. Either way, John continued, your lottery number in the game of life is up and your man and my brother looks very, very bad just when, as you know, he's considering a major career move. Your sudden demise would call unwanted attention to Frank's business affairs.

John now put his hands under the table. They were trembling and he didn't want his companions to notice. The waiter brought the pizza—John worried that he could not hold the slices steadily enough to eat.

Fat Tony then back-handed Dominic. "What the hell you doing? You crazy fuck." He's dense, John thought, but even he sees Dominic's courting serious peril.

Dominic waved his hand at Tony, but John surmised that the fat man's knowing made it likely that Dominic would have to give up his extracurricular activities, at least this version of them, at least for now. Dominic looked at John. "Why you? Why not let Frank handle this?"

John saw that no one was eating. Maybe everybody's hands are shaking under the table? "Couple of things. He already struck out once. Figured I owed him. Thought, too, maybe he didn't present it right. Maybe he was too protective of you. Thought I could make you see, better than he could, the risks involved." John knew he was giving Dominic both the benefit of the doubt and a way out.

"You mean like to him? Like this could queer his plan?"

"That's part of it. Could even be worse." From the side of his eye, John saw Tony slowly nod his big head.

Dominic stood and paced back and forth, occasionally bumping into the empty tables and chairs. He breathed heavily, grumbled fiercely in a conversation with himself. Once he stopped and pressed the sides of his head with each hand. John gazed at Tony, noisily chewing his food, plainly unworried. Like he had seen this behavior before, Dominic's interior struggle, physically displayed, before he decided to be sensible. What scared John, assured the fat man.

John got up and grabbed Dominic by each arm. He stooped to look his old rival in the face, as he used to do, sometimes still did, with his sons. "Not just for your own well-being, but for Frankie's sake. You fucking understand that?"

Dominic twisted out of John's grasp, not angrily, yet firmly, and returned to pacing. John sat down. "The only problem with this place," he heard Tony pontificate between bites, "there's no jukebox. Love to hear Sinatra, Dino, those guys while I'm eatin' Italian." Ordinarily, John might respond to such sentiments with a 'know what you mean' grin. Not when Dominic was about to combust in front of them. Is he a buffoon, John wondered about Tony, or just playing a role?

Dominic came back to his seat, stared at his untouched food. "Okay, Johnny, I'll bide my time, till Frank's out of the picture. You're not the only one who owes him. But not because I'm afraid of that black son of a bitch mother fucker." He hit the table with a closed fist, rattling the dishes.

John concluded it was smart he had not passed on Robeson Turner's reason for not whacking Dominic. It would set a bad example, he claimed, for his already too violence-prone boys. It was one thing to have your charges shoot up an automobile, John guessed. Aiming bullets at human flesh is another matter.

As John walked to the subway, he dangled his arms and wriggled his fingers, his way of getting rid of the nervous buzz his body still felt. He passed a mixed group of teens—black, brown, and white together. He couldn't avoid bumping into one of them who turned and apologized. Another boy pointed at John's shaking hands and giggled. John smiled too and picked up his pace toward the train that would take him home for the night.

He took a seat on the subway car, leaned his head back against the window, only half-listening to the clatter of the wheels on the track. Something still bothered him, a nagging doubt. Would Dominic, the crazy fuck, keep his word?

CHAPTER 10

Frank's major concession to Theresa was their house or, more precisely, its location: not in the old neighborhood in Brooklyn, but in comparatively posh Neponsit—secluded, at least by New York City standards, residential, bordering the Atlantic Ocean, just over the Marine Parkway Bridge in Queens. Mainly Jewish families lived there; husbands and wives were professionals: teachers, lawyers, doctors. Theresa had only a few friends in Neponsit, but preferred it to their old home in much noisier Bensonhurst and the stream of vulgar and coarse men who were Frank's associates.

Frank came to prize the place, the respite it brought him from the restaurant, his other business activities, people like Fat Tony and Dominic, whom he loved, but from whom, he found, he welcomed some separation. Each night leaving Rosario's, he felt a little lift getting into his car, saying good-bye to all that and driving home. It was a large white stucco house, on the front corner of a block that dead-ended at the beach. In the early mornings, almost any weather permitting, he took a walk down his street and along the sand before people in his family or the neighborhood saw fit to stir and come outside. This custom, in the solemn, quiet dawn of the day, the big black sea by his side, brought Frank more peace than any other part of his life.

The last Sunday afternoon in July, the small Rosario clan, including Angie and her mother Louise, gathered at Frank and Theresa's. It was an old-fashioned dinner and discussion—the women cooked and laid out the food and cleaned up afterwards and the men sat in a separate room and talked. Most of the children were absent but accounted for: Donnie was playing in a summer basketball league game; Sandy, the youngest of Frank and Theresa's three daughters, the aspiring dancer, had a summer job waitressing on Cape Cod; the oldest, Joanne, the nurse, whose personality was most like Theresa's, was working the week-end shift in the emergency room at Coney Island Hospital; and John's two sons still passed their time at camp.

The only off-spring there was Antoinette, Frank and Theresa's middle daughter, who so resembled her mother that John was still not used to her small, squeaky voice and compliant manner. He kept expecting a Theresa-like loudness to erupt from this child, who was now a young woman, but it never happened. He could not tell whether he was disappointed.

At the table, Whiney nudged John's ribs with his elbow and pointed to his full plate of pasta. "You know, John, how your mother and Theresa make the sauce so good?" He spoke a little too loudly. "It's just a plain sauce, right, so what makes it exceptional?"

"I don't know, Whiney. What does make the sauce exceptional?" John liked the sound and feel of 'exceptional' on his and his uncle's lips.

Whiney grinned, enjoying the spotlight. "Well, it's not the tomatoes, though, of course, they're important. And not the parsley, basil, parmesan cheese, salt and pepper, though you do have to get the right mix of those things." Whiney paused to make sure he had everyone's attention. "Not the bread crumbs and olive oil either, though you need the correct mix there too. You know, the crumbs can't be too dry...."

"Whiney, come out with it," John cried.

Whiney winked conspiratorially. "It's the eggplant oil. After frying the egg-plants, women pour the leftover juice in the sauce and those sweet drops give it the distinctive Sicilian flavor you and other men have had the good fortune to enjoy since the beginning of time. So, my boy, whadda ya think of that?" He brought his hand up to and away from his lips, blowing a kiss across the table.

The conversation turned to politics. Reversing what public polls reported, the men favored David Dinkins in the upcoming mayoral election and the women, except Angie, supported his opponent, Rudy Giuliani. Theresa expressed the female view that New York was "going down the toilet in a great big flush so loud you could hear it all over the city" and that Dinkins did noth-ing to stem the flow.

Whiney took offense that, as a law enforcement official, Giuliani made his bones by prosecuting—the word Whiney used was 'persecuting'—so-called organized crime figures, especially when the end result was, as you could read in the papers every day, a drug trade more violent and dangerous than in the old days. Frank said that, despite all the huffing and puffing about the Crown Heights disturbance, Dinkins' quiet bearing helped calm the City.

"What has Giuliani shown?" Angie remarked. "The man's given us no reason to vote for him, no program, no plan. Other than he used to be a prosecutor, and he's white."

"I'm not for Giuliani because he's white and I'm not against Dinkins because he's black," Antoinette said in a hurt tone.

Everyone was surprised she said anything, no less so clearly. Angie made amends. "I don't mean you or anybody is being, you know, racist, Antoinette, but there's a hidden message in Giuliani's campaign…."

"Have to agree," John said. "Rudy's counting on a large white vote, especially from people like us, from Bensonhurst."

Theresa aimed her hard, angry words at Angie. "You should be careful, girl, what you say around people because it might upset them. Ever since you went to night school and got that job in the city, you been acting superior. I don't think your liberal views become you myself."

"Theresa, what you mind is not what I think, but that I think at all."

Marie rose from the table, murmuring that was enough political talk for a while. It was time for the next course anyway, and everybody, meaning all the women present, should help clear the table. No one, except Theresa, minded the break in the discussion.

❧   ❧   ❧

Dessert was a cup of creamy cappuccino with a plate of even creamier cannolis. The men sat waiting for it on the house's back porch, a small deck made of brick and concrete. Overhead, big, grey clouds crawled slowly across the sky.

"Whew," John said mainly to Frank, "I know Theresa's no pussy cat, but she really bared her claws today." He hoped his brother would explain.

"She has only daggers for Angie," Whiney said. "I don't get it." When his nephew didn't speak, he asked, "What gives, Frankie?"

Frank squirmed in his chair. "Hard to put a finger on why Angie gets Theresa's goat. Could be a clash between the old and the new. Angie's like a new woman, single mother, full-time job, fancy clothes. And the way men take to her doesn't exactly win her a place in Theresa's heart."

Whiney and John exchanged looks, nodded their heads. Two dogs barked in the distance, in response to each other or the sounds of sea gulls circling over the ocean.

"In Theresa's defense," Frank said, "she's wanted to get away from here for years. Bet it'd make her a happier person." He paused, weighing his next words. "Now, with the help of you guys, that'll be my gift to her."

Nice segue, John thought.

Whiney was stung by Frank's challenge. "Spoke to Sally Broadway for you, didn't I?" Was that Whiney's mission when I interrupted the brisk game? John wondered. Not necessarily, those two old-timers must talk all the time.

A slice of sunshine cut through the heavy clouds. Frank looked up, squinted his eyes at the new light in the sky. "Yeah, old Sal was very understanding. Sure, Frankie boy, get out while you're still young, he said. Just don't look back and don't give away any secrets. We can trust the Rosarios, I know." Frank shook his head in disbelief. "That's all there was to it. He seemed, like, happy for me."

"It might not've been so easy," Whiney said, "if I hadn't made the case ahead of time."

"I know, Whine," Frank said. "You, Pop and Sal used to hang out on the beach together and flirt with the girls at Luna Park down on Coney Island at night. So we go way back with him and that counted for something."

John smiled. He loved it when his brother, when any Rosario man, talked about the past.

"But that's only part of the picture," Frank continued. "Sal's a tired horse now. His race almost over, his day about done. I'm thinking he hardly gives a shit about the business."

"Guess there's truth to that," Whiney said. "At Vito D'Onofio's wake last year, Paulie Shortchange pointed Sally out to me and said: 'The only numbers he cares about now are the old ones by Frank Loesser.'"

John trusted his brother and uncle's judgment about Sally. Still he was dubious. Even in its present state of decline, even with the old capo running interference, would the gang really be so nonchalant about a top lieutenant walking away from the life? He recalled his father's long ago warning. They'll exact a price....

"Now, the question is," Frank was saying, "who'll run the restaurant?" He turned toward John who sat back in his chair as if shoved.

John hesitated, wished he could avoid this encounter. "Can't do what you ask, Frankie." His brother's disappointed look annoyed him. "I have another job." He wanted to go on about how his own work was so demanding, more than a 50-hour week proposition, but figured it would only sound like whining.

He wanted to reveal his recent intervention with Dominic, how he finally entered Frank's universe and on Frank's behalf, and covered for him for once. Yeah, Johnny Once, like his brother knighted him. But that would've been way wrong as Teddy might say. Wrong-headed too. He did realize there was a selfish benefit to the action. He felt less guilt about his brother, greater ease in resisting Frank's pressure.

Frank's face hardened and he stared at nothing in particular, at the empty space filling his back yard. "Great, Johnny. For years, like a fucking tout at the track, you've been pushing me. Now I'm about to place the bet, and you leave me holding the bag. Shit."

John knew his uncle would welcome the chance to resolve things. "Got my own life, can't take on yours. But Whiney and I can share the responsibility for Rosario's...."

"Just say the word," Whiney put in.

A sweet whiff of cappuccino made its way from the kitchen to the back porch. The three men shifted their heads in unison, the warm aroma tickling their nostrils.

"We could hire a manager for the day to day stuff." John spoke rapidly, hoping his sense of Frank's growing openness was not a delusion. "He'd report to me on a weekly or monthly basis, whatever we work out. I'd consult with you down in Florida and others in the family like Whiney and even mom and Angie could touch base regularly with the place."

"I've got some time on my hands." Whiney leaned back in his chair. "Could stop by every day, keep an eye on things."

Frank gazed at one man, then the other. He nodded, but said nothing.

"Whaddya say, Frankie?" Whiney implored. "Let's hear from you."

"I'm thinking," Frank said.

"Should listen to your brother here. He's got some good ideas. Maybe all that college training paid off."

"We'll find someone with talent." John leaned over and put a hand on his brother's shoulder. "New blood can't hurt."

Frank slumped in his chair. "Haven't left me much choice." His self-pitying tone surprised the other men. His conduct lacked class.

Whiney stepped over to Frank's chair. "In your father's absence, it's my place to do this." He raised his arm and brought it down in a swinging arc that, in its upward curve, grazed the back of Frank's head.

Startled, but unhurt, Frank rubbed his head. "Trying to knock some sense into me, huh?"

From inside the house, the sounds of Sinatra reached the men. *Here I am, begging for, only five minutes more.* Bet Angie put on a record, John thought.

Frank sat up, cleared his throat, allowed a grin to crease his lips. "Okay, I'll do it, no if's, and's, or but's. Just the way you boys said."

The deal's done, John thought contentedly, or at least it's understood. Managed the Dominic crisis. Negotiated a compromise with Frank. Soon the old man can rest in his grave.

❦   ❦   ❦

The three men entered the house, headed for the dinning room, looking forward to dessert. Theresa picked up the ringing phone in the kitchen. "Jack Dorney," she shouted to Frank, her tone disapproving. "Claims it's urgent."

"Your old high school buddy," Frank frowned at John as he left to take the call. John recalled Dorney—a burly Irish kid, a scrub on the basketball team always willing to give a foul, and starting catcher on the baseball squad fearless of whatever came his way: bats, balls, or base runners. Now a cop, a lieutenant at the 81st precinct in Bensonhurst. John told Angie who Dorney was. "The acorn didn't fall very far from the tree," she said. He smiled, but was worried. Why'd Frank scowl? Why'd a local top cop call him on Sunday afternoon? Was it business or was it personal?

Frank returned to the company, walking stiffly. He stood behind the chair where he would have sat. "Sorry to pour cold water on the party…. I know dessert would've been delicious, ladies, but something important's come up." His eyes blinked, twitched. What the fuck is going on? John wondered. Frank said: "Whiney, Johnny, can I see you in the living room."

Theresa uttered an exasperated "C'mon, Frank…." before he cut her off with a gesture. She waved back, dismissing the men who were already leaving the room.

As they gathered, John gazed at the furniture: fancily embroidered, somehow intimidating, and, he was sure, rarely used—it reminded him of his mother's taste in things and gave him momentary comfort.

"Gentlemen," Frank said, "a call from Dorney often means bad news, but today's troubles are not the usual kind." He rubbed his hand across his face wearily. "Let's put our heads together, boys, this is a deep shit situation."

"How 'bout getting to the point?" Whiney said.

Frank spoke slowly, reluctant to part with the news. "Donnie's been in a fra-cas at the playground...."

"Oh, no," John groaned. "Not a black/white thing?"

"'Fraid so, Johnny, 'fraid so."

"Donnie hurt?"

"No, he wasn't. Others were, but not him."

Earlier that afternoon, after their league game, Donnie and some of his black friends showed up at the basketball courts on Bay Parkway and Bath Ave-nue. They were fooling around, shooting baskets when some of the local white boys started busting their chops about being on foreign turf. Donnie and his pals did not back down and hostile words turned into physical combat. Some-one got clobbered with a baseball bat, someone got stabbed. The cops got there quickly and prevented further damage—none of the injuries seem serious. Donnie and the other boys were at the police station being booked on various charges and most would probably be released if and when their parents showed up.

John felt queasy. This went way past deep shit. Another racial incident in Bensonhurst. Fucking disaster was more like it. Poor Donnie. Poor Angie.

Frank lowered his eyes and stared at the plush, blue carpet. "Damn kid, thought I had gotten through to him," he said under his breath.

Whiney leaned forward. "Easy, Frankie, easy...."

Frank lifted his eyes toward his uncle. "Just the other day, Donnie and I had this little talk." He clenched a fist in a kind of impotent anger. "Donnie, I told him, it's one thing to have different kinds of friends, got no problem with that, but don't bring your different worlds together because, you know, the chemi-cals might not mix. They can turn into dynamite, maybe blow up in your face." He held out his hands, palms upward, and dropped them into his lap.

Whiney and John stood together. Frank glanced up. "Handwringing time's over, huh?"

"I'll explain things to Angie." John was a reluctant volunteer, but knew his job. "What about the boy's father?"

"Dorney's men are calling around," Frank said. "They'll track Dominic down soon enough."

Whiney chuckled at John's questioning look. "Handy to have a friend at the local cop house, huh, Johnny?"

John passed the next five minutes calming a distraught Angie. She com-posed herself quickly only because she needed to join the men in the drive to the precinct. A sense of urgency pacified her—her recuperative powers were impressive. Her eyes were noticeably red, though, and her step unsteady as she left the house. Even Theresa gave her a sympathetic look.

❦   ❦   ❦

Over the years the brick of the two-story Bensonhurst police station had turned from bright red to sooty, greyish brown. The building looked drab and stupid, a sorry site for an agency charged with upholding society's laws. John recalled an old, familiar fantasy. He'd run for mayor on a single issue platform: a public works project employing the poor and jobless to steam clean and scrub every structure in the city. The plan's appeal lay in its simplicity and ambition—in one sweeping stroke, it would provide jobs, teach work habits, reduce drug abuse and crime, foster a sense of community, and produce a fresh and unsullied city. He wondered why no one else promoted such a sure-fire program.

The doors to the precinct were ponderous, creaking with the opening and closing. After entering the building, Angie and her companions adjusted their eyes to the dim interior light. Two uniform officers were guffawing with the sergeant who sat behind a huge, raised desk at the back wall. They heard the words "boobs" and "pussy," and the Rosario men were embarrassed for Angie, but she hardly cared. Over to the side, in a small open cubicle, a young couple complained loudly to a skinny officer about their recently stolen automobile. There were no signs of an unusual incident. John relaxed; maybe there'd be no messy fallout.

Angie's mother anxiety simmered. "Where's Donnie?" she asked. "Where they keeping my boy?"

Frank approached the desk sergeant who broke off the conversation with his fellow cops. A rough-looking, unshaven man, the sergeant, John thought, was like a defrocked, unkempt priest from a Graham Greene novel. The man dispensed wisdom, or, at least, information from behind his desk, which doubled for an altar. The ceremonious way the cleric/cop leaned over to greet him reflected Frank's standing in the parish/precinct. He'd likely come back with an answer to Angie's frantic question.

The cops held two groups of boys—Donnie and his black friends and the local Bensonhurst kids—upstairs on the second floor while detectives questioned them. They were the first relatives to arrive, but other people would show up soon. The sergeant didn't know what charges the boys faced—"You'll hafta ask Dorney about that one," he stated—but he reported unusual activity presumably relating to the case: calls into the precinct from One Police Plaza, the department's central headquarters in Manhattan. They're worried downtown, John thought.

The second floor consisted of a large open room with cubicled offices ringing its dull, grey walls. Chairs, small benches were carelessly arranged in the middle. The police kept the two sets of boys far away from each other in the string of cubicles at opposite sides of the room. John reflected: Virtually all these boys, sitting and standing in the small offices, talking among themselves and to the cops, looking around and over the short walls with sullen, frightened glances, share many things: their age and size; their borough; their interest in sports, girls and music—probably have similar tastes in these things—their fearful and defiant reaction to the crisis at hand. So what separates them, why are they so ready to despise and fight each other? Race and culture. Beautiful things, really, but too often at the root of the terrible human divide that rends this city's heart.

❈   ❈   ❈

Jack Dorney appeared well-dressed and well-fed, a stockier and smoother version of the boy John once knew, without the rough edges and awkward movements that marked not only his younger self, but most cops—young or middle-aged—John had ever met.

Smiling grimly, Dorney shook hands with the Rosario men and greeted John with a friendly nod. "I see you figured out how to keep trim. Bet you're still playing ball."

"Get to the gym once in a while."

"Wish I could say the same." Dorney patted his girth.

"This is Angie Roselli," John said, "the boy's mother. She's very worried at the moment." He wanted to cut short the small talk.

"I understand, I understand," Dorney muttered.

"Is Donnie alright, can we take him home?" Angie asked, pleading, demanding.

"He seems no worse for wear." Dorney adopted a hearty, slightly fake tone. "Surprisingly enough, none of the boys really got hurt bad, including the two we're counting as injuries."

"Can I see him?" Angie asked.

"Soon, dear, soon."

"So, Jack, how's this going to be handled?" John was annoyed with Dorney's stalling.

The cop looked uncomfortable. "The decision's not come down yet about charges or anything. I'm saying my piece to central office, but this one's outta my hands. And I think they're talking to City Hall, so we gotta wait."

"What advice are you offering?" Whiney asked.

"Me, I'm saying what's the obvious: Sunday in the summer, boys will be boys, nobody got hurt—although we still gotta get the final word from the hospital on that—let everybody walk outta here on DAT's for lightweight charges like misdemeanor assault, harassment, or unlawful assembly. And let's do it fast."

"Before the press, lawyers, or anybody from the community gets wind of it," John said.

"And blows the entire thing wide open splat," Dorney said, "like a melon hitting the ground."

Angie had enough of man talk and walked slowly away from the group toward the cubicles holding the black boys. John watched her go off; Dorney made no effort to stop her. She leaned her head inside one cubicle, then another, until she paused, took a step back, and let Donnie walk past her. Mother and son sat down facing each other, knees nearly touching, in chairs right outside the cubicle, and spoke in nervous bursts. Donnie from time to time messed up his hair, then patted it down; Angie occasionally tapped the boy's face with her fingers.

Other family members came and dispersed by race to opposite sides of the room. Several uniformed cops stationed themselves at different points in the large middle space, to prevent contact between the black and white adults. The Rosario men walked slowly over to Angie and Donnie, were reassured by the boy that he was "okay, considering everything that's gone down," and stood in a semi-circle, protecting mother and son from the ugly glares from some of the grown-ups across the way.

Chaos and noise took hold: recriminating shouts from both sides of the room, some table-pounding, even a slap or two, and some calming sounds—a few female voices urging people to "please shush." Frank kept his eye on the room's door. "There's Dominic," he soon announced. Donnie looked up, then shook his head and stared at the floor. He was like a patient, weary from his illness, who sees a bumbling, distracted nurse approach his bed.

Frank stepped forward to meet his old friend who seemed only slightly more wired than usual. The two men moved to an empty corner of the room where, John guessed, Frank made some suggestions about how to behave. When the two men joined the group, Dominic was matter of fact in his greetings, adopting a resigned air. He asked to speak alone with his son, who rose with a 'what now?' look on his face and strode with his father to the empty corner. John saw Dominic lift his hand and drop it to his side in frustration and read Donnie's lips saying: "Chill, Dad, chill."

Dorney came by appearing satisfied—word just came from downtown wrapping up this stage of the case. All the boys at the police station would get desk appearance tickets for disorderly conduct, roughly equivalent to a traffic summons. They could all leave now, their departure tightly controlled with cops escorting the white families out first, and making sure everybody had safe passage home. The two hospitalized boys—neither had either a serious injury or a criminal record—would receive bedside arraignments tomorrow and be released on third degree assault charges, a misdemeanor. "And," Dorney concluded, "as far as we know, the goddamn media knows nothing, nada."

Delivered to small groups by individual cops, this news traveled quickly around the room, accompanied by relieved sighs, an occasional happy hand slap, and "let's get outta here" mutterings. Donnie broke away from the adults around him and found his friends who high- and low-fived each other and promised to see each other at the next game, wherever that may be, some of them joked, but not in Bensonhurst.

On the way out, John and Dominic walked behind the others. Both understood there'd be no reference to their previous conversation. Not now, probably not ever. But because of it, they felt a bond. "Hope you have better luck with your boys," Dominic said.

"A tough situation," was all John could think to say.

"Don't mean just this shit. I can't talk to him about anything." Dominic sounded hopeless.

"Maybe if you give him time and some space...." John said weakly.

"Nah, Johnny, nothing seems to work." Dominic slapped his head and pushed his hand through his hair. "Banana," he growled. "Sometimes I could fucking kill the kid."

"Easy does it," John cautioned.

"Don't worry, Johnny, just a figure of speech I was using."

On the sidewalk, John noticed Marilyn Diaz, a *New York Newsday* reporter who occasionally called him for background on City Hall stories. He hurried past, trying to avoid her. "John Rosario," she called, "what are you doing here?"

He turned. "The real question, Marilyn, is: Why are you here?"

"Got a tip."

"Forget it," John said flatly. "Nothing happened. There's no story."

"Tell that to Bill Simon. Rumor has it the Reverend's called a press conference tomorrow to denounce Bensonhurst's latest racist outrage."

❦   ❦   ❦

All the television stations covered Bill Simon's call for a march through Brooklyn whose destination would be the playground, the "site of the fight." He invited "all the good people of the City, black, brown, and white," to join his rainbow ranks. This racially integrated action would show that, indeed, basketball was the entire City's game, that people of all colors—especially blacks who so exemplify and elevate the sport—should be able to play it in any park in the metropolitan area, including ethnic enclaves of any kind, and that "basketball should be a unifier, an activity that spreads harmony, rather than an occasion for driving a bitter wedge between us."

"The man has few peers in the rhetorical arts," John said to Angie as they watched the news.

"He's a big mouth, a blow-hard who's just gonna make things worse. Told you not to trust him." She shoved John's shoulder.

John held up his hands to ward off more blows. "He's probably only playing the part expected of him."

"Let's not waste too much sympathy on the guy," she said. "We gotta look out for Donnie."

"And we will." John knew his main task was to safeguard Angie and her son. Though worried about his charges, he embraced the job.

❦   ❦   ❦

Mayor David Dinkins supported Simon's right to march, but urged moderation on all sides and ordered cops deployed in full force along the march's route. Candidate Rudy Giuliani opposed Simon's plans. If the Reverend really wants to bring black and white together, he asked, why would he engage in such polarizing, in-your-face tactics?

Reporters bombarded Angie's house with phone calls, seeking comments from, and interviews with, the boy at the center of the disquieting incident. Donnie was willing to talk to only a few people, none of them reporters, so Angie either left the phone off the hook or asked John to field the calls. He explained to journalists that he was a family friend helping out in a crisis and that Donnie was a decent kid who loved basketball and played regularly with black friends he met through the league. The boys made the dubious judgment of celebrating a big win by showing up at the Bath Avenue playground, near Donnie's house, where, in fact, he grew up.

Most frightening for the Rosselli/Rosarios were the death threats, often laced with racist epithets, aimed at Donnie. Through the mail and on the phone, menacing messages from friendly, neighborhood "coon-hunters" promising to kill the "nigger-loving traitor" in their midst. Donnie wandered around the house, arms dangling, muttering rap lyrics nobody else got, or sat sullenly on the couch under his headphones lost to or in his music, but he did not seem afraid.

Maybe to compensate for her son's lack of affect, Angie became unnerved. She was given to snapping at the people around her, sudden breakdowns into sobs, and sleepless nights. The constant presence of the cops, in the house because of the death threats—whether they tried to be sociable or stay out of her way—aggravated her downcast and frazzled mood.

John was a mixed comfort—she loved him and wanted him around, but his relationship with Bill Simon irked her and she was frustrated, unreasonably she knew, when he couldn't eradicate the dangers besetting her and her child. Only after several days, and only after John organized Frank and Whiney to follow his stays in the house round the clock, and only when these men proved effective buffers between her and the cops and other foreign elements in her suddenly embattled world, did she center herself. After a night of fitful starts, when she cried herself back to sleep in John's arms, her head on his chest, as he dried the warm tears off her cheek, she awoke refreshed. She came out of the shower, washed hair wrapped in a towel high on her head, John's big bathrobe loosely draped over her body. "If those gutless gavonnes so much as lay a hand on my Donnie," she said, "I'm not gonna turn to Frank or Dominic or Fat Tony or you, and certainly not the cops. Gonna kill the bastards myself."

"Good to have you back, Angelina," John said.

Public interest friends and colleagues called John. They asked him to denounce the Bensonhurst boys and to endorse Simon's march which the preacher and his supporters billed not so much as a protest tactic, but as an expression of moral concern by enlightened people of the City. "First, your holier than thou tone pisses me off," John snarled at one associate. "Second, I got to be wherever Angie and her boy wind up that day."

The exception was Harry Glassman, executive director of the New York Civil Liberties Union. Harry was born and bred in Flatbush, Brooklyn, where working class and upwardly mobile Jews mingled. He was an occasional elbow-wielding player in the Monday night games, a smart, fast-and straight-talking lawyer devoted to transcending the legalistic limits of the NYCLU's traditional agenda, so he and it could take on the larger social issues of the day.

"What I wanna know," Harry asked on the phone, "is who's this woman that's causing you to abandon your cherished ideals?"

"An old friend, Harry, someone I grew up with," he said, pleased to explain.

"Returning to your roots for romance, eh, John? Listen, wouldn't have bothered you ordinarily, but Simon's been pushing me, thinks you can do something to diffuse the situation…. get the kid to make a statement, get your brother involved, that kind of thing."

John ignored Harry's specific points. "Why didn't Simon call me himself?"

"Establishing deniability, I guess." After silent moments passed, Harry asked: "So nu, Rosario? Whadda you say?"

"I'll think about it."

"Your call. Whatever you do, I'll still love you."

Charles phoned the next day, reaching John at his office. "I've hesitated contacting you. Didn't want you to think I was carrying Bill Simon's water."

"So, you're disabusing Simon of these foolish notions."

"Not really. He's got the nutty idea that Donnie can save the day here. You know, man, white boy, black friends, unusual kid, let him come forward, spotlight on, stand up for what's right and just, and the ignorant racist dogs will slink away."

"What?" They have no clue how deeply Bensonhurst Donnie is, John thought, black companions notwithstanding.

"Just giving you the Reverend's take on this." Charles spoke more rapidly now. "You should hear him wax eloquent about Donnie's potential mission quotient. Underneath all his militant bluster, the man still believes in the white man's ultimate goodness. And that's what Donnie represents to him."

"So you're disabusing Simon of these foolish notions."

"Of course," Charles said, "though the fantasy dies hard with him." John said nothing, so Charles continued: "But the Reverend's other idea could work."

"What other idea?" John sat at his desk, staring at the pictures hanging on the opposite wall. He eyed his collection's latest addition, a snapshot of Angie standing under a stone bridge in Central Park on a windy day, her unruly hair framing her smiling face. He couldn't recall the wisecrack he came up with to make her laugh.

"Where your brother plays the hero," Charles said.

"My brother? How?"

"Maybe he could march with us?"

"Not a chance. Simon's really grasping for ways to diffuse the time-bomb, isn't he?" Charles' evident anxiety stoked John's. How bad is this?

"Desperately, I'd say, like the rest of us."

"I'm out of touch with things. What are your people telling you?" John meant the neighborhood workers from the Human Rights Commission.

"It's fucking volatile," Charles said evenly.

"Is Robeson Turner, folks like that, a threat here?" John pictured bloody clashes between black radicals and Bensonhurst toughs. A fucking horror show.

"Promise you'll tell me someday why he's such a reference point."

"Ducking my question, are we?"

"He did announce intentions to bring his lost boys," Charles said. "But Simon advised otherwise, and Turner was cool with that."

Glad someone can influence that man, John thought. "Lost boys?"

"Some of them can fly, or so Robeson says." Charles chuckled. "All similarity to Peter Pan's troop ends there."

Was there poetry in Robeson Turner's soul? Corny thought. Perplexing man. Charles voice barreled through. "So, will you talk to Frank? Maybe he can fix it so at least their side stays calm. However wise guys do that."

"Okay," John said. "But don't bet the mortgage he'll help with this."

John, Frank, and Whiney sat in Angie's living room, tired and dazed. They lost track of whose shift it was to stand, or at least sit guard. Once they finished talking, they'd likely fall asleep in their chairs.

Dominic had left about an hour ago, after proposing the boy come stay with him, an offer Donnie rejected. He didn't want to cut and run, didn't want to leave his mother. On the way out Dominic stood by the door with Frank. "Please look out for my boy," he asked solemnly.

John saw his opportunity. When his brother sat down, he asked: "What do you say, Frankie? Can you persuade the local gumbahs to be good when folks march through here on Sunday?"

Frank's head jerked back. "What do you mean?" he asked sharply.

"You know, get a message out on the grapevine calling for restraint. You're not a lame duck yet."

"What are you fucking saying? Coming out of the blue like this?" Frank looked to Whiney for understanding, guidance. The old man shrugged, meaning maybe John's idea wasn't *so* crazy. "Nah," said Frank. "That's not me, not even for Angie and Donnie."

"That's too bad, Frank." John made a disappointed face.

Frank leaned forward, tapped his uncle's knee. "Talk to this child of the sixties. We're from the old school, keep a low profile, stay outta politics."

A door slammed upstairs, the sound of running water came from the bathroom. Donnie taking a late night shower.

Whiney finally spoke. "Whadda you got to lose, Frank? That's one way of lookin' at it. You're leaving town soon anyway, so whadda you got to lose?"

"All the more reason," Frank replied, "not to attract any notice."

"I think your old man would approve," Whiney said.

"Don't bullshit me, Whine."

"You know what he used to say," Whiney replied, unfazed. "Sometimes, you hafta give something back."

Pop espouse such a principle or Whiney make it up? John wondered. Either way, it was a good pitch.

Frank said nothing.

❧   ❧   ❧

Angie objected, but John decided to take Donnie for a nighttime drive—his response to her reporting the boy wanted his advice about what to do on the day of the march. It'll liberate Donnie from the round-the-clock sentinel, he explained, make it easier for them to talk. The boy shrugged, but was willing to go along. "Don't worry, babes," John said, "the cops'll follow us." She walked them to the door, patting them tenderly on their arms and shoulders as they left the house. "Be careful, and be wise," she whispered in John's ear.

John drove the van toward Flatbush, traveling down Ocean Parkway, past tidy apartment buildings and suburban-looking single-family homes. Unseen by Donnie, he smiled—they were headed for the same place his father brought him nearly 30 years ago for their talk about life's tough choices.

John treated Donnie to a couple of hot dogs and a side of fries at Nathan's in Coney Island, where Ocean Parkway ends its span of road. An old amusement park area on the ocean, Coney Island was no longer Brooklyn's recreational jewel. Still it had its honky-tonk charms, especially on warm summer nights: noisy with voices, traffic of young people in shorts and t-shirts, and a long boardwalk dotted with rickety rides, candy palaces, and video arcades. The crowd stood in the open air, on the broad sidewalk in front of the food counters, and shouted in different languages their orders for dinner, their commands to their children, their requests to friends to save a seat inside. It was a place of special memories for John, where he had eaten many salty, sloppy, hot and fast meals.

They found a quiet table in the back of a large glass enclosed room, a long ago addition to the original Nathan's. They breathed in deeply, enjoying the pungent blend, smells from fried fast foods, heated sandwich meats, and the mighty ocean at their backs.

Done eating, Donnie leaned against the glass wall, patted his stomach. "Thanks for the eats. Now what is it you want to talk about?"

"Word from your mama is *you* wanted to talk to me."

Donnie snickered. "Got some things on my mind."

"Can imagine." Not wanting to press the boy, John said nothing more. The ensuing silence, though brief, was like a tangible, expanding thing, a discourteous third presence at the table. When Donnie spoke, John thought it was because the quiet was more painful to the boy than the discomfort that might accompany his words.

"I thought, you know, because of your work…. Mom tells me you deal with City officials a lot…. you may be able to advise me on some stuff."

John made circling motions with his hand.

"What I should do on Sunday, should I like, make a statement?" Donnie's cheeks colored, first a light pink, then a brighter red.

"Piece of cake," John said.

A tiny smile creased Donnie's lips. John congratulated himself on a limited victory. "Piece of cake, sure," said the boy, "and John Starks doesn't have nightmares about shooting 2 for 18 in game seven against Houston."

John grinned. "Let's break the puzzle into small pieces. Then, maybe, you can decide how to handle yourself."

John expected a bewildered silence, instead got a question: What stake did Mayor Dinkins and candidate Giuliani have in the incident and the aftermath? John answered that Giuliani probably wanted some violence that showed on the six o'clock news how the City was spinning out of control under Dinkins. The Mayor obviously hoped for a peaceful day, and had to back the protest because it was "his people" who were abused and his principles that were violated. Giuliani, meanwhile, grabbed the chance to solidify his white base by knocking the Simon demonstration.

"My father and your brother don't say anything good about Bill Simon," the boy said.

"No surprise there."

"Yeah, but sometimes my father makes sense. He says, what's the big fucking deal, you know how he talks, with the rumble in the park. When he was coming up, the races and ethnics, you know like the Italians, the Irish, the Jews, they'd fight all the time. No front-page headlines then, so why alla noise now?"

"It's a different time." John was pleased, eager even, to pass on his views. "There's less tolerance for racial hatred, at least when it's so out in the open. Our leaders, including media people, say they value equality, so they hafta act upset when that value's breached, even if in their heart of hearts, they aren't fully committed to it. You know, Martin Luther King's a national saint nowadays, but lots of the folks who honor him wouldn't be so happy if he were still around, protesting this and that."

"So it's all bullshit?" The boy tried for a cynical sum-up.

John shook his head. "Much of the outrage is phony—Dominic's got a point—still it's important the value's taken hold. Know what I mean?"

The boy gave John a blank look.

"For whatever reasons," John continued, "that society objects to people getting beat up because they're black is a good thing. The world no longer shrugs its shoulders, and says"—John waved his hand—"Ah, so fucking what."

"So the march's important because it's, like, a protest against some wrong shit"

Yes, he's getting it, John thought.

"So I shouldn't hide away, like my father…he just wants me to stay in the house, him and his boys protecting me. But turning my back wouldn't be right…."

"That's how I see it."

A group of Latin youths gathered outside the glass wall. They pushed, yelled, giggled, gestured—several boy/girl couples tickling and slapping at each other in their midst. They all raised their arms in a Spanish cheer and ran toward the beach. John flicked his wrist in a thumb point. "There's a happy bunch," he said.

"Think there's gonna be trouble on Sunday?" Donnie asked. "I wanna be brave sure, but I don't wanna be stupid."

John rejected an impulse to coddle. "Disturbances, I'm afraid, are likely."

The boy's shoulders slumped. "Shit, can't I walk away from this?" He gazed at John like a sad puppy.

"I'll be with you. So, probably, will Frank."

"Yeah, that helps."

"The question is, where will you be?"

The boy shifted slowly in his seat and sat upright. "I'm gonna show up at the playground to greet the marchers. You know, some of my friends will be there."

"Salute," John said. They clicked their soda cups. "Good way to make your point."

Donnie shrugged. "Besides, it's what my mom thinks is best."

John was amused and hardly surprised. Another Angie talent, he supposed, the benign manipulation of people and circumstances.

❧   ❧   ❧

Saturday afternoon, it was quiet at the house. No calls from Harry, Charles, Simon or anyone associated with the upcoming march. Angie and Donnie were watching one of the boy's old favorite movies, the film equivalent of comfort food. John phoned his brother at the restaurant, but got Fat Tony instead.

"Hey, Johnny, how you doing? Everything alright?"

"Yes, Tony, I'm fine."

"Glad to hear that."

"Frankie there?"

"Oh, too bad, Johnny, you just missed him."

"He went out?"

"Yeah. Told me to take messages."

"Shit."

"Why? Is there a problem?"

"Not really.... well, I'm a little worried about what may happen tomorrow. You know, the protest march through Bensonhurst."

"Hey, I know, helluva thing."

He wondered why he was talking to Fat Tony, of all people, on this subject. Must be desperate for human contact. "I was hoping Frank might intercede in some way. Maybe suggest cool heads should prevail, enough damage has been done."

"Hear you, Johnny boy. These fuckin' gavonnes, guidos whatever they call them now, giving us all a bad name."

"Right on," John said in a bit of 60's irony lost on Tony.

"Got no problems with the blacks," Tony went on. "Used to look down on 'em, call 'em niggers and shit. Now I work with 'em everyday almost. Frank says you mark a man by his actions, not his skin color."

"Appears we have a common philosophy," John said, surprised. What did his brother say? Yeah, Tony has a head, but so do nails. Could we have underestimated the big man's intelligence?

The fat man, though, was no benign presence in John's bad dream that night. More like a hulking beast taller than in reality, more like Minx the Enforcer with body hair and claws. Tony kept thrusting at John, threatening him, backing him off from saving two women, UJI's Jeanette and Leslie, he thought they were, from an impending doom. Frankie was there too, not intervening, but giving directions to Fat Tony. His brother shook his head, mumbling tch, tch, poor Johnny, always wanted to save the world, now he can't even save his two friends.

CHAPTER 11

On Sunday, the grey, concrete playground became the setting for a festive urban picnic. Ringing the inside of its fence was a circle of tables filled with mainly hot, delicious looking dishes served by smiling people who on any other Sunday would be waiting on customers or working in the kitchen in Rosario's. For this one sunny afternoon, Frank devised a fool-proof means for diverting people from the violent course in their hearts—a complimentary banquet. The villain of John's dream was the hero of the day.

Clusters of people jammed the tables. Pastas cooked in six styles and with as many sauces, hot and sweet and thick and juicy sausages, Marie Rosario's celebrated meatballs, calamari fried and marinated, potatoes cooked deep and steeped in the finest olive oil, eggplants plain and Parmigiana and stuffed Sicilian style with soft ricotta cheese, Palermo pizza jammed with vegetables and meat, artichokes tenderly braised and baked. These concoctions were available to the mix of Bensonhurst denizens, marchers, police and journalists that convened in the park. The protesters and other people there were dumbstruck at finding a feast of flavors instead of tense stand-offs, clenched jaws and fists, pissed-off verbal exchanges and, perhaps, physical confrontations. The crowd buzzed and mingled, laughed and spoke and shouted, and nibbled and licked and chewed and swallowed.

With Donnie surrounded by a group of his friends and media, and Angie chatting with Frank under the basketball hoop with busy tables on each side, John felt free to wander through the happy mass of people. He brushed shoulders and bumped elbows, breathed in whiffs of food, tried futilely to identify the actual words coming from peoples' lips. One thing bothered him. Why hadn't his brother even dropped a hint that this was in the works?

He approached his mother, who was placing a hero sandwich in the out-stretched hand of a grinning black boy. "Why all the hush-hush?" he asked.

"Beats me, son," she said. "I had only one assignment, make and serve my meatballs."

"Right," he replied. "But did Frank tell you not to tell me?"

"He did," Marie remarked with a shrug. The boy bit into his sandwich and turned away from the table with a merry skip. "Everybody at Rosario's was given the strictest orders not to breathe a word about this. So my lips were sealed, even where you were concerned."

He gave her a sorrowful look which she deflected with a hand wave. "Look around you, Johnny. This is a great day for New York."

❦   ❦   ❦

"This is truly a grand day for all New Yorkers," Bill Simon declared to a small pack of reporters who trailed the minister as he strolled the playground greeting fans and putative foes alike. "I cannot take the lion's share of the credit for the success of this day," Simon continued magnanimously. "That honor must be bestowed on Frank Rosario, a heretofore unknown Italian-American restauranteur. But I am pleased to have played a part, to have called for the march that brought to this affair so many different people, a veritable human rainbow of colors. Yes, folks, this is unquestionably a wonderful day for this town, for all of us." Simon brought himself and his entourage to a full stop and accompanied his final words with a crisscross sweep of his arms. Even in this motley crowd, he stood out—his tall, gaunt, Lincolnesque frame, the trade-mark peace symbol dangling from his neck, glinting in the sun.

Later the Reverend spent a few private minutes with John. "It was, as today's youth might say, awesome," Simon said. "Shortly after we began marching, these white dudes, you know, now don't get offended, your people, from cen-tral casting, cut-off t-shirts and greasy hair, came out of the storefronts and off of the sidewalks and began dispensing without charge or fanfare all kinds of foods. Welcome to Bensonhurst, they were saying, smiling all the while like it was some big joke. And of course it was. And word is, with some help from Nick Caesar, who you probably know runs another restaurant around here, your brother organized the whole damn show."

John nodded and smiled.

"Why didn't you tell me this was coming down?" the Reverend asked.

"Because I didn't fucking know" was John's response. He hated being kept in the dark by his brother. Simon shifted his gaze, sparing John a minor humiliation.

"Fantastic, huh, Johnny?" Donnie said. They bumped bodies like teammates after a big play. The boy's complexion shone with pleasure. John realized sadly that it was the only time he had seen Donnie happy. The boy's smile, a dimple on his right cheek, reminded him of Angie's expression at glad times. Pretty people, he thought.

"Whadda ya staring at?" Donnie asked.

John ignored the question. "What have you been telling reporters?"

"I added some things to the stuff you wanted me to say. How it's important for people from all backgrounds to take a stand, however they feel like doing it. And how great it would be if people could live together in peace and stuff and how today we're showing that it can be done and how, because of that, it's a real good day, you know, for New York."

"Well done, Donnie," John said.

The boy nodded. "How about Frank," he said. "Really, did he ever come through!"

"Did you have an inkling about all this?"

"Maybe an inkling…. from something Frank said last night at the house."

"What? What did he say to you?"

"Something, you know, about how he had things covered."

Charles removed his light green Kansas City Monarchs baseball cap, rubbed his head with his hand, and smiled at John. The two men stared in each other's eyes and said in unison: "A great day for New York," their faces brightening at their shared satire. It was a fleeting reminder of their teenage silliness and excitement, when their instinct for teamwork and talent for the game enabled them to bring off a surprising basketball maneuver. They'd run in place facing each other, raise their knees high, shake their arms and torsos like monkeys, and emit happy, unintelligible woofing sounds of triumphant boys.

John saw Dominic approach Donnie, tap him on the shoulder and embrace him. Father and son chatted briefly, heads bobbing in friendly rhythm, and parted company.

John caught up with Dominic, whose bright black shirt with its folded short sleeves marked him as a neighborhood greaser. Slightly more sophisticated than most perhaps, but an identifiable type. The leopard won't change his spots, John thought.

"Who would've figured such a happy ending, huh, Johnny?" Dominic said, spreading out his hands. John asked how involved he was in planning the outdoor banquet that was winding down as they spoke.

"Had nothin' to do with this," Dominic said. "Frank asked me to give him a hand, but I told him not a chance." He made a thumbs down motion. "I hafta say," he summarized, "it all came off. My boy's alright, and Frank becomes Saint Racial Brotherhood for a day."

❦   ❦   ❦

The soft blue light of evening slowly settled over the scene and the crowd began to leave the park. John and Angie leaned on the tall fence at the back end of the playground and on each other, their first moment together of the day. Tired and elated, they snuck glances at Fat Tony who was silently standing guard at a table about forty feet away where Frank and Jack Dorney talked.

"Trust me, babes, if you looked at Tony for an extended period today, you were sure to catch him, at least for a minute or two, in the act of not chewing."

"Ya gotta admit," she giggled, silly with surviving the day, "he's very, very loyal."

"Probably Frank's best friend in that respect. Can always find him at the restaurant."

"Aha," she exclaimed, raising her finger in the air. "That's it, the reason for his loyalty."

"What's it?"

"Like any faithful dog, Tony's loyalty is based partly on food…. in this case, what he can get at Rosario's."

"Wow," he said, feigning dismay. "You really think so?"

"Indisputable, if you want my opinion."

"Wow, the dog."

"That's what we're saying."

Harry Glassman approached and shook John's hand with a hardy pump. John wriggled his fingers. "Take it easy, my man. You might hurt somebody."

"You're clearly a woman to be reckoned with," Harry said to Angie.

"What's that mean?" she asked, verbal dukes up.

"First you capture John's fancy," Harry replied with a grin, "and he's not an easy man to please. Then it turns out you're the mother of the only honorable white boy in all Bensonhurst."

"Guess these things are true," John jumped in, hoping to coax a positive reaction from Angie.

"Don't mince words much, do you?" Angie said.

"I may be outspoken," Harry responded, "but only with people I think can handle it." He lowered his head in a subtle bow which Angie returned in kind.

Harry turned toward John. "Your brother did a wonderful, brave thing."

"No two ways about it," Angie said. "He made it happen, didn't he, Johnny?"

John said nothing.

"Have you talked to him?" Angie asked.

"Not yet."

"Don't you think you better?" She was not so much asking as advising.

❦   ❦   ❦

On his way to Frank, John walked past an agitated Jack Dorney, reached out and grabbed the cop's arm. Startled, Dorney whirled around—moving lithely for a stout man—and saw the contact had a friendly source.

"Hey, buddy," Dorney said catching his breath. "How's life?"

"Counting today, pretty good."

"Listen, Johnny," Dorney said, suddenly solemn, "I'm glad our paths crossed. Can you repeat a message to your brother?"

"I'm listening, but not promising anything."

"Tell him," the police official whispered, "he's gotta look over his shoulder, and the road in front of him too."

John reached Frank at the table where Fat Tony kept his impassive post. "What's with the local carabiniere?" he asked. "Says to watch your back, but to keep your eyes on the road also."

Frank grunted. "Wanna know why he's got a bug up his ass? Some of Dorney's precinct cops—it goes pretty high up actually—they're pissed off because

I stopped my pay-offs. When I decided to leave town, I told them to take up their under-the-table transactions with Sally Broadway."

"A suggestion to which they did not take kindly?"

"So I hear. One of 'em even wanted to shut down our little picnic for today, can you imagine, because I didn't get the necessary permit, for a block party or whatever."

"So Jack's nervous maybe they're working up their so-called courage to teach you a lesson, break your legs, something like that?"

"Nah," Frank said, "he thinks they may try to harass me with traffic tickets. Call in health inspectors on the restaurant. That kind of thing."

"I don't have to lose sleep over this?"

"Just a blip on the screen of life." Frank smiled at his own clever expression.

John saw Fat Tony eat the last scrap of veal cutlet from the table. He turned toward his brother. "You pulled it off, Frank, a master stroke." He had in mind the grand gestures of mythic godfather figures, like Lucky Lucciano paying the full tab of rebuilding a Catholic school destroyed by fire. "You made everybody happy: Angie, Donnie, me, all my friends, even Bill Simon."

"Except for the last vegetable you mentioned, that was my plan. Guess I don't begrudge him either."

"You should feel proud," John said. "I know I do."

"Okay, Johnny. Basta."

"So why didn't you tell me about it?"

"Couldn't chance it, Johnny, given the gag order I put on everyone. Couldn't make you an exception."

"But you did drop a hint to Donnie?"

"Had to give the kid that much."

"Guess so," John conceded.

"Besides, I wanted to see the dumbfounded look on your face, that ga-ga look you still haven't shaken."

"At least I didn't disappoint you."

"Nor I you," Frank said.

Frank's moment, well earned, John knew. Time to let go of my beef.

Returning to Angie, he walked past Fat Tony. "What do you say, big man?"

Tony leaned a beefy hand on the table, ran his tongue across his teeth. "Great fucking day for the city, huh, Johnny?"

❦   ❦   ❦

Whiney wanted all the details. He had spent Sunday at home tending to his invalid wife Shirley and, at John's request, staying by the phone in case crises arose and they—John, Angie, Donnie, whoever—had to reach the outside world or to leave messages for each other.

"Your mom's gonna watch Shirley for me," Whiney told John over the phone on Monday morning. "So how 'bout later tonight, we take a ride, go for a walk in the park and you fill me in on everything?"

John, Whiney, and Angie rode in the van onto the Belt Parkway, winding beside the curves of the Narrows. They slipped into a small scenic parking area off the highway where later in the night lovers would furtively embrace, then walked along the promenade until they reached an intact park bench where Angie and Whiney sat down. John stood leaning against the railing, facing them.

The air off the sea felt warm, comforting. This was his favorite season, John said, recalling the safety zone of his youth when the weather was hot, school was out, and all he cared about was the Yankees. "Dad and I use to play catch in front of our apartment after supper. I'd pretend to be the Mick, or Yogi, or somebody, and he'd do the play by play. People would smile at us, and I'd be proud to be out there with him, my good-looking old man."

"Summer memories," Whiney said softly, "precious things." He ran his hand through his full head of white hair and looked at the sky past John's head. John glanced from his uncle to Angie, dressed in a sleeveless white blouse and beige shorts, her body turned toward the old man, the skin and flesh of her tanned crossed legs arousing him.

Whiney cleared his throat. "Your father and I had some great times here." He waved his hand, to his left toward Coney Island and to his right toward the Verrazano Bridge. "All this was beach when we were kids, no highway, no buildings, no fences, nothing but clean sand and water. What did we know then, just young, stupid kids, going swimming. No air conditioners then either, we were just getting out of the heat."

"Hey, Whiney," Angie cooed, "why so sad? Beautiful memories make you sad?"

"They're not just beautiful, darling. They're gone…. can't get them back." He leaned forward, stared out at the water. "When we were older, during the depression, maybe in our 20's, had no jobs, maybe drive a hack at night and earn a coupla bucks. Your father and me, Benny Porche, Nicky Bitts, Johnny Once now and then, and lotsa other guys, we'd spend the day at the beach, girls too, that's where Frank met your mother." Whiney paused, glanced at John. "She was looking him and me over, sizing us up, both of us dark from all the time in the sun, about the same height, and she says, I can't differentiate between the two of you, your mom being an intellectual at the time, liked to use big words and your father, he says laughing, 'You mean, you can't tell the difference between the two of us.'"

John smiled at Angie, wondered whether she was familiar with this part of Rosario family lore.

"What did we know?" Whiney said again. "We were so young. Don't mean just in years. No money worries either. All the boys'd harmonize on the beach.

> Please play for me/That sweet melody
> called Doodle-li-do, Doodle-li-do
> Simplest thing/Nothing much to it
> Don't have to sing/Just doodle-li-do it"

Whiney sang in a soft sandpaper voice, like Jimmy Durante crooning a lullabye. John half expected his uncle to do a tap dance and take a bow.

"Silly song," Whiney said. "One of our favorites, though." He rubbed the side of his head. "Helped us get through the day back then."

The steamy August sun settled into the horizon beyond the Narrow's bleak waters, tossing up streaks of purple into the twilight. Like an aging chorus dancer flashing her still shapely legs, old grey Brooklyn surprised John, Angie, and Whiney with the sudden beauty in its sky.

"Enough about the past," Whiney said. "Tell me what happened yesterday."

❧   ❧   ❧

On the following Friday, their first night alone after the demonstration, John and Angie strolled arm in arm up Amsterdam Avenue toward his apartment. The evening air was cool, but muggy, a rare summer combination. The street was busy with college kids still at home hanging out in front of suddenly popular singles bars; older couples chatting at outdoor cafe tables; homeless men, dirty and bearded, sprawled snoozing on the local library's stoop and on the sidewalks in front of abandoned storefronts; and teenagers of every color listening to loud music boxes outside pizza joints.

The nighttime chill had not made its way to John's apartment. The rooms felt stuffy and hot, as if a disgruntled landlord had the radiators blasting away at dead of winter levels. They rushed into the master bedroom, shut the door, and turned the air conditioner switch to high cool.

"Ah," he said, "my bedroom, an urban oasis."

She sat down heavily on the bed and complained about being worn out by the stresses of the week. She was so fatigued, in fact, she couldn't imagine rising from her current spot, getting undressed, brushing her teeth, removing her contacts....

"But it's early," John heard himself whine. "I wanted to play, babes, especially after the lovely dinner."

"Sorry, Johnny, I'm not up to it. Can barely move, no less you know what."

He swallowed his pride. "It's okay. We'll make love another time." But he nurtured a secret hope.

When she finally did get up and go into the bathroom, he quickly changed into a matching pair of light grey shorts and t-shirt that she bought for him and liked for their smart, tight look. She came out and murmured, "Oh, John, you're bad."

She had put on a mid-thigh length, brown cotton nightshirt. It fit her tightly enough to reveal the outlines of her nipples and the curve of her buttocks. "Oh, Angie," he said, "you're the bad one."

She smiled. "Maybe both of us are bad, baby, but it's not going to do you any good. I'm going to sleep."

"I'll just read a bit before turning off the light." He raised his hands midway into the air, showing he carried no weapons.

She climbed into bed. "That's a nice boy."

She lay on her side facing him and began to doze. He gently touched her—first caressing her nipples through the brown cotton in a soft circular motion and, when she didn't slap him away, fingering the tip of her vagina. He figured, at worst, she'd wake and scold him and forget his transgression by morning. The best outcome was physical bliss.

She moaned in pleasure. Eyes still shut, she whispered, "What are you doing, naughty Johnny? Now you're not bad, you're naughty."

With one hand he cupped and squeezed her breasts—ample breasts, ample bosom, he teased himself with the play of those words, and the image and wonder they conveyed. The fingers of his other hand reached lower into her pussy's growing wetness. He savored the slow hardening of his penis and the excitement coursing through his body.

She opened her eyes. "I want to sleep. You're waking me up. It's sooo nice, but you're waking me up."

"Soon you'll be able to sleep, babes, better than ever," he promised.

It was a night of sweet dreams for John, even as the details slipped away, the comforting feeling remained.... what was it his mom use to say at bedtime? Have pleasant dreams, my son. He woke and stretched, reaching out for Angie, but she was gone. He sat up like a fast bolt. She left so noiselessly.

He relaxed when he caught a whiff of food coming from the kitchen. He found her there, wearing his best dress shirt. She was making one of his favorite breakfasts, raisin bread french toast. "Hmmm," he said, "warm, sweet bread. Where'd you get the slices?"

"Frozen solid cold in the freezer. D'ya forget about 'em?"

"Must've put 'em there only about a hundred years ago. Can't remember why."

"Thought I'd turn them into a morning meal. So we could celebrate last night's lovemaking."

He moved toward the stove, hugged her from behind, nuzzled her neck. "Love of my life," he called her.

"Likewise," she said.

He stepped back and opened the refrigerator to take out the maple syrup. "Sex and sleep's better than just sleep, isn't it?" he said.

She pointed at him. "Used to call you Johnny the Rose. Johnny the Seducer's more like it."

He grinned, proud as a praised child.

CHAPTER 12

❊

"We have to talk about something important," Angie said. John and she had finished breakfast and were sitting across from one another in the old, comfortable chairs in his living room. John thought he never felt more content.

"Fire away."

"This might upset you."

"Whatever it is, I can handle it." Still, he felt a twinge of anxiety in his stomach.

"There's something you gotta know about me, about my life." She stopped, changed course. "You love me, right, Johnny?"

"Completely." But the twined ball in his belly tightened.

"No matter what, almost no matter what anyway, you won't leave me?"

He stared at her, saying nothing.

"Please stay for me, for us."

He was touched by her beseeching tone, but didn't move to hug her. He was scared. What was the awful secret? He motioned for her to continue.

"Dominic, you know Dominic," she started. In response to John's frown, she said, "Dominic's not Donnie's real father."

"Oh. Okay," he replied carefully. "Who is?"

She took a deep breath, released it. "Your brother Frank."

John felt his chair, heavy as it was, rise from the floor and fly wildly around the room, nearly banging into the walls before swerving to avoid the actual crash, tossing him like an unwanted object onto the floor. When he looked up, dizzy and nauseous, he sat in the chair across from Angie.

Barely opening his mouth, he said, "You had sex with my brother? You had a child with Frank?"

She was shaken by the abrupt change in his posture and appearance and by his accusing tone. "Johnny," she said, "what's going on? You're turning white. Jesus, come back to me, come back to me please."

"You had sex with Frank. Oh shit, you had his child." He leaned back, held his stomach, and moaned once in physical pain.

He went from ship-shape to shipwreck so fast that she was breathless at the sight of it. She became frantic to retrieve him.

"You had sex with my brother once or twice, or was it lots of times, over the years?"

"Why does it matter?" she asked. "I never loved him like I love you. I'm with only you now."

"I have a right to know." He yelled, his voice jolting her like a shove in the chest. "How often did you have sex with Frank? How long did you sleep with him?"

Reluctantly, she told her story. Lonely for companionship, Frank and she became friends and then secret lovers, the romance lasting, on and off, for about twelve years. The last time they made love was about ten years ago. They didn't 'do it' often, just once in a while, the sex being less important than the human kinship. "After all," she said, "especially after people like you left, Johnny, it was pretty much a desert out there in Brooklyn."

"And after one of these rare occasions," he asked, "you became pregnant?"

She bowed her head. "Yes."

"Why didn't you have an abortion?" He shook his head in disgust. "And, once you had the child, why didn't Frank acknowledge him?"

She still wanted to reach him, settle him, hold onto him. "Johnny, you're being so cold, so cruel." And she knew he wasn't a cruel man. "I know all this causes you pain," she said, "but it's in the past, the distant past. I'm a different person now, I'm with you."

The glare of hate and ache in his eyes chilled her. She shuddered, and thought maybe she had lost him. It had all been too good to be true—that'll teach the girl from Bensonhurst to dream so large.

"I'm with you," she said, "but only if you still want me."

🍁   🍁   🍁

For what remained of the morning, Angie begged John for understanding, for a sign he cared for her. Her efforts were useless. All he wanted were the details of the Bensonhurst drama he missed, her relationship with Frank, the child that resulted, the marriage with Dominic. Under his dogged pressure, she explained that she did not even think about an abortion—it repulsed her, it profoundly contradicted her beliefs, all that she had been taught in church and home, and, damnit, she *wanted* to have the baby. Frank did not take responsibility for the pregnancy, for the child—at least not openly—because "of the terrible suffering, and I mean suffering, it would've caused lots of people we loved, including our mothers and fathers, to say nothing of Theresa and the girls. Can you imagine, Johnny, what Theresa would've done? She would've gone completely ballistic, would've killed herself, or Frank, or all of us."

He was not moved by her predictions. I'm going ballistic myself, he thought. "And Dominic, how and why did he come to accept this very fucked-up arrangement?"

Dominic, Angie said, more than cooperated with the scheme—he helped with its design. "When Frank saw I wouldn't get an abortion and knew he couldn't come forward and that I didn't particularly want him to anyway, he approached Dominic to see if he'd let the word get out that he had, you know, knocked me up."

He groaned at the crude plotting. In a weary voice, she continued. "To our relief, believe it or not, Dominic agreed, but on one condition. It was the deal-breaker." She snickered bitterly. "He insisted him and me actually get married. Acted like it was his life's dream. Didn't even care much when I asked him about it, that one day I'd want to tell the kid the truth.... Oh, he did agree to be the father, spend time with the boy, you know, really raise him with me, take financial responsibility."

"And you, you went along with this sick, crazy charade? No one around there saw through it?"

A new tone crept into her voice, a tired annoyance. "What choice did I have? Couldn't up and leave Brooklyn like you. With what money, with what abilities, with what connections? I needed a situation, where I could have the baby, where our basic needs were cared for. I needed a situation, believe me."

"What about staying home with your folks?" Anything, he thought, would've been better than setting up house with Dominic.

"Wouldn't do, wouldn't do." She shook her head. "Too much shame, too many questions. You forget Bensonhurst is like a little village and I couldn't cause.... what's the name of that book.... a scarlet letter situation for my parents, not with all the trouble my wild ways already put my mother and father through. Oh, that's another reason Frank couldn't come clean. My father would've probably shot him."

She lowered her head, her full dark hair falling forward, her face covered in her cupped hands. He heard a voice inside his head, a remote part of him, not in possession of him: Don't be an asshole, don't let her slip away. But when she raised her head, showing a tear-tracked face, he was unmoved. She stretched her hand toward him. "Don't you see, I was trapped by these insane circumstances? I was a young, dumb girl then maybe, but I was doing my best to make the best of a sad, mad, bad thing."

Her words spun around in his brain, almost charming him. Doing my best to make the best of a sad, mad, bad thing. But he had sunk into a deep sulk. No word or gesture of hers nor distant voice inside him could restore him to her. He did not respond to her outstretched hand and she returned it to her lap.

"So your parents accepted your marriage to Dominic?" he asked flatly.

She wiped her cheeks with several flicks of her fingers. Her manner became reserved, contained. She'd tell him within reason what he needed, wanted to know. But she'd no longer implore him and she would not, for the moment at least, surrender to her despondency.

"What my folks wanted in the worst way was for me to settle down, have a child, become grandparents, that whole package. Dominic's faults seemed like small potatoes when stacked up along side that dish. Besides, my father counted on Frank to keep track of Dominic, in case he ever stepped out of line. And foolishly I suppose, given how things turned out, I had my own hopes about me and Dominic, thought maybe we could make a go of it."

"You and Dominic? You had to know better."

"Please listen," she said impatiently. "I said I had my hopes, not that I was sure of anything. But Dominic and I knew each other for years, even dated off and on after high school. He was handsome, had some style, you know the flashy smile and shiny shoes. He had left home, gotten away from his drunken shit of a father and was getting set up in some kind of arrangement with Frank who was like a new and better father to him, like, you know, a mentor. I was young, like I said, trying to make the best of things. If you weren't being such a judgmental asshole right now, you might understand I had to have my hopes. Otherwise it would've been impossible for me to keep going, to be there for the baby."

He pounced on the 'asshole' remark. It was like she had invaded his subconscious, grabbed a piece of it, and hurled it at his head. "You have a shitload of nerve," he barked, "calling me names after what you've done."

"You *are* being an asshole," she shouted. "Under your educated, middle-fucking-class ways, you're a Sicilian macho male asshole like the rest of them.

What I did was 20 years ago and had nothing to do with you. I was, we were just living, maybe screwing things up, but it was not...." She could not say what Frank, Dominic, and she did was not. She took a big breath. "But what you're doing now is hurting people, it's hurting us, is destroying us and I don't deserve it and we don't deserve it and you should fucking stop it."

"Don't turn this around on me, Angie. I'm not the sinner. I'm the sinned against." He swung at the air, rejecting her charge. "You fucked up and you fucked around and with my brother of all fucking people and, whether you know it or not or meant it or not, it was a betrayal. I can't accept it."

"Okay," she said. "You can't accept it. Then you can't accept me. I'll leave. Is that what you want? Will me walking out make you happy? 'Cause I'll leave. In fact, I'd be happy to leave. You can choke to fucking death on your jealousy."

He pressed his arms to his sides and tried to calm himself. They were standing now, in the middle of the living room, only a few inches apart and facing each other. He spoke softly. "It will not make me happy if you leave. Nothing can make me happy. But I do want you to leave. You have to."

She strode past him—he grabbed her arm and spun her around. "One last question," he spat out. "What about Donnie? Have you explained the real deal to Dominic Jr.?"

"Fuck you." Glaring at him, she said: "I expected you to be shaken, alright, but not splattered. I expected you to get past it and back to us. But you couldn't handle it. What's that expression you men use? You dropped the ball. You stupid, stupid bastard."

No, not bastard, the voice inside him said as she was opening the door. Asshole, asshole, it repeated after the door slammed, like a dull whisper throbbing inside his head.

Most of the time John did not feel the pain sharply; it was more like a heavy shroud enveloping him, making him numb, even dopey. For the first time in his life, he attempted to drown himself with drink, using a bottle of choice white wine that Charles had brought him two years ago—part of a misbegotten celebration of his divorce from Suzanne. He slept a lot, was hung over, but couldn't recall doing any of life's basic tasks like eating or going to the bathroom.

By Sunday night he was too sick to drink anymore. He emerged from his vaporous condition and immediately regretted it. He walked around his apartment holding and rubbing different parts of his body—trying simultaneously to ward off and relieve physical injury. He was beset by images of, and questions about, Angie's affair with his brother: How and why could they behave so badly, betraying him and all the people around them? He no longer thought of Angie and Frank as good people or trusted them. He did not see life as good or trust it. He hated them furiously, yet missed them. He was approaching a desperate place—no, he was already there and taking up residence. He wanted to leave, or, at least, to retreat from it, if only because his massive self-pity made him uncomfortable—it was never an emotion he indulged in, in anything but small measures.

On Sunday night he sat on his sofa and listened to Sinatra's mournful, lonesome-voiced albums about love's crack-ups, about losing out to another guy. Then he switched to a more rugged sound, Dion's "Runaround Sue"—*Here's my story, sad but true/About a girl that I once knew…. Hape, hape, bum da haydee/Hape hape, bum da haydee* went the rhythmic doo-wop chorus. That's wrong, he thought. It should go *Hurt, hurt*, bum da haydee.

Monday meant work, a departure from his private life, where the weekend's events left him banged-up and bitter. But at the office, it'd be a struggle to suppress his charged emotions, so he could be civil, could focus, could function.

His sons had convinced him to hang a large mirror in the hallway next to the front door, so they could conveniently check their looks before stepping into the street. On the way out, John took advantage of his concession to his sons' vanities and determined that he looked only slightly rumpled. Hair combed neatly with no more grey showing than before, clothes and dress presentable, face washed and clean-shaven, the traces of bleariness around the eyes the only thing giving him away. He'd done a pretty good job covering up the ruins.

He ducked Jeanette's efforts at Monday morning chatter about the weekend's highs and lows, and quickly mounted the stairs to his office where he closed the door—usually a sign that he was having a sensitive phone conversation with, say, a board member or the mayor's office or that he was doing a taped radio interview. He was not to be disturbed, the preferred arrangement for the time being. He sat at his desk and opened his day-at-a-glance book which was sent to him, personally monographed, by one of the few wealthy members of his board—the man's company manufactured these and other stationary products. What was on his calendar for the coming weeks? Not that much, a relatively light height of the summer schedule, ordinarily welcome but now a scary prospect. Who needs all this fucking found time? Keeping busy was one way he could get through the coming weeks.

He did look forward to a planned series of meetings with Leslie to discuss the status of her report on "progressive" welfare reform. For example, rather than penalize recipients for dropping out of a vocational training program or relapsing on drugs, support and reward their holding a job, keeping their children in school, maintaining a stable household. He wanted UJI to complete and publish the report by early fall. This way, its recommendations could shape the Dinkins/Giuliani debate about social issues as election day approached.

Other things—dinners and dates with Angie and a meeting with Bill Simon and his cohorts on nurturing the new harmony in Bensonhurst—were now out of the question. "Shit," he muttered, the pain returning at the sight of these markings in his book.

One of his regular lunches with Charles was coming up, though still days away. He thought about how he'd describe the intense misery of loving a woman he hated so much, he fantasized smashing her to death, of loathing the woman who had brought excitement and contentment into his life like unexpected gifts. He nourished a dim hope that Charles could be more than a receptacle for his woes, but that his friend could offer healing thoughts, words, whatever. Stirring in John faintly was the understanding he was ensnared in an old world response to the Angie and Frank business— my brother, he obsessed, goddamn, why did it have to be my brother. He wished he could forgive and forget, and reach the point of wanting Angie back.

John did not want to be home alone, where jealousy gnawed like an unsparing rodent on his psyche, but also wanted to avoid the forced civility of most social occasions. He spent much of his nighttime hours after work walking the City's warm, summer streets, making his way home slowly. He'd go from Gramercy Park with its tree-lined blocks and handsome, spacious one or two family brick homes, through the active bustle of midtown Manhattan with its tall buildings and honking taxis to the heavy pedestrian traffic, varied in ethnic mix and personal styles, of the West Side.

One night he stopped for dinner at a seafood restaurant on Columbus Ave—it had known seedier days as Joe's. He'd eaten there often twenty odd years ago after a day on the job at St. Matthew and St. Timothy's community center, where he supervised children of all ages, many troubled and/or in trouble.

He sipped an aromatic serving of lobster bisque from a tiny dish and thought of an earlier evening at the counter. He'd come from a long afternoon softball game where he had been more referee than coach. Suzanne was away that summer, traveling in Greece with a former college roommate who had grown up in that ancient land and he was lonesome and annoyed now that he couldn't unburden his frustrations. The Yankee game was on the radio, as usual at Joe's. Mulling over new ways for handling "his kids"—smaller groups, stricter rules, speaking more softly, shouting even more loudly—he munched on a burger and welcomed the familiar sounds of a baseball crowd buzzing and of Yankee announcer Mel Allen burbling. His ears did not fully attend to the game, though, until they picked up the home crowd roar that signaled Mickey Mantle was at the plate. The Mick had already homered, Mel Allen was saying, and wouldn't it be terrific if he could hit one out again, this being the bottom of the 8th and the Yankees being down 7-5, but having two men on base, and so many baseball pundits having written off the aging Mantle, what with his hobbled legs and irregular play.

John listened.

"There's one," Mel Allen hollered as the crowd's rumble grew louder. "It's going, going, gone."

The Mick delivered, John said under his breath. He slapped the counter and smiled at the waiter. The old cripple's still got it.

"How about that!" Mel Allen said.

John gazed at his soup. Ah, he thought, when a ballgame's outcome could lighten my pain.

❧   ❧   ❧

Coming home late, John discovered something rare among the scattered pieces of mail the building porter slipped under the door: a letter from Jake. He sat at his big, wooden dining table with a soothing cup of decaf cafe mocha and read….

"Dear Dad,

What is it with girls? How is it they can make you feel like the biggest star, then like shit a minute later?

Guess what? My Emily is driving me nuts, nuts, nuts. She's been so nasty lately, just in a lousy mood, that I asked her if she was having her period. Big Mistake!! She bit my nose. I really mean that—she took my head in her two hands, and held it tightly enough so it really hurt, and then bit my nose very, very hard. Girls!

Things started to go bad with us when I got mad at her last week for spending so much time with Teddy listening to hard rock music, Teddy's new favorite hobby. Emily scolded me, her French accent really coming out, calling me a jealous baby. I can still hear her say that and stamping her feet at the same time. I feel bad, bad about it because she was right. I was being a jealous baby and more so because it was Teddy not somebody else. Funny thing about brothers, huh?

Anyway now I'm being sensible, I think, trying to make up for things, but Emily's not going for it. She won't hang out with me and it's killing me, or at least really bugging me. Funny thing is I've gotten into the record they were listening to most, the album by Hole, Courtney Love's group. In my free time, which I got a lot of since Emily's playing hard to please or whatever she's doing, I'm listening to this tape and can they make a lot of noise and can this girl howl and I love it. Hey, Dad, am I becoming a normal teenager?

But let me get to my real reason for writing you. Last night I'm hanging out with my bunk's senior counselor, Andy Berger, an older guy, though not as old as you of course, who likes old rock and roll stuff. We're talking, and he's telling me to be cool about Emily, and the radio's on to the golden oldies station and on comes a live performance by the one and only Dion and Andy's real impressed because I even knew who Dion is because of you. Dion does this great bit, telling a story introducing a song, 'Ruby, Baby' I think it was, a cute song I'll give you that, catchy in fact, but what I loved was his rap leading up to it, how he and his friends in the neighborhood were all in love with this older girl. They were 14 like me and she was 22, and they'd wait for her to get off the bus six o'clock every night, and she walks right past them, of course, nose in the air and Dion has his boys follow her, serenading stalkers Dion called them, and righteous fox was what he called her. I loved that, righteous fox, and Dion says, before beginning his song, here's to all the righteous foxes in the world, what would we do without them?

So, Dad, try and answer that question for me.

Patiently Awaiting Your Reply,

Jake"

John dropped the letter on the table and licked the cafe mocha's last drops from his lips. Like father, like son, he thought.

❖   ❖   ❖

Over lunch, John described to Charles the mortar shell fired out of the past, how it blasted apart his romance with Angie and pelted him with shrapnel of images and emotions. They ate at Tony's, the world's tiniest delicatessen, located in a shallow, narrow storefront space on the border of Chinatown and Little Italy behind the criminal court building in lower Manhattan. The place was run by a small family of Phillipinos who greeted John and Charles with snappy chatter, and always seemed satisfied when the two men ordered their customary choice of a chicken salad sandwich, soft and crunchy.

John jumped quickly from the break-up with Angie, before Charles could even respond, to his son's unusual letter. "Could hear Jake's voice in my head, like he was in the room with me." He spoke in agitated tones. "But it wasn't like Jake, or it was a new Jake, not so closed, but expressive, even funny, or trying to be." He looked wide-eyed at Charles, expecting him to solve the riddle.

"Looks like your boy's going through some changes." Charles leaned back in his seat like a professor. "Teenagers are like toddlers, doing something different every week."

"But this was *so* different. Jake usually writes three lines, and only when he's asking for something."

"He was asking for something this time too."

John motioned to Charles to keep talking.

"Jake's felt distant from you for a coupla years, since the divorce. Now he's identifying with you. He's having girl troubles. You had girl troubles. He's in love, you're in love." Charles was wearing a dark brown beret, the kind John had seen on Dizzy Gillepsie in more than one photo. He put it down on the table next to his dish and scratched his head. "He's bonding with you, even listening to that hard rock white boy's shit he must associate with you. Like that band Mott the something."

"Mott the Hoople," John said. "And the Teddy thing?"

"Also new. He's been jealous of Teddy before, but not about a girl. That's a powerful brew, no need to tell you."

John nodded at two Legal Aid lawyers who came into the place, a man and woman, he in rumpled attire, she stylishly dressed, a married couple who passed on useful stories to him about their cases while he was writing an UJI proposal about mentally ill inmates on Rikers.

"Funny thing about brothers, Jake wrote." John shook his head. "Like he understood the creepy mix of love and envy. The fucking irony of it."

"Back to Angie," Charles said. "Do you still love her?"

"Don't know…. I know I hate her."

"Maybe that's a start." Charles leaned across the table and tugged gently on his friend's tie.

He's impatient, yet tender, John thought. "Start?" he said.

"That she's still important to you."

"What good is that?" John felt and looked miserable.

An old man came out from behind the counter—it was probably Tony himself—and pointed to John's barely eaten sandwich. "Is anything wrong?" he asked. John said, Oh, no and took a fast bite.

Charles chuckled. "See, you got everybody worrying…. Can you picture life without her?"

"Once in a while I hear a buzz in my ear like a gnat that won't quit"—John spoke *sotte voce*—"put it behind you, asshole, go back to her."

"And?"

"Can't do it. Putting it behind me is beyond me." John raised his arms, then let them fall against the sides of his chair. He was exasperated by his helplessness.

It was a hot, clammy August night, the air heavy and humid. John holed up in his bedroom with the air-conditioning on and watched the Yankees. He'd occasionally go to the Stadium with his father and Frank and, more recently, with Jake and Teddy. He loved sitting in the stands of the magnificent old ballpark, its manicured basepath diamond and outfield lawns and the choreographed moves of conditioned, coordinated athletes. His favorite moment: the white hardball, well-hit, rising in flight against the lighted yet darkening blue skies and descending in virtual slow motion to the outfielder's mitt, the playing field, or, best of all, the grandstands for a home-run.

The televised game was a modest diversion. Then the phone rang and he heard Frank's voice saying hello.

"What do you want?" he asked. His dull ache spread like a messy hurt, making his body tingle. Shit, do I have to talk to this fucking guy, formerly known as my brother? Hanging up would be giving in, but to what? He's the devil I have to confront, exorcize, right? John felt dizzy, a passing nausea.

"Just checking in," Frank said.

"Sure, like you always do."

"I wanna help make peace between you and Angie," Frank said.

"Don't think you're the man for the job."

"Please hear me out, Johnny."

John paused, then spoke. "Okay, shoot." Despite his unhappy, rancorous mood, he could not deny his curiosity. How would Frank try to heal the terrible rift between him and the woman who apparently was, at different times, the love of both their lives?

"People around here don't know what happened, but they're pretty broken-hearted about you and Angie. Mom, Louise, Whiney, I think even Donnie…. count myself in that number."

"You, of course, know what happened."

"Angie gave me the picture."

"Well, fuck you, Frank."

"C'mon, Johnny." Frank sounded hurt.

"You really fucked up, Frank." John said, his brain hot-wired. "Sleeping with Angie, getting her pregnant, what a complete, royal, A number one fuck-up."

"I'm sorry for what you're going through." Frank spoke with a tenderness that even John could recognize. "But I don't think about it that way. It's a desert out here in Bensonhurst when it comes to socializing with intelligent people, so Angie and I were, you know, drawn together. And besides, out of all that comes Donnie. A boy, a life."

"So you're a fucking saint, Frank," John said, his raised voice cracking.

"Remember what Dad wrote in our autograph books? When we graduated Our Lady of Perpetual Help?"

"What did he write?" John spit out. Though annoyed with the diversion, he recognized it took them to hallowed ground.

"'Keep cool,' with a capitol K for both words. And you're not being cool," Frank said gently.

"Easy for you to say."

"Remember what else he wrote?"

"What?" And why are we going through this stupid exercise?

"Love many/Trust few/And always paddle/Your own canoe."

After a pause, John said, "That's not bad. I do remember." A fire truck bel-lowed down the street below his apartment, with an ambulance, sirens wailing, following closely behind it. John flinched at the noise and covered his ear with his hand so he could make out his brother's words.

"Always thought you did that," Frank said, his tone seductive. "While I stayed back in Brooklyn, hanging out with the few I trusted, you stepped out into the world, tried to change it. You loved many like Pop told us. Didn't really know what he meant until you started leading your life."

"Glad to be of service," John said sarcastically.

"After your divorce, though, I figured the trust thing wasn't working out for you. Figured you missed your people."

"So I returned to Brooklyn?"

"Grant you, Angie was the main attraction. But I saw you wanting to be among your family again. For us, where you were concerned, there'd never be any questions asked."

"The prodigal son coming home?" More siren sounds came from the street. A police car—a little late, perhaps—rushing to the scene. "So that's why you brought up Pop and his 30 year-old poem." John's tone of voice was no longer edgy. It was resigned.

"I got more to say. So don't crush my head between your teeth like a damn lamb chop."

But John fired a pre-emptive strike. "Nobody, no thing from my other world, even Suzanne and all the bullshit around the divorce, hurt me like Angie and you."

"What crap, Johnny, it's hard for me to be patient with such crap." Frank raised his voice, not his usual way of speaking. "What me and Angie did was in another lifetime. It had nothing to do with you, except maybe that you were gone, gone, fucking gone, making everything even more empty."

"It's like a betrayal, Frankie, and, to put it in your terms, a betrayal by two people I trusted entirely."

"I just don't get it. You're smart, a college boy, and the truth here's not com-plicated." Frank still spoke in agitated tones. He breathed deeply. "Angie loves you, you fucking jerk, not me, not anyone else. If you ask me, that's the way it's always been, from the time the two of you were teenagers, for all I know, from the time you were fucking two years old. No matter who else she was seeing, she loved you."

John said nothing. What could he? Not rising above his jealousy seemed puny, low-class.

Frank spoke again, calmer now. "Johnny, I love you too."

John noted the emotion in his brother's voice, and the weariness. "Okay, Frankie. I hear you."

"Just please don't walk away from us again," Frank said before hanging up.

Wants me to shed the Johnny Once suit for good, John thought.

❦   ❦   ❦

Angie's phone call came during an UJI staff meeting, when all John could do was pick up the receiver and say he'd have to get back to her, when merely the sound of her sad, yet bright voice saying: "Okay, Johnny, but soon, huh?" caused a sharp, sudden pang in his heart at the sense of sweetness lost.

At the staff meeting, Leslie Kaplan said she'd made an unexpected discovery while preparing her report on welfare reform in New York and the nation. One of her policy wonk buddies from her student days at the Kennedy School on Government leaked suppressed research to her on a successful supported work program for welfare mothers that the first Dukakis Administration ran in Massachusetts. The next governor, a Republican who campaigned on an anti-government spending platform, deep-sixed the program and refused to let an outcome study be published.

The research's findings were powerful; after 18 months, 62% of the welfare mothers still held jobs paying at least double the minimum wage—they could support their households. And these women were not "creamed," meaning they were not screened first for such qualities as previous work experience and resolve to get off welfare. They were randomly selected, yet their success rate was 18% above the results any similarly designed program in New York or elsewhere produced. Leslie attributed it to the state's providing not only child care, parenting classes, and job training but also employment incentives for private businesses that took a chance on the women and decent-paying, job creation projects like publicly funded, supervised work crews to clean parks and repair government buildings.

Everyone around the table saw the study's value, but there were problems. The report was secret and virtually certain to be disputed if and when released. Also the program was short-lived and so was the research, there not being enough time to see whether the benefits would last over the long term and to determine why, even during its brief life, the program did so well.

After some hesitation, John told Leslie to submit the study to a small group of academic experts who would verify the document or not on a confidential basis. If they endorsed it, UJI would highlight the information in its own report, while describing the circumstances of uncovering it. John was happy with this approach. It was responsible and defensible, in case a board member or external enemy raised a question or a fuss, and would be a public relations coup for UJI. And, all the while, he and they, Leslie and his staff, pursued a righteous political course.

He was not so sanguine, however, about the pending phone call to Angie—that dilemma being much less susceptible to the concentrated vigors of rational analysis. He dialed the number with a feeling of dread leavened by what he identified as a small dose of hope.

❧   ❧   ❧

"At first she cooed, then she cried and ended the damn call by scolding me," John told Charles as they walked on a cool, drizzly evening in late August in an empty Riverside Park. He crossed his arms and shivered. "Whew, it's chilly out here. Where has summer gone?"

Charles grinned. "Slipped away like a hot summer romance?" He shook wetness off his Greek sea captain's hat.

John made a face. "So Angie describes how crestfallen she is at my conduct, at my cut and run impulse, how tears will form in her eyes, on her cheeks without notice, without her even knowing until someone asks why she's crying or does she just have a real bad case of hay fever." The two men had stopped walking and, facing Charles, John was leaning his backside on a leg-high stone wall overlooking the river. He shook his head in wonder. "Felt like smashing the guy who'd break her heart, who could fail her so miserably. How'd I turn out to be the bad guy here? Aren't I the aggrieved party?"

"Some folks might think you took your grievance a little too far." Charles spoke gently as if his words were like eggs placed on the table with the greatest care.

"Like Angie. Says she'd have forgiven me a sulk for a day or two or even three, in fact would've been understanding, even contrite, but this, what's this been, three weeks. Now she's indignant. If I come back, she'll make me pay. In a way I won't soon forget, she says."

"Poor Johnny," Charles clucked.

"Then my mother calls," John continued, "with her air of disappointment. I don't know the details, she tells me, but don't toss Angie aside like she's some topinara from the streets. I say Mom, I know Angie's not a stuck up little bit of nothing, but I got to work through these issues on my own and she says while I'm taking my own sweet time, I should know that Louise tells her, that's Angie's mother, that Angie has cried herself to sleep on more than one occasion although it does seem to be getting better, my mother is forced to admit."

A huge freighter rolled silently up the river below them, cutting a deep swath in the waters. Its lights shone through the rain, throwing off rays of mist midway into the sky.

"Pretty and spooky, isn't it?" Charles said, pointing to the boat. "So what are you gonna do?"

"Let's hear from you," John said, side-stepping the question. "Joining the chorus?"

"I'm really curious. Why is an at least 10 year-old affair so important? Is it a macho thing? Well, you're not such a macho guy, at least not in a stupid, chauvinistic sense." Charles' words came in a rush, hands opening and closing as he talked. Shit, John realized, he's passionate about this, maybe even pissed. Probably been holding back.

"Is it an Italian thing?" Charles went on. "I think maybe that's true, and then it's a brother thing too, sibling rivalry, a Cain and Able thing. I think that's part of it also and all that shit can run pretty deep…." He paused. John's face conveyed no signals, so he continued. "Where I come out, even understanding all that, is: So what? Know what I mean? So fucking what that Angie's had other men in her life? So fucking what that one of them, maybe the main one, was your brother? That was over a decade ago. Besides, she could have made a lot worse choices." Charles slowed down, spoke through nearly clenched teeth. "And she loves you now, man. She loves you."

"Intellectually," John said softly, with some shame, "I mainly see things the same way. But I still cringe. Don't want the disorder. Prefer a prettier package, with no muddy footprints, no mental pictures of Frank and Angie."

"John," Charles said, "at our age, there are no virgins left."

"I know that, but I'm still stuck."

"Move on, man, move on."

John patted Charles on the cheek, his way of expressing thanks.

The drizzle ceased as the two friends walked out of the park and the blurred rays of the setting sun became visible in the sky. They turned to look back at the beauty behind and above them.

CHAPTER 13

"Hiya, babes," John said, affecting a cavalier tone. "Long time no see."

He greeted Angie as she left her office building at a little past 5 PM on a weekday night in early September. She stepped out from a small group of co-workers and exclaimed, "Johnny, what…." She held a tiny red umbrella, protection from a light rain.

"What am I doing here?"

"Well, yeah."

"I want to get back into your life." He pulled a floppy rain hat out of his briefcase and fitted it on his head.

A smile radiated across her face. His doubts about returning dissolved like a morning fog routed by the strong light of dawn.

She punched him on the chest and arms to prove he wasn't merely an apparition. "Johnny the Rose Rosario, you're back?" she practically cried.

"I'm back."

"Johnny, J-o-h-n-n-y, you here to stay?"

"To stay." He put his briefcase down and slipped his arms around her. People hurried past without jostling them, permitting them a private moment in the crowd.

"You're passed all that bullshit that came between us?"

"I'm still a little sore. Brooded and suffered and got lots of unsolicited advice from folks you know well and I've worked it through. So, will you have me?"

"Have to think about it," she said, feigning a thoughtful air, gazing over his shoulder.

"Well?"

"I guess I'll take you back." She giggled.

"Whew!" His relief was genuine. "Of course I prefer no more surprises from your past."

"Oh, I'll save a few for you over time, but how should I put this…. none of the same magnitude."

They had dinner at an "of the moment" restaurant near Union Square. Despite its trendiness, John liked the Coffee Shop—crowded with beautiful people of many lineages. Eyeing the women customers and servers who strolled the aisles like slinky supermodels, Angie said, "I see why you wanted to come here."

"The food's not bad either," he said.

They traded news about their children. Donnie was returning to Xaverian for his senior year in a settled state of mind. His celebrity as symbol of the city's potential for racial harmony was a blessing—he was wearing it well and it was serving him well and he was practical enough to use it as an advantage in his college applications. He wanted to play basketball for a local school: Manhattan, Fordham, maybe that Big East powerhouse St. John's.

John's sons were in "a good space." They came home from camp getting along better than usual—he regularly heard them chortling in their room, about girls, maybe girlie magazines. Cheery as ever, Teddy was pleased with his improving athletic skills. And Jake was relieved that his stormy relationship with Emily survived the summer and he had already written her twice—the boy was turning into quite a correspondent. The boys had the habit, picked up from another camper, whenever they got annoyed, of slamming their right fist loudly into their left palm and saying, "Rats." Angie laughed and said she couldn't wait to see that—he was sure she'd have the chance, for better or worse.

Dessert was a brandied mango mousse that they ate together with tiny spoons. "Charles know about the Frank, Dominic, and me business?" Angie asked, swallowing the first bite.

"Yeah."

"Does he think poorly of me?"

"No. In fact, he was very sympathetic."

"That's good," she sighed, comforted, John saw, by the news.

"He basically told me I was an asshole to drive you away. In fact, there was a little voice inside my head saying the same thing."

She smiled. "You should listen when you talk to yourself."

"I did, finally," he said with a shrug.

She slid next to him in the booth, put her arm through his and wriggled close. "Tell me why you came back."

He tried to think of a witty response that touched on the truth and also got a laugh. But he couldn't come up with one. "You know this, but I hate to admit it. My reaction to your past was due pretty much to Italian male stuff I was raised on, thought I left behind." He turned toward her and held up his hands. "No justification, babes, but your hooking up with Frankie, even so long ago, pushed that button hard." He placed his hands on the table, palms upward. "But other things eventually took precedence."

"Like?"

"Like loneliness and desire. And love too." He squeezed her hand. "This precious thirty year old love."

"Yes, I know," she said huskily.

"Also, I wanted to see what would happen next."

❧   ❧   ❧

The following Friday, she announced the third coming of Angie the Librarian—they had returned to his apartment after a disappointing night at the movies, some Hollywood thriller with too much action and not enough personality. She sat with him on the couch in his living room and explained the rules. Although she usually did 'Angie the Librarian' as a reward, this time he'd be "punished too" for leaving her for so long. This time he'd get the royal treatment, "the queening," she called it. "I sit, full-flesh, on your face."

He caught his breath, excited and embarrassed by his reaction to her promised threat. Or was it a threatening promise?

Except for high heels, she'd be naked, no panties or g-strings to intrude on his pleasure. It was a "no frills" Angie, no book reading, just a poem she'd written special for the occasion. Oh yes, she'd apply spices, meaning perfumes, to her body, so there'd be "no yucky tastes or odors." She couldn't stand complaints about that.

John lay on his back. Angie advanced toward him and turned around by the side of the bed. She spread her legs slightly apart—the high heels gave her body a statuesque look, adding a tantalizing lift to her buttocks. She spoke over her shoulder. "You long for my round plump ass, don't you?"

He did not know what she wanted, so said nothing. "You long for it, don't you?" She said again with a raised voice.

"Yes, yes, I do long for it. Please." He felt giddy, worshipful. Yes, yes, he'd worship at the altar of Angie's ass. It'd be his new religion.

She sat facing him, astride his abdomen like a rider on a horse; then gripping his torso firmly with her thighs, she inched her way forward. "Move those pillows out of the way," she directed, and chuckled at his prompt compliance. She then sat on his face, covering his mouth and chin, applying her 'thigh vise' this time to the sides of his head. Staring up with scared and excited eyes, he saw her body, her belly, her breasts, especially her breasts with their large pink nipples, as magnified and magnificent things. She's humming something, he realized, not surprised his flesh-pressed ears couldn't make out the song.

Angie raised up on her knees and turned around so that her backside was above his face. "Are you ready for what happens next?" she asked ominously. "That's what you came back for, isn't it?" She's making me eat my words, and more than that, he thought.

Hands on his ribcage, she slowly lowered her ass toward John's face. She stopped at a strategic point above his eyes and purred: "Enjoy the view? Isn't it the most beautiful sight you've ever seen?" He said yes to her, oh, oh, I'm going under to himself, and she descended onto his face. She raised and lowered herself on him almost tenderly, as if she were riding a wave, and he thought groggily how deliciously supple her ass was.

Angie sat firmly on him, "cheek to cheek, so to speak," she tittered, and praised him for being such a comfortable seat. "Now for my poem," she said primly. "Please pay attention, Johnny.

> To forgive their lovers,
> Some women take them in their arms.
> Me? I have a different way.
> I smother them with my charms."

She picked up one of his hands and traced her finger in his palm. His body remained still, its only active part his throbbing, upright organ. "Surrender to me," she said. "Admit you've been beaten."

He nodded beneath her, and she laughed. "Not so fast, Johnny boy," she said, pinching his fingers. "You hafta say a special word. Now that shouldn't be hard, should it?"

What's she got in store for me, he worried. She continued in a meditative vein. "What do you boys say when you've lost a fight? Uncle, right? Well, I want you to say auntie." He did not respond, temporarily resisting this humiliation.

Angie pressed down a bit harder. "Now don't be a bad boy again, because I'll sit here all night."

A long deflating sigh came from him. Yes, he was thinking, you are a witch, and yes, that's what I want you to be, my witch. And yes, despite the pain of it, I love having your flesh on my face, love getting helplessly lost in it, love the taste, feel and smell of it. "Auntie," he tried to say, but the sound was muffled by her buttocks. She raised herself and he quickly repeated, "Auntie," before being smothered by her charms again.

She leaned forward and ran her hands over his torso, chatting with a seemingly idle, thoughtless air. "Your physique has such fine, what's the word, definition…. all that basketball you play must keep you trim. Guess I'd hafta say you're the best-looking specimen of a so-called man I've ever had the pleasure of queening."

At her reference to past conquests, he groaned loudly and raised his head and shoulders. She sat back on his face, grabbed his wrist, and stretched his fingers backwards. For a moment, they stalemated. "Ouch," he said, "you're hurting me." She did not relent. "You've already cried auntie," she said with a steely voice. "No fair going back on your word."

She continued bending his fingers and he could hold out no longer. Surrendering again, he said, "Auntie"; his head fell back on the bed with a soft thud. "Admit I've tamed you, Johnny," she said. "You must also agree never to leave me again." It was like she was ticking things off her fingers. "And you have to accept *my past*. That, I guess, turns out to be tonight's main lesson."

"Last night was the payback, huh?" John said to Angie in his kitchen on the following morning. "Just like you warned me."

"Only gave you what you had coming," she said lightly.

Guess that's true, he thought, but her sexual mastery rankled him.

Clad only in John's blue terry cloth bathrobe, Angie sat on the formica counter top covering the dishwasher and clothes dryer while John, in his loose red cotton pajamas, stood cooking at the stove. He was making a dish from his limited breakfast repertoire, scrambled eggs mixed with cream cheese which, when he got it right, was best eaten not by chewing, but by letting the spoonfuls rest on the tongue, then slip smoothly down the throat.

"The coming," he said, changing the meaning of her words, "that part I liked."

"It was fun for me too…. Besides I didn't wanna be too rough on you." If she were standing next to him, she would have pinched his cheek.

He shook his head as he mixed the eggs, then attempted a glare, and she winked. He felt provoked by her smugness, and safe from succumbing to her wiles so soon again. "Don't think you can subdue me that easily next time, sweetheart. There's my dignity to restore, you know."

Angie hopped down from her perch on the counter. She held the bathrobe's lapels and stretched out her hands, uncovering her naked body. She raised a leg on the ball of her foot and bent her knee in his direction, posing like a magazine pinup. The surprise attack began to work its effect. He gazed at her flesh, her stately, tapered form, her round pink nipples that lured and commanded him. Oh, shit, he thought. His knees sagged.

"Crumble, slave," she snarled playfully, "before your mistress." Tilting her head, she stared into his eyes, opened her mouth and rolled her tongue around her moist lips.

The weakness in him spread. Did a whimpering noise escape from his lips? Then Angie quickly closed the robe around her, jumped back on the counter, and gazed at him with innocent eyes. "Not to worry, Johnny, about your dignity or anything else." She crossed her legs and swung her foot, the back of it thumping the dishwasher.

He ran his hands down his torso and patted his thighs, trying to settle his roused libido and his ruffled nerves. "Thanks for putting the genie back in the bottle."

"No problem," she said with a shrug. "Enough is enough, right?"

"Yeah…. now get dressed please," he said. She left laughing, and he returned to making breakfast. He pondered the tremendous and elegant power and pulchritude of women, how Angie possessed and expressed them, how he'd be smart not to tangle with them again. Another lesson learned.

Angie gabbed happily over breakfast. The family and friends in Bensonhurst—her mother, his mother, Frank, Donnie, Whiney—were all "positively elated" about their renewed relationship. Whiney, he thought, I knew something was missing. Why didn't he call me during the breakup?

Angie rambled on about how John was, though not in a heavy way, kind of a mama's boy—and incidentally, that was a sign, along with being a devout Catholic in one's youth, that he'd go for dominant-woman sex. He said with some embarrassment that he'd plead guilty to that, but he didn't really see himself as a mama's boy, much as he loved his mother. Angie, surprised, told how when they were kids, she thought John's father saw him as, well, strange; how when she was over his house sometimes, she'd see the old man look at him with puzzled eyes and furrowed brow…. like he was trying to sort out just what forces produced you; you were so, well, sweet and intellectual, read books and were a serious—I mean serious—altar boy; it was a good thing you had a sports thing going, though, again, I don't think your old man understood your, I guess, pure approach to it, how you were so intense about it all—the practices, the responsibility to the school—all that was outside his purview, so to speak, beyond Bensonhurst. That's it Johnny, she wrapped up, you were more American than the rest of us, and more innocent, a strange mix.

You've thought a lot about us Rosarios, haven't you, he said self-consciously. Of course I have, you knucklehead, she came back. You were like part of my family and what happened to you—to you, Johnny, especially—would directly affect my life. Knew that like I knew blood flowed in my veins and skin covered my flesh.

He encouraged her to continue.

Where was I? Oh, yeah, your old man, he understood you were different, but not who you were or how you got to be whoever it was you were. I mean, he adored you, loved you totally, but it was, like, you weren't his, or certainly couldn't be for long, you weren't of his world. That was Frank, Frankie was his boy, maybe not as sharp and cool as the old man would've liked, but Frankie was his boy.

John wondered whether the opposite of Angie's theory was true, that Frank's being a papa's boy and halfhearted Catholic at best meant he had no predilection for dominant-woman sex. Maybe Angie the Librarian, or any similar exhibition of her powers, did *not* make an appearance during their long-ago affair. That's some kind of consolation, that we didn't share that part of her.

Speaking of Frank, he heard her say, you should give him a call.

"Yes, sweetheart, I will. Any day now."

"I mean it, Johnny. He was so low-down because of our split-up, guilty he caused it all. Besides, by calling him you'll show you've overcome your problems with jealousy, insecure male feelings and that shit."

He laughed. "Impressive, the different roles you play. Last night you did Madonna on a sexual spree. This morning you analyze my family and person like some kind of seasoned psychoanalyst."

"Interesting you say that," she mused. "Guess this is as good a time as any to tell you. I was in therapy once. Until quite recently in fact."

"That's impossible," John blurted. The unexpected strikes again, he thought. Sometimes revealing ways we're different, this time ways we're similar.

"Why?"

"Because you never mentioned it."

"I was embarrassed about it. You're actually the first person I've told."

"Embarrassed to tell me? Most of my friends have been in therapy…. I went for a while, during my divorce."

She gazed with concern at his still startled face. "You're alright about this, aren't you?"

"Yeah, sure," he said, annoyed at her solicitous tone. "But you are full of surprises."

"And you don't like surprises about my past."

"This is different."

"You gonna throw me out again?" she teased.

"This is different."

"Guess we see eye to eye on that," she said, persuaded the danger point, if there had really been one, was passed.

After a pause, he asked, "Did it help?"

"What?"

"Therapy. Did it help?"

❦   ❦   ❦

Riverside Park, Manhattan's west side boundary, stretches along the grey expanse of the Hudson River. John and Angie walked arm-in-arm on the promenade above the water, contentedly observing the thickly rolled clouds crawling across the sky.

Angie talked about the benefits of seeing a therapist regularly—she'd go every Tuesday right after work, enabling her to get home or wherever she had to be later without arousing suspicions. She valued the talking, ventilating if you will, and hearing back an informed response, a sympathetic voice. Then she'd go over it afterwards on her own and cover the same ground the next sessions until things became clearer, you know, more manageable and her understanding deepened.

They passed two couples pushing their toddlers, one squealing, one sleeping, in elaborate, silver chromed strollers. "Probably cost more than what people used to pay for cars," John joked.

Therapy, she told him, helped her get past and through Dominic and over Frank. She had valued herself virtually all her life on the basis of her relationships with men. She realized she was always a man's woman, knew automatically, intuitively how to win men over, it was like rolling off a log for her, she could get it done without being like her mother, a docile woman who knew her place. Her independence from her mom was a good thing, but her actions to gain men's favor were definitely *not* always a good thing. She learned that she didn't have to be Dominic's girl, she didn't have to be Frank's girl, and, probably most importantly and at the root of her problem, she didn't have to be her Daddy's girl, her old man being the resplendent and charming Eddie the Head Capobella, and what little girl from Bensonhurst wouldn't want to occupy a prime place in his heart.

John and Angie sat on a wooden bench. He leaned forward, elbows on his thighs, and turned to her. "You could finally be your own girl." She smiled, placed her head on his shoulder.

Several silent moments passed. "My therapist's name is Janet Kuerer," Angie said, sounding proud, like a teacher's pet happy with the status. They got up, climbed winding steps to a higher level in the park, and sat again on a bench, far back from a short stonewall overlooking the Hudson.

"Cure—a?"

"Yeah, like a person who cures or heals," she said. "Only it's spelled K-U-E-R-E-R."

"Fits her profession." He tugged at his ear lobe.

Two dogs ran around the patch of grass in front of them. The smaller one, a black, long-haired dachshund, chased the larger animal, dark brown, looked like a mix between a shepherd and setter. The big dog turned at the edge of the grass, sat, and shook his paw, attempting to fend off the yelping pest.

"I stopped going about a year ago, but I told her about you before we met again. Wanna know what she thinks of you?"

"Sure," he said despite his doubts.

"She thought you were probably a good man, understood why I was so damn stuck on you, but felt you had your faults. You were likely a self-righteous guy, self-involved too." Angie spoke rapidly, eager to impart assessments she obviously shared. "And maybe you were not always aware of things. You could hurt people without knowing it."

"Intriguing." John rubbed his cheek as if it felt sore.

"You hurt me, Johnny," she said. "That's why I hurt you last night. I pleased you too, but I also wanted to demean you."

"I know," he said.

"It helped me to, like, get it out of my system, but I still have anger in me."

"I know." He kissed her softly on the cheek.

"So beware," she said. "And be good to me."

"Definitely," he promised. He understood her threat and her appeal.

They walked up the hilly path out of the park, the full round sun descending in the sky behind their backs. The pollution in the air mixed with the sky's declining light to produce the purple shadows of an urban twilight.

Angie recalled starting therapy around the time she told Donnie the truth. He was thirteen years old. The boy began acting out at school and sullen at home, behavior that continued more or less, off and on, till his junior year in high school when his basketball game reached another level and he started working at the restaurant part-time. Though, she added, she knew from talking to both of them, Frank and Donnie never broached the father/son business.

They reached the city sidewalks and walked quickly towards his apartment. They shivered slightly from the early evening chill, the unwelcome successor to the day's Indian summer warmth.

"I know why Frankie did the picnic in the playground," John said. Angie nodded. He went on. "It wasn't just a favor, a gesture. It was a blood thing. For Donnie." They slowed their steps. "Stupid," John said. He slapped the side of his head, spoke with an aha! tone in his voice. "Now I get why after all those years of saying no, he's ready to leave Brooklyn. He's been mysterious with me, saying his reasons for staying were personal."

"Why?" Angie asked, stopping him so she could look into his eyes.

Because I'm on the scene," John said, finger pointed at himself. "Taking care of you and the boy. Figures you're in good hands, so he can make his goodbye."

"Sounds like Frankie to me," Angie said.

☙   ☙   ☙

Memories occupied John on the Sunday night he drove home after dropping Angie off in Brooklyn. The van offered solitude—though the evening temperatures were mild, he closed the windows to keep out the highway's noise.

Yankee was his childhood dog, a little, light brown cocker spaniel with short legs, floppy ears, and sad eyes. Why'd he think of her? Maybe it was the dogs they'd seen in Riverside Park.

They named her Yankee, but she was Marie Rosario's dog. They'd come home from a dinner or movie and the dog would greet them at the door with excited shakes and turns, all meant for Marie. Yankee made a stutter step or two in the boys' direction, but quickly turned to dance at the feet of their mother who bent over and poured out baby talk like Ella Fitzgerald scat-singing.

Their father didn't care, but the boys resented the dog's preference for their mother. Once they walked through the apartment switching off cradling her in their arms and whispering loudly in her ears didn't she know, dogs are supposed to be MAN'S best friend.

The old man raised his eyes from his newspaper and smiled. Marie shook her head and said, "My, my, you two boys are pathetic."

The van clung smoothly to the road as the Belt Parkway snaked around the edges of Brooklyn's modest shoreline. In the darkening night, John glimpsed the dim lights of the Fort Hamilton playgrounds, the only basketball court along the parkway, at least between Bensonhurst and the Battery Tunnel leading into Manhattan. He played there just once as a boy.

An autumn Sunday morning, his senior year in high school, he was getting dressed for mass, and Frank came into the room to ask a favor. He wanted John to join him in a game of basketball later that day, "maybe, actually, a coupla games" at Fort Hamilton playgrounds where local boys, including some hoodlum pretenders from surrounding neighborhoods, tried their hand "at the hoops."

Frank's game was baseball—he was a clumsy basketball player, hardly even a fan of the sport. "Why the sudden interest?" John asked.

"Like to do a few things here at once," Frank said. "One, play ball with my kid brother while he's still willing to step on the court with me, and two, spring a little surprise on some low-class ringoleveos who've been getting away with talking big about their game only because they haven't gone up against a real player."

"How come I haven't heard about these guys?"

"You and me don't travel the same circles."

"Guess not. How'd they get on your bad side?"

"Well, some of my boys from around here brought me to check things out last week. Sunday afternoon in the park and these other boys, Dad would probably call 'em salamis, from, you know, the other side of Fourth Ave, Bay Ridge, were there and licked all comers and were boisterous in bringing attention to their winning streak."

"Salamis, eh?" John said. "Real annoying, huh?"

"Extremely."

"And I come in….?"

"If you're half as good as you were last year when Xaverian beat Charminade—remember I saw that game—you'll embarrass these monkeys, I'll win a little moolah, and some deserving assholes will've been brought down a peg or two or three."

The basketball courts were bounded by benches where young men and boys congregated to watch the games and remark and bet on the goings-on. Frank soon joined those on the sidelines—after two games he was puffing heavily. He waved for someone to take his place, staggered to the nearest bench scattering the people blocking his way, and caught his breath.

John sustained more than his fair share of bruises, inflicted by frustrated Bay Ridge boys who could not match either his conditioning or his skills. They could not stop his jump shots, drives, dribbling, and tiny left-handed hookshots off a rebound. He was a dancer amid a gang of oafs. Frank hooted and pointed from his spectator's perch and collected his money.

After several losses, the Bay Ridge boys appointed an enforcer to harass John—a tall, broad, stocky fullback type, who wore a New Utrecht football jersey and short hair-cut and who snickered and cursed at John whenever he hacked him or grabbed his pants belt.

When the goon stepped on his feet, John stopped play, took him aside, and told him that, if there were another foul, there'd be a fight. John turned away and the Bay Ridger gave him a push that sent him sprawling onto the concrete. Frightened and furious, he jumped quickly to his feet and raised his hands. The fear was familiar, he'd felt it before other fights. But the fury, where'd that come from? The sense of betrayal? That the cheap shot from the back crossed a line, violated playground rules. Whatever, he was ready for action.

But he didn't have to take any. A basketball whizzed past his head and struck the face of his tormentor who fell back, putting his hand over his nose. John turned to see his brother standing on the court—Frank had thrown the basketball overhand and hard, as he might pitch a baseball. "Don't fuck with my brother," he shouted.

On the way home in the family car, Frank spoke from behind the wheel. "I was proud of you out there. You showed couragio, as Pop would say." John maintained a glum silence. Frank nudged his brother's shoulder. "Whatsa matter, Bob Cousy? Talk to me."

"You set me up today, Frankie," John said in a louder voice than he intended. "Okay, I knew the deal and got a kick out of showing those chumps a thing or two, but I didn't really understand, um, the dangers involved."

"Hey," Frank said with a defensive laugh, "I was watching out for you, that things didn't go too far. Put some money down for you too."

"Keep my winnings," John snapped. He sat up and leaned against the passenger seat's door. Frank swung the car off the highway. "Where we going?" John asked.

"Benson Avenue, to get that gloppy Sicilian pizza they sell by the carnival."

"I earned the treat, huh, Frankie?"

Twenty minutes later they stood outside Pete's Pizza Palace, less than two short blocks from the shore and parkway. It did a brisk business in the shadows of Bensonhurst's only amusement park, a honky tonk assortment of rides and games—noise, sawdust, lots of greasy fried food and smells of the same, and one gigantic ferris wheel that threatened to touch the sky as it ground round the height of its cycle.

Chomping on their slices, Frank and John gazed up at this great contraption and listened to the riders' screams as it churned and swayed. "You know, Johnny," Frank said, "I wanna apologize for bringing you to Fort Hamilton today. But you were beautiful to watch."

John grinned. "Thanks for stepping in when things got hairy." He felt like putting his arm around Frank, but didn't.

A hefty breeze bringing aromas of the sea beyond the nearby highway blew in their faces. The brothers smiled together. Frank waved his hand. "Got you into the scrape. The least I could do was get you out."

John steered his van through the tunnel and onto the thoroughfares of Manhattan's west side. He could hear in his head Frank's booming voice. "Don't fuck with my brother." It was time to keep his promise to Angie. Tomorrow night after work, he'd call Frank, his big brother, at home.

CHAPTER 14

John was half-dressed when he received the call.

"John," Whiney said simply.

"Whiney, how are you…. what's up?" It's Monday morning, John thought. Why's Whiney calling me now?

"I have bad news."

"Oh no." His mind raced. Had Shirley died?

"It's about Frank." Whiney's voice was flat and solemn.

"Oh shit." Not Frank, John thought. Always there Frank. He felt wobbly on his feet.

"Somebody put the chill on your brother early this morning, in front of his house."

"Somebody what?"

Whiney's words came slowly and clearly—the talking strains him, John realized. "Some guy or guys—it was guys, it had to be at least a two man job—put a coupla bullets into Frankie's head and heart this morning."

"He's dead?" He was choking on his words, on his very breath.

"Yes. Dead," Whiney said.

John felt a pain in his stomach like from a punch and grabbed his midsection. He fell in the easy chair across from the T.V. set. Silent sobs rose up from his gut. Frankie's dead, Frankie's dead, Frankie's dead?

My brain's rattled, he realized in incipient panic. I have to sit still, steady my mind, hold my head and stop the shaking, stop the mental noise. Have to see and hear through the blur. How could this fucking thing happen before I called him? The question burst like a scream inside his head. Before the panic took over, he forced himself to speak. "What happened? What fucking happened?" He heard his uncle's quiet sobbing on the other end of the line.

Both men held their grief at bay while they talked. They could not surrender to it. They had to think, to plan, to handle things.

First, Whiney reported. Gloria, Theresa's closest sister, called him about an hour ago. Gloria, overweight, overbearing, very energetic and competent. It always impressed John that two such loud and domineering people survived intact in the same family. Here they were at menopausal middle age, a loyal, loving and larger than life pair, each of whom scurried to the other's side at any inkling of need. After finding Frank's inert body sprawled on the front stoop, Theresa phoned Gloria who, surveying the scene, contacted the police and Whiney who in turn had his own telephone chats with the cops and Sally Broadway. John's heartbeat quickened at the mention of the old gangster and his estimate of his uncle's resolve increased. *You're making the right moves, Whiney.*

Frank was killed at about 6 o'clock when he left his house for his daily walk on the beach. He was taken down by two shots from a pistol, probably equipped with a silencer because nobody heard a thing, from the look of things and how quickly it all happened, fired by one man sitting in the back seat of a car driven away by another man at the wheel.

"No witnesses?" John asked.

"Right."

"Then how can you be sure about how it was done. I mean the car, rather than by someone on foot, two men, rather than one?"

"All I can tell you, Johnny, is that's how three sets of eyes see it. The detective I spoke to, Sally, and me…. If you're gonna do this thing and do it this fast and this clean and not be seen or heard, that's how you're gonna do it."

"Clean, Whiney? I'm stuck on that. What do you mean, clean?" He stared at the blank T.V. screen. No picture there, no sound, just emptiness.

"This was a neat job. No mess, no gore, no noise. Just small, dark holes, they tell me, one in your brother's forehead, one in his chest. A neat job."

John suppressed a moan.

"A very professional piece of work," Whiney added.

John wondered whether there were clues, suspicions. What did the cops think? What did Sally Broadway have to say? He dreaded that it was a mob hit to stop Frank from leaving town. *Did I fuck up here?*

The police are not officially pointing any fingers, Whiney said, but they figure it was the Mafia making a lesson of Frank's declaration of independence.

Sally denied any involvement and said that whoever wanted to get rid of Frank made it look like a gangland job as a matter of perverse convenience, as a way of diverting attention. We didn't do this, I swear on my mother's grave, Sally said. I don't care how it fucking looks. I'm almost as broken up as you, he claimed. And I'll tell ya another thing, Sally went on, I'll get the word out. We'll find the rotten sonuvabitch who did this and you'll be the first to know when we do.

"You believe him?" John asked. He pictured Sally, bent body at the table in his club's drab back room, the bitter sting of his talk and glance. Has a dark side, but murder like this, so treacherous, brutal? Not likely.

"Can't be sure," Whiney replied, "but I'm leaning that way."

"Then who else?"

"Who knows? The police Frank aggravated by welching on pay-offs, so they saw it, or pissed off political blacks…."

John remembered after the picnic in the park some African Americans of the militant stripe, Simon notably excluded, ripped Frank for his bread and circus act. Was Robeson Turner among them?

"Or maybe it was some dumb wops from the neighborhood," Whiney went on, "who were mad at Frank's stand on behalf of racial harmony?"

"Who would've thought, huh?" John said. "Shit, I want to know…." Images of possible killers banged around his brain like pin-balls. He raised his hand to his head to rub away the pain.

"I know, Johnny. I'm sorry…. this is very hard, but we have to tend to other things now. We can play Sherlock Holmes later."

He felt overwhelmingly sad and tired. "Yeah, first things first."

"The first thing," Whiney said, "is you have to tell your mother."

❧   ❧   ❧

John wandered through his apartment. He stood in front of the photograph of Frank, their father, and him on the white mantlepiece in the living room where all the pictures were. The two brothers were young men—mid to late 20's—the old man about sixty. Standing side by side on a sunny day, they were all smiling—Frank had told a funny story, the one about Fat Tony trying to pick up a girl at Raven Hall Pool in Coney Island. She asks him does he play drums and when he says no, she says, well beat it anyway.

John stared at his brother's smiling face—tears clouding his vision. He tried to conjure life, movements, words from Frank. Johnny, he wanted to hear him

say, could hear him say, tender, familiar, almost off-hand, sometimes beseeching. Like the last time they spoke on the phone. Johnny, he said, please don't
walk away from us again. Or something like that. Oh shit. What a fucked-up
thing. Geez Frank, say Johnny one last time. Please Frankie.

He moved away from the photos and stood in front of the blank white wall
next to the mantlepiece. He pounded it with the sides of his closed fists, groaning with each swing, once, twice, three times, cursing the scumbags who murdered Frank in front of his own house. The force of his blows did not even
crack the thick concrete.

Anger spent, sorrow remaining, he sat at the long wooden table in his dining room. A beloved piece of furniture, like a member of the family. He'd have
to get up soon, tend to business, as Whiney said. He lay his head in his folded
arms on the table and wept.

Angie was the first person he called. She gasped, sobbed, gasped and sobbed
again. She seemed to gulp down her breath. "Don't worry 'bout me, Johnny,"
she finally said. "I'm gonna be okay."

"It's alright, Angie, collapse and weep if you want. No shame in that."

"No, not now. Can't let go." Her fierce resolution to control her feelings baffled him. "It's Donnie," she said, "I hafta tell him. Luckily he hasn't left for
school yet."

After a pause, she accused Sally Broadway of sending two of his ugly thugs
to put an end to Frank. John said that appearances may point to the Brooklyn
capo, but that Whiney had already talked to the old hoodlum and was persuaded for now by his heated denials.

"Whiney was convinced, really? Whatever, whatever," she said. "Gotta go
talk to Donnie."

He interrupted her good-bye. "The thing of it is, Angie, I never got around
to making that call, the one I promised you."

"Damn, so Frank and you never connected?"

"No, the last time we spoke, it was pretty bad between us." John thought
she'd try to, but could not, absolve him of his sin.

"You know, Johnny, Frank knew you loved him, that you'd eventually come
around."

"Kind of you to say, babes."

❧   ❧   ❧

He drove up Bath Avenue toward his old house, Marie's house now, past the mom and pop shops—little cleaning places and candy and grocery stores that weren't much bigger still predominated. He saw three elderly women dressed in black turn up 19th Avenue, going to morning mass at St. Finbar's. Professional widows, caricatures in their own community, old and overweight, defined by the deaths of the men in their lives, incomprehensible to the outside world and uncomprehending of it. Could my mother turn out like that? he asked himself. Nah, he said out loud. She's too self-conscious, too sophisticated. Even as a boy, he was proud of his mother's ways, more modern than most other Bensonhurst women. She'd occasionally watch discussion shows on Channel 13 and read the books his school assigned, so she could keep up her end of the conversation with him. Nah, it was unlikely that even the blow of a son's sudden death would knock her loose from her moorings. Yet he was concerned that a primitive Sicilian urge would overcome her, rout her lady-like, contemporary manners, and transform her into a human relic, a mourning, antediluvian spirit returned to and trapped forever in the old country's ways.

Marie didn't seem surprised when he told her about the shooting and death of Frank. She sat in a big chair in her small living room, head bent, crying softly. Between sobs she recounted a recent dream: Frank, her husband, had appeared at the apartment one morning and warned her not to go out because some crazy man would try to kill her, by running her down with a car. She thought twice about leaving the apartment every morning since that dream, but now she knew what it meant, except that her husband got the victim and the weapon wrong. Still, it was close enough, wasn't it, Johnny? she asked.

"Yes, Mom," he agreed. "It was close enough."

Marie cried for her first-born child for what remained of the morning. She didn't ask about who might have committed the murder, wouldn't accept John's offerings of a drink of water or a tissue, and barely responded to his embraces. She remained beyond his reach, alone in her misery.

Around noon, Louise, Angie's mother, phoned and when he told Marie she didn't have to take the call, she waved him away and spoke to her old friend for a quick moment.

"Louise's coming over," she said, "to keep me company. Angie told her about my dear boy. Sweet Louise."

"Good, mama. That'll help."

"Yes, Johnny…. now excuse me. I hafta wash up and change my clothes."

"Why? You don't have to dress up for Louise. She understands how terrible you feel." Everyone, Whiney, Angie, and now his mother resisted giving way to their grief. It annoyed him.

Marie explained that she was leaving that place of total sorrow not because of any sense of duty, but because if she lingered there much longer, she might never have the strength to come back.

❦   ❦   ❦

"Theresa said you might be there," Gloria said to John over the phone. He was still at his mother's.

"How are you, Gloria?" He was pleased to hear her gruff voice.

"I'm bad, very bad," she responded. "Don't mind telling you I'm not prepared for this. This is a very gruesome thing, what happened here and if my sister Theresa didn't need me to be here for her…."

"This is a very bad day for all of us," he said. "How's Theresa?"

"My sister Theresa's like a rock, but today the rock broke open like an egg you drop on the floor. She's bad, John, very bad." Words of the day, he thought. "Practically tripping over your husband's body on your front steps," she continued, "shot dead by some goddamn animals."

He flinched at the image of Theresa finding Frank, already dead and gone, no chance of parting words. What a cruel, twisted experience—he could see it driving Theresa into a demented state. "What can I do?" he asked. He twirled the telephone cord around his fingers and looked at the pictures on the living room walls: holy men and pastoral scenes.

"The press people and the politicians"—Gloria used these words like they were slurs—"are starting to gather, like vultures, and Theresa said that was your department. They're clogging the phone lines and standing around the house out here packing their cameras like guns I swear. Get them to back off, Theresa says. To stop bothering us."

"Give me a few minutes," he said.

When they spoke again, he told her to record a message on the answering machine which he'd written. He'd drive to Theresa's house and read a similar statement to the press on the lawn. The journalists would disperse and Theresa, Gloria, and whoever else was in the house could leave with a minimum of hassle.

The statement read:

The family of Frank Rosario appreciates the concern and curiosity that the media and others have regarding the shocking circumstances of his death. For now, however, the shooting is a police matter and the family will answer no questions on the subject. We request that no journalists pressure us, that no cameras stalk us, that no politicians contact us. The family of Frank Rosario also requests the space and time it needs to properly mourn, along with his friends, the untimely passing of this good and honorable man.

❦   ❦   ❦

Suzanne gave him the warmest hug he'd gotten from her since their break-up two years ago. He was at the doorway of her apartment, stopping by there Monday night to talk to his sons. He wanted the boys with him during the wake on the next two days and at the funeral on Thursday and the lunch gathering to follow.

"Oh, John, I'm so, so sorry," she said. "This is so awful." She shook her head and her eyes moistened.

He gave her a surprised look. "I always liked your brother," she said. "I could actually converse with him. Besides, you look so…. affected by it."

"It's a nightmare, especially how it happened." They were in the front foyer—with its narrow walls and high ceiling, he felt his words reverberate.

"How's your mother?" she asked.

"Holding up so far, I think. But Theresa, never your favorite person I know, she's on the verge of a crack-up. She found the body."

She raised her hand to her mouth. "How very horrible."

She led him to their children who were eating their evening meal in the small white room off the kitchen. He wondered whether her usual 'those who live by the sword die by the sword' attitude toward his family prevailed in her mind at the moment. Clad in a silky pale green pants suit that rippled as she moved, she looked appealingly elegant. Cool, he thought, she's coolly attractive. In the ying and yang of women's looks, she's the epitome of cool. What's Angie? The height of hot? These momentary distractions ended when he came upon Jake and Teddy wiping their mouths after their last bites of take-home Chinese food.

The whiff of the remaining food's aroma was distasteful to him. His appetite had vanished with the first news of Frank's death and it had not returned. They're just about done eating, he thought, so my timing's good. But what the fuck am I going to say to them?

Jake walked over to John, and embraced him. Teddy followed suit, burying his head in John's shoulder. "We're sorry about Uncle Frank," Jake said with weighty seriousness.

The three males sat down at the table. "There's broccoli and chicken left, Dad," Teddy said. "Want some?"

"Thanks," he replied, "but I'll pass for now." He winked at them. "Might've gone for some pizza, you know how that is, but this stuff, nah."

Suzanne hovered, pacing from the room into the kitchen and back again in the guise of cleaning up and serving dessert for Jake and Teddy and coffee for John. "Joshua Burns called to tell me he just saw you on the television news, Dad," Teddy started. "On Channel One or something. You were reading some kind of statement, basically, he said, telling everybody to chill. You know, to give you all space to mourn. He said you looked pretty used up."

John grimaced. "What does stupid Joshua Burns expect dad to look like when Uncle Frank's been killed?" Jake put in. "That dweeb would cry himself to sleep if his hamster died."

Teddy looked sheepishly at his father. "Forget it," John said.

He plunged in, succinctly telling what had happened to Frank and that though there were suspicions, no one really knew who did the crime. The boys nodded their heads and patted their father on the arm.

"There is one thing," Jake said in a halting voice. "We asked Mom and she said talk to you."

He looked at Suzanne for a clue about what was coming. But her eyes were on Jake. "Go on, son," John said. "Ask."

"Joshua said you called Uncle Frank a good and honorable man and he said the guy on the news kinda sneered and he asked Teddy about it and I know he's a stone jerk, Joshua Burns is, but still it's a good question I think. I mean if Uncle Frank was a gangster and was in the Mafia like they say and did bad things and maybe even had people shot, then how can you call him a good and honorable man?"

The sixty-four thousand fucking dollar question, John thought. And could anyone outside my Bensonhurst family understand my answer?

John shifted his weight from one buttock to the other. His two boys also squirmed uneasily. Suzanne leaned on the window sill across from John, arms folded and gazing at him.

"They referred to him as a gangster on T.V.?" John asked.

Suzanne spoke. "The television newspeople called Frank that even when he saved the day with the picnic in the park last month. They said alleged or reputed, but left no doubt…"

John held up his hand and Suzanne stopped. She sees I'm in pain, he thought, and probably even feels twinges of sympathy. "Can't we have this chat some other time?" he asked. "I mean, my brother's not cold in his coffin and I have to defend his value as a person? Come on."

The two boys sunk in their chairs. They were about to let their father off the hook.

"John, this thing, this gangster Italian thing, is part of you," Suzanne said. "Part of your family and part of the boys too. You've never really talked about it with them, helped them think it through. I think you owe it to them, especially at this particular point in time."

Point in time, particular point in time. Never liked that expression, he thought, its stiff formality bordering on arrogance. Shit, though, she's right.

"Okay," he said.

Everyone breathed more easily. John caught Suzanne's eye and motioned her to sit down in the remaining empty chair.

✿ ✿ ✿

"Yes, your Uncle Frank was in the Mafia," John began. Why the stunned silence? They can't be surprised by the news, maybe just surprised I said it, he realized. "Your grandfather was in the Mafia." What was that sound? My old man turning over in his grave? No, just the wings of autumn pigeons flapping outside the window. "The Rosarios were a Mafia family." Guess I'm a little surprised myself that I've said it. And now what's left to disclose?

Around the table, heads turned, everyone eyed each other, and the silence held. It's like they need time, John thought, to absorb the revelation. "What did they actually do?" Suzanne finally asked. Can't shake the feeling she's trying to help, John thought.

The first thing to understand, he said, choosing his words carefully, was that the Rosarios plied their trade in the least objectionable arenas. Without knowing the details, he guessed his father, uncle, and brother did some loan-sharking, operated book and other gambling ventures, and ran clubs where men relaxed, drank, played cards for money, and did other illegal things. He wondered whether the boys knew that meant prostitution, thought that, unfortunately, they probably did, and moved on.

The men in his family avoided all but the absolutely necessary use of force. Some mob guys were hit men or button men and some were not. Some made lots of money in drug smuggling and dealing and others did not. Some tried to expand their base of power and money and readily killed to do so and others were content to conduct their business within identifiable communities like, say, Bensonhurst. Some used violence and intimidation to coerce welshers to pay their debts to loan-sharks or bookies and others employed gentle arts of persuasion. Some, more and more in fact, were low-lifes, skunks of the earth like the hoods in "Goodfellas", and others were men of respect, who were loyal to family and friends, who followed a code of honor.

"Like the Corleone family in the "Godfather"?" Suzanne asked with a dab of sarcasm.

"Well, like the Brando character at least." John tried not to sound defensive.

Jake and Teddy gazed steadily at their father, nodding. At least my boys seem to accept it, John thought. He flashed on a years ago conversation with Suzanne about his family's affairs and how she dismissed his "Godfather" comparisons as Hollywood hogwash, as convenient rationales for illicit behaviors she was disappointed he didn't condemn. Would there be a similar challenge now?

"What you're saying, John, is that the boys' grandfather and uncle were decent people, though their activities were criminal." There was no hint of irony in Suzanne's voice. "They didn't engage in gratuitous violence, for instance. They profited from what many in society see as harmless vices."

John's eyes lit with gratitude. "That's what I'm saying. Though you said it better."

"What about the point," she continued, "that, unlike you, the first Rosario to go to college, they didn't really have options offering anything like the earning power or control over their lives the mob gave them."

"That, too," John said, thinking: my ex-wife, professor of Mafia sociology. "They didn't choose to become involved with evil, but to rise to the top, or close to it, of the limited world they knew." He realized her game finally, the reason for the switch in attitude. She didn't want her sons, at their tender ages, to feel ashamed of their father's family and past.

John explained that men like his father and brother were often benevolent leaders in the community, settling disputes, finding jobs for people, locating affordable apartments, that kind of thing.

"Cool, Dad," Teddy said.

"Regular saints, your relatives," Jake deadpanned.

"Maybe I'm laying it on thick," John said, "but, remember, they're your family too."

At the elevator, John asked Suzanne, "How d'you think it went?"

"It was good you told them, even if you did put a very positive spin on things." Her tone was condescending.

"With more than a little help from you. What happened, got you in a weak moment?" He grinned.

"Considering everything, a benign view seemed best."

He pressed the elevator button.

"I'll take them shopping tomorrow morning," she said. "They'll need dark suits."

"Shit, didn't think of that. Thanks"

They kissed each other on the cheek and squeezed hands. He stepped into the elevator that would take him down and out of her building.

Frank *was* an honorable man, John mused. No doubt. He didn't belong in the dirty Mafia trade, and now it may have killed him. Can't fucking stand the truth of that.

❦   ❦   ❦

On the way to his car, John window-gazed the shops along Madison Avenue—cluttered ornate antiques; self-conscious and strange paintings; and women's dresses dangling seductively on ceiling hangers. Merchants catering to the wealthy, streets orderly for an city thoughfare and quiet too—tidy and tasteful, like Suzanne. In heart, soul, and bone, she's an east-side girl.

He drove through Central Park under a dark, tranquil sky, the night lamps giving the tree-filled place the romantic look of a vacant movie set. He felt unsettling mood sways, pride in his mother's sad valor, jolting hurt at the thought of bullets thwacking his brother's flesh. They hit Frank's head and heart.

He pictured Frank falling back hard against the front door, the boom of that sound heard by no one, body slowly sliding down, hitting the small concrete stoop, rolling over, face up, arms stretched out, heart and breath failing. What was he thinking? Who the fuck did this to me, or so this is it, how it had to end? About his girls, how their lives'd turn out? The grandkids he'd never see? About his brother, how he missed him the last couple of weeks? No, his last thoughts were about Theresa, John was sure. And about the slam to the heart she'd feel when she opened the door and found him there, shot up, crumpled, dead to her forever.

At home, John called Angie, his day's last act before sleep. They wept—initial attempts at conversation failing—then soothed each other. "Tomorrow'll be better," he said. "Meeting and greeting at Danny George's, going through the rituals, you know, there'll even be a few laughs. How's Donnie, by the way?"

"Not bad," she said with relief. "Maybe we were all lucky, Donnie especially, that Frank never claimed him as his own. He's being cool, detached, like I'm not sure what he's feeling."

"Could be worse, right?" John could make out music in the background. A horn player doing "Embraceable You." A new interest of Donnie's?

"The only problem," Angie said, "was explaining to the school that he was taking off a few days. He took on a tone then. 'Ma,' he said, 'like I can't tell them my father got killed, can I?'"

"And you came up with....?" John got worried. What story could they devise on the quick?

"We told the truth, or at least a fair version of it. The brother of his mother's fiancé died a horrible death and he'd be spending the next few days with his mother and family."

"QED."

After a pause, she asked, "Was it alright what I called you?"

"Did I miss something?"

"I called you my fiancé. Such an affected word," she said with a shudder. "Was I being, well, presumptuous?"

"Not at all." He thought a moment. "That's not right. You were, but if it was your presumption, it was my honor."

"Oh, Johnny," she said, pleased at his gallantry.

CHAPTER 15

Theresa was subdued during most of the wake. She sat or walked with stooped shoulders, supported by members of the family, her complexion pale, her movements unsteady. She asked for a private meeting with Whiney and John, both ready to agree to any requests she made.

In blue pin-striped suits, the two sat waiting in the glass enclosed office of Danny George. They didn't like the room's warm fragrance—it reminded them of the embalming purposes of the place—and stood when Theresa entered, accompanied by Gloria who held her sister's arm and took up a position, sentinel-like, beside Theresa's chair.

Theresa had two requests, both for John, but she wanted Whiney there too. She expected them to share responsibility for solving problems that fell within the masculine province. John felt the sarcasm Theresa had frequently directed toward Frank was now pointed at him.

"I'd like you to do a eulogy for Frank at the funeral, John," Theresa said. "And please make it have weight and beauty…. You're good with words. You can do that."

"Done, Theresa." John turned his palms upward, meaning no problem, a piece of cake. At his mother's behest, he had spoken at his father's funeral, and did well, telling how his father taught him to use an electric shaver and about the seductive appeal of Old Spice; describing the old man's love for pasta, FDR, and the Mills Brothers and the tunes they harmonized. "You rose to the occasion before," Theresa said. "I thought you could repeat the favor for your brother." There was an edge to Theresa's voice.

"What's next on the agenda?" John asked.

"I want you to find Frank's murderers. And I want you to kill them." No longer a shriveled figure, Theresa grew in height while sitting, like a trick carnival snake curling skyward, ominous and deadly, hissing her words too.

Taken aback by Theresa's vehemence, John instinctively shook his head. Thoughts came to him which he could not, dared not share with her. He wanted to avenge his brother's murder, but would be treading unknown turf. Sure, if Frank's killer or killers stood before him and he had a bat in his hand, he'd smash their skulls, but how could *he* make that happen? Besides that's why he left Bensonhurst and the old way of life, that's why his father wanted him out, to avoid getting caught up in reckless macho scenarios. Growing anxiety rolled around in his gut. Shit, he thought, I know Theresa can't make me take this on, but she can make me feel like a piece of garbage.

She leaned forward and pointed her finger at him—the snake was about to bite. "Listen to me, Johnny Rosario," she said, in still sibilant tones, "You walked away from the family and its affairs and they all fell on Frank's shoulders. And still he loved you and he understood you and would defend you…. and where did it get him? This, this, this, foul, ugly dying, on the stoop of his own home, his own home, before he could even…." Theresa's sobs became the only sounds she could make.

He felt miserable and desolate, unable to protect himself from the assault of her words and weeping. He noticed Whiney looking downcast too. Gloria patted Theresa's shoulders and said, "There, there, that's alright, dear." She glowered, especially at John.

Theresa pushed up on the arms of her chair and checked her sobs. "Before he could even see his daughters' grandchildren, before he could even enjoy a new life in a new place."

She was smaller again, terribly sad and no longer ferocious.

John couldn't stop shaking his head. "I'm sorry, Theresa, wish I could give you what you want…."

Gloria cut in bitterly. "You owe Frank, John. You owe Theresa."

"True," he said, "but I cannot pay my debt by stalking Frank's killers. Rough justice is not my way." His tone was angry, frustrated. "Frank would understand, and so would our father. Neither would expect this of me." He looked at Whiney who nodded in agreement.

Theresa spoke in a hoarse whisper. "Time for you to step up, Johnny."

John and Whiney remained silent for several minutes after Theresa and Gloria left.

"You know, I'm tempted," John said. Maybe I *can* do this thing, he thought. Might be better than shouldering the guilt.

"What, to go after Frank's killers?"

"Yeah."

Whiney's voice was determined, almost fierce. "Don't even think about it."

John hung out with Whiney and other 'vecchios', as his uncle called them, venerable gangsters who had achieved a kind of retirement status within the mob, men like Johnny Bathbeach and Joey the Judge DeSanto. They told him what a stand-up guy his father was. His favorite story· The car carrying Frank Rosario Sr. and his colleagues in crime to select gaming tables up in Harlem stalled at a stoplight on the same corner as a notorious nightclub. The automobile's motor coughed loudly two or three times just before conking out, attracting a crowd of sharply dressed black men who either laughed or scowled at the young whites. Frank Sr.'s pals, Whiney and Joey the Judge in their number, turned various shades of green in their fear and embarrassment and wondered what would become of their life and limbs, when Frank opened the door and coolly stepped out of the car. He approached the most fearsome scowler and spoke politely. "I know it's late, but would you tell us where we can get a good cup of coffee around here?"

The upshot was that the Italian men were feted, amid warm guffaws and back slaps, coffee and crumb cake in the back room of the nearby club and the best car man in the neighborhood was brought around to repair the frayed wire connecting the fuel pipe to the carburetor. "Your old man," Joey the Judge said to John, "taught me more that night about race relations than any priest or politician ever did."

Dominic and Fat Tony wore their best simonized suits, rings on many fingers, thumbs sparkling with golden or silver sheen. Still their expressions were dull, uncertain. They stayed at the back of the funeral parlor's large room, sad puppies abandoned by the leader of the pack—at the front Frank was laid out in a closed coffin. John valued these men as never before—they loved Frank purely, fully. He approached them where they stood.

After they exchanged mutual condolences, Dominic said that Sally Broadway's foot soldiers had questioned him about his whereabouts when Frank was shot. He chuckled in disbelief.

"So what d'ya tell them?" Fat Tony asked, meaning to commiserate.

"What d'ya think? Where would any normal person be that early on Monday morning? Told them I was asleep in my bed."

"They got a lotta nerve grilling you," the fat man said.

"I didn't take it that way and I'll tell you fellas why. Sally Broadway's our best hope here. I don't believe he had anything to do with it, no matter what the cops are saying in the papers. And he's pissed off enough to pull out all the stops to solve this thing. Naturally he's gotta check out all possibilities including me as crazy as that seems."

"Why didn't they pay me a visit?" Tony asked. He seemed insulted.

Dominic waved his hand. "Once they ruled me out, they ruled you out too."

"Oh," Fat Tony said. John thought the rotund man did understand.

"Me, frankly," Dominic continued, "I believe it had something to do with the Mollen Commission. They're investigating graft among the cops, ya know, cops with their hands in the cocaine jar, cops taking pay-offs to look the other way when the dope was passed, or dice gamed rolled."

"Yeah, so, what does it have to do with Frank?" John had already guessed the answer.

"Thought you knew. Mollen was pressing Frank to be what they call a cooperative witness. Wanted him to rat on all the cops who played ball nice and cozy, ya know, with the wise guys around here."

"But no matter what Frank thought about the police," John said, "he'd never fink on them." My brother's ethos, he reflected, bequeathed by the old man.

"You know that, I fucking know that, but maybe somebody out there was not so sure…. I told Sally's boys, the Mollen Commission's your best bet."

"And….?"

"They're gonna pursue it," Dominic said. "And Tony and me are gonna nose around a little bit too, aren't we, big guy?" Fat Tony nodded. Dominic slipped into a Jimmy Cagney accent. "If we find those dirty coppers who did Frank in, we're gonna do them in too, slam, bam, no thank you, sam."

❦   ❦   ❦

With no time for tailoring, the new suits their mother bought them—dark brown for Teddy and black for Jake—fit too loosely. John loved even their awkward appearance, was pleased just having them there.

They stood in the rear of the large main room and he pointed out some local customs. People lining up and kneeling before the casket, the placing of mass cards in the claps of metal vises on the golden stands near the coffin, the aromatic and blowsy flower arrangements, the hushed tone muffling every sound. The boys stood stiffly, nodded solemnly at their father's explanations, hardly willing to move or speak, John realized. Probably afraid to embarrass themselves or me.

The boys bent their heads, whispered to each other, Teddy gently poking Jake who finally said, "Any real life gangsters here, Dad?"

John saw Sally Broadway approaching, Minx the Enforcer by his side. "Here comes one now." Jake raised his eyebrows, made gulping sounds. Teddy actually rocked back on his heels. "Steady now, fellas," John said from the side of his mouth. "He puts his pants on one leg at a time like everyone else."

Sally smiled warmly and shook the boys' hands—they managed to hold their grips and to mumble that it was good to meet him too. Sally said he was pleased to see the Rosario male line continue, then asked John to step outside for a little chat. John pointed his still shaky sons in the direction of Whiney and Marie—he was counting on their soothing effect. He joined the old capo on the sidewalk in front of the funeral parlor.

"Seem like nice boys," Sally said.

"Thanks, they are," John said. "You're looking good." He was commenting on Sally's healthier appearance, shoulders more or less upright, color back in his complexion.

"Yeah, time's being kind to me for now." He took out his wallet, flashed a hefty roll of bills, gave one to Minx the Enforcer and directed the obedient bodyguard to a well-known cigar store on nearby 86th street. To John, he said, "Let's walk," and they headed the opposite way.

Sally raised his arm, flicking his thumb over his shoulder. "There he goes, my main man," he said about Minx the Enforcer. "Dumb as Big Julie, you know, from "Guys and Dolls". And as strong. And good at his job. I love the man." He stopped, looked at the ground for no apparent reason, then at John.

"What's more important, he loves me." He's used to command, John realized, to an attentive audience. I won't break with custom.

They resumed walking. "I also loved your old man and your brother," Sally went on, waving his hand expansively as if to say just being on this block, he felt more in touch with them. "Didn't always see eye to eye, but always respected each other. They were unusual men."

"Share your assessment about that," John put in. He felt awkward in the old capo's presence and annoyed about it.

"Wasn't sure about you," Sally continued. Walked away from la famiglia and all that. But when you shoved Minx the Enforcer that time…." he shook his head. "Saw you in a new light."

They passed two men, small in stature, wearing baggy suits and hats too big for their heads. "Buona Sera," Sally said. Going to Danny George's, John figured.

They stopped again, faced one another. Sally put a hand on John's shoulder. "Anything I can do, John. Fucking anything. Don't worry about the cosa nostra side of things—Dominic and I got that in hand. And I'll find the son of a bitch bastard that ambushed Frankie, on my papa's grave, I swear."

They walked back to Danny George's. The aging godfather asked about the restaurant. For now, John explained, he'd leave it to Theresa and his mother. It'd provide a daily distraction from the loss and pain, a way to heal. Sally promised to update Whiney on his manhunt's progress. "If you wanna learn or report anything," Sally wrapped up, "go through your uncle."

Despite himself, John felt grateful and satisfied, like one of the mob fold. A strange sensation, he reflected, wonder how long it'll last? He chuckled lowly. Probably till the next time I'm with Angie.

John sat with Charles and Harry on the deep red leather chairs Danny George had placed in one corner of his large outer room. They talked eagerly about politics, agreeing Giuliani had built a sizeable lead over Dinkins in the pending mayoral contest. Moderate and conservative whites would unite behind the former prosecutor along with many liberals who saw Dinkins as too soft-headed, not tending to the job of government. And black support for Dinkins was largely lukewarm because he hadn't become their energetic champion while mayor. With their diverse mix of lifestyles and idealogies, Latinos would split their ballots roughly down the middle. When all the shouting and

TV ads stopped, and the numbers were counted, the trends favored the Italian-American candidate.

"Rudy's one of my people," John said in a mock confessional tone, "but I'm not happy about this."

"Rejecting our first black mayor's re-election bid," Harry said. "A sorry legacy."

"Amen," Charles said. He looked sternly at his two companions as if they were to blame.

❧   ❧   ❧

Dominic and Fat Tony strolled past, and John introduced them to his friends. He steered the conversation to sports, a common interest.

"Just being a fan is too frustrating," Dominic said. "That's why I've taken up my own sport, skiing."

"You ski, Dominic?" John did not conceal his surprise.

"Yeah, why not? Gets me outta the city. Keeps my mind offa things. Keeps me in shape." He looked at Fat Tony, and punched him in the arm. "Mainly it gets me away from the big fella over here."

Tony grinned, brushed his friend's hand away. "It's okay with me, baby boy. I hate the snow. It's fucking unnatural. Give me concrete anytime. You couldn't get me on skis for 10 million bucks."

John was pleased to see Charles and Harry smile. Ah, he thought, in the convention that is my personal history, the delegates from Manhattan recognize the entertainment value of the Bensonhurst spokesmen.

Later that evening, as John and Angie sipped wine in her living room, she recounted the origins of Dominic's passion for skiing. "We tried it together years ago, in upstate New York, near the Berkshires. Crazy Dominic wanted to recapture the romance in our marriage, if there had been anything there in the first place. Well, he loved it, got hooked on it and I just got hurt. Twisted my knee trying to avoid some six year old on the beginners' hill." Angie laughed at the memory. "Yeah, Dominic on skis. It's a funny image, I know. Gangster on the slopes."

❧   ❧   ❧

The Reverend Bill Simon sent his condolences in a note, written in florid penmanship, that Charles delivered to John.

∾

"Dear John,

I know you would be graciously receptive if I arrived at the funeral home to pay my respects to your brother and his family. But I considered that the rest of his kin might not be as benevolently disposed, and determined, therefore, that it would be best to express my sympathies in a written message conveyed to you by our mutual friend Mr. Buford. I believe that your brother was a good man, despite some aspects of his reputation and some of his associations and, perhaps, even deeds. I believe, too, that our lives, and the quality of life in this city, are diminished by his death, achieved by such wrenching, violent means. Given the circumstances too often prevalent on the streets of my own community, I know first-hand what it is like to 'lose' a loved one to sudden violence and can readily identify with the emotional havoc such an unwelcome experience wrecks upon friends and blood relatives. I wish only that I could relieve your pain during what must, unavoidably, be a very difficult time. I wish, too, that I could be there with you if only for a short time and that I could personally offer my regards and respects to your brother Frank's mother, wife, and daughters.

Yours in Sorrow,

William Simon"

John could hear the minister's sonorous voice speaking the letter's words. The man was a powerful presence in person or on the page. He asked Charles, "Is Simon close to anyone who was shot or killed?"

"A nephew was murdered and a brother paralyzed in separate shooting incidents."

"Shit, didn't know."

"Some things he keeps in the background."

❦   ❦   ❦

Wearing a fashionable short jacket buttoned to the top and a long, black dress loosely draped on her tall frame, Suzanne arrived at Danny George's on the second night of the wake. Her demeanor was friendly and her charm determined as she greeted people like Theresa and Gloria who, once she'd left John, she did not want to see or be touched by again. She came without Kenneth, mainly for Jake and Teddy, to show that the important people in their lives, though separated, were still responsive to one another in a crisis.

Suzanne embraced Marie with feeling—she was her favorite person in the family. She laughed warmly at Whiney's remarks about first there being Katherine Hepburn, then Audrey Hepburn, and then Suzanne, the loveliest lady of the three.

Angie appeared wearing a straight skirt, dark blue blouse, and short jacket not unlike Suzanne's in color and style. Angie and Suzanne were politely chilly to each other at first, then more cordial—they discovered the common ground of being mothers of moody adolescent boys who loved basketball, music, and girls. Suzanne was sympathetic to Angie because by next September Donnie would leave home for college. Angie told Suzanne not to worry—she was relieved the boy had gotten his act together and could now make plans for moving on.

Afterwards, when most mourners had departed, John and Angie sat alone in the large room where Frank's casket remained in unattended stillness.

"The two of you were so amiable," he said.

"We do have certain mutual interests. Sorry there were no fireworks?"

"Just wondered about the friendliness of it all."

"This is how it is, Johnny," she said. "Unlike me and Dominic, you still like Suzanne, don't you?"

"Uh-huh," he said cautiously.

"So any friend of yours," she said, "is a friend of mine."

He recalled a previous occasion when she espoused a similar principle. It was with Charles long ago, at the pizza parlor, when she welcomed another foreigner to their world.

"Uncle Johnny," called the sad young woman. John stood in the funeral parlor's outer room, checking the names in the guest book. He turned and took two steps toward the girl coming to greet him—Sandy Rosario, small in stature for one of their tribe, her most distinctive features her bushy jet black hair and her full lips. She was Frank's youngest daughter, still tan from her summer in Cape Cod, the family member most like John, a kindred wandering spirit among a rooted, parochial clan. She tried to smile as they embraced, but her face trembled, her body shook, and she broke into sobs, dampening the shoulder of John's suit jacket.

He could not think of words to ease her grief, so he simply held her without speaking for a long time. Later they sat downstairs where the rooms were mainly empty. She talked about studying dance at a state college in Westchester. "My ambition after school is to perform for Ballet Hispanico. It's a modern dance company in the City."

"I knew that, I think." A man and woman John did not recognize came down the stairs. They shared a vague, uncertain look and he pointed them toward the bathrooms.

"They have energy and style," Sandy said. "A Spanish flavor to everything."

"Sounds like a good fit, given your personality and interests." He was trying to be a supportive uncle.

"Yeah," she said, "especially since with a last name like Rosario and my dark complexion, I can pass for a real Latina."

"Your mother will be proud." He smiled, leaned toward her. "Note the tongue planted firmly in cheek."

"I know, I know," she said, "Mommy will be a problem. It's not that she's hostile exactly but she's so, like suspicious of my dream to dance professionally."

"There's no Ballet Italiano dance troupe?" he asked, teasing.

Sandy did not joke back. "I'll have to work hard on her, real hard.... especially with my father gone." She was ambushed suddenly by her own words and thoughts. She sat still and bit her lips, much like her mother might.

He patted her shoulder. "Now your old man, he'd be proud of you without reservation."

"Oh, I know," she muttered. She leaned forward, placed her head on his shoulder again, and dissolved into tears. "Oh Daddy, Daddy, Daddy," she moaned.

To help her shake her grief and to relieve his own anxiety, John asked Sandy to look out for Donnie and his boys. My kids haven't visited Bensonhurst often, so they're like strangers in a strange land, and I can't be with them every moment. And Donnie apparently felt real close to your father, working in the restaurant as he did. "Gotcha," Sandy said.

Later John went looking for his sons and found them with Sandy and Donnie in the same downstairs area where he had sat with his niece, guffawing in controlled volume. He stood in front of them, hands in his pocket, and tried to appear casual, but authoritative. He asked what was going on.

"Here's what happened," Sandy volunteered. "We wanted to find out what things we all liked, whether we had any, you know, shared passions, considering our family ties and all."

Sandy and the boys tittered in unison. John slipped into the spirit of the moment, smiled.

Sandy continued. "First we tried music, but we have different favorites. I like the classy softer stuff, like Freedy Johnston and Richard Thompson, but your boys dig hard things like rap or Hole with, you know, that wild blonde girl, while Donnie here has grown religious about jazz, did you know, Miles Davis and his "Kind of Blue" period, very sad and elegant sounds to hear the boy tell it."

Sandy was on a roll and the three boys, wide-eyed, were enjoying her performance. She discussed films which they disagreed about, then moved onto comedy where they finally found a common bond in their love for Monty Python. When John requested a sample of the troop's genius, Jake and Teddy acted out the *Karate School Fruit Sketch*. The bit ended with Jake pretending to shoot Teddy who pretended to lunge at him with a banana. Teddy crumbled to the floor and Donnie let out a soft whoop at his new friends' antics.

As he mounted the stairs to join the other grown-ups, John felt relieved, pleased. That Donnie and his boys were hitting it off, that Donnie seemed to feel no terrible pain at Frank's death. He's a sweet, smart kid, John mused. With her intense mother love and attention, Angie protected him, insulated him from Frank's rejection, from Dominic's crudeness. Another mama's boy turns out okay.

❦   ❦   ❦

Although grief-stricken, Marie talked like a genial queen with all the people who visited Danny George's. Tears occasionally made their way down her cheek before she patted them away with a tissue, and a companion of the moment took hold of her hand or made another gesture of support.

At times, even in the lushly sedate funeral parlor, Marie smiled, most often at a remark by Whiney who told stories about the two Franks in her life, her departed husband and son. Though he carried off the role with apparent ease, Whiney was hard put to entertain Marie and others he felt responsible for comforting. Frank's death had stunned him, leaving a gap in his soul that no one, not John, not anyone, could fill, a wound that Whiney's rich store of memories could soothe only partially. The childless old man worried about where he'd find the emotional stamina to go on once the wake and related festivities were over.

Marie motioned to John when he entered Danny George's on the wake's last night. He sat next to her and kissed her cheek. "How you doing, Johnny?" she asked.

Marie's tone was pointed, not polite. "Good as could be expected." John said. "What's up?"

"I'm very upset with Theresa," Marie said. "I know it'll be hard to say no to her." John was not surprised that his mother had heard about Theresa's expectations—the topic had to be the talk of the wake. Marie was fearful. "Promise me you won't do anything stupid."

"You can stop worrying, Mom." John's voice was tender. "I know it'd be crazy, risky. I'll let the cops do their job." He chose not to mention Sally Broadway's sidewalk pledge.

"Good. That's settled." Marie patted her son's arm. "I couldn't survive the passing of my two boys. I would die. The blood would drain out of my heart and I know I would die."

Marie grew silent, a soft, sad hum slipping past her lips. John inched closer and made out the notes to a familiar tune, "Take Me Out to the Ballgame." He'd never heard her sing it before. "What are you doing?" he whispered. "Somebody might hear."

"Oops," Marie said with an embarrassed smile. In a slow, careful movement, she raised her hand to her mouth and hushed her own foolish noisemaking. "I was just thinking of Frankie and Yankee. Your brother whistled that song to let the dog know he was about to take her out."

"Funny," John said, "I don't remember it."

"Frankie and Yankee, Yankee and Frankie. Your brother would hold her in his arms like a baby in a cradle. I loved to say their names together. That's why I agreed to the dog's name, not because of baseball...."

Marie drifted into a nostalgic haze, seeing beyond and through John. He squeezed her hands as she talked and silently wished her godspeed on her trip back in time.

"Such a sweet, sweet dog, Yankee was," Marie said. "There was no anger in her. That always struck me.... if another dog barked at her, she'd hold her ground, but not snarl back. I once said this to your brother and Frankie just said, 'Well, mama, that's who Yankee is, she has no anger in her.'" Marie paused and wiped away tears. "There was no anger in my boy either. Not out of any weakness, mind you, but because that's just who he was. You, Johnny, were always a good boy, but you had ansiatas, worries, that you kept from us. You were just more complicated, because that's who *you* are. Frankie, he was simpler. You always knew where he was."

"A stand-up guy, like Pop," John said.

Marie fluttered her hand. Her husband and older son were different—Frankie didn't possess his father's pride and flash. "Without a trace of anger," she said. "I want you to tell them that, when you speak at the funeral. Tell them that about my sweet, sweet boy." Marie's weeping vibrated softly through her body. "My sweet, sweet boy," she moaned. "Figlio di mi cuore, son of my heart." She leaned forward, laid her head against John's chest and allowed him to place his consoling arms around her.

❧   ❧   ❧

Whiney's wife Shirley made an unexpected appearance at the wake. She was the family invalid, the tribe's sole Jewish member, a woman of sympathetic mystery, a reclusive victim of multiple sclerosis. Whiney parked her wheelchair against the wall in the middle of Danny George's main room. The sight of her there spooked more than a few mourners who remembered that the last time they saw her she was sitting in the same spot, at the wake for the recently deceased Frank Rosario Sr. Ironic and fitting that this woman, who was so absent from their lives that many Rosarios considered her as having passed on, would renew her presence at such times. When John approached her later in the evening and, trying to be matter-of-fact, asked, "What are you doing here, lady?" Shirley replied, "It takes the dead to bring me back to life, don't ya' know."

For much of the night, Shirley attracted more attention than the coffin—appropriately so, John figured, since the living dead ought every time to draw more interest than the truly gone. Her illness had worsened—at the elder Rosario's wake she could manage a little lift of her hand to salute her companions, but now her arms lay inertly across the sides of her wheelchair, her hands resting without a flicker of movement on her lap. Shirley could still rotate her head, but she was paralyzed from the neck down.

John rested his forearms on the side of the wheelchair. "What's on your mind, aunt?"

Breathing deeply, her expression turning serious, Shirley spoke in a rapid whisper. "Look, I'm practically spent for the night, so I'll make this short. Two things I hafta say to you. One is that your Uncle Whiney, my Ernie, is on the verge of a deep depression, and I'm scared for him and want you to come 'round the house as much as possible after Frank is buried and you can bring that girlfriend of yours, that Angelina, because, when it comes to females, next to me, I like to think, he's most sweet on her."

John nodded. "Next."

"Next, for all our sakes, including that bigmouth Theresa, I urge you, wish I could forbid you. Don't go after the guys who shot Frank. You could get yourself killed."

"Okay," John said.

"We've had enough macho bullshit in this family over the years," she went on. "Enough blood's been spilt and there's been enough worrying about blood being spilt to last too many lifetimes."

"No argument, aunt," he said.

"That was easier than I thought." She seemed perplexed.

"My mother and your husband paved the way," John said, patting her hand.

One party was not yet heard from, that girlfriend of his, Angelina.

On the night before the funeral, John and Angie sat across from each other in the living room of her house, where they had stood together talking nervously the night of their first date the summer just past. John wasn't sitting normally—he was sprawled on the couch, his back where his butt should be, his legs extended on the floor, knees upright. He looked like a praying mantis—a ramshackle one, with his tie loosened, eyes nearly shut from tiredness, and hair mussed. The pressure to maintain ceremony passed, the energy leaked out of him, and he deflated before her eyes.

"Whatsa matter, big guy?" Angie asked. "You sink any deeper into that couch, I'll hafta count you as one of the cushions."

He sat upright. "Sorry…. I'm just wrung out."

"Don't apologize."

Their sons were upstairs in Donnie's room watching taped re-runs of the Simpsons—another mutual interest. Louise had accompanied Marie to Whiney and Shirley's house.

Angie joined John on the couch. She placed her hand on his thigh and asked for an update on the investigation into Frank's murder.

John said that his old pal, police lieutenant Jack Dorney, had stopped by Danny George's. When Angie wondered why she hadn't seen Dorney there, he explained the cop probably didn't want to be observed hanging out with the likes of them, the notorious Rosario family, and had made a quick exit. Angie made a face—she had little regard for Dorney since their encounter at the precinct after the playground skirmish.

Dorney had promised that, even if Frank had been gunned down by a mafia hitman, the police would put the case on the 'A' list. John doubted it was a mob hit. He said some folks, not usually dumb about such things, thought it might be cops worried about Frank testifying before the Mollen Commission. Dorney raised his eyes toward the ceiling, and said even the most ignorant cops knew an old-time wise guy like Frank would never turn rat.

Dorney swore the police would check out all leads and possible scenarios, including the rumor that black militants of some kind had a hand in it. John thought of Robeson Turner, then dismissed him as a possible suspect. Doesn't compute, he judged. Too base an act.

The homicide detective handling the case was Pat Devlin, one of the best men in the Department, according to Dorney. "I suggested he be in touch first thing after the funeral," the lieutenant said. "I know what a difficult time this must be for all of you, and figured you wouldn't want to be bothered during this period of, you know, your official sorrow."

John recalled thinking at the time that Dorney's last remark sounded phony. Maybe Angie's right. He might just be a smarmy son of a bitch.

"That it?" she asked.

"No," he said. "There's the other white hope, Sally Broadway." Before she could show her displeasure, he held up a hand. "I know when he passes, he won't sit at the right hand of God."

Angie groaned. "He maybe charmed you the other night. Still gives me crawly skin."

"Whiney trusts him too," John went on. "Word's out everywhere, Sally says. If it's a cop or mob guy or just some punk, he says, we'll find him. Only a matter of time."

"Old Sal and Dorney." Angie frowned. "Hate having to depend on them. For all we know, they're the fucking princes of darkness."

"Then there's Dominic and Fat Tony. They're gonna see what they can turn up." Angie put a hand over her mouth, suppressing laughter. But he grinned too. "I thought," he said, "that news would reassure you."

His expression turned woeful again. Angie gently tapped his head with her fingertips. She saw wetness around his eyes and tears form. "What is it, baby?" she said, startled to see him weep.

He shook his head—it was difficult for him to speak.

"Talk to me, Johnny, please."

"I have this great love for Dominic and Tony now," he said with effort, "because they were a part of Frank I hardly knew, a part I discounted. I feel so bad about that." He lowered his head, his body shaking. A dam of sorrow and regret poured out. Angie rested her head on his back and put her arms around him from behind.

"We all feel bad," she murmured.

"No, no, it's not just that. I want to do something"—his voice sounded angry—"I want to hurt the men who killed Frank. I want to hug him too, like I never did in life. Want to tell him I know he died for our sins, that I know he was a good man, that it wasn't fair, not fucking fair that he died too soon, before he could get outta Brooklyn."

He sat back on the couch, not bothering to dry the tears off his face. She kept an arm around him. The boys found them asleep that way in the morning.

John and Angie quickly showered, changed into their second outfits of dark apparel, and stepped onto the porch on the way to Danny George's for the prayer with family and friends over Frank's casket. Funeral mass at the church would follow.

"I was gonna raise this last night," she said, "but...."

"My breakdown intervened. Go ahead. What's up?"

She touched his cheek. "I'm scared for you, Johnny, you wanting to get those men."

"Relax. I'm not chasing anybody."

"Frank wouldn't want it. Taking care of Donnie and me, that's the way to make things up to him."

John sighed. "I'm taking a pass. Already promised my mom, Whiney, and Shirley." The league to keep John Rosario alive, he thought.

"You won't change your mind. Theresa won't be able...."

He interrupted. "Theresa's a heavy, but the rest of you outweigh her."

Relieved, she took his hand and led him off the porch. "There's something else," she said. They paused on the sidewalk. "What you said last night about Frank dying for our sins. I heard Whiney saying the same thing to Shirley when he wheeled her into Danny George's."

✤   ✤   ✤

St. Finbar's was packed with people for the funeral. Statues of saints known and obscure occupied every nook on the ground level of the dark-grey and cavernous old church; ornate stained-glass windows depicting the 14 stations of the cross encircled the higher reaches of its side walls. Perfect setting for sad and ceremonious occasions, John thought, not for the first time in his life.

He realized that sitting in the crowd could be the person or persons responsible for Frank's bloody death. It was a chilling thought, but if it were a gangland shooting, that's the time-honored way wise guys carried it off. They attended the funeral, sent flowers with a brief note of condolences, donated money to the family and kissed the widow's cheek.

The main vocalist for the mass was Caroline Caesar, daughter of Nick Caesar, proprietor of Un Villa Paradiso, principal rival of Rosario's among Bensonhurst restaurants. Caroline had studied voice in Italy, was renowned in the local community for having sung with Pavorotti as a stand-in for some established star of a soprano at a rehearsal for some opera or another. At Theresa's request, Caroline sang "Un Belle Di," from Puccini's *Madame Butterfly*. According to Theresa, it was Frank's favorite opera piece—it was really the only aria Frank cared for.

Caroline sang from the balcony above and behind the wooden pews where the mourners and curious sat. Her singing filled the high-ceilinged church with poignant melody and surprised people with its power and loveliness. They looked up to see where on the walls and pillars of St. Finbar's the loudspeakers were, but found none. The impressive sounds came only from her voice, amplified by the cathedral's natural acoustics. Theresa's pretensions to the high brow worked. The splendid aria evoked a yearning and sense of loss in most of the good people there, and even some of the bad.

✤   ✤   ✤

His voice cracking intermittently, John spoke about his brother, their shared experiences and emotions—three musketeer candy bars and black jack chewing gum were preferred tastes as kids and vanilla egg creams too; their unshakable love for the Yankees and DiMaggio, Mantle, and Mattingly; the pleasure they took in Sinatra's singing; the passion they had for their mother's pasta meals on Thursday nights and Sunday afternoons.

He talked about Frank's good and estimable character; his dutifulness as a son, friend, and brother; despite disappointments in life, his lack of anger or bitterness—in that way he was like a beloved dog at his best: kind, loyal, and tough; his physical and moral courage shown by his judging people mainly by their character and actions and by his bold decision to organize a banquet outdoors in Bensonhurst that, wonder of wonders, brought people together for at least a day.

John ended with a conversation Frank and he had 30 or so years ago when they lived at home and shared a room. Frank was stepping into his manhood, spending more and more nights with a girl he'd been dating for about six months, Theresa Milazzo, who eventually became his wife and mother of his three daughters.

Theresa was sick for about two weeks. It turned out to be just an uncommon strain of the flu, but it was misdiagnosed and treated with medicine that made her sicker, until some smart resident at the hospital where she wound up discovered the error and reversed the prescriptive course. During this period of pain and anxiety, Frank visited Theresa every day, sometimes twice a day.

The brothers were in their room. The older boy sat on a stool and polished his shoes in a distracted fashion. The younger boy sat on his bed and asked questions about the ill girlfriend. Frank described the confusing twists and turns of Theresa's condition and what the doctors were saying, and how he, Frank, was saying things, bringing her things to ease her suffering, to show his affection.

"So," John said in a gently teasing tone, "the tough guy's got a soft spot for this girl."

"No big deal, Johnny," Frank said. "It's the things you do for the ones you love."

When John finished, many people in the church were crying and Theresa's sobs could be heard above the rest. As he stepped down the pulpit, he patted tears off his face with his handkerchief. Maybe, he thought, this will temper my sister-in-laws's rancor.

As Theresa wished, the luncheon following the burial took place at Nick Caesar's restaurant. Hands together, body bowing, Nick greeted family members as they entered, paying special attention to Marie the mother, Theresa the wife and Joanne the oldest daughter. He was heavy-hearted, naturally, but honored they picked his restaurant. He hoped Un Villa Paradiso's food would provide some small comfort during this unhappy time.

Marie virtually ignored Nick while her daughter-in-law seemed flattered by the man's fawning. "He's pouring it on, isn't he?" Angie said sotto vocce to John. "And Theresa's lapping it up."

"Nick Caesar, the showman of solicitude," John commented. He thought: The guy's probably more smug than usual because now he can stand uncontested as *the* godfather of Bensonhurst trattorias.

Whatever Nick's character defects, he ran a superb kitchen. Its delectable dishes were laid out on a horse-shoe arrangement of tables filling the restaurant's long and narrow side room where private parties were held. Amidst smells of garlic and oil, sausage and seafood, the Rosarios and friends enjoyed the pasta plates, spinach and eggplant lasagna with sun-dried tomato sauce and shells stuffed with succulent ricotta cheese soaked in a pesto sauce. Spotted around the tables were smaller specialties of the house: a crabmeat appetizer, a sweet desert of juicy raspberries covered by a thick zabaglione cream.

John stood aside for a moment, took in the scene. Angie and Suzanne chatting again, smiling together at some shared insight; Jake and Teddy, hands in pockets, standing and talking with Marie and Donnie—his boys seemed at ease, growing accustomed to my customs, he thought; Fat Tony gesturing, guffawing with Whiney—is he trying to cheer up the old man? And Sally Broadway conferring with Dominic—are they divying up Frank's Mafia spoils? Well, let them.

The guests talked loudly and laughed hard—that's what they were supposed to do on such occasions. For this brief time, they would forget their terrible loss. They knew in their hearts, as people seasoned to mourning, that later that night, that tomorrow, that for as far as they could see into the future, they would have to work—and it would be very hard work—to accommodate the gaping absence in their lives caused by the death of Frank Rosario.

CHAPTER 16

❀

John was haunted by the gory nature of his brother's death. Worse, the sadness at Frank being gone rarely left. He felt it when he was at his desk alone and needed to touch his brother one last time, at a meeting or restaurant when people were calling names, when someone close to him used a reminiscent phrase or gesture.

John returned to a more or less normal working schedule, but mainly he tended to his family. He called or visited his mother every day, keeping a watchful eye, ready to bolster her at depression's first sign.

Marie welcomed her son's attentions. Her heart broken and bleeding, she felt a numbness, deep and wide. But she did not give up her will to live. Over the first month following Frank's death, she gradually emerged from the darkness in her life to see light in the company of her grandchildren, in the romance between John and Angie, and in her stints at Rosario's where she joined Theresa in preparing the day's menu.

"How'd you say Theresa's doing?" Angie asked during a visit with John. She bit into a simmering sausage Marie placed on her plate.

"Not badly," Marie replied, "considering. Luckily she's got the restaurant. It keeps her going. Me too, for that matter."

"After the funeral, Dominic offered to help," John said. "I asked him to drop by Rosario's. Have you seen him, Mom?"

"He comes around with Fat Tony. Once or twice Donnie was with him. They sit in the back alcove by the kitchen like Frank used to."

"Reliving memories," John said. He chewed on a meatball and relived some of his own.

"Makes himself useful," Marie continued. "Helps Theresa with the accounts and orders, manages the staff a bit. I'll say one thing for Dominic. He learned something, sitting at Frank's elbow all those years."

"And they're getting along, Dominic and Theresa?" John asked.

"Seems so, and when he's not there, Nick Caesar stops in and places himself at Theresa's disposal. Offers advice on this and that, color of the table cloths, what wines to have on hand."

"A regular good samaritan," Angie said.

"A slippery man, if you ask me," Marie said. "Greased from head to toe. I'm happier when Dominic's there. Keeps Nick away."

"Strange business, hah, Mom? Dominic, a welcome presence?" Though irked by Nick Caesar's pseudo courtesies, John was pleased—less pressure on him to turn up a manager to run the place.

"But don't bother about me or Theresa either," Marie said. "It's your Uncle Whiney who's completely miserable. Visits the restaurant, sits down alone and hardly says a thing. No jokes, nothing."

"Sounds like he's lost his twinkle," Angie said with her own twinkle directed at John.

Bet she's got an idea for lifting my uncle's spirits, he thought.

❧   ❧   ❧

John and Angie sat with Whiney in the small living room. Shirley lay in the master bedroom upstairs, having withdrawn again from human contact. Sounds came from the VCR of a shoot 'em up western, a film genre the sick old woman preferred, especially if Barbara Stanwyck had a lead role.

Whiney slumped over on the dark, red couch, resting his elbows on his thighs. He spoke of his youth in clear and colorful detail, and stumbled when the conversation returned to the present. He recalled dates his brother Frank and he had with pretty girls at the Like a Melody Lounge on West 14th Street by the water; the daytime parties at the beach on Coney Island during the depression and the songs harmonized and card tricks played; their dreams for a safe and serene life and the achievements they imagined for their children—Whiney, of course, never having any and now Frankie, Frank's older boy, taken from them probably by one of their own.

Three times Whiney got up to point to an old photograph on the large polished wood table next to the couch, his brother and he standing together in bathing suits, young and invincible in their tanned skins and dimpled smiles.

"That's your father over there," Whiney sighed. "A pair of devils, we were. Had fun.... didn't hurt nobody then."

"I've been thinking," John interrupted. "Pop wasn't prejudiced. Frankie neither. How come?" He wanted to rouse his uncle from his sorrow.

Whiney grinned like a child offered extra dessert. It didn't matter that John and Angie heard this story before. He'd tell them again—it was a temporary lifeline out of his desolation. Hesitating, he struggled to scoop the incident whole and precise out of the haze clouding his memory.

"Whiney?" John said.

"I know," the old man responded. "What was that boy's name? Thought I'd never forget it, how it fit him." Another pause. "Yeah, yeah, it was Ezekiel, and everybody called him Zeke. Zeke, the toughest Jewish kid in the school yard."

Whiney chuckled and smiled throughout the memory play. He used hand and leg gestures to act out the parts. Frank and Whiney Rosario, nine and seven year old brothers, inseparable—eating, playing games, going to school, returning from school together, sleeping in the same room and sometimes the same bed—were collaborators in many forms of mischief. Chief among their crimes was anti-semitism, their community's dishonorable sin. The Rosarios put their own stamp on it, as explained by Frank: "We're not gonna pick on crybaby, eyeglass-wearing Jews. We're going after the tough ones, who could maybe belt us around a little bit if they caught us."

The boys tapped Ezekiel Rabinowitz as their target. Zeke the Rough, Frank dubbed him with a laugh that Whiney could recall as clearly as if his brother were sitting in the room. The action took place in their public school's playground on the Lower East Side. During lunch recess, little Frankie and Whiney inflicted sneak kicks on the butt and limbs of Zeke during a game, say, of ring-a-levio or punch ball, when the older boy's attention was elsewhere. These guerrilla attacks worked for the better part of the fall before Zeke, alert to the coming blitz, snatched Whiney by the belt of his pants as the boy tried to make his getaway. Frank returned to rescue him and pummeled the big, bad captor.

Zeke, God bless him, Whiney said, did not return a blow. He held tightly onto Whiney and eventually seized Frank by his jacket and pushed him away. "Stop all your jumping around," Zeke screamed, shaking both boys.

Recognizing defeat, the Rosario brothers stood still and stared sullenly at the larger, stronger boy.

"What are you crazy kids doing?" Zeke shouted. "Every day almost you come in here and hit me while I'm not looking. Why? What did I ever do to you?"

"Nuthin," Frank, the defiant spokesperson, said. "You ain't done nuthin' to us."

"So why make me an enemy?"

"Because you're Jewish," Frank said. "Because of what you people did to Jesus."

Whiney could still hear the Jewish boy's laugh too, as plainly as one of the car horns that occasionally beeped outside his house. "Did you know that Jesus Christ himself was a Jew?" Zeke asked.

"Can't be," Frank assured his brother as they hurried home, "cause if Christ was a Jew, why do we hate them so much." Whiney nodded his head. How could anybody deny such logic? They were in such a rush to find an adult to discredit Zeke that they passed up their regular afterschool treat in the chilly fall of hot chocolate and cannolli that old Mr. Funiciello, a shopkeeper friend of the family, was pleased to serve them. "The Jew's a liar, no doubt about it," the little brothers swore to each other.

Whiney's story triggered John's memory. On the second or third day of his try-out for Xaverian's basketball team, he was standing to one side under the boards, Charles driving down a clear lane to the hoop when the defender on John moved away to guard him. Charles, eyes averted, dished a pretty little pass to John and John banked the easy shot off the glass into the basket. It was like a gift, a connection, an act of friendship. Charles showed he was a classy and selfless teammate, and no amount of racist images and comments bombarding John in his environment could alter that view. It was like a clear light flashing on the truth, that unexpected no-look pass from Charles, like his father and Whiney's run-in with Zeke.

John started to tell his story, thinking it'd help keep up his uncle's spirits. But the old man slumped over again and covered his face with his hands. "I tell ya' something, Johnny," he said with a clutched sob, "my memories are killing me."

Angie's plan was to buy the old man a dog, a loving pet. John thought it was silly and might even backfire—his uncle already had enough worry and woe in caring for Shirley. They sat in his apartment's living room on a weekend night in October, shortly after their last visit with Whiney and debated the question. Jake and Teddy were sleeping at their mother's, so the house was otherwise empty and John was more interested in lovemaking than arguing. Besides he was on the verge of conceding.

Angie had the details worked out. To drive with John to City Island, off Orchard Beach in the Bronx, to eyeball and purchase one of the tiny hounds raised by a breeder who lived in that funky ocean place, an old woman who one of Angie's co-workers knew well and vouched for. Her name was Rose Mastrangelo, her being Italian lent more weight to Angie's scheme in John's eyes. She specialized in raising and training shih tzus for several months until she could sell these friendly house-broken creatures at sensible prices to lonely old people.

John and Angie sat next to each other, he at the end of the big brown couch, she in a small black leather chair. "You know, Angie the Librarian hasn't been heard from lately," he said, making a poor try at sounding matter of fact.

Angie moved his hand back to his lap. "Why, Johnny, do you feel the need for further instruction?"

"Oh," he said, sitting back. "I thought she bestowed rewards for good behavior, for being cooperative."

"Hmm, I see where you're coming from, and where you'd like to go." She laughed softly, got up from her chair, and led her compliant man into the bedroom.

John spent much of the evening entrapped in a leg scissors. Angie the Librarian squeezed his face between her full-fleshed thighs, so much so that his jaws hurt. Now and then she patted him on the top of his protruding head and pinched his nose. She relaxed and read the book review section of the Sunday paper, opening her thighs from time to time so he could gasp for breath before firmly embracing him again.

She sang lowly, *My baby calls me when he wants to sado* (pronounced say-dough). An old Mott the Hoople song he forgot he taught her. A little joke on me, he thought.

John followed Angie's bidding the next day. He took the trip to Rose Mastrangelo's City Island pet hideaway and joined in the choosing of a small grey and white female puppy. The instrument of my uncle's hoped-for revival, he reflected as he carried the sweet, furry thing to the van.... and a contributor to no small amount of merriment for me and my girl last night.

❧   ❧   ❧

Charles called John early the following Monday and said they had to talk. They met for a quick lunch at the Sunburst Espresso Bar, a new coffee and sandwich place a few blocks north of John's office, on Third Avenue in the Gramercy Park section of town. They sat in a quiet corner at the window counter, watching the people and automobiles go by.

"You're looking very dapper," John said. Charles's handsome felt hat was nothing new, but not so typical was the dark blue and unrumpled suit, light blue shirt with white collar, and subdued red tie sprinkled with dots of blue.

"Thank you, I think," Charles replied. "I'm doing more work for the Dinkins campaign and have to dress the part." He sipped his cream of spinach soup. "Rev. Simon and I talked it over and decided it was important to help get David elected, despite his ah, imperfections, as Bill might say."

Calling them David and Bill now, John noted.

"I've had fun with it," Charles went on. "Been on some Sunday morning shows explaining the merits of the city's community relations program."

"Missed that." John was sorry about it too, not being able to see his friend perform.

"Well, you've been preoccupied," Charles said.

Outside, an old black woman begged from passersby, wishing a nice day to everyone, including the many who ignored her.

"This may be a painful subject," Charles said, "so don't feel you have to answer. I'll understand completely. But I'm curious: Any clues turning up about Frank's killers?"

John saw his friend's tense expression and realized they had come to the reason Charles wanted to see him ASAP. He finished his sandwich. "Don't mind talking about it, not with you. But I don't have much to report. There are no leads pointing anywhere."

"They still have no idea?"

"Nothing anybody's telling me. My high school pal Dorney says they've uncovered no evidence. So does a Captain Pat Devlin, the lead cop on the case, who at least has the courtesy to call me once in a while with an update."

"Polite police," Charles said with a whistle. "Don't knock it."

"I'm not, but how about producing something, a trail heading somewhere, a theory about the who and why of it?"

"What do your friends of the family have to say?" Charles was like a lawyer wanting to learn the cards his adversary holds before showing his own hand.

John answered in his best casual tone. "Just saw my uncle, stopped off at his place to deliver a dog yesterday in fact. Angie's idea—the animal is supposed to get Whiney back in touch with the positive side of life." The two men shook their heads in shared skepticism. "Whiney talks regularly to Sally Broadway who's giving up nothing yet. Sally's still upset about Frank, but Whiney points out that Sally's also upset about racism in contemporary theater, just look at the recent productions of "Showboat" and the "Merchant of Venice"."

"Quite a character, that Sally."

"Fair to say. You going to tell me why you're asking these questions?"

"I was coming to that." Charles hesitated, swallowed more of his soup. "We have a clue to pass on to you which we haven't told the police or anybody else yet—figure the word'll get to them sooner rather than later anyway."

John tapped his fingers on the counter and jiggled the ball of his foot on the metal bar running along the floor. "Out with it, Charles. What's up?" Nerves in the belly, John thought. Been a while since I felt them.

"Last night Bill Simon met with some of his radical friends who are pissed off about his support for Dinkins. They fear Bill's going soft and want to pressure him into more of a protest from the sidelines mode."

John shrugged. "A fair debate, right, as far as it goes?"

"But last night it went further than that. Tempers frayed, heated words were spoken." Charles paused—the sudden silence seeming like dead air on the radio to John. "By Robeson Turner, your old friend."

John rubbed his neck back and around, like that's where the ache associated with Robeson Turner bothered him most. He remembered the Bensonhurst shooting, their troubling chance meeting at his son's camp. The man's a fucking irritant, he thought. Worse, a dark specter that shows up periodically to disturb, in good times and bad. None of which he said. "How come I'm not surprised," was his response.

"Well, what might surprise you is that brother Turner's a former mentee of the good reverend. Also one of his severest critics whenever he strays from the militant fold. And last night, when it became clear that Simon was sticking to his moderate course, he issued a threat and walked out of the meeting with a homeboy or two in tow."

"The threat being?"

"Something along the lines of 'Remember what happened to your honky pal Frank Rosario? A similar fate could await you, my dear reverend.'"

"Shit," John said. A few moments passed. "Honky pal?" he asked. "Do people still talk that way?" Much as I revere the sixties, he thought, some of its customs should stay buried.

"Robeson Turner does."

John and Charles dropped coins in the hands of the old woman beggar and parted company, each preoccupied. Charles, about the inevitable media coverage of Robeson Turner's remarks and the damage to the Dinkins campaign. John, about whether Turner could be the guilty party. Did he kill not for this or any political reason, but for some snafu around the drug dealing thing? Did Dominic reneg and Turner go off about that and pop Frankie? Not likely, John thought. Too far-fetched for me, for now.

As he walked back to his office, he considered telling Charles about the guerrilla attack on Dominic's car. He opted against it, figuring we never determined that the man was responsible and if he was, it was almost evidence against concluding he could draw the final curtain on Frank or anybody else.

He stood in front of Jeanette's desk reading his phone messages. He was eager to see whether word had leaked out about the Bill Simon/Robeson Turner exchange.

"What happened at lunch?" Jeanette asked. "You have that pale, cold look you get before Finance Committee meetings." She spoke lightly, hoping to draw a smile from him. John ignored her. He found a message from Marilyn Diaz, a young, energetic *New York Newsday* reporter whom he had worked with when she was covering City Hall, before she moved to the guts and gore of the paper's police beat. She was the first person to inform him of Simon's plans to march on Bensonhurst last summer.

"Damn," he said, more to the world than to Jeanette, slamming the fist of one hand into the palm of the other. "The shit's about to hit the fan."

❦   ❦   ❦

Marilyn Diaz was one of a handful of smart and persistent reporters that *New York Newsday* hired to burnish its local coverage. Pretty, dark-haired, with a penchant for dark clothes and dramatic affect in her talk and gestures, Marilyn wore her Latin ethnicity proudly, and sometimes loudly, and had integrated it seamlessly into the presentation of her self. Even if she wasn't in the habit of quoting him on budget stories when she covered City Hall, John would have found Marilyn Diaz immensely appealing. Jeanette adored her and always pressed John to respond to her phone messages first. "The Rosie Perez of the newsworld," Jeanette dubbed her. John returned her call.

"So, Rosario," she said, her tone friendly, but peremptory, "have you heard the rumor about Robeson Turner's confrontation with Bill Simon? Is it true? And if so, what'd you make of it?"

"How come you're the only reporter who's called me on this?"

"Because," she shot back, "I'm a damn good news hound and because my blood brothers at police headquarters tend to favor all the cute Spanish girls on the beat with the best news leaks." John could picture Marilyn's wink. "But you better get ready, my friend," she continued, "because others will pick up the scent, I'm sure, and bother you soon."

"I'm not happy about this," he said.

"I'm sorry, John, that you're in the middle of this story and that your brother bought the farm the way he did." She spoke honestly, yet hastily. "But *this is a story*, maybe a big one, and I want a scoop if you can help me. So how about it? What can you tell me?"

"Not to be so fucking blunt, for starters." Stung, he wanted to sting back.

"Ouch," she responded. "Said I'm sorry. I really am, Rosario."

"Okay," he relented. Still he held back, counting several beats in his head before speaking. "It's true."

"Wow," Marilyn said, breathless for a moment. "Turner really told Simon if he stayed in the mayor's camp, he better watch his back because what happened to Frank Rosario could happen to him?" She seemed shocked, upset and John mused in a passing way that reporters are not a entirely cynical lot.

"Something like that," he said.

"Robeson Turner must be one crazy sucker, a one man bomb squad blowing up the Dinkins campaign."

"Still doesn't mean he murdered my brother." John's tone was matter of fact.

"Then what does it mean?" Marilyn said sharply. "Why say something like that?"

"Don't know. Maybe he was just trying to scare the preacher."

"Too pointed, man," Marilyn said. "He just pushed himself to the head of the line. The main suspect now."

"The only suspect." John looked out the window in his office. Clouds covered the sun, turning the day's bright light grey. Just like his mood.

"Like I said, I'm sorry, but I gotta jump on this and put something together by deadline." She paused. "Tell you what. If I come up with anything on Turner or on anything else, I'll call you right away. My promise, John."

"Before you hang up, let me ask you something. You know cops right, their thinking, their behavior?" He trusted her and thought she might favor him with an insider's wisdom.

She shook off her impatience, as a dog might dry off her fur after a walk in the rain. He could practically hear her shudder on the other end of the line. "What's your question?"

"Could the cops be the culprits here? In my brother's death?"

"Why think that? Where's the motive?"

"Fear of his testimony, in the open or behind closed doors, at the Mollen Commission."

"You're reaching," she said. "Word on the street is your brother was an old-fashioned capo, lived by the code. Even the jerks in blue would understand that Frank Rosario, with his pedigree, would never flip."

"But maybe one of them got drunk…." he persisted.

"And," Marilyn said, "in an inebriated state, drove out to Neponsit at 6 o'clock in the morning and pulled off a virtually perfect hit. No way, John, the whole job was too neat, well-planned to fit that theory. In fact, it was too well-done and planned for most cops I know to even have thought of it."

"Okay," he said, impressed but not entirely convinced.

"Listen, Rosario," Marilyn adopted the scolding tone of a teacher fond of the student she's trying to set straight. "I mostly share your sympathies about social injustice, but based on all I've seen and heard, Robeson Turner is the more likely perpetrator here than some mentally deficient rogue cop. Maybe I'm stepping over a line, but I like you so I'll take the chance. My advice is don't let your politics cloud your thinking."

John did not know whether it was his politics, emotional denseness, or some other personal inadequacy beclouding his mind, but he could not fully embrace the proposition that Robeson Turner 'did it'. He didn't like the man and didn't dismiss the theory. But it did not have the clear, sharp snap of truth he expected to feel if and when the killer or killers were revealed. That's what was missing—that bracing sense of certainty.

Other reporters called him that afternoon, from *The New York Times*, the *Daily News*, and the *Associated Press*, from *WCBS All-News Radio* and a local T.V. station—he gave them all a terse "no comment." Other than his favor to Marilyn, he'd do nothing to feed the media. Maybe without much to chomp on, they'd move on to other matters—a lame hope, but one he entertained.

He made a few calls of his own: one to Whiney who agreed Robeson Turner's remarks didn't necessarily mean the man was culpable, though he had no other explanation. Whiney promised to talk to Sally Broadway to see what the mobster's sources could turn up on the black militant. The dog Twinkle—Angie's name for her which Whiney accepted—was yelping in the background. "Gotta see to my new pet," Whiney said. "But stay in touch, Johnny, and stay outta this. Let's just see what unfolds."

Angie and Marie could both see Robeson Turner as the killer.

"Sure he might be the one," Angie said. "In my book, he's a degenerate bastard just for saying such a thing. If he's the guy, I hope they nail him and jail him fast." She had far less patience than he for the offensive conduct of radical African-Americans.

Marie was more philosophical. "It'd be painful, wouldn't it, if it was a colored man." It still bothered John when his mother called black people 'colored.' But he didn't correct her—she used the language she grew up with and meant no harm. "I want them to catch the man and put him away," she went on, "but it'd make me sad if it was a colored man."

The women were united on one issue. "Whatever the case may be, Johnny," Angie said, "you don't hafta get to the truth of it. Just let the cops handle it."

"And what am I supposed to do?" He was miffed that everyone was so protective, so sure he couldn't handle an encounter with the menacing likes of Robeson Turner.

"You're supposed to go to work everyday," Angie snapped, "take care of your kids, be a good son to your still grieving mother, and a faithful, living and breathing lover to me. We don't need two dead Rosarios in the same fucking season."

"Okay, okay, doll," he said, backing off. "Case closed."

"We don't need you to turn into a brave mafia asshole all of a sudden," she raved on.

Theresa held a different view. She called him at home, late at night; he was alone, about to slip into bed. But sleep and dreams would have to wait.

"Whatcha gonna do about this?" she pounced. Nothing he said mollified her. Not how a man's hateful words need not reflect his actions. Not how the case was still better left to the police, especially now that there was a prime suspect. "For Chrissakes," he said, "some of these detectives are real old-hands, been doing this kind of thing for years."

"Bullshit," she cried. "Sometimes I wish I was a man. I'd grab a gun and shoot the sonavabitch myself."

❉   ❉   ❉

John learned a lot in the next few days about the man Theresa would have loved to shoot. About time, John thought, after all he has come to mean to me. Bill Simon, who seemed uncomfortable talking, told him that Turner ran rec- reation programs like a midnight basketball league—did you know, Simon huffed, that the mayor of Kansas City claims crime drops 25% on the nights they sponsor midnight basketball—and organized street patrols of young men that kept the local drug dealers at bay. Simon had no good answer for why Turner spoke so harshly to him. "Always thought of him as a good man," the Reverend said. "A hard-head, maybe, but not a hot-head. It is my belief that deadly violence is beyond him. I'm sorry, though, about all this."

From Harry Glasser, John found out that Turner was the lead plaintive in a prisoners' rights case—Turner in the midst of a misspent youth having sold narcotics to an undercover cop and wound up in prison on a five years to life Rockefeller Drug Law conviction. While locked up, Turner got not religion, but politics and became an outspoken critic of arbitrary and degrading prison practices. Harry had argued a class action lawsuit in federal court on behalf of inmates organized by Turner. They won the claim that conditions of confine- ment in the disciplinary housing unit of an upstate maximum security prison violated the eighth amendment prohibition against cruel and unusual punish- ment. "Remember him well," Harry said, "a real character. Fearless. I liked him, but I'd guess he was capable of violence if he decided that's what it took to advance his cause." Violence is not the question, John thought. Homicide is.

Media sources completed the picture—phone conversations with Marilyn Diaz and press accounts of Robeson Turner, the man, the ex-con, the black nationalist, the community activist and rabble-rouser and former mentee of the Rev. Bill Simon. Turner grew up in the blighted projects of Brownsville, Brooklyn, the oldest child and only son of a hard-working mother and mainly absent and alcoholic father. The mother supported the family first on her sec- retary's salary and then as a fully registered nurse. But she couldn't keep tabs on her beloved son who, though sticking in school and attending City College, ran the streets and earned the reputation for being a rough and daring fellow. He had several run-ins with the law, from which the mother, with the help of local clergy, extricated him until the sale to a narcotics officer and the state's mandatory sentencing laws intervened.

Turner then came under the sway of Bill Simon who operated a prison min-istry—visiting and counseling and performing church services at several pris-ons in New York's Hudson Valley. Because of Turner's spotty institutional record, the Parole Board did not release him until he served more than 10 years—by which time, speculation was, prison officials were anxious to get rid of him.

Back in the City, Turner worked with Church groups and others to help the high-risk boys he probably identified with, those out of work and out of school kids who were most liable to end up in jail. He got high-marks for these efforts, but scared off his community's more moderate members by his habit, in the name of protecting the boys, of facing-off with cops and pushers. John, of course, had his own source of knowledge about that activity.

Though generally ignoring electoral politics, Turner did join the first Din-kins campaign, organizing youths to distribute literature throughout the projects and to get out the vote on election day. Once Dinkins took office, however, the organizer turned on the mayor, criticizing him for kowtowing to the City's moneyed interests, for going too far in accommodating mainstream editorial boards and white voting blocks, for beefing up the police force and expanding the jails, while cutting other government programs. Turner saw the Mayor as a sell-out, decided to sit-out the current campaign and thought all right-thinking blacks should do the same.

Robeson Turner, a classic American story, John reflected. A trouble-maker, with a penchant for acting tough, for doing violence. But a principled man, too. "A soldier for justice," the *Amsterdam News* called him. The profile of his brother's murderer? Maybe. John leaned toward maybe not.

❦   ❦   ❦

On a grey overcast day, over another quick lunch at the Sunburst Espresso Cafe, Charles passed on more useful information. "Did you know," he said, "that Robeson Turner's not actually the man's name?"

"No," John responded. "Didn't see any reference to it in the news bios."

"Somehow the reporters missed it."

"Didn't miss much else. Feel like I know the guy well."

"It wasn't actually a change," Charles said, "more like minor surgery. His real name was Robeson Turner Williams. But he hated his father's weakness, his inability to cope, so while in prison, he lopped off the old man's name."

"Simon told you this?"

"The one and only."

Jeanette and Leslie sat at a nearby table. John leaned over and advised them to try the carrot soup. "It'll keep you warm," he said.

"So Robeson Turner was left with, not coincidentally," Charles went on, "the names of two African-American heroes, Paul Robeson and Nat Turner."

John nodded.

"There's one more thing," Charles said. "Turner's not like you and me."

"Sounds like a line from a Michael Jackson video," John said. He thought of the short movie they made for "Thriller", title cut from the Michael Jackson album. The transformation of the star from a benign young man into a werewolf so terrified Teddy that the boy shivered with fright whenever he saw or heard Michael Jackson for several years afterwards.

"I'm serious," Charles said. "You work for social justice, a better world, but eventually you go home. Maybe you take some of your work home, but, basically, there you turn to other things, Angie, your kids, the fucking Sinatra Duets album, whatever." It had started to rain heavily. The steady patter of drops on the sidewalks accompanied Charles's words. "As a black man, I probably take more of my work home than you do. But still I go home and find a haven. Have dinner out with my wife. Play video basketball with my sons. Home is my time-out zone, my cherished private space."

"Got to have it," John said.

"Not men like Robeson Turner, and Bill Simon too. They're so engrossed with the lives and problems of their people, black people, with all the inhumane unjust shit, that they can't or won't create that separate space for themselves, that time apart at their own private supper table. They're compelled to devote their entire energy to the struggle."

"And this extraordinary dedication sets Turner apart, marks him as different from other people?"

"That's right."

"Are you also saying," John asked, "that this total immersion in the cause might drive him over the edge into a kind of volatile monomania?" Maybe Turner is the guy, John thought. His fierce outburst during their encounter at the camp. The twisted look on his face. Maybe he is wound just tight enough to commit homicidal violence.

"Volatile monomania? What the fuck are you getting at, man?"

"Is he kind of mad? So mad, he could actually kill?"

"I'm not claiming they're holy men or denying they're capable of bad shit." Charles was emphatic, but spoke softly. "I'm just saying that by choice *and* instinct their lives are completely political. There is no time for them, or room, for the personal."

Later that afternoon, at his desk, John received an unexpected phone call. "I swear, Johnny," Dominic said, "just say the word, I'll bump him off. Got more than one score to settle with that fucking creep." John saw again the bullets ripping into Dominic's car, shredding the tires, busting open the gas tank.

"Let's be cool for now," he cautioned. The rain had turned into a downpour, hitting hard against John's office window. Lightning cracked the sky. It's a violent world, he thought.

"Sally Broadway's telling everybody, no brash behavior before we know what the deal is with this Robeson guy," Dominic rolled on. "We want no race wars in this city, Sally says." Dominic chuckled, for no reason John could see.

"Hold your powder for now, my man," John said firmly, backing up Sally Broadway.

"Alright, alright," Dominic said agreeably enough. "Thought maybe I should take this Robeson guy out, but then I don't want to be wildly reckless. After all, I'm on this new kick, trying to be mature."

John stared at the receiver back in its cradle. He wondered whether he could express his conflicting emotions in a single sound combining laughter and weeping. Dominic, what a sweet, dumb, and just a little scary guy. Imagine his making such an offer that I *could* refuse. The real poignancy of his experimenting with growing up. Was he serious or kidding? But mention of a race war, now that would be unlikely, wouldn't it, even if Dominic did rub out Robeson Turner. Holy shit, how did things get to the insane point that we can even talk about a race war? How does Frank, his life and death, honorable and terrible, relate to such a horrifying possibility? And, finally, I gotta wonder whether my sister-in-law Theresa has been egging Dominic on.

It was a beautiful Sunday afternoon in early November, sunlight filling a glossy blue sky. John and Angie took their three sons to Whiney's house. From the van's back seat, Donnie discoursed on Miles Davis.

"Except for his last few records when he was going for a more pop sound, everything Miles did was special, took you to a new place. Not only what he did with his own instrument, you know, making music that was so delicate and soft, yet so present and strong, but what he got out of his musicians, his bands. They took flight—his modal jazz idea was new and forced their solos to be more creative, more searching. And they came down, only after the feeling was done, only after this cool and harmonious trip."

The boy must be swallowing *Downbeat* magazine whole, John thought. He glanced at Angie who nodded at him with pride.

"Until his genius deserted him at the end," Donnie said to Jake and Teddy, "Miles was a superhero of jazz, you know, the most 'beautiful cat' of all." Donnie's tone was reverential.

"I'd like to hear some of his albums," Jake said politely.

"I'm ready to get into it," Teddy said. "Can you make us a tape of his best cuts, Donnie?"

"I'll do that for you guys," Donnie said. "Rap and rock is alright, but you really ought to try this stuff out. I'm telling ya', it'll change how you listen to music."

"You should hear Donnie play himself," Angie said. "After only, what is it, two months, he can do "My Funny Valentine" on the trumpet, and "These Foolish Things" too. The way the music floats through the house.... I can almost cry."

Donnie waved his hand. "Ah, Mom. Don't listen to her, guys. I'm really not much of a player. That's just a mother talking."

Angie's cheeks reddened. It was only the second or third time John could recall seeing her blush.

The four adults sat in the tiny front yard—including Shirley whose wheelchair John and Whiney had guided down the few stairs of the front stoop. They watched the three boys play with the new puppy.

Twinkle crawled over the boys' bodies rolling on the ground like a sure-footed donkey crossing a rocky terrain; she yelped at them to start a chase; she eluded them with quick feints punt return specialists would envy; when she got tired, she sprawled in the cool grass, panting heavily, and gazed at the boys with an open face; and when they lay still enough, she climbed onto their torsos, licked their hands and faces, and nosed around gingerly until she found a place, on their chests and under their chins, to snuggle in.

Whiney and Shirley chuckled at their pet's high jinks—evidence that the little dog had driven the black dog of depression from the old man's life.

Whiney had some news to report: Theresa and Dominic had worked out an informal arrangement about running the restaurant. They were getting along, the old man said, God bless 'em, un miraculo che, who knows how long it will last? She'll handle the kitchen and menus, with some help from Marie, and Dominic will tend to the business side of things, the workers, the books, the vendors, the size and shape of the spice dispensers, and so on.

The unlikely compact had the advantage of cutting Nick Caesar out of the picture—his continuing attentions to Theresa bothered the entire family. At least the oily snake in the grass will keep in his hole for now, Angie said.

John did not find the next bit of information so comforting. Sally Broadway had just told Whiney they had come across "an interesting development", that's what the musical comedy lover called it, that could steer them to Frank's killer. It was too early to tell whether it would amount to anything, so Sally was tight-lipped about it, Whiney said, but there you are, Johnny, thought you should know.

"Thanks," John replied, "I guess."

"Don't ask me if this new clue of Sally's points the finger at Robeson Turner," Whiney said, "because I don't know."

On the drive home, anxiety rippled through John's frame like a fretful electric current. "Why am I so rattled by the prospect of learning who shot my brother?" he whispered to Angie, expecting, for once, no answer from her that would help. Maybe, though, Theresa was right. Time for me to step up.

CHAPTER 17

A couple of days after Giuliani won the election, John got a late night call. "Yo, Rosario, this is Robeson Turner." John settled into the big reclining chair in his bedroom, phone to his ear. Nothing clever came to mind, so he remained quiet.

"Rosario, are you there?" Turner talked in a slow cadence, slurring his words, almost as if he were drunk.

"You must be pleased," John said, his opening thrust.

"Why? Oh, because of Tuesday's so-called vote," Turner replied lazily. "No, not really."

"Your man won, didn't he?"

"Come on, Rosario, Rudy the Gee man is not my man. I'd call it another way. It wasn't that my man won. It was that I lost my man years ago."

"You mean when Dinkins began, as you see it, selling out."

"That's as I see it," Turner said. "And I'm not alone. What about your op ed in *The Times* slagging the man for building jails just like that honky Koch would have."

Honky, John thought, that dumb, old word again. It made his caller seem less intimidating. He did not like the way Turner used his analysis. "Dinkins and his people turned things around. Jail population's going down."

"Yeah, they told the cops to back off all those mickey mouse narcotics arrests that did nothing but send lots of young brothers and sisters to Rikers."

John got that Turner was wise to the ways of city government. The shift away from drug sweeps was supposed to be a well-guarded secret.

"But," Turner continued, "though they were doing the right thing, the little people at City Hall didn't want anybody to know." He seemed bitter and righteous.

"Not everybody around Dinkins," John said, "can be dismissed as 'little people.'"

"Like who?"

"Charles Buford for one," John said. "Rudy's new Human Rights Commissioner will show him the door."

"Guess he will lose his job," Turner said thoughtfully. "I know Charles…. he's a good man. It's a loss for city government, maybe, but not for the City as a whole, know what I mean?"

"You tell him that."

"Maybe I will. Maybe I'll even offer him a job out in Brownsville."

You couldn't even begin to meet his salary needs, John thought. He could make out the low sounds of jazz on the other end of the line. Turner must have the radio on. "Just Friends," was it? A saxophone played it with a hint of blues, evoking sad romance.

In the conversation's pause, John flashed on Donnie. Why? The music? Thoughts of Turner's lost boys? Despite his real father's death, Donnie's not so lost, is he? Wrapped in a mother love that shielded him too from harm from his half-assed second father Dominic. Ended up keeping a safe distance from both men. Still needs an old man, though, who's accepting and accepted. Maybe me, his third father?

"Rudy the Gee man's an Italian like you," Turner finally said, "and, like I told you once, I dig your people, always have." The man follows his own stream of consciousness, John reflected. But he paid attention. "Got along with them in prison better than with some of my own kind. Those old don types, you always knew where you stood with them. Their politics sucked, but they were loyal to their friends, and you knew they were warm-hearted, just from the way they greeted folks on family days in the joint. But Rudy, don't know what it is with him, got too much education, became a Republican. Whatever it is, he's a cold-hearted sonofabitch."

"Well, he's everybody's mayor now," John said with his own snip of bitterness. "And your going AWOL didn't help."

"How about that," Turner replied. "Look, you and I could go on for hours, but I didn't call you to apologize for my political actions."

"Why did you call?"

"To tell you I didn't kill your brother, man."

"Why threaten Simon?" Turner offended John, yet he did want to hear his explanation, first-hand.

"That's just what it was, Rosario, a threat." Turner sounded impatient with John's thickheadedness. "Wasn't supposed to mean I committed violence, or however people took it. I was only pointing out that your brother was shot down by his own people and that a similar fate could be in store for the good reverend if he wasn't, you know, careful."

Why should I fucking believe you? John thought. And why are you calling me *now* anyway? He didn't ask these questions. He turned, instead, to another subject. "You were being just a little hard on Bill Simon, weren't you?"

"Oh, forgot, you're one of those clean-thinking white liberals he's won over now," Turner said. "Now that he's being reasonable. I liked him better when he was mad and bad." Turner chuckled and sang in a softly swaying voice an old soul standard. "*Yeah, Big, Bad Bill is Sweet William now.*" He chuckled again. "*Yeah, Big, Bad Bill is Sweet William now....* so long, Rosario," he said and hung up.

John looked at the phone. The song, I guess, is over.

❦   ❦   ❦

"Next to Latins, your people make the best food," Marilyn Diaz told John. She chewed on her half of the sweet sausages and onion hero they shared. "So greasy and intense." She wiped her mouth with one hand and held the sandwich away from her with the other, to avoid the dripping sauce.

They sat on a wooden bench in City Hall Park, the small patch of grass and trees surrounded and criss-crossed by concrete walkways, on the south side of the sturdy stone structure where the Mayor of the City of New York and its council of elected representatives conducted their business. John had just met with police Captain Pat Devlin at One Police Plaza. Afterwards, he dropped in at the police beat press room and asked Marilyn out for lunch—they bought a sandwich at a nearby open air food stand.

"Remember walking through this park last summer," Marilyn said with a shiver, "after the police riot which Giuliani stoked with the hoarse screech of his that passes for fiery rhetoric." She was referring to a brief and destructive rampage of police officers after an outdoors rally against Dinkins. "Walked past cops who where still milling around, saw them gulping down their beers and overheard their words: fuck the niggers and faggots."

"A nasty business," John said.

"After Rudy gets through cutting services," Marilyn said, "there'll be lots of other people out here protesting in the coming years." Even as a news reporter, she seemed unhappy at the prospect.

"And then," John said, "the cops will protect City Hall, not attack it."

"Amen. So how'd your little chat with Devlin go?"

"Interesting. But not because I learned anything new." Marilyn gave John a quizzical look. "Liked him despite myself," he said. "He's dignified, courtly even, and smart. Not my idea of a cop, even one in the upper echelons."

"Yeah, Pat's a good guy, and competent." Her tone intimated that you couldn't say that about many people in the Department.

"He tells me they have nothing on Robeson Turner, though they'd like to collar the guy for something, anything. But, besides having a loose cannon for a mouth, he seems completely clean."

Marilyn swallowed her last bite of sandwich. "So I've heard. And don't think they weren't all over the guy. Like bark on a tree. Tailing him, staking out his apartment and office, probably breaking in too. But nada, nothing. Entirely empty-handed."

John recounted his phone conversation with Turner. Marilyn smiled. "'Big, Bad Bill is Sweet William Now', hah. That's good."

"I thought so," he said. "So Devlin apologizes and tells me, although he has nothing, rumor is Sally Broadway does."

"At least he knows enough to be sorry." Marilyn frowned. Two men walked past, one skinny, one chubby, both with shoulders scrunched up, the skinny one with a hat pulled down over his forehead. Marilyn waved at them. Must be reporters, John thought.

"But he's got no idea what Sally Broadway, the uncommunicative old bastard, has," John said. "He shrugs and says he'll keep in touch."

"Ain't that shit?" Marilyn said. "Crooks better detectives than cops."

They walked out of the park, she heading to the press room, he to the subway. She told him about a news wire story: A male corpse found buried in upstate New York; not many details, but the man was probably murdered by a professional because the hands, head, and feet were either missing or so mangled it was impossible to identify the body.

"You got a reason for telling me this?" John asked with a grimace.

"People make fun of me," Marilyn said matter-of-factly, "but I believe in the significance of coincidence. Here we have two murders, very possibly by mob hit men, and both unsolved. And though not in the same place, at least in the same state. So I figure maybe there's a connection. And if there is one, I don't expect the police to make it. Maybe your mob pals can."

"I'll see it gets passed on to Sally Broadway," John said. And he'd press Whiney to get some hard intelligence from the Brooklyn capo about those precious clues he keeps so close to his chest. Maybe he'd call the secretive old godfather himself.

❧   ❧   ❧

The Rosario family gathered at Angie's house for Thanksgiving dinner. Missing was Theresa and her clan, though Sandy showed up later. John and his sons, Marie, Angie and her mother and son, and Whiney and the dog Twinkle were there for the whole day.

Assorted heaps of side selections crowded the table. Meatballs, sausages, soft chunks of marinated pork, cooked eggplant, and roasted, sliced potatoes steeped in sundry pungent sauces. Marie, Louise, and their sometimes apprentice Angelina cooked two main dishes: two huge casseroles of baked ziti with layers of pasta carefully placed on top of and below thick slices of mozzarella cheese, laced with onion, pepper and basil spices; and two small capons—the Italian substitute for the traditional holiday turkey—stuffed with bits of sausage, ground veal and beef, sweet currants, and bacon.

His belly aching with pleasure, John was about to stand and applaud the cooks. But it'd be too showy, and likely embarrass the women he wanted to honor.

His uncle filled the breach. Whiney pushed his chair away from the table, sighed with contentment, raised his fingers to his mouth, then extended his hand in the air and smacked his lips. "Delizioso," he said. "Words like 'meal' or 'dinner' don't do justice to an occasion like this. 'Feast' falls short. It's more like an Olympic event, a marathon. They, the women, keep making and bringing on the food, and we, all of us, keep on eating and eating until we finish, ready to drop."

People smiled. "An epic contest," John agreed, patting his stomach. "I like that image, Whine."

"Yes, a test of endurance," Whiney intoned with a W.C. Fields affect. "And I must retire to the salon for a rest."

"Suppose I'll join you," John said. He started to rise from his chair until a frown from Angie reminded him that though he just ate like a prince, he would have to help clean up the dishes like the rest of the peasants.

Sandy arrived in time for the cannolli, sweet and crunchy. Afterwards, anyone who could walk made it into the large living room for the debate and argument portion of the day. As they sat around the room, in couch or easy chair, Sandy claimed that America was in the throes of a post-counter-culture Italian obsession. John wanted to hear more, but figured his boys, who were leaning forward in their seats, could fill him in later.

John led Whiney onto the enclosed front porch. As they walked out of the room, they caught some of Sandy's words. In the 1970's and 80's, after America's love affair with young, affluent college students ran its course, the nation turned its lonely eyes toward Italian heroes, rougher men with a working-class manner, like John Travolta, Robert De Niro, Al Pacino, and, of all people, Columbo and the Fonz.

The two men sat on wicker furniture, white frames holding green pillows. Twinkle jumped into Whiney's lap and nuzzled her head under one of his arms.

"Why didn't you leave the pooch back with Shirley?" John asked.

"Thought I would, but my lovely wife said the dog'd be happier here, with all the company, the kids, and me."

"And so it is," John said.

"And so it is," Whiney nodded.

They talked about Frank. Whiney explained his theories of homicide, how you always look for the motive, who stood to gain, personally or business-wise, from the victim's death; how this wisdom didn't apply in this case, because no evidence had came to light as to motive yet, and it was already past time that such clues should surface, even hinting at the killer or killers' identity. Only improbable scenarios, like the one implicating Robeson Turner, suggested someone had any reason for gunning Frank down.

"What do you figure Sally Broadway has locked up in the safety deposit box of his brain?" John asked.

"Whatever it is," Whiney said, "it's factual. Doesn't show motive, but may help solve the puzzle."

"If Sally does have something, why's he sitting on it so damn long?" John pumped a clinched fist, like a punch pulled back in mid-air. He wanted to intervene directly.

Whiney would now insist on getting the full story from Sally Broadway. After all, who more than family had a right to know. But, no, John should stay at least once removed from the conversation for now, in case things suddenly turned, you know, not so friendly. And, though sharing John's doubts about its value, the old man said he'd pass on Marilyn Diaz' tip about the cadaver discovered upstate.

A satisfactory plan, John supposed. But are we mistaking motion for action?

❦   ❦   ❦

On the Sunday afternoon following Thanksgiving, the rain went from a light drizzle to a pounding downpour that the van's wipers slapped at with noisy futility. His foot light on the gas, John steered carefully through the storm on the way to his uncle's house. Whiney wanted Angie and him over there right away. They guessed the old man finally got "the skinny" from Sally Broadway.

"Is that why we're creeping along at a tortoise pace here?" Angie prodded. "You still dread finding out who might've killed your brother?"

"No," John said. "Just want to avoid an accident, if you don't mind. Let's see what Whiney's got. Who knows, it may be nothing. Someone heard the car pull away and thinks they remember one or two letters from the license plate. But whatever it is, let's deal with it. If I need someone to hold my hand, you'll be there."

"You can count on me, kiddo." She was impressed with his change of heart, pleased she had something to do with it.

On the tape deck, Dion sang with a raspy, playful growl. *I want you all to understand/That I'm a man/So turn me loose.*

Even as they shook off the rain they couldn't evade during their fast dash up the driveway, John could see the worry on the old man's face. His complexion was pale, the color of his white hair, the twinkle gone again from his eyes. This was not depression, but distress based on some kind of hard reality. Shit, John thought, this is going to be bad.

There was no sign of Shirley, not even the usual television sounds. Must be in the upstairs bedroom, behind a closed door, John guessed. The dog lay down by Whiney's feet after the old man sat in the big chair in the small living room.

"Let's have it, Whine," John said after Angie and he sat together on the couch.

Whiney hesitated, then began. "You two remember Guido Arlotta?"

John and Angie looked at one another, then stared blankly at Whiney. "No," John said.

"We called him Weedie," Whiney said. "A classy guy, gave wide berth to the rougher boys like your father and me. Made money in an antique business. A real collector."

"What about him?" John asked sharply, showing impatience.

"He had a younger brother, much younger, who he tried to watch over. The parents had passed on, and the job fell to Weedie."

Angie shook a finger at Whiney, spoke excitedly. "The younger brother, his name was Tommy, right? Tommy Arlotta?"

"That's him," the old man said. "Weedie was always embarrassed by Tommy's antics. A foolish kid, everybody picked on him." John remembered Tommy now. He had sat at the table with Dominic in the pizza parlor when Angie saved Charles and him from the wrath of the local boys.

"Weedie didn't like Tommy's friends, he'd get upset with how far he'd go to impress them," Whiney said.

"Yeah," Angie said. "He hung out with gavonnes like Dominic."

John recalled Frank thinking Dominic and Tommy were a dangerous mix, prone to reckless behavior. Batman and Robin, he called them with contempt.

"Arlotta shit," Angie said. "That's the name Dominic and his stupid pals gave him, Tommy Arlotta shit."

"Well," Whiney said, "Sally Broadway says the body they found upstate is probably him, probably Tommy Arlotta."

"Oh no," Angie said.

Why such a fervent "oh no"? John thought. "How does he figure it, uncle?" he asked. "An identification was supposed to be impossible."

"Sally says Tommy's been missing for a month and a half, since about the time Frank got shot. Tommy had moved up to Boston years ago, you know, where his reputation as a frankfurter had not preceded him. Tried to make a new life, I guess. Weedie told me about it once. Anyway, Tommy was a hanger-on with the wise guys up there and they told Sally he was missing for awhile, but Sally didn't come to any conclusions because Tommy, according to the locals, disappeared like alacazam from time to time." Whiney paused, snapped his fingers. "Then returned ready for action."

"So the Boston people," John said, "didn't necessarily make anything of it."

"But Sally, the old bloodhound," Whiney said, "he was suspicious."

"And when the body turned up...."

"Bingo, especially since they found a New Utrecht High School ring in the pants."

"Jesus," Angie said. Her body had gone cold and was trembling. John placed his hand on her arm in a vain effort to comfort her. A ring in his pocket—John wondered whether Tommy had the presence of mind to put it there when he realized what was going to happen to him.

"So," John remarked carefully, "the finger of suspicion points to?" He resisted Angie's judgment. It was too terrible not to be absolutely certain.

His face expressionless, Whiney stared at John. "Dominic," he said. "He recruited Tommy to help him with his fucked-up plan to cut Frank down and when it was done, he snuffed the poor jerk, destroyed the body parts that could identify him, and buried him upstate."

"Where upstate?" Angie asked.

"The town of New Lebanon."

Angie raised her hand to her mouth and John asked, "What is it, babes?"

"That's where Dominic rents his ski house about 20 minutes from the mountains." Angie seemed numb and spoke without affect.

John stood up and paced the room. Angie and he had been hit by the same lightning strike, but it had flattened her and roused him. It was Dominic. Of course, it was Dominic. This was not a strange and disaffected man of color, or a hopped up, disgruntled cop no one had ever met, or some cold-blooded contract killer of the mob. This was Dominic whom they all knew, whom his brother embraced.

His fury mounting, John pictured Dominic with Frank, huddling with his buddy, mentor and boss, nodding at every word. Dominic with Donnie, patting and hugging him at Frank's picnic in the park. Dominic with Fat Tony at the wake, joking with Charles and Harry. Dominic with Theresa and Marie, helping them run Rosario's, *his family's* restaurant.

This was an act of betrayal and violence, fierce and savage and beyond understanding, that would have to be matched in kind. He'd find Dominic soon and smash him to smithereens. He felt no hesitation, no concern about consequences. It was a blood imperative.

"How much time is Sally giving us?" he calmly asked his uncle.

"Today, that's it. As we speak, arrangements are being made to take Dominic out tomorrow. That's if nobody, you know, has gotten to him first."

"Oh no," Angie said weakly, still sitting on the couch, her head back and rolling from one side to another. "Oh no, oh no, oh no, oh no, oh no."

❦   ❦   ❦

Whiney and John stood in the hallway by the house's front door. The older man's face—his whole body—drooped. John wanted to bolster him, but couldn't think of the right words, if there were any.

"Funny about Dominic," Whiney said, almost matter-of-factly.

"Son of a bitch," John said.

"Never seemed to mind being under Frank's hand." Whiney sounded emotionally removed.

"Who knows?" John said brusquely. "Maybe he did it because Frank was leaving, deserting him, or because I moved in on Angie and his kid, or just because he wanted to sit at the back table in Rosario's like he was a true fucking don."

After a pause, Whiney said, "Wasn't supposed to come to this. Your father…." The old man was now close to tears.

"But my father would lead the charge, wouldn't he?" John said firmly.

Whiney didn't argue. He suggested an alternative plan. "You know, you don't have to be the one. I could take it on. After all, at my age there's less to lose, and I've had some experience with these sorts of things."

"Frank was my brother," John said. "End of story." He turned up the palms of his hands. Whiney nodded.

Twinkle was at their feet. She scratched gently at Whiney's leg, whether to get his attention or to soothe him was not clear. Whiney bent down to pat her, saying take it easy, pet. He asked John to wait a moment and reached into the closet at his back. Meanwhile, Angie approached the two men. Whiney held out a gun and told John, "Here, you might need this."

"What are you, crazy?" Angie screamed. And then in the same loud, mad voice: "This cannot happen, please, not with Johnny."

Angie's howl reverberated in the small hallway and in John's head. She stood in a crouch, hands at her mid-section, her shouts and sobs coming up from her gut. "Pass on this mafia mission, please," she yelled. "It's the fucking cops' job, we agreed."

She got in front of him, blocking his exit. He was touched by her frenzy, even confused, but not deterred. He knew no words of his about his course of action could reach her. I won't try to kill Dominic, he offered coolly, only subdue him, then maybe call the police. The concession did not soothe her. Her eyes showed in quick succession her terror, then defeat. John gently turned her around and left her weeping in Whiney's arms.

"Take good care of her," he said softly. Since for now, he thought, I can't.

❦   ❦   ❦

On Sunday afternoons Dominic worked on the accounts at Rosario's—more information courtesy of Sally—and that's where John headed. In his jacket's inside pocket was Whiney's gun, a little thing, a weapon he never handled in his life and could barely imagine using even now. Dion's "Turn Me Loose" boomed from the tape deck and John's blood pulsed along with the rhythmic beats filling the car. Hands on the steering wheel, he wriggled his body, shaking off the remnants of his encounter with Angie, juiced by a high rapid rush of emotion. *Turn me loose*, damn fucking right, he thought. I'm going to squash that sonavabitch like a bug.

The recurring memories came in rapid sequence: His old man near death in the hospital, visited by Frank and him, barely able to speak, mouthing the words "my sons" with an awesome tenderness. Frank calling him Johnny, smiling sadly at one thing or another. Dad and Frankie dead, he thought, and Dominic alive, a walking, breathing traitor in our midst.

Love many, trust few, his father had written Frank and him. And he had come to trust Dominic. What a fucking fool he'd been. Now Dominic'd pay the price. Time's up for you, bastard.

In the restaurant, busy with weekend customers, John spotted Dominic sitting at the table in the back alcove in front of the kitchen's swinging doors, the same place of honor Frank occupied in his heyday. Dominic, the new godfather of Bensonhurst, his dark blue suit gleaming even to John's eyes from across the restaurant. Fat Tony sat next to him, eating and chatting.

Dominic wanted all things Frank, John's mind flashed. Angie and his son, but he lost them. Most of all he lusted after this, to be the big-time mobster with the common touch. If Frank had left town on his own, I might be sitting there on a Sunday. *And Dominic, the sick fuck, must've despised both of us.*

John called out Dominic's name and, in a single motion, picked up a large, glass sugar dispenser from a nearby table and threw it at him. It hit the plate of spaghetti in front of Dominic and splashed red sauce on him and his glittering clothes.

Dominic jumped up and, as the diners scattered either to hug the walls or leave the place, he shouted: "John, are you fucking nuts?"

John advanced toward Dominic. "You killed Frankie!" he shouted back. "You killed my brother, you fucking son of a bitch!" The loud sound of his own scream startled him, filled the room—it was a roar from the bottom of his belly, a great release. At that moment, given the chance, despite his pledge to Angie, he'd have murdered Dominic.

Tears of rage filled John's eyes—he jerked his head to see clearly. A brief eerie silence ensued. Fat Tony got up and stood by the table.

Dominic said, "That's crazy.... why would I shoot Frank?"

Tony looked perplexed and said to John, "Yeah, why would Dominic fucking do that?"

Tony speaks, John thought, a good thing. He suddenly viewed the fat man as a possible confederate, a buffer against the death he saw staring out at him from Dominic's furious glare.

John quickly related Sally Broadway's news about Tommy Arlotta, his death by violence brutal and well-planned and the site of his uncermonial burial and the conclusion that any sentient being would draw from such things. Tommy being Dominic's well-known partner in crime and New Lebanon being where Dominic rented his ski house.

Tony rubbed his eyes to dispel his confusion. Growing more nervous, John felt time had stopped. Shit, he thought, Dominic's got to be carrying a piece. I could die here. John still felt fury, and now, abruptly, also fear. A sense of dire consequences.

Then Tony seemed to receive the terrible truth of it, not, John guessed, from anything he, John, said, but from the wild, scared, and guilt-ridden eyes the fat man's old friend Dominic could not conceal. In slow-motion, Tony raised one of his hands, stretched it out, and pointed a finger at Dominic. The finger hung in air, it trembled, but the fat man said nothing.

Dominic took a gun from the shoulder holster his jacket hid from view. John thought sadly and helplessly of his uncle's gun, that simply could not be of any use to him now, if it ever could. He backed up and told everyone to "calm down and back up", but he was not really sure whom he was talking to. Tony grabbed his head in his hands, emitted a mournful growl. John was struck, was moved by Tony's intense hurt. The fat man lowered his head and charged at Dominic who pulled the trigger of his pistol. The gunshot's blare shocked John's ears and added to his fright. He saw Tony stagger back, clutch his bleeding shoulder where the bullet hit. Despite his fear, John made a move toward the gunman. But Dominic now pointed his weapon at John and warned him not to take one step closer.

"Frank was like my father," Dominic said.

"And who did you hate and wanna kill?" John cried. "But your old man."

Dominic held the gun in his steady, outstretched hand. John said, "What are you gonna do, Dominic? Kill all of us?"

"Don't try me, man."

Time was suspended. John was living, maybe about to die in an unreal, slow-motion dream. That dreadful prospect had been with him for the last 10 minutes and his body and psyche more or less adjusted to it. He was able to make judgments: I can't walk away because Dominic would almost certainly shoot me in the back. Gonna rush him, jump him, scared as I am.

Another body materialized. John's vision was blurred by the quick movement, by the sweat from his forehead dripping onto his eyelids. Dominic did not pull the trigger again. Something, someone suddenly knocked him down, propelling him and his gun to the floor. Theresa had come out of the kitchen and smacked him in the head with one of the biggest frying pans John had ever seen.

The blow did not knock Dominic out cold. He scrambled for the gun that was jolted from his hand and now lay under a nearby table. But Fat Tony was quicker, knocked over the furniture in his way, and got to the gun first. Standing over Dominic, he held his wounded arm with one hand and the gun with the other.

Theresa was screaming at Dominic. "You killed Frankie, you fucking punk! He loved you." John stepped in front of her, placed his hands on both her upper arms, looked into her face, and tried to calm her. She was still shouting, sobbing, saying "Son of a bitch" at Dominic who was laying, bloodied head, sullied clothes, frightened, twitching eyes, on the floor.

John hugged Theresa and she cried on his shoulder. He repeated, like a mantra, "Easy, sweetheart, easy sweetheart. It's over now, it's alright, it's over now."

Weeping in John's arms, Theresa mumbled, "Fucking two-bit, greaseball punk." She looked at Dominic once more and spat past John at her fallen foe.

John became conscious of sirens, bustle, the presence of cops. Someone must have called them, he thought hazily: Whiney, Angie, maybe someone at the restaurant. John noticed that Tony still held the gun on Dominic and looked like he was about to use it. Tony's face was flushed red with hurt and anger, his eyes bugged out, his world ripped to bits by an unimaginable act of betrayal.

John moved away from Theresa towards Tony. "No," he said softly, reaching out his hand. "No, Tony. I know how you feel, believe me, but it's not the way to go."

The cops approached the two men. John was grateful to see Jack Dorney in civilian clothes leading the pack of blue uniforms, some with pistols drawn. "What gives here, John?" Jack shouted. "Dominic, the guy on the floor," John shouted back, less to Dorney, than to the officers behind him. "He did my brother Frank. He's the killer."

Tony gazed a final long moment at Dominic, raised his head, ignored the cops, and looked at John who shook his head. Tony hesitated, then lowered the gun slowly to his side. "Sorry, fat man," John said.

CHAPTER 18

John felt the difference when he stepped into Angie's house. It was strangely quiet, somber, like a wake where nobody laughed. Whiney and John's mother, who had come over to be with the family, greeted him.

Her face white with worry, Marie wept even as she smiled. She embraced her son tightly, and held onto him for several minutes. "Giovanni, Giovanni," she said softly. Whiney smiled too and patted him on one cheek and kissed him on the other.

"Where is everybody?" John asked.

"Angie's in her bedroom with her mother," Whiney said. "And Donnie's alone in his room."

"Why such long faces on you two?" John said. "I'm all right, and the bad guy's been captured. The news is good, right?" He saw it was a foolish question. The looks on his mother and uncle made him want to stuff the words back down his mouth. "Angie's bad, huh?" he asked.

"Low-down, Johnny," Marie said. "So low-down."

"How's Donnie?"

"Mesa, mesa," Whiney answered with a hand gesture. "Seems more upset about his mother than anything."

On his way up the stairs to see Angie, he heard the woeful sounds of some unknown jazz song coming from Donnie's room. He thought the boy would probably listen to a lot of music like that in the coming weeks.

Angie looked like a sick, pale old woman. "Hiya Johnny," she said weakly.

He sat by her on the edge of the bed and described the showdown at Rosario's, keeping it light, matter-of-fact. He emphasized the bravery of Theresa and Tony, past thorns in his side or butts of his jokes. "No doubt about it," he said. "They were heroes, like you in the pizza parlor."

Barely a murmur from Angie, although her mother Louise, who sat in a chair by the foot of the bed, grinned when he described with hand motions the gigantic frying pan Theresa used to slam Dominic in the head.

John leaned forward, his face close to Angie's. "C'mon, babes," he whispered, "I'm here, we're here, we can put this shit behind us."

"No, we can't," she hissed, for the moment animated with a powerful sentiment. "This shit was too much. People died, died because of me. People I loved. People I loved acted like possessed madmen because of me. I can't…. won't…. don't want this….comfort. Don't deserve it." Her fervor subsided as abruptly as it appeared.

He began to speak, but she held up her hand. "No more, Johnny," she said. "No more talk tonight."

Louise motioned to John that she would stay with her daughter. He kissed Angie on the forehead, and left the room.

❀   ❀   ❀

For the cold December weeks, John kept a vigil at the Capobella house. He visited every day, sat and talked with Angie although she didn't always respond, and tended to Donnic. He tried different ways of reaching her. Once he put "Sweet Angeline" on, the Mott the Hoople track, hoping its rocking energy would touch her, stir healing memories. She groused at him to turn the music off. "It's just giving me a headache," she said.

Sometimes he'd discuss the work at UJI. He stayed heavily involved—his main diversion in the face of her great pain. He described the rampant scuttlebutt about the government services Giuliani was expected to cut when he took office. "He's going to drive the poor from the City," John said. He was trying to provoke the political ire in her. She shrugged off the news. "Knew this was coming, didn't we?"

He told her Charles was working with him as a consultant, on a conference UJI was co-sponsoring with the New School for Social Research on the need for government programs to boost the declining economy and shrinking job market in the inner cities. The project even now excited him and would have interested her in better days. "Lotsa luck, brother," she said.

❧   ❧   ❧

The measured, sad, mellifluous sounds of jazz filled the house, slinking through the hallways, drifting like airborne smoke from room to room. Sometimes Donnie played the trumpet himself, making melancholy music while John sat in his room and listened. Gloomy slow numbers were the norm, like "Don't Get Around Much Anymore" and "Guess I'll Hang My Tears Out to Dry," songs Sinatra did that man and boy hoped would draw a response, physical or verbal, from Angie, but never did.

One night Donnie explained to John the basic technique for playing the trumpet. "Gotta breathe in through the mouth, can't be through the nostrils. Gotta fill the air in the lower part of your gut, so it comes up and out naturally, instead of you forcing it out."

"Sounds like you know your way around that horn." John pointed to the instrument in the boy's hand.

Donnie shook his head. "Technique's important, but not the main deal. The secret's in the attitude." He affected a low, raspy voice close enough to Miles Davis' that John understood the reference. "You got to make it your own thing."

❧   ❧   ❧

John and Whiney stood together, arms folded, leaning against the back of wooden benches that looked out onto the gray flowing Narrows. On a mild Sunday in December, they were spectators to the dog's sport as she cavorted with her canine mates on the sprawling meadow separating the Belt Parkway from the water behind them. John marveled how a tiny creature like Twinkle, fluffy and feminine, could scamper and roughhouse with the rest of the dogs. "She's downright athletic," he said.

"Twinkle's a bundle, alright…. loves to cuddle and be held like a baby cat and still can hold her own with the boys out there. Look at her now."

They watched the little shih tzu flounce and shimmy up to another, slightly larger white dog. She flitted back and forth in front of the other hound, pausing occasionally to splay herself on the ground and yelp.

John chuckled and looked at Whiney. "That's Bailey," the old man said. "A sealyham terrier, you might say a steady acquaintance of Twinkle…. So, how you doing?"

"Hanging in," John said.

"How's Angie?"

"Not great."

Whiney frowned. "Ah, that's too bad."

John spoke in a distracted tone as if he were recalling a distant memory. "The other night I was coming home from parking my car in the garage on 110th street. It wasn't too late, not too cold, so I walked the 30 blocks or so to my apartment. Been doing that a lot lately, going for walks whenever I can, weather permitting. At about 100th street I notice this black kid in front of me on roller blades, gliding down the street with a hockey stick in his hands, bending his knees and swaying his body like he knows the moves, wearing a Mark Messier shirt, you know the Ranger hockey player. It doesn't occur to me for a few blocks that this is a highly unusual sight, a black kid who's into hockey."

"Like an Italian from Bensonhurst who only eats vegetarian," Whiney said with a guffaw.

"Exactly. So the boy skates up to three older, bigger kids, black also, who are walking towards us, scowls on their faces in the custom of the street, and as he passes them, the one on the outside suddenly smiles sweetly at him, holds out his hand for a slap, and says, 'What's up?'"

"Pretty good New York moment, huh?" Whiney said.

"The thing of it is," John replied, "I can't share it with Angie. Can tell her about it, but she'll just stare right past me."

Whiney squeezed his nephew's shoulder. "She'll be back."

"I believe that too, but what makes *you* so sure?"

Running full speed, Twinkle returned. She sat at Whiney's feet, panting happily. He picked her up, kissed her on the head. "You and the boy," he said. "She'll come back for you two. Besides, it's December. Angie won't want to miss Christmas."

John's eyes roamed Angie's bedroom, the walls and ceilings painted bright white, the white, wicker furniture to match—a bureau, the shelves cluttered with books, photos, and knick-knacks, the small love seat where they now sat, the lacy, white bedspread and pillow cases as fluffy as a fat bushy-haired cat. He realized that Angie the Librarian had not appeared there once. Not even Angie at her liberated peak could overcome the room's aura of girlish purity.

"You know I'm never going to leave you," John said.

She patted him on the arm, but did not speak. As was often the case now, she wore pajamas and a washed-out, body-length house coat.

"Remember we reached an understanding," he tried again, "that night you sat on my face."

Still nothing.

"You got me to promise never to leave you again." He chuckled. "That's hardly an exaggeration. You sat on my face and I surrendered to you not just for the night, but forever. Remember?"

She spoke with a mixture of sympathy and sarcasm that encouraged him—any display of affect struck him as a good sign. "Oh, poor Johnny, you must miss Angie the Librarian terribly."

"Not really," he said. "Miss other things more."

"But I can't hold you to that understanding, reached under those circumstances." He noted her choice of words. Was she making a stab at humor? "Can't hold you to that understanding," she went on. "Considering my current situation."

He guessed she meant that she was not about to have sex of any kind, now or in the foreseeable future. He held his ground. "Sorry, babes," he said. "A deal's a deal."

❦   ❦   ❦

John felt awkward visiting Janet Kuerer. Angie's therapist lived and worked only a few blocks from his west side apartment. She used her spacious living room as her office, with two floor to ceiling wooden shelves at either end of one wall filled with books on psychological theory and treatment methods. There were two comfortable couches, one large and one small, and scattered chairs that John guessed were for group sessions and/or small gatherings of family and friends.

He felt like Nick Nolte in "Prince of Tides" and wondered whether Janet Kuerer resembled the Barbra Streisand character. When she entered the room, he checked the skirt length and found it normal. Ditto, the fingernails.

He sat on the small couch, legs crossed, fingers tapping nervously on his thigh. She sat in a large swivel chair and rolled it away from her desk, stopping a few feet from him. They talked about looking familiar—maybe they had seen each other in the neighborhood: in a supermarket aisle, on a line at the movies, or a path in Riverside Park.

"It's hard," she said, "when someone you love and depend on, especially someone as lively as Angie, sinks into depression."

"Like watching the prettiest flower in the garden wither and fade," he responded.

"Painful, but true," she said.

"Just so you know," he said, "Angie gave me the go-ahead to call you."

"I checked with her too, before agreeing to speak with you."

He raised a finger to his forehead and tipped it. "Touche, doctor."

She smiled. She had a pretty round-shaped face with tiny wrinkles around the eyes, traces of advancing middle-age. Her expression reminded him of Angie's. They say over the years people begin resembling their mates or pets. Maybe it also applies to patients and their shrinks? Or maybe his imagination was getting loopy because he was so desperate to get Angie back into his life?

So how are *you* doing, John, she asked, and he talked about Angie's troubles and she interrupted him, saying no, tell me how *you're* doing. You mean about Frank being gone, about Dominic's treachery? he asked. She nodded and he said he'd never get over it, not so much the Dominic thing, but the loss of his brother, the meanness of it, the crushing unfairness of it, the gap in his life because of it, but with his worries over Angie, he'd nearly forgotten about it....

"So her condition's in a way therapeutic *for you*?"

John went to speak, paused, thought for a moment. "Good point, doctor. But about Angie, your prescription?"

"You have to stay by her side, John, visit her often," Dr. Kuerer said. "That's the best therapy *for her*."

"I'm there everyday." He gazed at a photo on the wall. Freud, legs crossed, in jacket and vest, hand to his chin, looking wise.

"Good. Fair or not, she thinks you abandoned her before. She's putting you to the test now."

John said he understood. It was his way of being a stand-up guy as his father had advised.

"And the boy," she continued, "he must be devastated, probably furious too, but, for her sake, he has to bear up. He may crash later and you'll have to care for him then."

"But my priority's Angie for now," he said, asking a question and making a statement.

Unlike Whiney, Janet Kuerer made no predictions about Angie's mental health. John left wondering what she really thought.

❦   ❦   ❦

John and Angie sat on the benches in the old gym at Xaverian High School and watched Donnie play basketball. John loved the scene and smell of the place. The faint odor of locker room sweat, the bright antiseptic light making the players feel like they are part of a stage drama, the buzz and hoots of a friendly crowd, the efforts of boys under pressure to perform. He remembered the camaraderie and teamwork of his own squad at its best: the quick passes, the swish shots, the glad-handing by Charles and him and the others.

Angie insisted he bring her, saying she had already been absent for three home games and could not let Donnie down any more than she already had. He knew she was referring to greater maternal sins than missing a couple of basketball games.

Though pleased Angie wanted to go, he had misgivings. She seemed so, well, frail—merely putting her clothes on wore her out. She stumbled coming down the stairs, and fastened her hands on his arm like an old person walking on slippery ground. He just didn't know whether she was going to make it.

Donnie played well, inspired by his mother's presence, John figured—though the boy made no gesture acknowledging it. Whenever he hit an outside shot—he had four 3-pointers by half-time—or made a quick-stepping move that caught the opposing players flat-footed, a coterie of his fans—a boisterous mix of black and white boys—blew on noisy party horns and shouted out in unison: "There's nothing like tooting your own horn."

Angie smiled and clapped at times, but soon began to shake, her body reacting to the booming din, which grew louder with each home team basket. When John saw Angie tremble, like a child coming down with chills, he decided her psyche, her sensibility was too brittle to sustain a prolonged exposure to the clamor. He told her he'd take her home at half-time. She demurred, but only lamely. Still, when the time came, she refused to go until John agreed to explain to Donnie why they were leaving. While reluctant to violate long-standing tradition and be the non-combatant who enters a locker-room, John did her bidding.

When he looked into the locker-room, the excited chatter of resting players and encouraging coaches stopped cold. Virtually all eyes turned toward the door. He saw Donnie's cheerful, perspiring face turn sour as the boy rose from the bench in the center of the room.

They stood in the dimly lit, drab hallway outside the locker-room that John remembered as a shinier, cleaner place. "Whatsa matter, now?" the boy squawked. "Why can't she stay? Why can't she be strong just once?"

"Your mother's very fragile now, but, even so, I'm the one who forced the issue. She was shaking so much, I was afraid she'd break into little pieces."

"Shit," the boy cried, running his hand through his hair still moist with sweat. "I can't handle this." He shook his head and squeezed his eyes shut. "I'm not sure I can handle this, John."

John leaned his head closer to the boy's. "Donnie, you and I have to hold on. She's been there for us. Now, hard as it is, we have to be there for her."

The boy said nothing, rubbed his forehead. Is he taking this in? John wondered. Donnie turned to go back to his teammates. "Terrific playing, your mom wanted me to tell you," John said to his back.

"Tell her thanks," Donnie said over his shoulder and shut the locker-room door behind him.

Later that night, John went into Donnie's room, walls lined with posters of jazz performers and basketball players, the boy laying on his bed, under a small overhanging light, listening to Miles Davis and holding the cover art for "Sketches of Spain."

"How was the game?" John asked.

"All right," the boy said flatly. "We held on for the win."

"Good," John said, and then: "Your little fan club was a kick to watch." Donnie looked puzzled. "The boys who were blowing the horns," John explained.

"Yeah, they're cool," the boy said. "We listen to jazz together. Some of them are pretty good musicians." John sat on the boy's bed. They talked over the soft tremor of Miles Davis' trumpet. "This goes beyond 'Shit Happens', right?" Donnie asked. "That's what one of my friends said. He was just trying to be helpful."

John nodded. "Our family's recent troubles cut much deeper than that. Life usually can't be reduced to slogans on bumper stickers."

"You're not going to leave, are you, John?"

"No." John couldn't track Donnie's shifting emotions, but he was trying. Hold steady, he told himself. Be there for the boy.

Donnie moaned. "I've been hurting a lot," he said and looked directly at John.

"Have to be made of steel not to." John's own gut began to ache.

"What the fuck was going on with Dominic? Why'd he do it?" The boy spoke in a raised, intense voice. "My fake father murders my real father. That really rips me up. Why the fuck did he do it?"

John was relieved by the boy's contempt for Dominic—the bond was clearly broken. He returned Donnie's gaze, held his attention. "Dominic was sick and twisted," John said. "There was a dark side in him, though we didn't know the extent of it, did we? And, you know, we can't always sort out the malignant things in life, the bad, barbarous things people, people who walk and talk and see and hear and eat and feel like us, do. Maybe with Dominic it was a power thing, a jealousy thing. Like the gangster life got inside his head and made him even more violent." John did not mention he also thought that it might have been a weird father transference. Dominic felt cheated, injured and, finally, enraged when John and not he took possession of the things Frank was passing on.

"I hate him for it," Donnie said. "Wish I could kill him myself." The boy's hands balled up into fists and he pounded the bed with them once, then again.

"I don't hate him anymore," John said. "Maybe because I saw him that day at the restaurant on the floor, smeared with sauce and blood, a scared mess of a man and I felt pity and disgust, but no longer loathing." John didn't pass on his other association at that sight. Some other time, he thought. "And then I got so worried, preoccupied about your mother and trying to help her that I practically forgot about Dominic and my fury at him."

"My mother, she's given up on life, hasn't she?" the boy said bitterly. "Just checked out on us."

"I don't see it that way," John said. "I've been thinking about this a lot…. your mother's been carrying the weight for us."

Donnie shot John a startled expression. "What'd you mean?"

"When we learned the terrible news about Dominic and Frank, we had no ritual to help us process it or to express our emotional response to it. A truly horrendous thing had happened and we had no way to absorb it." John spoke slowly, careful to get his words right. "You know, like the purpose a wake and funeral serve after a death. Your mom's been working it through, and, by her sadness and withdrawal, been forcing a vigil on us, making us work through the pain and confusion of it too."

"Like when you grieve," Donnie said. "At a wake, like you said? And mom's obviously not dead, but…." The music stopped, and Donnie stared at the soundless CD player. His words, his unfinished thought hung in the silent air.

"She's at the center of it, feeling the emotional brunt of it," John said.

"I miss her so much." The boy sobbed softly. "That's what hurts so much. I've lost the two men who were my fathers, and now I'm losing her too."

John hugged the boy, then released him, patting him on the leg as he spoke. "You've got to tell her, Donnie. That, more than anything, will help bring her back." He loved Donnie now, felt a deep connection. Angie's son. My brother's son. Now my boy too. A third father for a third son.

"I have," the boy said.

"Then tell her again."

❈   ❈   ❈

On the Saturday afternoon before Christmas, John got a phone call from Angie's mother Louise. "Angie asked me to make sure you were coming over tonight."

"That's my plan."

"I think she wants you over here right away." Louise whispered as if she possessed a great secret.

"I'm leaving soon," John responded. "What's up?"

"Angie's different. I think she's, you know, better." Louise's whisper grew more excited.

"What makes you say that?" John was dubious, but ready to be convinced.

"Well, first of all, she comes downstairs this morning dressed like it was a regular day and that's different. And the first thing she does is put Christmas music on the record player."

Louise will probably always call the CD machine a record player, John thought. "Christmas music," he said, "that's great!"

"Donch ya think? By that Italian guy from the Bronx you two are so crazy about."

John's ambivalence about Bensonhurst dissolved entirely during Christmas. The elaborate lawn ornaments depicting Santa Claus and the reindeers or Frosty the Snowman or the Three Wise Men and the Christ Child—the red, blue, green and yellow holiday lights strung on porches and windows and on rooves and fence railings give the neighborhood a festive look that seduced him. It was the best time of the year, by far, for this, the most parochial of Brooklyn's little villages. He loved the spectacle as he took it in again on his drive to Angie's house.

No one was there when he entered the living room—from the coffee table he picked up the CD holder for Dion's "Rock 'n Roll Christmas" album. Angie appeared at the top of the stairs and started to descend. "Didn't even know Dion made a Christmas album," he called out.

"Neither did I," she said. "Donnie came across it while shopping for jazz albums. Wrapped it up like a pre-Christmas gift."

John could imagine her delighted surprise when she opened it. Way to go, Donnie. "How is it?" He held up Dion's picture on the CD package.

"It's fun. Reverent, but, you know, very good-natured." She snapped her fingers two or three times and shimmied her shoulders. *"Rocking around the christmas tree* and all that."

He was happy to see the life in her. "Can't wait to hear it," he said and sat on the couch where she joined him. She'd obviously been waiting for him, he was pleased to think. She had just washed her hair, still damp and stringy, and, with an air blast from her mouth, blew the bangs off her forehead like Popeye puffing his pipe. She wore jeans and a light blue blouse.

"I have an announcement." Angie looked down, hands on her thighs like a prim schoolgirl. "I'm back, and wanted you to be the first to know." Her face almost broke into a smile, but couldn't quite get there.

"Wonderful," he said skeptically. "I thought it was just a matter of time."

"But you were worried about me, right?"

"I was. After all, what happened, what you had to go through was…."

"Heavy, right?"

"It was very heavy, sweetheart."

"I mean the man I married, who raised my son, shoots and kills my boy's actual father and then the man who I truly love, you, you nincompoop, takes it in his head to almost get shot and killed too…. and I thought I caused it all." She seemed breathless.

He grew anxious that she was slipping again into her deep sadness.

"You know, Johnny," she went on. "I knew, I thought Dominic had harmed, maybe even killed people." She stared at him, a plea in her eyes. She's seeking absolution, he thought.

"We all knew," John replied. "We just never thought he'd cross the line." He meant from professional violence to personal. "Nobody could have predicted that." He raised his hand toward her face, and she tilted her head, resting it in his palm. "You didn't cause it," he said tenderly.

"Not really, not fully. I was just…."

"Living, trying, and it went bad for you, and those men." He hurried to help her come up with a way to forgive and understand her life.

"Then it crashed down on me with a horrible thud," Angie said. "And I took a trip out of town for a while."

"Now you're back." He held his joy at bay, concerned about her mood, whether she could hold it together. "And you have Donnie and me and other people in your life."

"Right, and I'm gonna be okay."

"No buts about it." He tried for a playful tone.

"You're sweet."

The house was still, no other signs of life. Where are Donnie and Louise? he thought. Left the field to me? He heard a toilet flush upstairs. Guess not entirely.

"So, how are your boys?" she asked. "I've been neglecting the people and things in my world…. How are your boys?"

"They're good. Enjoying the holiday break. Jake's made the junior varsity basketball team and getting lots of playing time, scoring some points."

"And Teddy. Still the cheerful kid?"

"More or less. His latest thing is to say at every Remotely appropriate opportunity: 'Yabba, dabba, dooffus.' Heard it on some Saturday morning T.V. show."

"Whiney? Still happy with the dog?"

"Yes, you should be pleased to know. The depression passed with no lapses to my knowledge. Maybe we should rename the pooch Prozac."

"That's a thought," Angie said. "And the restaurant? What's going on there?"

She wants to know everything, is hungry for news, he reflected. Well, that's just terrific. "Rosario's doing well," he said. "Theresa's in charge now, with help from my mom, Whiney, even Fat Tony, but mainly from Nick Caesar."

Angie grimaced. "I share your opinion," he said, "but Theresa seems content for now."

"And that's important. Theresa's a piece of work, isn't she? Saved your life, didn't she?"

"You are correct, babes. With help from Fat Tony, but Theresa did strike the critical blow. She hit Dominic"—John lifted his hands, like a fisherman showing the size of a monster fish he's just caught, and noticed the look of anticipation on Angie's face—"with the biggest, fucking frying pan on the planet."

Her face broke into a real smile, slightly off-kilter—her facial muscles were out of shape.

"You know," he said, "when I first told you that story, using very similar words if I'm not mistaken, you didn't react."

"I wanted to," she said, "but couldn't. Everything around me was like a distant echo I couldn't get to, couldn't touch."

"Sorry, babes."

"Don't be," she said. "Tell me about politics. What's the latest news?"

"You know Giuliani won. Republicans won in other places as well. And they all have their budget machetes in hand, eager to cut services for the poor to get the economy going again."

"Ugh, the Republicans," she shuddered. "Their hearts would set off a government building's metal detector."

John smiled. "Well, they're certainly taking over. All the more reason for folks like us to stick together."

Angie grinned too, still off-kilter.

"Your smile's crooked now," he said. "Like Ellen Barkin's."

"Could do worse, right?" she responded without missing a beat. "She's tough, isn't she, and good-looking and sexy too, right?"

"Absolutely," he said. "In "Sea of Love" with Pacino, she wore that short, straight skirt, with high heels on"—like a neighborhood gombah, he shook his hand before him. "Ma-donne, I'd follow her anywhere."

Her lopsided grin remained. She moved toward the corner of the couch, pulled him towards her, and coohed, "C'mere, Johnny Rosario." She caressed his cheek. I'm glad Theresa and the fat man came to your rescue. I'm glad…."

EPILOGUE

John sat with Sally Broadway at the table in the back room of the old capo's Little Italy Social Club. It was January, a few days past New Year's. Here's where Whiney and Sally played brisk, John thought. Seems like another age. Minx the Enforcer stood back, half in the dark, leaning against the grey wall next to the bathroom. *Can't have one without the other*, the line from an old Sinatra song played in John's head.

"Glad you called," Sally said. "Been waiting."

"Well, I've been preoccupied."

Sally didn't ask with what. "Wanted to thank you for helping my niece Anne Marie. My sister tells me she's doing well at...."

"The Department of Employment," John helped out. "I'm getting good reports too. Happy to do it."

"Still owe you for that.... I know you said we had to tie up some loose ends, but first, about Fat Tony. Was he really gonna plug Dominic the sonavabitch point blank till you advised otherwise?"

Sally making Mafia small talk, John thought. "Yeah, he was. I did advise otherwise. More for the fat man's sake than Dominic's."

The conversation paused. John was conscious of how quiet things were; no sounds coming from the club's front room, no sounds from anywhere. *Now*, he thought. He fumbled inside his jacket, took out Whiney's gun, first pointing it at Sally, then motioning with it to Minx the Enforcer to sit down.

"What?" the old gangster said, raising his hands then dropping them. He sighed. "Should have patted you down this time."

"Definitely," Minx the Enforcer said.

First words I've heard him speak? John wondered. His body, his arms mainly, trembled with anger and fear. His voice cracked when he spoke. "I'm not fucking around." The two men sat stiffly, gazed at John, at his gun. He had achieved a sudden new status in their world.

"When I saw Dominic laying bloodied on the floor," John went on, "so fucked up and frightened, eyes so scared they practically rolled around in their sockets…. it struck me. Was he big and bad enough inside to bring down Frankie on his own? Then there was something the fat man said."

"What was that?" Sally sounded really curious.

"How Dominic was mainly bluff and bluster. When Frank was around, did nothing without his say so. After my brother's death, when you took over things, nothing without your say so. Not a fucking thing, Tony said."

"And?" Was Sally's one word question.

"Made me think." John figured it was sufficient explanation.

"Plan on shooting us?" Sally asked, this time seeming less interested.

John stayed on course. "Like why Dominic kept trading drugs in Brownsville, Mr. Robeson Turner's territory, even after Frank warned him to desist."

"Who could tell Dominic anything?" Sally shrugged, and his bodyguard followed suit.

"I'm thinking you."

"I'd want your brother's blood because…."

"No one walks away from the life?" Uncertain of Sally's motive, John offered up the obvious one.

Sally tilted his head, looked squarely at the gun in John's now steadier hand. "Not it. That was a cover, if the higher-ups asked which they never did. You Rosarios always pissed me off…. Starting with your old man. His fucking Cary Grant manners, his fucking there is some shit we will not eat. Like he wasn't a criminal headed for hell's basement like the rest of us."

John raised the gun, barrel stub pointed at Sally's head. He squeezed the handle so tightly, his muscles tingled, hurt. His hand shook again. Fucking prince of darkness, Angie called him. He wanted to cry and cry out. Hang tough, he told himself. Almost done. "Got some questions of my own."

"Shoot…. oops, poor choice of words." Sally laughed, joined by Minx the Enforcer.

John envied their coolness, hated them a little more. "So why not let Dominic be?" Probably will make their move soon, he thought tensely.

Sally answered. "He had big dreams, little talent to back them up. Became a liability."

"Should apply higher standards before choosing the help."

"You weren't available." Sally almost seemed sad.

John snickered. "Why not take Dominic out yourself?"

"Violating the code might've roused suspicion. Besides, couldn't resist making you the instrument. Hoped you'd end up killing each other."

John was finished, felt, to his surprise, relaxed. "You fucking motherless bastard," he spat out.

Minx the Enforcer rose, intent unclear. John fired twice at the space between the two men—they lowered their heads, covered their ears. The bullets crashed into the wall behind them, bits of plaster flew off, little white and grey splinters filling the air, descending slowly to the floor.

Captain Pat Devlin banged through the door, uniformed officers following him with guns in hand. The frigging calvary again, thought John.

Sally, standing now, looked at John. "You're wired too?"

John nodded. "You're a cooked goose, Sal."

The old capo glared at the police surrounding him. His body slouched. He eyed John again. "Better if you shot me."

"Not for your sake, I didn't." For mine, for Angie's. For Donnie's. She'd be up when he got home, eager to hear about it all. They'd eat, talk, lay together. He longed for such an evening in her company.

Devlin motioned Sally Broadway to place his hands behind his back. An officer cuffed him. "You're under arrest for the murder of Frank Rosario," Devlin pronounced. Don't remember him having that high-pitched Irish voice, John thought.

He remained seated, returned the gun to his jacket's inside pocket. Be glad to get it back into Whincy's hands. He watched Devlin direct Sally out the door. The captain stopped, turned. "You alright?"

"Just great," John said.

"Good work here, Rosario. We'll talk tomorrow."

"Sure." John made a soldier's salute.

Several officers lingered inside the clubhouse. John sat at the table with Minx the Enforcer who stared at the open door where his godfather just disappeared. He looked stunned, profoundly forlorn.

John lifted his hands wearily to the sides of his head, rubbed his temples. Case finally fucking closed.

THE END

0-595-33305-2